The Dogwoods Academy

By

Carolyn Tyree Feagans

Cover Photographs by
the author taken on
the Blue Ridge Mountains

Published by
Warwick House Publishing
720 Court Street
Lynchburg, Virginia 24504
1990

FIFTH PRINTING 1994

Library of Congress Catalog Card Number: 91-66078

ISBN 0-9634627-0-9

*This book is about a mountain,
a family and many valleys...*

I dedicate this book to...

"The Lily of the Valleys."

Table of Contents

Author's Note

I'm not sure I wrote this book. Once started (and that was the big step), the characters took over and led me on an interesting journey through the mountains of Virginia and the plains of South Dakota, through joys and sorrows, through despair and hope. It was fascinating to watch them develop and "say what I was going to say." I believe they will touch you as they touched me through excitement, mystery and beauty.

Having had the privilege of growing up and spending most of my life at the foothills of the Blue Ridge Mountains, you might know that the setting of this novel is none other than the majestic and beautiful Blue Ridge Mountains, and the time—the early 1900s. The story unfolds with the turn of the century, and the Barrett family is followed through three generations.

Some years ago, an old man died, a funeral wreath hung beside the door, an old woman was left. I wanted to tell the story—a story of life, death and love. What more is there? So in a simple way, I began. Heath and Emily emerged. How many times have Heath and Emily walked through the mountains of Virginia, the plains of South Dakota, the deserts of Arizona or the bayous of Louisiana? How many generations have Heath and Emily lived through? As long as there is a thing called "time," there will be a Heath and Emily.

What about Spring? That fragile, fragrant sign of time that rejuvenates and creates within us a longing...or that strong and determined spirit of the Indian princess that draws a sharp contrast to

Emily's quiet and contented manner. They both appear and reappear to add depth to the pages and give hope to the reader.

Finally, the purpose of this book was to fulfill a dream. I did! But now I have another dream. A dream that *you* will find faith, hope and love within these pages....

Carolyn T. Feagans

Chapter I

Till Death Us Do Part

The preacher's voice rolled on monotonously as the young couple stood before him, apparently with little concern. But behind the masks they wore were two very confused and scared kids.

Heath Barrett didn't look much like a groom, standing there tall and slim, resting his slight weight on first one foot, then the other. His boyish features gave him the appearance of one having grown too fast too suddenly. He looked more like a teenager going on his first date with his black shoes shining from heel to toe and the unbuttoned sport coat revealing his new navy blue tie.

He glanced at the small, frail girl beside him. Somehow she looked different...not like the sweetheart he'd been courting for almost two years now. There was a graveness behind her smile that gave her the appearance of maturity. Heath didn't feel very mature. He felt like running—running from responsibility—running from all of this. But that was stupid. He loved Emily. Why did he feel so uncomfortable?

Emily was amazed at herself—how could she be so composed on the outside while all the while she trembled within? Fragmentary thoughts bounced around in her brain as a butterfly flutters from one twig to another on a rose bush. Soon she would be saying those words...I DO...the beginning of a new life...the end of her old life. Was she ready? Yes, of course. Maybe Heath wasn't yet. He still seemed a bit mixed up, but she would help him get over that. She knew he loved her and she surely loved him. Isn't that all that matters?

But why did it have to be this way? Why did she feel like the victim instead of a glowing bride? She noticed her Mother looking at her. Poor Mother, she was so worn and tired-looking. Her marriage would not be that way! She remembered her Father lying on the bed drunk back home. No, her marriage would not be that way. Hers would be like those she read about in books—happy all the time. Of course, hers would be different. Why, Heath Barrett was a gentleman with well-to-do folks.

She remembered Heath breaking the news to her that his folks refused to attend the wedding. They didn't approve of her. It had really hurt, but she had not let him know it. So what if they didn't care for her—Heath did! She saw her Mother wipe her eyes with a handkerchief. Mother was their only witness outside of the parson and his wife. Again, Emily forced a smile. She didn't want her Mother to suspect anything. But that was foolish. How could she? Mother and everyone else had been expecting this marriage for a long time. Why, she and Heath had been engaged for almost a year. But that old feeling of fear and helplessness filled her again as she remembered it wasn't just she and Heath standing there with the preacher...but the unborn child she was carrying!

The preacher's words interrupted her thoughts..."for better, for worse...for richer, for poorer...in sickness and in health...to love, cherish, and to obey...till death us do part...."

She repeated the words automatically, but her mind was still hung up on the last part..."till death us do part"..."till death us do part." ...Suddenly she realized how powerful this vow was to God. She glanced up at Heath. It didn't seem to be getting the same reaction from him. She looked at her Mother—her head was bowed. She looked at the preacher's short, rather heavy wife who was witnessing the whole affair as one would an everyday sight, like the sun coming up. Didn't anyone feel the power of those words? Here she was, changing her whole life!

As Heath slipped the ring on her tiny finger, she noticed a small lamp burning on the desk in the corner, casting shadows about the room. Heavy velveteen drapes kept the light out of this room, but she could see through an opening that it was dusk outside anyway.

Driving off into the night, Heath pulled his watch out of his pocket. It was only half past eight. Why, it had only taken 30 minutes. He lifted the whip and brought it down upon the old horse's back, rousing him from his lazy trot. Heath didn't understand why, but he felt the need to get away from the seriousness and solemnity of the ceremony that had just taken place, and away from the gloom of the parsonage and the death-rattling voice of that preacher. He must have preached too many funerals and now the solemn tone was part of him. Once down the road a few miles, he let up on the reins and relaxed, letting the tired old horse retreat into its easy pace.

Darkness swept the forest now. Tall pines lined the winding, dirt road and the moon rose slowly ahead of them, sending out a soft glow. The air was damp with fresh fallen dew and a heavy pine fragrance.

They drove on...two figures quietly jostled about on the wooden bench of the wagon. A few potatoes rolled around in the back. Emily wanted to cry out, breaking this silence, but couldn't think of the right words to say. The wagon pulled up the mountainside slowly now, the old horse panting as the saliva ran out of his open mouth.

"Isn't it kind'a hard on him?" Emily asked timidly.

"He's used to it."

She looked at him with love, but wondered why sometimes he was so abrupt. Of course, she had gotten used to it and loved him in spite of it. He could be so gentle and sweet and fun when he wanted to. It seemed like she had loved him from the first moment she'd seen him at Mary Palmer's birthday party. All the girls were making fools of themselves that day, tugging on him to dance with them, laughing and giggling. She remembered Alice Freeman spilling half her punch on his new trousers in her awful eagerness to be near him.

She never dreamed that day he would ever give her a second look. But to her amazement, he had done more. The very next day was a Saturday, and he had driven all the way over to her place to see her. She recalled how embarassed she was to see him drive up and know how she really lived. She had heard that he lived in a big, fine home, with a maid. But he seemed at home right from the beginning, not appearing to notice anything different.

She felt his hand reach out for hers, bringing her back to reality. "We're almost there," he said, smiling down at her.

While she had been thinking, they had put some distance between them and the little parsonage in the valley. Now they were enveloped in a maze of trees, some tall and erect, others twisting and wrapping themselves around each other. The thick brush sent forth hideous imaginations as its weird shapes and forms took on unusual disguises in the moonlight. And then quite suddenly, a tiny cabin appeared, perched on the side of the mountain as if it had grown there along with the trees.

"There it is!" Heath pointed.

"It's beautiful!" she whispered, disregarding the broken shutters and crumbling chimney.

"Of course, it needs a lot of work," Heath continued, "but we can fix it up."

He jumped out of the wagon as soon as they pulled to a stop right in front of the porch, and tenderly lifted her out. As he went about putting the tired old horse up, Emily stood still. Knowing the cabin was old, she wondered what kind of people had lived here. Of course, she knew Heath's elderly Aunt had lived here the past few years and had died here. But before that, there must have been babies born here and laughter echoing throughout its tiny walls. She wondered what life held for her here. This was to be her home, her very own, hers and Heath's. She shivered a bit in the damp, night air, and pulling her shawl more snugly around her small shoulders, she walked up to the cabin and stepped up on the porch. It creaked under her step as she moved toward a hanging porch swing. All of a sudden, she felt very tired and slumped into it.

Heath came around the corner of the house and heard the rhythmic squeak of the swing as Emily slowly pushed it back and forth.

The glow of the moon brought out the red high-lights in her shiny auburn hair and showed off the creamy complexion of her youth. She was a pretty, little thing, he thought to himself. He swung up on the porch and sat down beside her, cuddling her in his arms. He caressed her and kissed her and led her from the swing into the house.

THE BRIGHT MORNING SUN streamed through the dusty window panes, falling on the faded quilt that covered the newlyweds, bringing it alive with glowing designs. As the sun rose higher, its warm rays crept up on the long lashes and faint smile of a girl no longer a girl. She opened her eyes and looked around the cabin, a bit confused. Where was she?

The realization of what had taken place the evening before came back. She turned to the empty spot beside her and then questioningly searched the room for the one who had been so close only hours before. All was still except for the ticking of the little clock beside the bed. Of course, she remembered, he's already gone to haul lumber. She silently chastised herself for not getting up to fix his breakfast, but she hadn't even heard him get up. He must have purposely left her asleep. Bringing her knees up under her chin, she sat up smiling. She felt happy, and warm all over, and full of energy. Why, she had a lot to do! Just look at this place—and she couldn't wait to begin. How in the world did Heath's Aunt stand it? Of course, she was old and life was ending for her, but life was just beginning for Emily. She jumped out of bed and after a scanty breakfast, dug into cleaning and completely turning the cabin inside out.

By noon the cabin was taking on a new look. Emily had just run down the hill to the spring when Heath arrived for lunch.

"Emily, Sweetheart, Emily," he called as he entered. The savory aroma from the pot of vegetable soup met his nostrils. He walked over to the old wood stove and leaned close to the pot, inhaling the sweet smell and feeling the hot steam warm his body. He sat down in the little green rocking chair by the door and took in all the changes with a smile. The windows were bare but shining. Gosh, he hadn't noticed how dirty they were before! The floors had been swept clean and scrubbed. The big bed they had shared was now stripped, revealing the worn mattress and exposing a few rips where the feathers were poking out,

some already on the floor. Even the wooden table in
the center of the small kitchen was bare, because the
faded dingy cloth had been discarded. Wow, that little
girl of his had been busy! His stomach growled, inter-
rupting his thoughts and he was glad to hear the back
door open.

"Is that you, Heath?"

Jumping out from behind the door, he placed his
hands over her eyes.

"It is a tall and handsome prince come to sweep
you off your feet, My Love."

"Oh, Heath," she laughed, turning and embracing him.

After sopping up the last remains of his soup
with the hot biscuit, Heath pushed his chair back
from the table and admired Emily as she mended the
holes in the mattress. She was some cook also! He
sure was glad that Annie had stocked the cupboards
with food. Yes, married life was gonna be all right!

Days passed, all alike—Heath going out every
morning to haul lumber and Emily busy converting
the drab, old cabin into a warm and cozy home for the
two of them...and the little one on the way. She
worked from daybreak till Heath came home at night,
and loved every minute of it. By the end of the first
week, she had it looking like a different place. Yellow
and white, ruffled, gingham curtains blew softly in
the mountain breezes that continually penetrated the
cabin. They matched the cloth that now graced the
kitchen table. A delicate glass vase stood in the center
with a bouquet of cut, wild flowers of rainbow colors.
Even the old quilt covering the bed looked newer after
many washings and soakings. The afghan her Mother

had given her lay folded at the foot of the bed. Every piece of furniture had been shined.

The second week found her painting the front porch and swing. She managed to talk Heath into buying enough paint for her to do the window shutters, too. He was amazed at her boundless energy to accomplish all of this and then to be waiting for him each night, fresh and sweet. How did she do it? The love between them grew, and many nights Emily lay wondering if this could be real. She was so happy and so content.

THE LONG HOT SUMMER for most folks was short for Heath and Emily. Their days were filled with work and laughter and fun. But the summer soon faded into fall, turning the forest into a mystic fairyland.

They took long walks each evening, examining the beauty of every tree as they formed a colorful banner over their heads. Drawn together as the only two humans in the enchanting forest, they talked a lot, revealing their inner selves to one another as never before. On one such evening, they were discussing their childhoods.

"Heath, with such a happy childhood as you had, don't you miss all that? I mean the plentyness of everything, the easy lifestyle, the luxuries you don't have now."

"No, " he answered abruptly. "It was a happy childhood, I guess, but if you want to know the truth of it, I'm really a rebel at heart." He winked at her.

Emily laughed. "Oh Heath, what do you mean?"

His countenance became more serious. "Well, I

didn't like the formality, the double standards, always being on your best behavior for guests who were constantly being entertained. I don't know...it seemed a farce to me. We never really spent time together as a family. We were always too busy presenting the right image for the county. I guess my insisting on moving into the cabin was an act of rebellion really, against all the frivolity back home."

"Was marrying me an act of rebellion also, Heath?"

"Of course not, Silly." He hugged her to him. "You were the first real thing to come into my life. I loved what you stood for and still do. Well, there was Annie, too. You'll love her when you meet her. *She's* real all right." He smiled at the thought of her.

"When will I get to meet her, Heath? And the rest of your family...when will I?"

"Soon, Honey, soon."

"But you've been saying that ever since we got married. Heath, are you ashamed of me?"

"Of course not, why would I be? If you want the truth...it's because I don't want you hurt. You see, they blame you for us getting married. I know it's ridiculous, but they do. Unfortunately, Mother doesn't think I can do any wrong. They had big plans for me...you know...college and all...and, well, they think you spoiled all that."

"I see," Emily said thoughtfully. "Heath, do you regret not being able to fulfill those plans?"

"Are you kidding? I never wanted to go to college anyway. I'm not college material like brother Robert, but Mother has never been able to accept that. I'm doing just what I want to do. Why, I wouldn't trade this life with you for a hundred of the other." He looked at her tenderly. "I love you, Sweetheart."

She found out just how true his words were a couple of months later when Mrs. Barrett called on her. Winter had settled down into a long, dreary season.

Emily was busy stoking the little potbelly stove in the kitchen when she heard someone drive up. Catching hold of the end of the table, she slowly pulled herself up. It was becoming quite a chore now to do this with her stomach as swollen as it was. She made her way to the window and, much to her surprise, saw Mrs. Barrett stepping down out of the fanciest surrey she had ever seen. She knew it was her because of the picture Heath had tucked away in the top bureau drawer. Quickly, she straightened her smock and smoothed back her hair, making her way to the door.

Mrs. Barrett knocked firmly. Emily opened.

Mrs. Barrett entered briskly, immediately making the cabin seem smaller with her tall, robust frame.

"You must be Emily," she said dryly.

"Yes, I am, and you're Heath's Mother. I know you by your picture," Emily answered with a smile.

"Oh really? I didn't know he had one," she added sarcastically, although Emily noticed the hint of pleasure this brought her.

"Won't you sit down, Mrs. Barrett?" Emily led her over to the couch.

After being seated, they sat looking at each other in awkward silence. Mrs. Barrett finally broke it. "Well, I must get to the point...the reason I'm here...I mean. Frankly, I'm worried about Heath. How long has he been without work, Dear?"

"Well, only for a couple of weeks, and I'm sure he will find something soon. In fact, he's gone over to Ridge Mountain today to see somebody about work."

"Do you realize, Dear, how hard it is to find work right now, especially the kind of work he's been doing?"

Emily sat still, feeling very uncomfortable. She couldn't help noticing the fine material of Mrs. Barrett's suit.

"You see, Dear, I talked with Heath only day before yesterday. I don't know whether he told you that he came by the house."

"No, he didn't." Emily observed a wave of satisfaction brush across Mrs. Barrett's face.

"Well, we talked about his being out of work. I suggested he forget about trying to find work now. You see, I still have his college money saved up, and I don't see why he can't go ahead with his plans and enter college next semester. He could probably find a part-time job near the campus. You know, John did that. And, of course, you could stay with us. It would work out. I'm sure it would."

"Mrs. Barrett, what did Heath say about it?" Emily asked reluctantly.

"That's why I'm here. He would not agree. In fact, he wouldn't even discuss it. I thought maybe you could help make him see it my way. Of course, you understand that if he gets his education, he will be able to find a much better job. You will be able to have some hope for the future. The way it is now, the lumber business, why a body cannot count on it, as you well know by now."

"Well, I don't know, Mrs. Barrett. I have never tried to tell Heath what to do. He has a mind of his own."

"How well I know, Dear."

Emily sensed that coldness she had felt when Mrs. Barrett arrived. She really didn't know what to say or do. Of course, *she* was concerned, too, about Heath being out of work. In fact, she hadn't been able to think about much else for the past few days, but for Heath to go away, away from her, off to college, and for her to have to stay with the Barretts…. She couldn't think of anything worse.

"I will talk to him, Mrs. Barrett. I'll talk to him about it. Now, wouldn't you like to have some coffee with me?"

"I reckon so."

They had coffee, talking about various unimportant things, but mostly Mrs. Barrett bragged on her grandchildren—how bright they were, how talented, and on and on. But never once did she mention the baby that was so obviously between them! Emily wanted to say something about the baby but dared not. That evening when Heath came home, she told him all about his Mother's visit. He didn't seem pleased at all.

"You remember what I told you that day in the woods. I meant it, and I don't care to discuss it with you or my Mother."

Emily felt relief flood over her.

"She didn't try to give you any money, did she?" he asked.

"No. Why?"

"I just wondered. The other day when I stopped

by, I was cornered with this same thing, but not only this, she wanted me to take some money. Emily, I will not take money from them. When I left home, it was completely an act of faith in myself. They refused to have anything to do with you or the marriage. They practically refused to have anything to do with me for a while. Now, I'm going to make it on my own or bust trying!"

Emily put her arms around him. "And you *will* make it. I know you will."

But the days passed and still he found no work. The cupboards were beginning to look very bare. Heath became more and more cross. They had planned to have someone come in and stay with them for a while now that the baby was just about due, but with Heath being home most of the time himself, they decided against it.

On a Tuesday night, Will Davis, one of Heath's former coworkers, stopped by and asked him if he wanted to go to Spottswood the next morning to look for work. Of course, Heath agreed. Before leaving, he asked Emily, "Are you sure you'll be all right alone?"

"Of course, Honey. The baby isn't due for another couple of weeks yet. Don't worry. Anyway, if anything happens, I can always drive over to Mrs. Campbell's."

Emily had just heard the wagon wheels rumble off in the distance when a sudden sharp pain caught her as she was clearing the kitchen table. It just about took her breath. Catching onto the door, she held herself up gasping. "It can't be," she thought.

But before she could decide what to do, another pain struck, doubling her over on the floor. Between the pains that continued and the dizziness that now enveloped her, she found herself struggling and groping on the floor toward the bed. She made it to the bed but couldn't get the strength to pull herself up on it. Again and again she tried, always falling back on the floor. Now she was wet with perspiration as she lay moaning on the floor. When the pains eased for a few seconds at a time, she was aware of the wind whistling through the cracks in the cabin. And as the pains increased the winds increased, now howling and shaking the front door.

Each pain seemed to grasp her whole body within its power, twisting it, tormenting it and then releasing it suddenly, leaving it limp and waiting— waiting for the next. She now cried softly, except when the pains hit, and then she let out a shrill, piercing scream that echoed off the cabin walls and united with the haunting whistling of the wind. Why couldn't she just pass out! Why *couldn't* she, then she wouldn't feel the pains! She felt the water trickling down her neck. She was hot and clammy. Now she hung on the verge of unconsciousness—hoping she would pass out. But what seemed like hours later, she still lay there in that semi-consciousness. The sounds of the wind now muffled through to her brain, disguised and distorted. She visualized tall, wretched creatures pounding on her door, forcing themselves against the windows, peering through and laughing hysterically at her plight. The intensity of the pains now were choking all reasoning out, and she couldn't distinguish between reality and imagination. "Oh God, help me!" she screamed.

Just then another pain caught her. Reaching

upward, she caught hold of the mattress, ripping it and sending feathers floating about the room. Sinking back to the floor, panting for breath, she thought she heard footsteps, or was it the wind again? Someone was knocking! She tried to move toward the door. It was useless. But the door was opening, and in walked Mrs. Campbell. Emily passed out.

The old lady immediately set about getting things ready. When Emily regained consciousness, she caught glimpses of Mrs. Campbell flitting about the room fussing over her, talking to her and wiping her forehead every now and then. Each time a new pain arrived, she would hold onto Emily's hand tightly, and smiling, would coach her with just the right words. Things weren't going too well. Mrs. Campbell was worried. It looked as if the baby was turned the wrong way and the only way to get it turned around was for Emily to do the work herself.

"Breath in deeply, now hold it!" Mrs. Campbell repeated over and over again. But Emily was growing weaker and weaker.

"I'm hot...so hot..." she whispered, but Mrs. Campbell didn't hear her. Emily stared at the wall. It was a golden crimson as the setting sun cast its flaming rays there. Feeling as if she were midst the flames, being engulfed with fire and pain, she let go the choking sobs.

"That's all right, Honey. You go ahead and cry all you want to. Let it out. It won't be long now though, Child," Mrs. Campbell said with a smile.

Emily seemed to be drifting from consciousness to unconsciousness again. She yearned to sleep and wanted to escape it all. Just as her eyes were closing, she noticed Mrs. Campbell down on her knees beside the bed. What was she doing? It seemed as if she were fading not only out but backwards in time, and it was her Grandmother that she was seeing down there on her knees. Yes, she remembered her doing that...praying. Was Mrs. Campbell praying?

Another pain seized her, flinging her abruptly back to reality. She grasped Mrs. Campbell's ready hand.

"Breath in, Dear, breath in...and hold it...hold it."

Emily obeyed and over and over again they repeated the ritual until she no longer had the strength to obey. But Mrs. Campbell continued, "Breath in, now, push, push, push, Dear...."

Emily formed the word "can't" on her dry lips but couldn't get it out. She felt dizzy, so dizzy and weak.

"The little one's fighting to be born," whispered Mrs. Campbell.

"Fighting to be born?" Emily let the words soak in. I never knew the baby tried too, she thought. And as she thought about those words, visualizing the tiny infant struggling and fighting its way into the world, she suddenly had renewed strength. She must help him!

As the twilight deepened, a cry came forth from the remote cabin. All was well—a son was born.

THE NEXT MORNING, Emily awoke to the warm sun oozing in through the window. Now in the brightness of the morning, she could see her Son really well for the first time. He's beautiful, she thought. Mrs. Campbell was still asleep on the couch.

But where was Heath? Fear crept upon her. Hadn't he been home all night? Why was Mrs. Campbell still here and sleeping so soundly? Didn't she know Heath hadn't come home?

The baby began to cry, and Mrs. Campbell immediately sat up. She came over to the crib and picked him up.

"My, what a fine son you have!" the old lady declared as she placed the tiny bundle in his Mother's arms.

"But Mrs. Campbell...where is Heath?"

A worried look came to Mrs. Campbell's eyes. "Why, I don't know, Child. I thought you knew because you kept saying, 'Heath'll be here soon, Heath'll be here soon' when you were out of your head."

"He should be here now...he just went over to Spottswood with Will Davis to look for work. But that was yesterday morning."

"If you think you'll be alright while I get home, I'll get someone to check on him for you."

But as Mrs. Campbell was preparing to leave, they heard a wagon pull up out front.

"It's him!" Mrs. Campbell said with a smile, looking from the window to Emily. Heath walked in and looked confused, seeing Mrs. Campbell and Emily in bed all at once. Rushing over to the bed, he didn't notice the small bundle. "Are you alright, Honey?"

But then his eyes fell upon the baby. Looking from the baby to Emily, a big smile spread over his face.

"Your son," Emily said, smiling up at him.

"Well, I think I'll be moseying on home now," Mrs. Campbell said, going to the door. "I'll be back to check on you. In fact, if you need me, I'll be back today."

"Oh no, Mrs. Campbell, you've done enough already. I'll be fine."

The door closed behind her.

"Where have you been, Heath?"

He buried his head in his hands. "I'm sorry, Honey. I had no idea you would deliver this early and..."

"And what..." Emily inquired, looking confused.

"Well, you know how worried I've been about finding a job and all. Things didn't work out over at Spottswood either and...well, frankly, I got drunk."

"Heath!"

"Well, I did. Will had a bottle with him...I didn't know about that in the beginning. I guess he was prepared for the worst, and the worst came."

He looked up at her and the baby. "But Honey, I'm sorry...I really am. It won't happen again, I promise."

Emily looked down at the tiny head resting in her arms and was quiet for a moment. Then she looked at him. "He has your eyes," she said.

CHRISTMAS CAME and went almost unnoticed. Still Heath found no work except for a day or two here and there to keep them from starving. And still he would accept no help from his Mother. Emily stayed busy taking care of Little David. They had named him David Edward Barrett after Heath's Grandfather, who had died the year before. Strangely enough, none of Heath's family had been to see him. Heath had become very bitter about it and refused to visit them now or even talk about them. In fact, Heath talked very little about anything these days. Emily was becoming quite worried about him. He wasn't himself at all. The only time he seemed to escape his depressed state of mind was when he held Little David or sat by his cradle watching him. Then he would smile and talk about him with the pride only a father can have for a son. But more often than not, he came in late, and more than once, Emily had caught the smell of alcohol. But what could she do? If only he could find work! She began to wonder if maybe they shouldn't take the Barretts up on their offer. They couldn't keep on this way much longer, and they must think about Little David. Maybe Heath ought to reconsider! When he came in that afternoon, she approached the subject. But he reeled around and looked at her with more anger than she'd ever seen.

"Leave me alone!" he yelled.

Emily backed off and stared at him as if he were a stranger.

But he continued to let it all out while pacing back and forth. He talked about how hard he'd been looking for work and that he was doing all he could do. But that under no circumstances would they ask for help in *any* way from his folks! He accused her of having no faith in him, which she tried to deny, but she couldn't get a word in. After he'd blown off all the steam that had been simmering in him, he concluded by storming out the door.

Emily sat down and cried. What was happening to them? After a while she got up and went about putting on the last of the pinto beans. He probably would be back soon, and she would have him a good hot meal. They would sit down and talk, and it would be like it used to be. But the evening dragged by with the ticking of the little clock keeping her constantly aware that it was getting later and later, and still Heath had not come home.

Finally she sat down alone at the table and ate a bowl of beans. She couldn't taste them, but finished them anyway. They certainly couldn't be wasted. After washing up the few dishes, she sat down by the window. It had begun to snow again. She watched it falling gracefully on the path she'd just shoveled the day before. She sighed. It would have to be shoveled again tomorrow before they could get back down to the spring. Where was Heath? She whispered to herself. Little David woke and began to cry. She went to him. "What's wrong with Mama's little man? Are you hungry? Mama will take care of that in just a minute." Sitting down with the baby snuggled up close to her, she proceeded to feed him, and smiled down at him, enjoying the tenderness and closeness of the moment. What happiness this small bundle of life had brought to her.

After he finished eating, he lay in her arms contented, his big blue eyes looking into hers. It was the same look he'd had when she held him for the first time. She would never forget that. Mrs. Campbell had laid him beside her, and that tiny piece of life that had just been separated from her own body looked at her with an understanding that convinced her that he knew who she was. Slowly now his little eyelids closed, and she put him back in his cradle. The cradle—Heath had spent hours working on, wanting it to be just right for his son. Where is he? She whispered again. She went back and sat beside the window, straining to see any sign of him. But it was dark now and the minute snowflakes were barely visible descending from the blackened sky.

Tired from a busy day, she soon dropped off into a restless sleep there in the chair, and dreamed that she was all alone out in a horrible storm. She was lost and couldn't find Heath. She kept running and running, calling his name. The slam of the door awakened her suddenly and sitting up straight, she saw Heath stumble into the room, with snow falling off him. He headed for the bed and nearly fell across it sideways. Completely bewildered, she called out, "Heath!"

Running to his side, she found out immediately what his problem was. He was already out...stone drunk!

The scene was repeated over and over in the next few months. Emily found herself alone night after night and cried herself to sleep most of the time. Heath worked enough to keep the bare essentials coming in, but that was all. Emily didn't blame him for the lack of work, but for the way he wasted what little they *did* have on drinking. At first she was sad and yearned for the relationship they'd once had, but eventually this turned into disgust. How could he continually damage their marriage this way? How could he abandon his tiny son time after time?

One night she had been dwelling on these thoughts as she sat alone, wondering where he might be, when he came in. Suddenly all the pent-up emotions within her exploded and she flew at him, demanding to know where he'd been and exactly what was so important to take him away from his family night after night. He swung around like lightning, catching her in the abdomen with his right fist before tumbling to the floor himself. The blow doubled her over beside him. Everything was swimming before her eyes as she tried to steady herself. She attempted to straighten up but couldn't. Fear seized her. What was wrong? Why couldn't she straighten up? What was that noise? She looked down at Heath and saw that he was snoring. Why, he was sound asleep! She then realized that he was drunk and had passed out. Why hadn't she seen that before? Heath would never hit her, but this thing on the floor...this thing that he'd become under the influence of alcohol would...it was not Heath! She made it to the couch walking ever so slowly, still doubled over, and lay down in the same position. She lay still and motionless throughout the night, never closing her eyes.

She saw Heath get up after awhile, go into the kitchen, fix himself something to eat, then go to bed. He never once noticed her. The pain in her stomach caused her to cry softly in the night. But worse than the pain was the fear of death. For the first time in her life, she really felt close to death. It was different even from when she'd given birth to Little David. Somehow she felt as if she were tasting of death and that soon she would eat of it and be a part of it herself. But she *couldn't*! She couldn't *die*! What about Little David? Who would take care of Little David? She *must* live! She remembered her words when she was about to give birth to Little David..."Oh God, help me!" It was strange that she hadn't thought of it since his birth. But she *was* helped! Mrs. Campbell had come to help her. She wondered...did He really hear me...was it God who sent Mrs. Campbell? If so, He might hear me again. She began to repeat over and over again, "Help me God, please help me, God." Over and over those same words were whispered into the night until the first rays of light pierced the darkened sky and found her sleeping peacefully.

She was okay the next day except for the soreness. Heath didn't remember the episode at all but was deeply sorry and begged her forgiveness, which she readily gave when he promised to stay home in the future. But this promise, like all the others, was not kept. He continued staying out late at night and coming home intoxicated. But Emily avoided him from then on, keeping still whenever he was drinking.

During those unhappy days, she found much joy in the baby. He could make her smile when she felt like crying. He turned her tears of sadness into tears of joy. How dreadful and empty would her life be without him!

THE WINTER dragged by. But as all things must pass, this lonely and disappointing winter also passed into spring. It arrived all at once, splashing the mountainside with gold wherever forsythia was found. The daffodils poked their welcomed heads out from the brush that had grown up around the cabin. I wonder who planted those daffodils? Emily thought to herself as she wandered around the cabin. Was it Heath's Aunt or someone else who had lived here many years ago? Whoever it was—they must have loved beauty as she did. She sensed a closeness to the forgotten past that clung to the cabin walls as the moss did to the old oak tree.

Without as much to keep her busy, she found more time to ramble around the mountainside surrounding the cabin. She didn't have to be constantly bringing in the wood that Heath had cut and stacked up out back. They only needed a fire in the mornings now, and she didn't have to worry about the fire going out during the day. She would wrap up Little David and carry him with her, exclaiming over all the beauty to him as if he knew exactly what she was talking about. She walked slowly, not to miss a thing, taking in all the new life exploding in every corner and crevice. What a joy to discover tiny, wild flowers budding beneath old, rotten stumps, or bushes bursting forth in color. What peace to hear the birds singing all around her.

One day she was sitting on a hillside enjoying all of this, yet feeling lonely inside because Heath had not come home. This time he had not come home all night. All of a sudden, a strange sense of awakening overwhelmed her, and she sensed the presence of one very near—one who had brought all this new life into being. What was the saying she had heard once? Yes, it was her Grandmother who used to say it, when she held her on her knee. Let's see, "Lo, the winter is past ...the rain is over and gone...the flowers appear on the earth, the time of the singing of birds has come." How beautiful! I wonder if it is an old poem or song, or could it be from the Bible? I remember seeing her read it often—but it all seemed so long ago. Her Grandmother had died when she was only seven years old. Just then, more words came to her from the past. "In the beginning...God created the heaven and the earth."

She was amazed how she could recall those words spoken to her so long ago. Yes, all this beauty she enjoyed, the earth coming alive with it, was made by God. Not only the earth but the heaven...gazing up into the clear, blue sky, she watched the feathery white clouds glide silently past. "I wonder about this God."

Just then she heard someone calling her. It was Heath! Glancing down at Little David, she saw that he had fallen asleep in her arms. Pressing him to her breast, she arose and made her way back to the cabin.

Heath was all excited about something—she could tell that before she reached him. "What is it?" she called, afraid of the unknown.

"We don't have to worry about money no more! I've got a part-time job now."

Very calmly but firmly, she spoke, "Heath, I'm not as worried about money as I am about us...where have you been?"

He tucked his head as a small boy would on being caught with his hand in the cookie jar. "I'm sorry, Honey. I was out with some of the guys, and we had a few drinks. The time got away from me and, believe it or not...I fell asleep. I'm sorry...really I am. Honey, it won't happen again. You see, with this part-time job, I won't be worrying about how to make ends meet the way I have been. Things are gonna get better. Just you wait and see."

"What kind of part-time job is it?"

"You know Dan Saunders. Well, he's got this band, you know...called "The Oak Mountain Boys"...and he needs a banjo player."

Emily interrupted. "And *you're* gonna be the

banjo player."

"That's right. That is, if you don't mind, of course. They make pretty good money for just standing up there and playing, and we can sure use the money…what do you think, Honey?"

Emily felt confused. She didn't want Heath playing in a band and being gone even more, but the truth was, they really did need the money.

"Well, don't you think it's a good idea?"

Reluctantly, she agreed.

EMILY'S FEARS TURNED into reality. The band did bring in more money, for which she was grateful, but Heath was away most of the time now, and what hurt her the most was, he seemed to be enjoying it. She tried going with him a couple of times but Little David was awfully irritable and couldn't sleep amid all the noise. She soon gave up that idea and sadly, she noticed Heath's relief.

It all ended, or rather began, with the fourth dance he played for, over at Bill Moore's barn. A large crowd showed up, and there was plenty of laughter and dancing and drinking, as usual. Heath found himself feeling young and free, not very married and certainly not very fatherly. He watched the young girls swirling around to the music and felt like dancing himself. Dan had brought a jug of moonshine with him, and they all partook of it between numbers. By the time Heath took a break, he was really feeling a part of things. He made his way over to the homemade bar and sat down on an empty stool, wondering who had gone to all the trouble to rig up the bar. It sure couldn't have been Bill Moore. Why, there wasn't a lazier man in all these here mountains than Bill Moore.

"What'll ya have, Mr. Barrett?" a young voice boomed.

Looking around, he saw a tall, robust fellow, not much younger than himself.

"Don't need anything, thank you," Heath answered, waving his glass in the young fellow's direction. "I brought my own."

"So did just about everybody else. Shucks, I won't learn how to be a bartender at this rate."

"Who rigged up this bar anyway?"

"Sis, I mean, Mrs. Moore. She's my big Sister. She figured we could make more money this way...you know, for the cause."

"What cause? I'm just playing here."

"For the Charity Sisters. You know, the group that comes up with all the help for the people in need."

"That so? Well, I'm afraid I can't help you out tonight. This here 'shine is about all I can handle tonight."

The young fellow moved off looking around for other prospects. Heath finished his glass and was about to get up when a small hand rested lightly on his shoulder. He looked up into two of the blackest eyes he'd ever seen. They resembled two wells of black water, and he felt as if he were falling way down into the depths of them.

"My name is Betty Lou. I don't believe I know yours."

"Heath...Heath Barrett."

She sat down beside him, crossing her long slender legs. He wondered how he knew they were long and slender beneath that long dress. But, of course, they had to be to go with the rest of her. She was tall. He figured she must be the tallest girl he'd ever seen. With both hands, she swooped back her thick black hair and smiled at him teasingly. "I believe you're the most handsome man I've seen tonight."

Heath smiled back. "That could go both ways...I don't mean man, though."

They laughed.

"What *do* you mean?" she asked as she moved closer.

He felt like he was drowning and didn't know whether it was the sweet fragrance coming from her and surrounding him or the stuff he'd been drinking. He was experiencing desires, both good and bad, and couldn't distinguish between the two.

"I mean you are a pretty doggone good-looking woman."

She smiled at him again and ran her long fingers up and down his arm.

LITTLE DAVID WAS SLEEPING at last, and Emily resigned herself to an evening alone. She felt restless recalling how Heath had looked when he walked out the door—handsome and sweet. She yearned for him. Oh well, she must not think of him. She was lonely enough. Looking at the cradle, she smiled at the little form sound asleep now. How precious he is! How can anyone refuse to see him? She remembered Heath's words, "They just won't come. They keep making excuses. Who the heck cares anyway!" She wondered if it was because they had gotten married against their wishes and they now blamed this tiny, innocent baby as the cause of it all. They would probably never believe that Heath would have married her anyway. It didn't really matter whether they believed it or not.

Of course, Heath seems to think that most of the problem lies in the fact that he still refuses help from them. His Mother, as possessive as she is, cannot accept the idea that he will not even take money from her. And, of course, with him refusing her money, it takes away her rights to manipulate him as she had always done. She had no strings with which to work— what was she to do? But to refuse to see their Grandchild! How could people who claimed to be Christians do that? Heath said they went to church every Sunday and that Mr. Barrett even served as Sunday School superintendent. It was all so confusing. Just then, she heard a soft knock at the door. She hadn't heard anyone drive up. Pulling back the curtain and peering out, she saw Mrs. Campbell. Quickly she opened the door to welcome her.

"Oh, I'm so glad you've come, Mrs. Campbell. I was just sitting here wishing I had someone to talk to. Heath is playing in the band tonight."

"Well Child, I thought I'd mosey over for a short spell. Can't stay too long, don't like to be out late, you know. What kind of band is Heath playing in?"

"Oh, he's playing with Dan Saunders and their group called the Oak Mountain Boys. They're playing over at Bill Moore's tonight, I think."

Mrs. Campbell didn't comment, but Emily sensed her disapproval.

Emily got out the cups and saucers for coffee and cake. Sitting at the kitchen table, they talked about the weather, the neighbors, but mostly about Little David. Mrs. Campbell marveled at how he was growing.

"Going to be a big boy, he sure is."

"Yes, I think so, too. You know, Mrs. Campbell, I've often wondered why you were out that day, at just the right time. It was almost as if you knew that I needed you. I sure am glad that you happened along, though."

"I *did* know that you needed me, Child, or at least that *somebody* needed me."

Emily looked at her with growing interest. "Why, how could you have known?"

"Well, you see, that day I had just gone out on my back porch and was a fixin' to go down to the cellar to bring up some potatoes for supper. But before I opened the screen door, I heard this strange sound. It sorta' sounded like the wind, but yet and still it didn't. I could have sworn it sounded like somebody calling me, and it was'a coming from this direction. I stood there a spell trying to collect my thoughts. Suddenly, I thought about you! I wondered if you were alright, knowing your time was drawing nigh and all. I started out the door to get those potatoes again, and I don't know if you remember or not but the wind was something terrible that day. Well'sa, before I could reach the cellar door, that powerful wind was a'whippin' me around and toward this direction again. I found myself being drawn—almost forced—here. Well, by that time, I knew something strange was a'happening, but all I could think about was that I had to get over here and see 'bout you young folk. I went back to the house and grabbed up my coat and scarf and headed this'a way. Well, you know the rest of the story."

Emily sat very still and quiet.

Mrs. Campbell continued. "Course, I didn't know who it was. He works in mysterious ways sometimes. Maybe nobody else knew you needed help, but He did."

Emily didn't know whether to ask or not but couldn't hold it in any longer. "Who?"

Mrs. Campbell looked at her, rather surprised. "Why, God, of course, Child."

This was just too much for Emily. Her mind was racing. Could this really be true? That day when she had called on Him for help, had He actually spoken to Mrs. Campbell, calling her over here? She wanted to tell Mrs. Campbell about calling on God for help, but couldn't get the words out. Instead, she asked, "Do you really think He...God...knows all about us and our needs?"

"Course, Child. His Word tells us so. 'The eyes of the Lord run to and fro over the whole earth.' He don't miss nothing."

"Another thing, Mrs. Campbell, when I was in such pain and so very weak, I saw you down on your knees by my bed. Were you...were you talking to Him then?"

"I sho was. I was really bothered 'bout you. You didn't seem to have no strength left in you—but I knew God had the strength and could give it to you. God says to call upon Him in our day of trouble, and I figured you were in trouble."

"He answered, too," Emily said as she watched Little David rousing from sleep. He let out a strong, healthy cry, and she and Mrs. Campbell laughed.

Emily enjoyed Mrs. Campbell's visit, though it was brief. She stood watching her disappear through the woods, just as dusk was settling in. Little David squirmed in her arms as she pondered all that had been said.

AT THE BARN DANCE the music was a little louder than before, the dancing much livelier, and the moonshine disappearing. Some of the couples had left the boisterous barn for quieter surroundings outside. They lounged on the bales of straw stacked up beside the barn, snuggling closer all the time. Heath watched the intimate fondling between strangers with increasing interest and while his fingers still moved automatically over the strings of his banjo, his thoughts were elsewhere. They followed his roving eyes, which never lost sight of those swishing, black skirts that darted from one end of the dance floor to the other as Betty Lou wallowed in the attention she was getting from most of the men there. She was the belle of the party all right, and she knew it. But as a cat goes after its prey, she nervously watched Heath from the corner of her eye throughout the night.

He fell into her trap and found himself feeling rather jealous but couldn't understand why. As he played the last number, she was just in front of him, her thick dark hair resting on her half bare shoulders. Her tall, slender body moved with the beat of the music. As her partner drew her closer to him, she looked up at Heath with those piercing eyes and a slight smile on her lips. He smiled back, and laying his banjo down, stepped down off the platform and strode across the floor, dodging couples. He walked outside into the moonless night toward his wagon. She followed.

Emily had gone to bed, figuring it would be late before Heath got home. Those dances did stretch on very late sometimes. It wasn't too long before she was sleeping soundly. The little clock beside the bed ticked on into the silent night. But about three o'clock, Little David woke, crying. He was hungry. Emily dragged herself out of bed and picked him up, wrapping him in his big blanket. She carried him over to the little, green rocker and sat down to feed him. Would he ever sleep through a whole night? Though busy with the baby, she had not failed to notice the empty spot beside her in the bed and the sickening feeling way down in her stomach. After Little David was satisfied and sleeping again, she put him back in his cradle and walked over to the window, gazing into the black night. She was fighting the inevitable tears. Why? Why? Why? All of a sudden the tears she had been holding back began to flow, first slowly and then more rapidly.

She cried so hard and so long that she felt sick all over, her whole body jerking with each sob. Finally, exhausted from crying, she fell back on the bed and stared up at the ceiling. How could she cope with this? How could she sit idly by and watch her marriage dissolve? She must do something! Then she remembered Mrs. Campbell's words again: "Call upon me in your day of trouble." She had called once and He had answered. The words spilled forth…"God, please help me!"

She waited and nothing happened. She waited

for what seemed like hours and nothing happened. All the while, she became more and more anxious. But then she thought of something. If Mrs. Campbell got all of her faith from the Bible—and she said that she did—maybe if she read it, she would find her answers also. She got up again. "Now, let's see. I know there's one around here somewhere. I remember seeing it when we first moved in." She went through a few drawers but couldn't find it. "Oh, now I remember." She went over to the bed and pulled a large, heavy trunk out from under it. She recalled she had put it in the trunk when cleaning up one day. Opening the old trunk, she found the Bible underneath some papers. It wasn't in the best shape, rather old and worn. It must have belonged to Heath's Aunt. "I wonder if she ever found help from it," she whispered aloud.

Letting the pages fall open, she began to read, first slowly, then more quickly. It all sounded good, but still she found nothing that seemed to be an answer for *her*. Some of it she understood, some she didn't. She was just about to lay it down when her eyes caught something..."Trust in the Lord with all thine heart, and lean not unto thine own understanding." She reread it again and again. "That's it! I've been trying to understand why Heath is acting the way he is, why he's so changed, why everything is such a mess. But this says don't *try* to understand, instead, to trust in the Lord. But *how* do I trust in the Lord?" She couldn't wait for Mrs. Campbell to come again so she could ask her. Crawling back into bed, she kept repeating those words to herself, and while thinking to herself that she didn't understand, she found peace in the words and drifted off to sleep.

The next morning, the steady tapping of raindrops hitting the tin roof awakened her. She knew before she looked that Heath wouldn't be beside her. It was barely daybreak though the sky was gray with rain. She pulled the covers up around her and lay there listening to the rhythmic patter-patter as it hit the roof. She wondered to herself why she loved the rain so. It made her feel warm and cozy. It made her feel happy. But that was strange when most people complained that it caused them to feel sad and depressed. She supposed it was because basically she was insecure and was most happy when comfortably and privately enclosed within walls, whether they be of wood, mountains, or even rain—just as long as they separated her from the sometimes frightening outside world as the rain did just now. The patter-patter increased until the rain began to pour. The harder it rained, the more complacent Emily felt. Why should she get up? Little David had not awakened. Heath was gone. She slept.

Chapter II
I Hear His Tender Angelic Voice as He Sings

Two years passed. This was Little David's third summer and it was passing fast. One morning Emily awoke to another familiar sound. This time it wasn't raindrops, but acorns falling from the big oak trees towering above the tiny cabin. They hit the tin roof and bounced off, ricocheting downward until they shot off the roof and sailed into the tangled mass of rose bushes behind the cabin. Could it be fall again? How time flew. The warm rays of sun drifted through the window. It was going to be a beautiful day!

Being Saturday and all her work done, at least most of it, why not do something special with Little David? No telling when Heath would show up. He often stayed gone from Friday night 'til Sunday morning. It had become a way of life for her by now. He still played for the barn dances, but she knew there was more to it than that. Night after night, her heart ached with loneliness and her pride was crushed. But what could she do? Often, when anger overruled all other emotions, she thought about leaving. But where could she go? She couldn't go back home. Her Father was drinking heavily now, and it would be worse there. Of course, Heath's folks were out of the question. They had grown more and more distant since Little David was born. Finally, she gave up thinking about leaving altogether and settled into a passive lifestyle—taking what comes. Her only joy was Little David. After breakfast, she asked, "How would you like to go on a picnic today, Little David?"

"Me go pic'a'nic...me go pic'a'nic," he repeated, clapping his chubby little hands.

"Mama will pack us a lunch and then we will go. We will climb *way* up the mountain where the birds live."

While it was still early, they set out. Emily carried the old, worn-out picnic basket which had belonged to her Mother. She remembered her Mother taking her for picnics when she was little. But that was so long ago—her Mother had changed. She was quite young when the changes began. Suddenly there were no more picnics, no more laughter. She seemed to drift away from them, away from reality.

"Mommy!" Little David squealed with delight as he pushed the low branches out of his way and trudged along beside her.

She laughed at him. He was so cute climbing up the mountain with such effort, his short, stubby legs pushing onward.

Poor Mother, she thought again, remembering

her visit the other day. It's strange how we see things in a different light when we grow up. Now I can see what happened to her. Her whole life was Daddy and when he went down, he took her with him. She lost all hope and happiness. That will *not* happen to me, she thought, pushing forth with more vigor than ever. No matter what happens, I will *enjoy* life…I will *love* life…I will *be happy*!

Little David smiled up at her as if he knew her thoughts.

"I bet you don't know what I put in this here basket for you."

"Ham bickets," he said, grinning.

"Besides ham biscuits, I bet you don't know."

"Doggy!" he exclaimed with his big eyes lighting up.

"A doggy! Now, Little David, how could a doggy be in this small basket?" All he talked about lately was a dog. He sure did want one. "No, guess again."

"But I wants a doggy, Mommy."

"Well, there's no doggy in the basket, Little David, but there are some sugar cookies in here for you."

"Goodie," he said, forgetting about the doggy for a while.

They finally reached the spot Emily remembered— a beautiful meadow way up looking down over the valley. It was grassy and had a mountain stream flowing behind it. There were masses of tall pine trees surrounding it. She had climbed up here right after they were first married and, inspired with its beauty, had returned several times. The last time was before Little David was born, though. Now it really looked like a fairyland with the trees beginning to turn colors. While Little David sat on the edge of the stream and patted his bare feet in the cold water, Emily began to put together the thoughts that came rushing into her head whenever she felt inspired with the beauty of nature. After several attempts, she whispered the finished product as if afraid of the disapproval of the tall pine trees and their sisters and brothers of nature.

> The maiden of Spring may wear her roses
> The maiden of Winter—her soft white coat,
> But they cannot compare to that little Miss
> Who arrives each year on her rainbow float,
>
> Upon her arrival—she quickly spreads
> Her colorful dress all over the land
> With sequins of gold and crimson reds
> Its beauty increases as it expands
>
> Yes, she is here—here again
> The prettiest maiden of all,
> But bringing death to all the land
> She makes her departure—this maiden of Fall!

"Mommy!" Little David called. "Come'ere Mommy."

What fun he was having. She pulled off her shoes and joined him in the water. Catching his hand, they waded the stream, stepping on the smooth, slippery rocks. It was so peaceful, with only the sounds of the rushing water through the big rocks, the soft, gentle breeze rustling the leaves that hung over the stream on both sides, and the birds singing way up in the tall trees.

"This where birds live, Mommy?"

"Yes, Little David, this is where the birds live way away from all the noise of people. They don't have to worry about someone shooting them or shooing them away."

"Daddy shoo bird 'way—I see him."

"Well, that's because Daddy didn't want them to eat up the seeds he'd planted in the garden. Look way up there, Little David, in that big oak tree—see that pretty red bird? That's a robin—probably a daddy robin. The daddy robins are always the prettiest."

He watched the bird intently for a short while, then went back to splashing the water with his feet. They spent most of the day enjoying the wonders of nature and each other. The food was delicious. The fresh mountain air seemed to have increased their appetites. Shortly after lunch, Little David fell asleep with his head on her lap as she leaned against a tree trunk. Emily also drifted between reality and a pacifying semi-sleep forgetting all her trouble back home. After their rest, and more playing and walking in the woods, they began their little journey back down the mountainside to home.

SOON ALL THE BEAUTY of autumn disappeared and death did fall over the land. The trees stood bare except for a few oaks whose crisp, brown leaves clung on desperately as the fierce, winter winds began to blow. It was a long, cold winter with only Christmas breaking the monotony. This Christmas was especially great with Little David just old enough to really understand all the excitement and anticipation. Emily spent hours making little decorations for the cabin while he watched and helped. She hung paper ornaments over the doors and windows. Little David exclaimed over each new thing. Heath even came back to his old self a bit with all the festivity. He stayed home more and seemed to enjoy watching Little David and Emily getting ready for Christmas.

Finally Christmas Eve arrived and Heath took her and Little David with him to find the Christmas tree. The three of them trudged around in the snow looking for just the right one.

"There it is!" Heath yelled.

Sure enough, it was the prettiest one they'd seen yet...tall and full, just waiting for someone to come along and chop it down so that it could adorn a home for Christmas.

And how it did! It stood tall and proud in the corner of the living room, filling the small cabin with its strong cedar scent. Emily had popped several bowls of popcorn, and she and Heath kept busy stringing it. After they had hung all the popcorn and the other ornaments she and Little David had made, they sat down to enjoy their beautiful tree. Heath had a good fire going in the fireplace which warmed the cabin comfortably even though the winds rattled the shutters outside. Anyone peering through a window would have seen a beautiful sight...the three of them huddled together on the couch, Heath in the middle with Emily tucked under one arm and Little David, just about to fall asleep, hanging onto his other arm...all watching the Christmas tree as the shadows from the fire danced upon it making it come alive.

"Guess what, Honey?" Heath asked suddenly.

"What?"

"We're invited over to my folks' tomorrow."

Emily sat a bit stunned. Could it be true? Were they finally coming around after all this time?

"When did you find this out?"

"Yesterday."

"Well, why didn't you tell me sooner?"

"I figured it would get you in too much of a stir. You know, you'd worry about it and all."

"I reckon you're right about that. But, gosh, what will I wear, and what can we take them? We should have gifts for them, you know."

"Now just settle down. See, I *knew* you would get all excited. That's why I didn't tell you sooner. No, we don't have to take gifts. They understand, and anything you wear will be fine. You look beautiful in anything."

Emily smiled at him and sat back and relaxed, at least on the surface. But inside, her mind was racing with all kinds of thoughts. What would it be like? How would they treat her? She had never even met his Sisters and Brother!

Christmas Day dawned cloudy and gray with a few snow flakes beginning to fall. Emily jumped out of bed, shivering as her bare feet touched the cold wood floor. She quickly drew her big shawl around her tightly as she went to make the fire. Her skillful hands soon had a good warm fire blazing in the fireplace and also in the kitchen stove. The Christmas tree now proudly displayed the gifts beneath it. It had been a wonderful Christmas Eve! After putting Little David to bed, they tipped around, placing his gifts under the tree, bumping into each other in their eagerness to have it look just right for him. The little wooden wagon stood out among the rest of the gifts. How proud she was of Heath. He had spent hours making it and then painting it that bright red. Next to it was the furry teddy bear she had scrimped to buy—even if it had been the smallest and most scraggly compared to the other bears in the store. Now, here at home under the tree, he was beautiful. Then there lay the mittens she had made for him out of the yarn Mrs. Barrett had sent her quite some time ago. Maybe she wasn't so bad after all. Maybe she was just being silly worrying about today. Suddenly she felt happy all over.

She couldn't wait for Little David to wake up, but knowing they had a big day ahead, she quietly went about breakfast, hoping he would get as much sleep as possible. She noticed the snow still coming down out of the kitchen window, and remembered Heath's predictions. He had said last night that it was going to snow today and he was right. He had stood at the window looking out, "We'll have snow for Christmas, and it's going to be the best Christmas ever." It had already been the best Christmas for her, even if there were no more.

After eating breakfast and watching Little David play with his toys, they made ready for the trip to the Barretts. Soon they were in the wagon with blankets wrapped around them, making their way through the lightly falling snow, and singing *"jingle bells, jingle bells, jingle all the way...."* Little David laughed and sang all the way.

"Put your hands in your pockets, Little David," Emily instructed, smiling at him as he kept waving his little hands in the air, enjoying his new mittens. "Your potatoes will get cold."

"You know, that's a pretty good idea. I wonder why we never did that," Heath said.

"Probably because you never had the need to." Emily smiled up at him. "Many a day when I had to walk clear from home over Spears Mountain to find Daddy for Mama, she would give me two hot potatoes to put in my pockets. I remember one time in particular. I know it must have been twenty below zero, and I'm sure I would have frozen if it hadn't been for those potatoes."

Heath looked at her with love and understanding, as he did whenever she spoke of her childhood.

THE BIG SOLID OAK DOOR stood as a barrier between her world and the Barretts'. Could the two meet? Emily wondered as she stood holding Little David in her arms while Heath rapped the shiny brass knocker.

"Darling!" Mrs. Barrett exclaimed as she opened the door, pulling Heath inside and hugging him to her at the same time. Emily followed, and stood unnoticed for what seemed like hours before Mrs. Barrett finally turned to her. "Oh, Dear, do come into the parlor…where we can all have a look at this fine young man." While saying this, she put out her hand to touch him, but Little David turned away. Withdrawing her hand, she turned to Heath.

"Heath, Darling, you look like you've lost weight! Have you been eating enough? No, it's probably that job of yours. I know you're probably working too hard."

Before giving him time to answer, she turned to Emily, "You know, he always was such a delicate boy, not as tough as Robert. Oh, I don't mean that he couldn't keep up with Robert—he sure did, but he was always one to fall sick more easily and oftentimes lost weight when he was too caught up in school activities and such."

"Oh, Mother, for Pete's sake, don't go on and on," Heath broke in.

Failing to notice his irritation, his Mother continued. "I always did keep a special eye out for him, you know. Whenever he started looking a bit pale or somewhat thinner, I would pile the potatoes higher on his plate and chase him to bed earlier. Of course, that wasn't always so easy. Now, Heath, Son, you just sit down right there in Papa's chair while I fix you something warm to drink. Emily, you might like to sit there by the east window. It's a lovely view."

She was right about that. The view was breathtaking. The lazy, sloping hills rolled down to a small lake that was frozen over. Old, twisted, willow trees bordered it on two sides with their naked branches hanging low, some caught fast in the ice. Starting back up the hill on the other side, there was a small building, now leaning with age. It looked like a house, but was very roughhewn. What had it been? Who had lived there?

"Look what Annie's got for her big man!" A loud, bass voice entered the room, accompanied by a short, heavy, black woman.

"Annie!" Heath exclaimed, rising from his chair. "Where've you been? The last time I was over, you had taken off somewhere."

"Now, Son, you knows I don't goes far. But I had'ta make a call on ol' Mrs. Brown. She's been failing fast." Turning to Emily, she said with a hearty smile, "This'ere must be Miss Emily. I's heard much 'bout ya."

She waddled over to Emily and grabbed her small hands in her big dark ones. "Why, Child, you is the littlest thing I's ever seen. Heath, you feedin' your little woman good?" she asked, turning to him again with a smile.

Just then Little David peeped out from behind Emily to see this person with the big voice.

"Well, jumpin' grasshoppers, look who's I see!" Annie boomed as she caught sight of him. "If it ain't Heath all over again when he was a youngster."

"Now I wouldn't go so far as to say that, Annie. There is some resemblance, of course, but Heath was much more wiry at that age and much darker," Mrs. Barrett broke in as she entered the room with hot drinks. "Frankly, I think he looks more like his Mother."

"You're right, Mother. He *is* more like Emily and we're sure glad of that," Heath added with a laugh.

Mr. Barrett was a very quiet man, hardly speaking at all. Maybe it was because he couldn't get a word in between Mrs. Barrett and Annie. The women kept Heath busy with questions and talk of the past. He seemed to be enjoying it. Little David had laid his head over on Emily and was just about asleep. She guessed the trip had been a little much for him. Now she was left alone to take in the room and its massive furniture. No one seemed to notice her as her eyes roamed from one corner of the room to another. It was very large, almost as large as their whole cabin. There were six big windows from the ceiling to the floor, with heavy, crimson, velvet drapes adorning each one. The furniture was old, but she could tell that each piece was very fine. It was extremely formal, not very "comfy" looking. She didn't care for the massive, formal furniture, but loved the soft, delicate wallpaper with its intricate design. She studied it, trying to make out what the design represented, but finally decided it was nothing unless the eye of the beholder chose to create his own answer. All in all, the room had class. Everything about it had class.

She wondered how Heath could be happy in their little mountain cabin after all of this. Suddenly she heard a multitude of voices, and looking out the window, saw a herd of children racing past the window, jumping onto sleds and skidding down the lazy, sloping hills that had just moments before been so tranquil. Then the front door opened, and she heard more voices in the entrance hall. And before she was ready, she was being introduced to the rest of the family.

"Emily, this is Elizabeth, Heath's oldest sister, and her husband, John. Where are the children?" Mrs. Barrett asked.

"Oh, they're sleigh-riding already, Mother," answered Elizabeth, a tall, handsome lady.

"Oh, of course. And this here is Robert, Heath's big brother, and his wife, Constance."

"How do you do," Robert reached his big hand out

for a hearty shake. Emily shook his hand but noticed that Constance forced a slight grin on her cold face and then walked away.

"And last but not least is Karen and her husband, William. Karen comes just before Heath." Karen smiled more warmly than any of them as she shook Emily's hand.

After the introductions, everyone was talking and laughing and she found herself alone again, but this time she welcomed it. Gosh, what a family! If she had been in enemy territory, she wouldn't have felt more alien. The screams of laughter coming from outside again caught her attention. The hillside was covered with little people all hooded and wrapped up so that she couldn't tell whether they were males or females. She began to count them...one...two...three...four...five... six...seven...eight...nine...ten...eleven...twelve. Wow, twelve kids, she had forgotten there were so many. Heath had told her all about them, but seeing them was something else. Before they had just been numbers. Now, they were live, moving people all around her, inside and out. She looked down at her own. Little David was sleeping soundly midst all the excitement. Heath had wanted to wake him up when everyone first arrived, but they had decided against it. In fact, no one really seemed that interested in Little David anyway. It was downright disgusting how they ignored him. She wondered if Heath had noticed it. If so, he wasn't letting on.

She looked back out the window. It was snowing more now. She hoped it wouldn't get too bad before they had to go home. Suddenly, one of the larger children pushed a smaller one down and then began the fight which ended in a free-for-all snow battle. Captivated, Emily didn't notice when someone sat down beside her.

"Miss Emily, I's sho glad to meet you," Annie said with a smile from ear to ear.

"Well, so am I, Annie. Heath's told me a lot about you."

"He has, has he...well'sa, he was my baby for sho. I loved'm like my own. Course, I loved'm all but Heath boy was sort'a special, you know."

"I know," Emily agreed with a knowing smile.

Annie leaned over, looking out the window also. "Look't them chilluns, would you. If they ain't havin' the time of their life. I remember watching their Mamas and Papas doing the same thing." She laughed. "Course, they done multiplied!"

"Yes, I hadn't realized there were so many. I just counted twelve."

"Yes'm, and yourn makes thirteen...the more there is...the better I likes it."

She was the first to really include Little David and Emily was immediately drawn to her.

"I haven't been able to make out whether they're boys or girls."

"Well'sa I can't rightly either, the way they're bundled up. But six of the biggest out there is Robert's boys. They're all big like him. And then four of 'em belongs to Lizabeth...she has two boys and two girls. And the other two be Karen's. They're twins, you know...both girls...identical. I finds it hard to tell 'em apart."

"Do you know what that old building is out there?

Emily asked. "I've been sitting here wondering about it."

Suddenly Annie's countenance changed, and she had a far away look. She was quiet for a while before answering. "Yes'm, I sho do. That tha's my home. I was born right tha, long with my brothers and sisters. That was in the slavery days before yo' time, Child. Them's was hard days...yes'm...hard working days. You see, Mr. Barrett's Pa before him wasn't a nice man like himself. No'sa, he was a fierce man, Mr. Barrett was...whippin' his slaves and making 'em work from daybreak to dark...my Ma and Pa had a hard life, God rest their po' souls."

Emily noticed a tear fall down the old woman's face. "You see that tha' horseshoe hanging over the door upside down?"

Emily strained her eyes to see it but really couldn't. It was too far away. "Well'sa, maybe you can't, but it's tha'. My Pa put it tha' when I wasn't much bigger than your baby. He said it was to bring 'em good luck. That's why it's hung upside down, you see, so that tha' good luck can't leak off." She wiped the tear off her brown face. "Course, it never did work, but maybe it helped Pa...you know...gave 'em hope."

"Well, Annie, how come you're still here? How come you didn't leave when you could?"

Annie looked at her and smiled her big smile. "Well'sa, my Brothers and Sisters all did. But you see, my poor Papa was still livin', but hardly. He was right near death, and I stayed on to take care of 'em. And, God rest his soul, when he left this'ere ol' world for a better one...well'sa, I just stayed on. I didn't have no home nowheres else, and the young Mr. Barrett was'a then taking over the place just 'bout. He was a sight better'n the old man, and his young wife, Mrs. Barrett tha, took a fancy to me...she wanted me to stay on. Then the young 'uns kept'a coming. You know, Mrs. Barrett, she lost two babies. One was'a dead when 'twas born and the other, well it died when it was only a couple of weeks old...don't know what happened to't. Course, them four kept us a runnin'. They's were a hardy bunch...'specially that'n of yours."

She laughed again. "Yes'm I kin member one day when he was 'bout four years old, he took't on himself to..."

"Annie!" Mrs. Barrett called, "Annie, come help me. It's time for dinner."

Annie jumped up without finishing her story and took off after Mrs. Barrett. "I's be back later," she called to Emily over her humped shoulder.

Emily noticed Heath was engaged in a deep conversation with his Father and Brother. He seemed to be enjoying himself. She was glad of that. The women folk were all trying to talk at the same time, and she was glad somehow that they hadn't included her. She turned again to look out the window. The children had gone back to sledding. Everything was a bit more peaceful now. She looked at the old shack again, but now it took on a whole different appearance. It wasn't just an old shack anymore. No, it contained memories— so many memories—within its tired walls. She wondered why it hadn't been torn down. Why was it left to stand as a reminder, a sad reminder? Emily slipped out of the noisy room through the familiar avenues of

her mind and paced the corridors of time composing her
thoughts ....

> Why are you still standing there?
> Oh little shack of slavery
> The snows of today you proudly wear
> How many snows will this be?
>
> You sheltered the babes of slavery
> You heard their cries of hunger
> But now they lie in history
> So why do you still linger?
>
> Your walls are decayed...your roof torn
> But still hanging is the good luck shoe!
> Which over your door you've always worn
> And now has proven true!
>
> Yes the babes of slaves are now free!
> So let your walls fall in peace
> How many snows will this be
> Oh little shack of slavery!

After a sumptuous Christmas dinner with turkey,
dressing, giblet gravy, hot sweet potatoes, butter beans,
homemade rolls and on and on, everyone left the formal
dining room with its large oak table and chairs. They
made their way back into the parlor, passing by the
open kitchen door where the laughter of the children
floated out to them. They were still enjoying seconds of
lemon pie and chocolate cake. Emily returned to her
spot beside the east window. Heath joined her briefly

before he was called to join in a game of checkers William had set up.

Karen rushed over and asked her to join her and the twins in some more sleigh-riding, but Emily declined, not wanting to leave Little David. He was wide awake now and sitting at Heath's feet, turning the pages of a big catalog very slowly. She could tell that he wasn't completely at home here. The stern faces from out of the past looked down upon him as they hung over the fireplace. They were his ancestors, too, Emily thought to herself as she studied the proud but distant portraits. The painter had caught more than the actual appearance—he had captured the proud, cold look of the Barretts. They were all that way for the most part...except for Heath...and Karen. She appreciated Karen's offer and had told her so. She turned to watch her and the twins through the window and saw the three of them go over the hill and disappear for a moment before emerging as a dark spot against the fluffy, white snow.

"Well, it won't be long now and we'll have our fifth, Constance," Elizabeth bragged. "We're going to catch up with you yet," she rubbed her swollen stomach.

"How far along are you exactly, Elizabeth?" Mrs. Barrett asked, not looking up from her knitting.

"Six months tomorrow. Oh, by the way, did you hear that Ethel Drinkard had her baby day before yesterday?"

"Why, they've only been married eight months!" Constance exclaimed. With this, she looked directly at Emily, who had finally tuned in on the conversation.

All eyes turned in her direction.

Emily could feel the blood rushing to her face, and she knew it would soon be as crimson as the curtains. But Mrs. Barrett changed the subject by asking if anyone would care for some tea.

There was a combined echo of yes, and as everyone focused their attention on being served, they forgot the previous conversation. All that is, but Emily. She sat looking out the window again, feeling her face cool off, and suddenly she felt like crying. But, no, she wouldn't! "You will *not* cry!" she told herself silently. "Maybe they will never like you or accept you, but you still have your pride. You will *not* cry!"

Emily hadn't seen Annie standing in the background, but she was there and soon as she'd finished serving the tea, she came over to her. "Won't you come with me to the kitchen? I's got my special surprise back there and if you like, you can he'p me with it."

Emily looked up and smiled. "I'd love to, Annie."

Once in the kitchen, Annie pulled down two big boxes from the cupboards and opened them up carefully. "My fruit cakes. They all loves my fruit cakes."

"Wow, they're *beautiful*, Annie. You sure know how to cook."

"Well'sa, I ought to. That's all I've ever done 'cept for runnin' after the young 'uns."

"I know that must have kept you busy."

Annie laughed. "You kin bet your bottom britches it did...'specially that Heath. I wouldn't have tha rest of 'em know't but he was my favorite, you know...being tha baby had some'in to do with't, but, well'sa, he had a way bout 'em that jest won ya' heart."

"And he loved *you* too, something special, Annie."

Annie chuckled. "He tell ya' that? Yes'm I was might worried 'bout 'em tha for a while though. He jest took to runnin' 'round with tha wrong kind, you know…troublemakers. He'd come in all hours of tha night. The folks couldn't do nothin' with 'em. I tried a talkin' with 'em but he wouldn't listen to no man. Well'sa, I commenced to prayin' for 'em. I prayed and prayed and jest like the good book says, He sho done answered my prayers. He up'n got himself a fine little woman and now a fine son. Yes'm he's gonna be all right."

Emily kept quiet, wanting to tell this good old honest woman about Heath's problems now, but yet afraid somehow.

All of a sudden they heard a strange yelping.

"What in tha worlds tha' noise?" Annie asked, running to the kitchen door and meeting Heath coming in with a little bundle of fur.

"What's that you got in yo' hands, Boy?" she asked, standing in front of him with her hands on her hips.

Heath dropped the furry little creature on the floor. It shook the snow off itself and then looked up at them all with big brown eyes.

"A puppy! Heath Boy, you git that animal out'a here. You knows I don't 'lows no animals in my kitchen!"

"Hold on, Annie, I am. What do you think, Emily?"

"For Little David?" she asked, rather surprised.

"Yep. It's my Christmas present to him."

Emily quickly knelt to the floor, rubbing the furry little body. "Oh Heath, he'll be so happy! Where did you get him?"

"Robert brought him over for us. I asked him about one a few weeks ago. You know ol' Lucy, Annie...it's one of her puppies."

"Well'sa, I thought I saw a resemblance of something. And, you know, ol' Lucy's Mama was the best dog we ever did have."

"So you see, Emily, he comes from a long history of Barrett dogs," Heath said, laughing. "Well, come on with me...let's take him in to Little David."

"Doggy! Doggy!" exclaimed Little David as soon as his eyes focused on the furry little creature. He ran to Heath with his little arms outstretched. The rest of the family looked on quietly as the three of them sat on the floor playing with their new addition.

"Would you look at that snow come down!" John said, breaking the silence.

"I believe there's gonna be a storm," Mr. Barrett added as he puffed on his pipe.

"A storm!" everyone exclaimed at once.

"Well, we better be headin' home," Heath lifted himself off the floor.

"Oh no, you can't go out in a storm, Son," Mrs. Barrett said in her commanding voice.

"There is no storm yet, Mother, only a little snow. We can make it. Emily, get Little David ready. You'll have something better than potatoes to keep you warm on the way home now," he smiled at Little David. The puppy was curled up in his arms already.

"There's no way I'd go out in this kind of snow," John added forcefully. Robert agreed and then William shared his view on the subject. "I think we all better stay here until we see what the weather is going to be."

Heath continued putting on his coat and went outside to get the wagon ready. Emily was tugging on Little David, trying to get his feet into the boots that were almost too little for him. She wondered why Heath was so set on getting home. The rest of the family spent several days at a time here anytime. At least, that's what she understood from little things Heath would say from time to time. He had never stayed very long when he visited here alone, but she had always figured that was because he wanted to get back home to her and Little David...but they were here, too. Oh well, she couldn't figure him out, that was for sure. Of course, she was anxious to get back home. She certainly didn't want to be snowbound *here*! One day was quite enough, but she still felt uneasy about going out into the snow, especially after what Mr. Barrett said about the storm. And then there was that little nagging fear because Heath had been doing a little too much nipping at the cider throughout the day. He *seemed* alright, but she wasn't really sure. Of course, no one else seemed to notice anything, but she could sense even the slightest change in him. Oh, there she was worrying again. Heath told her often enough that she worried too much. Maybe she did.

The wagon wheels began to turn, making long narrow tracks in the snow. They were on their way, huddled together as the wagon jolted back and forth down the winding road while the tiny flakes sprayed it white. The puppy snuggled closer to Little David.

The Barretts stood watching them from the long, wide windows.

"Well, I still think it was foolish of Heath to insist on going out in this snow, Edward. Why didn't you stop him?" Mrs. Barrett whined.

"Now, Mama, you know I can't stop him from doing anything he sets his mind to."

"Amen to that!" Elizabeth piped in. "Just like when he made up his mind to marry his little mountain girl."

"Elizabeth!" Karen retorted. "You shouldn't talk about her like that. I think she's rather sweet."

"I have to agree with Elizabeth, Karen," Constance said in her critical tone. "She no more fits into this family than...."

"Than what?" Robert asked suddenly. "I don't see anything wrong with her. Maybe not quite as much class as you ladies of society, but she's real quiet...and I'll vote for that anytime. How about you fellows?"

"I'll second it," John answered, laughing.

"Well, it does worry me whether or not Heath is really happy living in that little mountain cabin and all...after all, he's not used to that sort of life," Mrs. Barrett complained.

"Well, he looks happy enough for me, Honey," Mr. Barrett put his arm around her, "and it was certainly his decision to live there."

"If you ask me, he was probably ashamed to bring her out of the mountains. Can you imagine her entertaining a few guests?" Elizabeth asked sarcastically.

"Sure, wearing her little gingham dress she made out of a flour sack," Constance answered laughing.

"Wouldn't see a thing wrong with that," Annie spoke up as she busied herself around them clearing off the tables. "She's such'a pretty li'l thing. I 'spect she'd outshine most, don't matter what she have on."

"Well, well, I see that she's won the heart of someone around here." Elizabeth said, turning around to Annie.

"Sho has!" Annie declared as she left the room muttering to herself and shaking her head. "Now why did they have to talk 'bout her that'a way?" she mumbled as she entered the kitchen. "Well'sa, I reckon long as tha good Lord leaves us down here, there's gonna be those that think themselves better'n other folk."

Annie began to hum her favorite hymn, *The Old Rugged Cross*, as she set about cleaning up the kitchen. This way she wouldn't hear the conversation going on in the other room as the wagon disappeared into a heavy blanket of snow.

Finally out of sight of the house, Heath asked, "Well, what did you think?"

"Not as bad as I thought. It's a really big family."

"Sure is. Did you enjoy the day?"

"Yes," Emily answered slowly. "It was different from anything I've been used to. You sure have a beautiful home. I had no idea it would be so…so nice."

"Yeah, it's right nice…the pride and joy of Mother…and Father too, I guess."

"I especially liked Karen. She's my favorite."

"I figured you'd say that. She's my favorite, too. We were always closer. Of course, the others were alright in their own way. I hope you didn't pay any attention to Elizabeth and Constance. Those two have a habit of running their mouths too much and usually saying the wrong things."

"Well, to be honest, I wouldn't want to be around them too long. You know, you and your Brother sure are different. I would never take you for brothers if I didn't know it."

"You're right about that. Robert has always done everything right, and I've always done everything wrong."

"Heath, you shouldn't say that."

"Why not? It's the truth, but who cares?" He laughed and began singing. *"She'll be coming 'round the mountain when she comes, she'll be coming 'round the mountain when she comes, she'll be driving six white horses, she'll be driving six white horses...."* His voice rose higher and higher. Emily laughed at him but began to feel more uneasy. The snow was coming down much harder now and the wind was getting up, blowing it into their faces. She could hardly see ahead of them, but it didn't seem to bother Heath as he slapped the reins and sang louder.... *"She'll be coming 'round the mountain when she comes...she'll be coming 'round the mountain when she comes...she'll be wearing polka-dot pajamas, she'll be wearing polka-dot pajamas, she'll be wearing polka-dot pajamas when she comes...."*

Emily noticed the sky becoming very dark. The canvas over the wagon wasn't keeping the snow off them now as it blew in with each new gust of wind. Tucking Little David deeper inside the blanket which covered them both, she held him close. Heath just didn't seem to be aware of these changes. Blowing the snow off his face, he continued singing, *"She'll be coming 'round the mountain when she comes...."*

"Heath, Honey, don't you think you'd better slow down...."

"Who's driving this here wagon, Honey? Don't you start worrying. I've driven many a wagon in weather like this. Come on, sing with me."

But Emily didn't feel like singing. She realized Heath had had too much to drink. Why hadn't she seen this before? Why didn't she insist on them staying at the Barretts? She knew why. She had been too busy thinking about getting away from there. Oh, how she wished they were back there now, safe behind those massive doors, sheltered from the wind and snow and cold. She looked up into the huge, dark sky and whispered, "God, please take care of us!"

The snow was now turning into ice. It was sleeting. Emily realized they hadn't passed anyone on the road for miles. Oh, why couldn't they be safe at home like everybody else? She looked down at Little David who was asleep in spite of the snow and cold. The puppy was tucked in his arms, also asleep. What a beautiful picture. Of all the Barrett grandchildren, he was the most handsome. She smiled to herself—well, she was a little prejudiced.

She thought of how spoiled Elizabeth's children were...and when that little one threw that temper-tantrum. Boy, she would never let Little David get *that* spoiled! Suddenly she felt very tired. What a day! What a family! Looking at Heath as he sang, she was glad he was different. She thought about the things Annie had said about him. He was still like that mischievious little boy...only now he was a few feet taller. And Annie—she liked Annie. What a joy it must have been for Heath to grow up with her taking care of him. She thought of the little slavery shack and puzzled over how it depended on just where you happened to be born and to what parents as to how and what your life would be. Suppose by chance she had been born in the Barrett household, or on the other hand in the little slavery shack—how different her life would have been. Was it chance? She remembered the good luck shoe over the door of the shack. Was it luck? Somehow she felt like there was more to it than chance or luck. As she thought, Heath kept on singing…*"She'll be coming 'round the mountain when she comes, she'll be coming 'round the mountain when she comes, she'll be driving six white horses, she'll be driving six white horses, she'll be…."*

Suddenly the song stopped. Heath yelled, "Whoa!"

The wagon was sliding toward a steep cliff. Old Tom was doing his best to hold it back while Heath yanked on the reins. But it continued to slide. Emily was frozen with fear as she clutched Little David to her. Heath yelled and yelled and slapped Old Tom over and over with the whip, but the wagon kept sliding closer and closer to the cliff. Heath stood up, pulling Emily up to jump out of the wagon. There was a snap and the wagon tore away from Old Tom. It went over.

JUST A LITTLE WAYS down the road, Dan Johnson was carefully trying to make it home for Christmas when he heard a scream. It was such a wretched scream that it seemed to curdle his blood. His head, bent down against the wind and snow, jerked up suddenly. He immediately sat up straight and insisted on his tired horse going a little bit faster. As they rounded a sharp curve, he thought he saw something dark against the white snow. It was moving toward him. He finally saw through the blowing snow that it was a man waving his arms.

"Help, help…" Heath called.

Dan Johnson pulled up beside him.

"Please…Mister…please…help my wife, help my baby."

Dan had never seen such a look of terror on one man's face. His eyes bulged with fright as they turned from him toward the cliff.

"Oh, no!" Dan gasped when he saw why. There was a wagon turned bottom side up. After climbing down the slippery bank holding onto the frozen branches of bushes, he stepped on solid ground and made his way toward the wagon. He noticed the man had beat him down, practically sliding all the way and now he was sitting there by the wagon holding a young child. There was a young girl lying beside him covered with a blanket. He walked over to her and bending down could tell that she was only unconscious. But when his eyes fell on the young child in the man's arms, he could tell that it was dead. The man was sitting there rocking the child back and forth in his arms.

"Please help them, sir…my wife…my baby…please sir…" he pleaded.

Dan could see that he was in shock. He patted him on the shoulder. "You stay here…. I'm going to get the wagon…. I'll be right back."

Dan Johnson knew this land as well as his own back yard. He had roamed it as a little boy often and now he remembered a little, narrow road that used to lead off the main road and down toward where the overturned wagon was. Climbing back up the bank to his wagon, he remembered it used to lead to old Mack Jones' cabin. But old Mack had been dead for years now, and he didn't know if it would be passable at all. He expected it to be overgrown but headed for it anyway. Driving on as fast as he could in the blinding snow, he soon found it. Yes, it was still there and it seemed quite passable. He figured it was most likely being used now by some moonshiner. After winding round the narrow road, ducking branches and overgrown brush, he finally came to an opening and saw the overturned wagon just up ahead of him. The young man was still sitting in the same position he'd left him, and he was still holding the child.

After getting them into the wagon, Dan started back up the winding road. He was making his horse go as fast as possible against the snow storm that was now beating fiercely against them. Several times the old horse almost lost his way. The road was practically indistinguishable now. If it wasn't for the fact that Dan had driven this road so many times that he could almost drive it blindfolded, they would never have a chance. He didn't have time to check on the young girl, but every now and then he noticed the young man bent over her smoothing the blanket or something. He still held the child in his arms. He really thinks this child is alive, Dan thought to himself.

He breathed a sigh of relief when he saw the faint light shining through the snow. It was Doc Harris' house.

After leaving them safely in the doctor's care, Dan Johnson set out again for home. He was determined to make it home on Christmas Day.

Dr. Harris was working over Emily in the back room while Mrs. Harris sat facing Heath in the parlor. He held the small bundle close to him.

"Why don't you let me take the child for a while, Son," Mrs. Harris suggested tenderly, "and you can lie down there on the couch and rest." She had been trying for almost an hour now to get the baby away from him, but he had so far stubbornly refused. He still sat looking down into the face of the child with that blank expression. In all their years of practice, she had never before seen anyone in his shape. She had heard of cases like his, though. She wondered how long it would be before his mind would accept the fact.

She walked over to him, laying her hand gently on his shoulder. "I'll take care of him. You just lie down." She extended her arms, hoping he would yield the child. Still in a daze, he handed the small bundle to her and lay down.

Throughout the night while the storm raged on, piling the snow against the neat white cottage, Emily and Heath slept, not knowing what the morning held for them.

The doctor was up before daybreak, plowing the snow out in hopes to get word to the Barretts. He was able to make it to Matt Rhodes' place on Prince, the young stallion his son had left behind when he'd gone off to college this past fall. He knew he'd better not try to make it all the way, remembering his heart condition.

Matt was only too glad to help out and was soon on

his way to the Barretts' place. Everyone was seated around the large dining room table eating breakfast when he arrived. Annie answered the door and while Matt brushed the snow off in the foyer, everyone gathered around, sensing there was trouble.

"Doc Harris sent me here," he finally blurted out between coughs and trying to catch his breath. "It seems Heath and his family had an accident...."

Mrs. Barrett turned white and for once was speechless.

"Heath's alright and so's his wife," he hurriedly explained.

"What about the child?" Mr. Barrett asked.

"The child's dead."

Mrs. Barrett gasped and fainted. Mr. Barrett and Annie took her upstairs. The rest of the family just stood there.

Robert broke the silence by grabbing his coat and asking, "Who's coming with me?"

John and William began pulling their boots on.

"I'm going too," Ellen announced.

"We'll take the big sleigh. It'll hold us all," Mr. Barrett said, coming back down the steps.

When they entered the Doc's house, they found Heath at the kitchen table sobbing uncontrollably. Mrs. Harris was doing her best to console him. He didn't look up when they entered.

Dr. Harris had closed the door behind them and followed them into the kitchen.

"We were mighty worried about him," he practically whispered to Robert. "He wouldn't believe the child was dead when they first got here. But this morning, when he first woke up, it must have hit him all at once. He let out a'hollering and woke us all up. Been sitting there in that chair ever since, his heart breaking, poor thing."

"What about his wife, Emily," Robert asked, looking around for her.

"Well, that's what I was leading up to. She's yonder in the parlor sitting at the window. It's her we're worried about now. You know if a body can let it out...you know...let it all out...well, then they will commence to healing. But she hasn't shed the first tear yet. She just sits there staring out the window."

"Did you tell her? I understand she was unconscious."

"This morning after we were awakened by Heath's hollering, I went in to her and found her lying there, eyes wide open, staring at the ceiling. I commenced to break the terrible news to her but she stopped me, lifting one hand up and saying softly, *'I know.'*"

"And she didn't cry or anything?"

"Nope. Just sits there."

Robert followed the doctor to the door of the parlor. At first he gasped when he saw all the bandages on her head and arms.

"I thought she wasn't hurt?"

"There's nothing there that won't heal itself in a few weeks except for the broken arm, and that, too, will be fine in time. It's not the physical harm I'm worried about, though."

If Emily heard their hushed voices, she made no sign of it. She just stared out the window.

Once back at the Barretts', all the funeral arrangements were made by the family. Heath seemed to have grown old overnight. He moved around the big house silently, every now and then approaching Emily, gently putting his arm around her tiny shoulders, but she didn't seem aware of him or anyone else. She didn't talk and hardly ate. Once in a while Annie was able to coax her to eat a little soup or something.

The funeral was quick and small, only the family and a few close friends of the Barretts.

"I'm aghast that none of her folks have shown up!" Constance whispered to Elizabeth over Annie's head as they were being seated.

"Robert went over there and told them about it," Elizabeth said haughtily.

"And it turned out that her Mama's sick in bed with tha flu!" Annie interrupted.

"And her Father is gone off drunk!" Constance added with a sarcastic smile.

"Don't make no difference nohow," Annie looked over to Emily, "she won't know who's here and who ain't."

Emily sat up straight without a tear as the minister read on.

THE WINTER SNOWS SUBSIDED and soon it was spring. Emily stood looking out her small kitchen window. "Spring is here!" she said to herself. Can it be? She had been living in a daze for the past few months. A beautiful robin caught her attention and held it as she continued washing the breakfast dishes. As usual, Heath had left early for work. After seriously engaging itself in its search for food, the robin finally looked up toward the window and cocked its head sideways as if to proudly display its success. A fishing worm dangled from its beak. Emily felt like laughing for the first time in months. Then the robin lifted itself gracefully from the ground with its expanded wings and swooped up into a nearby oak, coming to rest on a nest with several tiny babies in it.

All of a sudden, Emily felt an overwhelming sadness take control of her, wiping out the laughter and replacing it with an emptiness greater than she could bear. The tears so long imprisoned broke forth, first slowly and then more rapidly. She cried out in grief and ran out of the cabin and up the hill to that clump of trees that sheltered the small grave. She threw herself down on the mound of dirt, sparsely covered with grass, and wept. She loosed those tears that had been stored up for months, and as they fell, her heart wrenched within. Hours later, she still sat beside the small grave, still and quiet. The tears had been shed at last and now the healing began.

Heath was puzzled as he stood watching her from the kitchen window. He remembered the days of the funeral, how she had nothing to do with anything or anybody but when it came to the burial, she demanded that he be buried here. In fact, she had even picked out the spot, there yonder on the hill, that they could see from the window here. But never once had she gone to the grave and when he had tried a couple of times to get her to go with him, she silently left the room. What had happened that now after all this time, he would come home and find her there? He left the house without eating lunch and returned to work.

Back at the lumber mill, he began loading the heavy timber, but the scene he'd witnessed under the clump of trees kept returning. He had been trying so hard for these past few months to forget the tragedy and escape the guilt that hung over him, but to no avail. When the lifeless body of their son was lowered into that grave, so was their love. Emily fixed his meals, washed his clothes, cleaned his house, but she was no longer his. She slept in the bedroom and he in the living room on the couch. At first he had tried persuading her, but when he felt her flesh cringe and withdraw each time he touched her, he soon gave up. They now moved about the cabin as two strangers might, avoiding each other, performing the daily tasks without conversation.

He threw the last piece of timber on the wagon and walked away announcing he was taking off early. He went into the millhouse to wash up and change clothes. After changing, he stood in front of the mirror smoothing back his hair. Yep, he was still proud of his looks. Everything had changed, but he still looked the same. Somehow he felt like he should look different. He took out his comb and began to comb the thick, wavy locks. He remembered when he had first discovered himself and how handsome he was. He had just gotten ready for Sally Brightwell's birthday party. It was the first time he'd worn the blue suit that his Mother had bought him for his fourteenth birthday. He remembered standing in his bedroom modeling the suit in front of his full-length mirror when Annie had knocked. She had come in and started fussing over him as usual.

"Now, Honey, you can't go with ya collar all turned up and sech. Look at ya!" she fussed, turning the collar down.

"I *am* looking, Annie," he answered, pulling away from her and straightening himself in front of the mirror. "What do you think?"

He remembered the look in Annie's eyes as if she were seeing him for the first time.

"Mercy, mercy me, Child, you done grown up and right under my own eyes, too."

"Well, what do you think?" he had asked again, impatiently.

"Well, I thinks any other young man in this 'ere county gonna have a hard time matchin' them looks," she said, smiling with her hands on her hips. No sooner than she'd gotten those words out, her expression changed to a frown, "but don't ya go gettin' no big head 'bout them looks now...tha good book says that God don't care 'bout them looks on the outside. No'sa, He looks down in'ta tha heart...."

He had walked out of the room while she was still talking. He didn't want to hear any more.

Now, years later, he stood looking at himself again. "Any other young man in this 'ere county gonna have a hard time matchin' them looks." He smiled to himself, turned to the door, and left for Tom's place.

He had been sitting there for about an hour drinking and trying to forget what he'd left at home out under the clump of trees when he felt a familiar hand rest lightly on his shoulder.

"Well, if it isn't little ol' Heath, Darling!" Betty Lou whined in her southern drawl. "Where have you been so long, Honey?"

HOURS LATER WHEN he pulled up in front of the cabin, he saw the faint glow from the lantern burning on the little table beside the window facing him. Why did she always do that? To make him feel guilty? Didn't he already feel guilty enough? Didn't he kill his own son? Didn't he kill their marriage? Didn't he do everything wrong? Wasn't he a failure? He sat there on the wagon looking up into the blackened sky that was gradually becoming gray with dawn. Why had he been with Betty Lou? Of course! She made him feel like the man he wasn't. She helped him escape reality. But how long could he go on escaping reality? When would it catch up with him? After putting the horse away, he reluctantly opened the door hoping she would be asleep. The house was still. He picked up the lantern, moved into the kitchen, poured himself a tall glass of buttermilk and sat down at the table. A small piece of paper neatly folded and tucked under the sugar bowl caught his attention. He picked it up, unfolded it and recognized Emily's handwriting as he read...

> Those whispering winds that we did hear
> Silently filled with sweet melodies the atmosphere
> That surrounded my only love and me
> As we lay beside the slumbering sea,
>
> The pine trees swayed above our heads
> And left mysterious shadows around our beds
> Which were made of mosses and flowers
> But we did not cringe from nature's powers

For the work of nature was our hearth
And to take its place was none on earth
With my love beside me I shed no tear
Devotion absorbed my soul when he was near,

Together we would climb the highest mountains
And silently drink from mother nature's fountains
Then descending, the tree tops we would view
As they glistened under a film of dew,

Gliding over a remote and desolate meadow
We were enchanted by the murmuring stream as it did flow
I was bound with happiness till I seemed to strain
When thoughts of ever losing my love brought me pain,

As we stood gazing at the sun
Which was steadily creeping beyond the horizon
His tiny and divine head I did behold
Turned toward Heaven with eyes aglow,

Now I sometimes wonder if
He was sent from Heaven as a gift
To lift my spirits up from despair
That seemed to have dropped beyond repair,

For his presence presented me with happiness
Far beyond any known or unknown bliss
But now I roam the fields alone
For my little baby has gone home,

I pour out my sorrows for the one I miss
As I clutch his little tomb, so cold and lifeless

But I know my baby is soaring in wings
For I hear his tender angelic voice as he sings....

He laid the paper down. This was what it was all about, why she had been out there today. He stood up and started for the living room, but the tears that were stinging his eyes now blinded him, and he groped for something to hold onto. His hands touched something warm and soft. Emily put her arm around him and led him to the couch where he buried his head in the pillows and smothered his cries. She lay down beside him and held him to her.

"Emily, oh Emily...."

Chapter III
The Decision

She inhaled the crisp, spring air deeply and looked around. "The dogwoods are blooming," Emily said out loud and reached to touch the delicate flower of one of the many blooming dogwoods that surrounded the cabin. She gently caressed each of the four ends of the flower and remembered the old legend that her Mother told her.

Many believed the dogwood to be the tree that the cross of calvary had been hewn from. And because of that, a curse was placed upon the tree, causing it to grow spindly and crooked, never again strong and tall. She thought about that. Did it take pain and tragedy to create this unique work of nature so beautiful? She stood and again inhaled the crisp, mountain air, and determined in her heart to make her marriage beautiful no matter what.

That spring and summer, she and Heath renewed their vows...falling in love all over again, but this time they drove the stakes even deeper into the fertile soil and fulfilled each other's emptiness, the emptiness that Little David had left. They went on picnics and hikes throughout the mountains. They fished and swam in the streams and lakes. They spent all their time together, except when Heath was at work. He was always home on time, never staying out late. They experienced the heat of the long summer and the heat of their own passion, but the days began to shorten and hints of autumn were everywhere. Emily hated to see the summer end, the flowers die and the trees lose their leaves, but at the same time, she yearned once more to experience the "Alice in Wonderland" existence brought on by autumn on Oak Mountain.

She pushed the swing slowly with her feet and rubbed her growing stomach, feeling a surge of happiness. Four more months and the cabin would once more ring with the joyful sounds of a baby's cry. Suddenly she heard wagon wheels making their way up the rough mountainside and heard the tumbling of rocks that were being sent downward by the visitor, whoever it might be. She strained to see beyond the maze of trees, but it was useless until one made the last bend in the winding road and then suddenly they would burst forth in full view, just as Annie did right now. She was waving one arm while holding onto the reins with the other. She had a grin from ear to ear, a happy sight as she pulled to a halt in front of the porch, while the fringe of miniature balls danced from the roof of the Barretts' fancy, new surrey.

"Annie!" Emily shouted, rising to her feet.

"Why Child, you look like ya gonna pop jest any minute...no way ya gonna make 't ta December. I bet this 'ere arm full'a peach preserves that tha's more'n one in tha...."

"Oh, Annie, you don't mean twins?" Emily asked, smiling.

"And why's not? You knows the Mrs. was a twin?"

"Mrs. Barrett? I didn't know that."

"For's a fact...she sho was...course the other'n died 'rectly after birth. How do'ya like this'ere fancy rig?" she asked as she climbed down from the surrey.

"It's really nice. Heath told me his folks had bought a new one."

"I didn't figure on them lettin' me drive't tho...you know it being all new and sech...but tha Mrs....she knows I kin outdrive the most of 'em. I'll be in 'rectly...gonna water Suzie here...she done worked up a powerful thirst comin' up this'ere mountain."

She handed Emily the preserves and began unhitching the horse from the rig. "The Mrs. sent ya' these 'ere preserves...theys the best...be careful with tha bag there...I done brought ya some'in too."

Emily pulled out a tiny, porcelain cup with an intricate design of blue flowers.

"Oh Annie, it's beautiful!"

"That's for tha baby. Course now if'n it's two, I 'spect I's havin' to come'up with'a second. That'n tha's special tho. Twas Heath's when he was a baby. He loved that li'l cup some'in special." Annie smiled remembering the past.

"Mrs. Barrett doesn't mind parting with it?"

"Twasn't the Mrs....I bought't myself for'em on his first birthday. It was his most favorite. The Mrs. done went an' got'em a silver cup, but no'sa, he was gonna have mine. I kin still see 'em sittin tha with it clutched in his li'l hands."

"Annie, this is so nice of you. I will take good care of it."

"Now it'll belong to Heath's baby." The old, black lady looked into Emily's eyes sadly. "I wanted to give 't to Little David but things wasn't so's that I could."

"I understand. Come on up on the porch and sit a spell. It's so nice out here. I was just sitting here thinking about how it feels like fall in the air."

"Sho does."

They talked about the family and caught up on all the news. Then Emily spoke up with determination, as if she'd been waiting all this while for just the right moment.

"Annie, all babies *do* go to heaven, don't they?"

"Why sho, Child."

"You know, Annie, back in the spring, I was so torn and broken-hearted over Little David that one day I just sort of collapsed and spent most of the day beside his grave crying."

"Ain't nothing wrong with that, Honey."

"Well, the most wonderful thing happened. I haven't told anyone about this...not even Heath. I suddenly seemed to hear him singing among the birds way up, way up in the sky. You probably never heard him, but he used to sing a lot and so sweetly. And it was just like that...just like when he'd sing sitting on the floor beside me...but instead it was like he was way up there with the birds singing. I believe...well, I've thought about it a lot, and I believe it was God letting me know that he lives and is still singing way up there somewhere."

Annie wiped the tears from her eyes.

"He probably was, Child. God works in mysterious ways...tha good book says His ways are far 'bove our little ways an' we can't for nothin' understand all of His ways. But our God knows our hearts and He knowed how broken your'n was an' maybe He jest wanted to soothe it'a little by lettin' you know that Little David is up tha with 'em. Yes, Child, he sho is...he's up tha in tha wide open arms of God an' one'a these days you gonna see 'em agin."

Emily looked up at Annie with a troubled look in her clear, blue eyes.

"I don't know, Annie. I would really like to believe that, but...."

"But what, Child?"

"Well, I don't think I'm good enough to go, Annie. You really don't know me. I have carried so much hate and bitterness in my heart ever since Little David died...well...you have no idea. I hated Heath. I hated the Barretts. I hated everyone. I even hated God for a while. Not only that, but I broke one of God's ten commandments when Heath and I had to get married...."

"You's got it all wrong...you don'ts get to Heaven by being good. Why shucks, Child, if that was so, heaven'd be a mighty empty place. No folks are good 'nough to get to Heaven. Tha good book says that all'uv our righteousness are like filthy rags."

"I never heard that before. I've always heard that

we have to be good and live the Christian life."

"Gracious sakes, Child...we can'ts do nothin' to get to Heaven. Why, you kin try to be tha best person in tha whole wide world...you kin try to keep tha ten commandments an' all the rest...but'ya still won't make 't through those pearly gates 'cause tha good book says...For by grace are'ya saved through faith...and that not 'uv yourselves, it is tha gift of God...not 'uv works, lest any man should boast."

"You mean God just gives it to us?"

"That's right. He said, 'Whosoever shall call 'pon tha name of tha lord shall be saved.' Course we gots to believe in 'em."

"Well everybody believes in Him, I'm sure. We've all heard about Him."

"That's a different kind 'uv believing, Child. He don't means to believe with ya' *head* but with ya' *heart*. If ya' really believe in 'em with ya' heart, you'll trust 'em with ya' life and soul. You see, it's kind'a like this'ere swing I'm sittin' in. I could'a stood thar when ya' asked me to sit down an' said to myself—now I believe it'll hold me but never sit down in 'it...but when I comes over here and sits in it, then that really proves I believe it'll really hold me."

"Oh, I see. You mean to really believe in him is to trust Him."

"Yes'm, trust in what He did for us when He died on tha' cross. You see, God made a way for us t'git to Heaven by sendin' His only Son, Jesus, down 'ere to die for our sins...my sins...yo sins...everybody's sins. All we have t'do is believe that Jesus was tha Son 'uv God an' that He *did* die for our sins an' then jest receive 'em as our Lord and Savior."

"It sounds so simple."

"It sho is."

Emily sat in deep thought, pondering those things as Annie gently pushed the swing back and forth.

"You know, Annie, you're the second real Christian I've ever met. No, I can't say that. There was my Grandmother, but I hardly remember her. She died when I was so young. But I was speaking of Mrs. Campbell that used to live near here."

"Mrs. Douglas Campbell...yes'm, I knows who ya speakin'uv. 'Course I never knew 'er personal but I understan' she was a mighty fine Christian. She up an' moved away...didn't she?"

"Yes, her sister was taken ill all of a sudden, and she had to move in with her to take care of her. I believe she still lives somewhere close to Richmond. I was planning on asking her some questions when she came back to see me, but she never came back."

"What kind'a questions, Child?"

Suddenly they heard the rumbling of a wagon approaching at a rather fast speed.

"Lord, have mercy...who ya reckon that be burlin' 'round these 'ere mountains?"

Emily laughed, "Just Heath, Annie. Don't you remember how he drives?"

The old lady slapped her knee and laughed with her. "I plum nelly fergot...you mean I done stayed 'till dinner time? I got's to be gettin' home...the folks'll think I done run off with this 'ere new surrey and ain't comin back."

Heath rounded the bend, pulled to an abrupt halt

and jumped out of the wagon and onto the porch with one leap. He grabbed Annie and nearly pulled her out of the swing with a hug.

"Well, it's about time you started visiting us, Old Lady."

"What you talkin' 'bout, Boy. I done been here two times before an' you never home...an' ain't I done told you 'bout drivin' that wagon like the fires a Hell are lappin' at your rear?"

Heath laughed harder than Emily had seen him do in a long time. He and Annie had fun teasing each other at the dinner table while Emily watched them with a smile. It didn't take too much coaxing from Heath to get her to stay for dinner, but then she had always been an old softy when it came to Heath. After dinner, though, she immediately set out for home and Heath went back to work.

Emily picked up her shawl and started out of the cabin with a purpose in her heart. She walked up the hill toward Little David's grave, paused for a moment, and then passed on. The sun felt good as its beaming rays shot down from the clear, blue sky through the tall, pine trees and caressed her shoulders underneath the shawl. The mountain breezes tossed her hair gently as she climbed higher up the mountain. After a while her destination came in view as she pushed forward the last few yards. By now she carried her shawl over her arm and perspiration dripped from her forehead. She wondered if maybe she shouldn't have tried to come so far. Sitting down on a rotting log, she caught her breath as she still looked ahead. Just a little farther and she would be there. She wondered what Heath would say if he knew where she was and how far she'd climbed up the mountain. He would probably scold her pretty good, but she just had to get to that spot. She didn't understand herself why it was so important to her, but she wanted a special place to do what she intended to do and this was it. She got up, wiped her forehead, and proceeded on. She finally arrived at the spot...the very spot where she and Little David had their last picnic. Picking out a shady tree, she sat down under it and looked up to heaven.

"God, I don't really know how to pray. So, I'm just going to talk to you. It looks like I've made a mess of my life from the beginning. I realize now that it's not your fault, or Heath's fault, or anybody's fault but mine. Yes, God, I have sinned against you. But God, I want to go to Heaven one day...I want to see Little David again, and you said that whoever would call upon You...call upon the name of the Lord...would be saved. I want to be saved, God."

She began to cry softly. "Please, God, save me...please come into my life. I believe in your Son, God...and I'm giving my life to you."

She found herself trembling as she finished talking—so intense had she been, so sincere. She realized as she sat back relaxing that she had made a decision— an eternal decision. She didn't know how, but she knew her life was going to be different.

CHRISTMAS HAD COME and gone once more. The new year was here, and it was snowing again. Emily watched each tiny flake descend from the hazy sky and thought to herself that no matter how much trouble it was, no matter how hard it made traveling in these mountains, she still loved it. She still felt that same excitement that she'd experienced as a young child upon waking up in the morning and discovering that her world had turned white overnight. Suddenly her thoughts were interrupted by the loud cries of a baby, and she rushed to the bedroom and picked up Patrick, hugging him close.

"Now, now, Son...it's alright...Mama's here, and I know you're hungry...'course you're always hungry," she laughed. She sat down in the rocker with him and putting him to her breast, she began to softly hum a tune. He was content, and soon he was sleeping again, but she continued to hold him, enjoying every moment. God had been so good to her. He had given her another son, but not only a son. She listened to the little sighs from the bedroom. Yes, Annie had been right! Twins! She never dreamed that she would have twins. She got up and took Patrick back to his crib and then leaned over the other, straightening the covers.

"What a beautiful, little girl you are, Prudence Katherine Barrett!" The infant stirred in her sleep. "You too, Little Man." She turned and went out of the room. Yes, God had been so good to her. He had given her two babies to soothe the ache within. She went into the kitchen to put on some coffee. Heath should be home any minute now, and he loved his coffee.

Dusk was just settling in as Heath drove homeward. The wagon was almost silent as its wheels rolled over the new fallen snow. He pulled his cap down over his ears. The temperature was dropping fast. He thought of the cabin and the family that awaited him.

It was a happy place these days, with the joy of the twins filling it, and Emily hustling around like a little mother hen. She sure was content—yes, that's the word for it—content.

Somehow he found himself feeling envious and very much discontented. Oh yes, he was certainly happy to have the twins, and of course, he wanted Emily happy and was really glad to see her that way, but what about himself? Why couldn't he be happy and content like her? What was wrong with him? He had never really been content. He had never had the peace Emily seemed to have. He couldn't understand what had happened to her, but he figured it must have had something to do with that day he'd come home and found her out there beside Little David's grave. Ever since then she'd been different, like she'd found herself. And he'd caught her reading the Bible often. Somehow, this bothered him. He'd never been around anyone who just sat and read like that. It was like she was trying to digest as much of it as she could and enjoying it, too. Why, he'd never even been able to understand it, much less enjoy it.

The more he thought on these things, the less he felt like going home. The wagon came to a stop. Darkness surrounded him now, but the bright, white snow illuminated the night. He looked to the right and knew he should continue home, but his eyes were drawn straight ahead, knowing where that narrow, curvy road led. Well, why shouldn't he? He'd worked hard all day! And he hadn't been anywhere for a lot longer than that. Why shouldn't he? A couple of drinks might be the very thing to perk him up a little.

He pulled the reins. "Git'up, Tom." His voice rang
out in the silent night as the wagon lunged forward
down the curvy, narrow road. The snow was coming
down heavier now, almost blinding. Suddenly he imagined it was he and Emily and Little David again. The
snow was blinding him, but it didn't scare him. He
could hear himself singing again, "She'll be coming
'round the mountain when she comes, she'll be coming
'round the mountain when she comes...." He saw the
lights in the distance, bringing him back to reality.

Once more, he'd escaped the nightmare that constantly sought him, but not the guilt. His shoulders
sagged beneath the weight of it as he entered the
smoke-filled tavern. Will Walters was at the old piano
as usual, his nimble fingers bouncing over the keyboard
to the tune of *Oh Susanna*. The crowd welcomed him
back with a few slaps on the back and the rest just
nodded from their tables, some already showing signs
of how long they'd been there. Heath pulled up a chair
at an empty table and ordered his first drink. He
wanted to be among them and yet he wanted to be alone.
What was with him?

Sometime later he noticed Betty Lou come in with
Buck Bryant, their arms entwined. Well, how about
that? The old bachelor of the mountains! He wondered
what she saw in him besides his monstrous body. He
was for a fact the biggest dude in these here mountains.

Jake Floyd sidled over to his table, blocking his
view, and sat down in front of him.

"Where'ya been, Boy? Haven't seen you around
for quite some time."

"Been busy." Heath answered briefly, not really

feeling like talking.

"Yeah, I heard." Jake laughed in his boisterous way. "Got ya'self a set of newborn twins. That's the way ta do it, two at a time."

Heath turned up his glass in front of him, taking a drink and wishing Jake would get lost. He'd never been too fond of Jake. But he stayed there for about an hour, rattling on while Heath kept on drinking, once in a while uttering some comment.

"Looks like it's time for me to mosey on," Jake said suddenly, and he got up and walked over to the bar.

Heath looked after him and met the piercing eyes of Betty Lou coming his way. So that's why the sudden exit.

"Hello, Darling, I thought you'd died and been buried long ago."

"No way. I'm very much alive."

"I can see that, and still the most handsome man in these parts, too." She sat down in front of him.

"Aren't you afraid ol' Buck boy will get jealous?"

"Shucks no, he's too busy playing poker. He's forgotten I'm here."

"I don't see how he could do that."

She slowly slid her hand across the table to his. "I sure have missed you."

Feeling somewhat uncomfortable, he removed his hand and took another drink.

"You know, I feel a sick headache coming on...I wouldn't be surprised if I have to go home early." Her black eyes danced.

"Where's home?" Heath asked while watching her toss her long, black curls.

"The same place, at least for now. I'll be moving back home in a couple'a weeks...much to my dread. You remember, don't you?" she teased.

"Yeah, the place where you have to pipe the moonlight in," he grinned.

"Oh, it's not that far back in the woods, Silly Boy."

She stood up, smiled down at him, and walked back over to where the poker game was in session, swishing her white skirts. Shortly after, Heath noticed, she and Buck left.

About an hour later, he traveled down that lonely road remembering his words about the moonlight. It was true. The trees were so thick that they were just a towering maze against the sky, blocking out any light that might have helped a poor traveler. A poor traveler! Was he a poor traveler? Of course not! The trees seemed to echo...not a poor traveler...but a deceiving sneak stealing through the forest at night in quest of the forbidden fruit. Where was it that he'd heard about the forbidden fruit? It seems there was punishment that went along with that story. What was it? His mind was playing tricks on him. He couldn't think straight. Had he really drunk that much? Turn back...turn back...the trees seemed to call out. A thorny branch reached out, stabbing his eye.

He cursed it aloud, and it seemed as if the whole forest picked up those horrible words and flung them back and forth in a cruel and sinister fashion. He was about to turn around and head home when the small, familiar house appeared suddenly out of nowhere, and there was just barely enough moonlight for him to distinguish the white skirts on the porch. She was waiting.

IT WAS DAWN when the strange surrey pulled up in front of the cabin, but Emily was already up. Who can that be, she wondered. The man coming to her door was also a stranger. She could tell that he was colored, but that was all. She opened the door cautiously.

"Hello, Mrs. Barrett. Doc Harris sent me here to fetch ya. Mr. Barrett done had'a accident."

Emily turned white.

"Oh, tha doctor say he gonna be all right—it's jest his arm, Mrs. Barrett."

"What's wrong with it?"

"Don't know, Ma'am, but he can't move't a'tall."

Emily began to hustle around, throwing things together. "I don't know about the twins. It will be difficult taking them."

"That's why I brought the Mrs. along. She's yonder in tha surrey. She'll help ya take'm or she'll stay here with'em...with tha snow piled up tha way it tis we figured ya might not want to take'm out."

"You're right. I'd rather leave them. Please tell your wife to come on in. I will feed them and then we'll go."

All kinds of thoughts raced through her mind as they rode down the snow-packed road to Dr. Harris' place. Where was he all night? She felt guilty because she hadn't worried about his welfare really. She just figured he was back to his old ways.

"How did he get here?" she asked the doctor once there.

"Well, some friends of his brought him."

Emily noticed the strain in those words and asked no more. She never found out, but Heath retraced the event over and over in his mind while lying there in pain. How could he be so stupid? He remembered stepping up on the porch that night kidding with Betty Lou about the moonlight. He remembered her reaching out for him with that seductive smile and that was it. That was all he remembered except for the blow itself. That excruciating blow that had come from nowhere knocking him off the porch and out of his senses. It had to have been Buck Bryant. Though he didn't see him, he knew it was him. Well, he'd asked for it! But now what? How could he work at the lumber mill with a no-good arm? What was he going to do?

A FEW WEEKS LATER, he was still asking himself that same question. He stood watching Emily and the babies disappear around the curve. The snows had finally melted, leaving the road almost impassable, mud ankle deep and ruts that no wagon could conquer—but the sun had appeared yesterday hardening all this and Annie had made her way through. It was Sunday, and they were all going to church—to Annie's church. He wondered what his folks would think of it if they knew. Of course, they didn't, and he really didn't care if they did. He thought of the offer his Father had made him only yesterday. It sounded good, to get away from all of this…a new start, but yet, he didn't want to accept charity from his family. He hadn't had to yet, and he didn't want to start now. But what was he going to do? He went into the kitchen to fix himself a cup of coffee and started to reach for the cupboard door before thinking. Darn this arm. How many times he'd tried to use it and how many times he'd had the rude awakening—it was no good! Who would hire a man with a no-good arm? Somebody would...somebody *must*.

The wagon bounced down the road, digging the deepest ruts.

"My goodness, Child. You sho look nice all purtied up."

"Thank you, Annie." She was glad she'd worn her best gingham.

"And tha babies—if they ain't tha most beautiful sight in this 'ere whole wide world!"

Emily looked down at the little, ruffled dresses. She was glad now that she had scrimped and saved to buy that material. They were beautiful.

"You sho sew a fine stitch, Honey."

"Thank you again, Annie. But you know, Heath didn't want me to put Patrick in this little, ruffled dress, but I wanted them to look just alike...I guess I could have left the ruffles off, but aren't they pretty?"

"Sho are...don't pay no mind to Heath, Honey. Menfolks always that a'way 'bout their sons. Don't worry...there's time 'nough for 'em to be a man...let 'em be a baby now. How's Heath doin' anyway?"

Emily's countenance changed abruptly. "Annie, I'm very worried about him. He's withdrawing into some sort of shell. He just walks around like he's in another world most of the time, ignoring me and the babies."

"I ain't surprised, Child. A man needs t'feel he's a man. Now with only one good arm and no way'uv takin care'uv his family...why he sho to be down and out."

"I know.   But I'm concerned about what we're going to do."

"I know you must be, Child. You know Mr. Barrett done offered to help 'em out but Heath's got a hard head 'bout 'ceptin' help."

"Really! He didn't mention anything to me about it."

"Well, tha she is!" Annie pointed to a small, white church, its steeple rising sharply through the pine trees. It sat down in a valley with a mountain towering just behind it. A stream of cold, clear water was rushing down the mountainside, curving around the little church, then making its way off into the dense forest. Someone had built a bridge just big enough for two people to walk across. After taking care of the wagon and the horse, they walked across the bridge. It was beginning to show its age. The planks sagged and creaked as they crossed over. But Emily was inspired with the fresh beauty of this old place. She stood beside the small bridge, inhaling the cold, mountain air that the stream brought with it from way up off that rugged mountain. She listened to the gurgling sounds it made while pushing its way over and between the large stones blocking its path. Every now and then, there was a crunching sound when a large piece of ice floated downstream and collided with one of these stones. She looked up and found herself alone with Prudence in her arms. Annie had disappeared. She started for the church and then saw her with Patrick, proudly displaying him before an old couple.

"Ain't he a fine lookin' baby? Here comes his twin

sister...now she be tha prettiest baby girl anywhere in these'ere parts," she bragged, turning to Emily. "Miss Emily, meet brother and sister Tomlin...this 'ere my boy's fine young wife."

Emily awkwardly shook hands with the old, friendly couple.

"Let's go inside to the fire," the old man suggested.

Emily wasn't used to churches and felt a little hesitation about going in, but Annie grabbed onto her and the next minute she was in. A couple of nice, older men smiled and greeted them warmly. After being seated, Emily cautiously glanced around, taking in the small, cozy room. The pews were rather rough-hewn but worn smoothly in spots where many folk had spent time sitting. She wondered who all those people must have been. The church wasn't very full today, probably because of the cold weather. There was a pot-belly stove in the center of the room. A nice fire blazed within, knocking the chill off the room. The few windows were partially covered with ice, but still they let in enough light.

Over in the left corner was a piano, shiny and new-looking. Later on, she found out that it was a gift to the church from more prominent members. It certainly looked out of place. A pretty, young girl sat at it as if waiting for a clue to start any minute. Then suddenly she began to play with such ease that the melody filled the church, causing everyone to relax and grow quiet. Emily wondered about that girl. How did she ever learn to play so beautifully? It must be wonderful to be able to play like that! Emily noticed that all eyes were on the girl playing the piano. She wasn't the only one in awe.

Most of the people were dressed quite simply, like herself. There were no frills, but they were all neat and clean, and happy. Yes, that was it. They all seemed so happy. She looked at Annie. She was smiling and keeping rhythm with her foot. Emily glanced around again. Yes, Annie was the only colored person there. She wondered how it had come about. Patrick seemed very content in Annie's arms, benefitting from the lulling movement caused by her foot. She looked down at the sleeping face in her own arms. Well, they certainly were at home. Suddenly there was a commotion from the back of the room. She turned to see several half-grown boys pulling a curtain around a small area. It hung from the ceiling and when pulled, covered three sides, uniting with a wall, and becoming a room in itself. The girl at the piano began a lively note as the children from all over the room jumped up and made their way to the curtained-off room.

"That's tha chillun's Sunday School," Annie whispered with pride. "Now we'll have our'n right where we be."

Before she had the words out of her mouth, a tall, thin man with graying hair stood at the pulpit. He lowered his head and spoke with a soft, pleasant voice, "Our Father hath said, 'Be still and know that I am God.'" A hush fell over the congregation and Emily noticed all heads immediately bowed. Then there was complete silence for the next fifteen minutes except for an occasional rustle or movement from the curtained area. It concluded with the preacher praying the most beautiful prayer she'd ever heard. It was as if he were talking to someone right next to him. When he finished, he looked up with a big smile that spread from ear to ear and said, "It's now time for our Bible drill."

Emily saw that everyone was grabbing for their Bibles, and she remembered she'd left hers on the kitchen table. For the next fifteen minutes, the preacher called out a verse and the first one to find it would stand and read it aloud. She was glad to be holding Prudence, thus having an excuse not to participate, but the longer she witnessed this drill, the more she had a desire to be able to use the Bible skillfully herself. After this, they began to sing. Everyone sang out loud and clear as if they meant every word in the songs. It was a happy time for them all, she sensed. Emily gradually began to feel at home here in this place among strangers—but somehow they didn't seem like strangers. *"Amazing Grace...how sweet the sound that saved a wretch like me...."* She joined in with all her heart. *"I once was lost but now I'm found, was blind but now I see...."*

Just when she was getting used to Sunday School, it was over. The preacher sat with his head bowed. She figured he must be talking to God again. Soon there was a commotion at the back of the room again, and she noticed children coming toward the front, taking their places beside their parents. Then the preacher stood and began to read from the big Bible in front of him. The sermon was all about how *we* might die for our loved ones, but the Lord Jesus died for His enemies also...the unmeasureable love of God!

Emily sat glued to the pew listening intently. The preacher concluded with an invitation for all who had not trusted in the cleansing blood of Jesus to come down the aisle and publicly confess Him with their mouths if they had believed in their hearts. Emily felt a strong tugging at her heart. She knew she was right with the Lord. They had gotten that straight that day alone there on the mountain, but what about publicly confessing him? Everyone stood and began to sing softly, *"Have thine own way Lord, thou art the Potter...I am the clay...mold me and make me after thy will...."* Emily found herself stepping out from the pew and making her way down the aisle. Was it really her? It was as if a powerful hand was shoving her along. She held Prudence tightly to her breast as she approached the preacher who kneeled with her as they prayed.

"My heart 'twas 'bout ta break when I saw ya' take to tha aisle," Annie turned the wagon back on to the road home. "This sho be a happy day in my life."

"That makes two of us, Annie. You remember that day we talked about God, and you told me about the swing?"

"Sho do."

"Well, I have sat in the swing and I'm trusting Him with my life and my soul. I did it a while back before Heath got hurt, but today when the preacher talked about confessing Him with our mouth publicly...well, I just felt like I had to do it."

"Why sho, Honey. The good book say, 'if'n thou shalt confess with thy mouth tha Lord Jesus an' shalt believe'n thine heart that God done raise him from tha dead, you shalt be saved.' "

This was just the beginning of Emily's tie to the little Baptist church in the valley. She didn't miss a Sunday from then on. Of course, when the Barretts heard, they were dismayed and Mrs. Barrett herself made a trip over to awaken Emily to what she was doing.

"Emily, Honey, the Barretts have always attended Mount Moriah Baptist Church. I really can't see any reason to change things," she laughed uncomfortably.

"I'm not trying to change things, Mrs. Barrett. It's just that Mountain Creek Baptist is closer for us, and...well, Heath doesn't care to go to any at this time."

"I know that, but he was raised in Mount Moriah and all of his friends are there. His Great Grandfather was an original deacon there. Why, we go back a long way at Mount Moriah."

"Well, I'm sure you do, but strangely enough, Mrs. Barrett, I like Annie's little church."

"We all love Annie. Why, she's just one of the family, but to attend church with her might make for gossip. You know how these mountain people do talk."

Emily sat up straight trying very hard to conceal her anger. Why did the Barretts always have to be so downright self-righteous?

"Annie is a wonderful Christian, Mrs. Barrett, and I hope one day I can be as good."

"Oh, no doubt about that. She is that, but she is still a colored woman and...."

Emily stood up abruptly. "Mrs. Barrett, would you care for some coffee?"

The conversation ended and was never spoken of again. Not only did Emily continue attending the little church in the valley but eventually began teaching Sunday School. She found herself not satisfied to sit in the pew Sunday after Sunday drinking in all this wonderful news about her Lord. She wanted to do something. Every time she heard the curtain being drawn in the back, she felt an urge to be back with the children, but she couldn't teach! Why, she was only learning herself.

But one Sunday after church was over, Marianne Smith caught up with her just before she left. "I'm glad you're still here. Mother asked me to talk to you."

Emily had already met Marianne. She was the pretty, young pianist. "Oh, what about?"

"I guess you noticed she wasn't here this morning. That's why I had to take her class. Mother will be laid up for a while. She twisted her ankle trying to chase a stray cat out of the barn yesterday while milking."

"I'm sorry," Emily said, wondering what in the world this had to do with her.

"Well, you know I play the piano, and I don't think I'll be able to do both. Mother suggested I speak to you. She thinks you would be really good with the children."

"Me?" Emily asked with a puzzled expression. "But I don't know the Bible...."

"That's the best way to learn," Marianne interrupted.

"But I'm not worthy to teach," Emily added earnestly.

"Who is?" Marianne asked with a smile. "Mother would like to talk with you, and if you're interested, she can give you all the materials she has and also a few tips. We just live over in the hollow."

"Well, I'd have to check with Annie, and I'd have to go back home first to see Heath."

"Great, we'll look for you. Please try to come.

Mother will be delighted."

Annie was tickled over the prospect of Emily becoming a Sunday School teacher and encouraged her all the way back home.

Marianne pulled up in front of the old, rambling farm house that had been their home for more than a century and noticed the upstairs windows on the east side. The curtains were still drawn! Bitterness swept over her.

When she turned the doorknob, she could hear her Mother calling from the kitchen, "Betty Lou, Betty Lou, are you up yet?"

No sound came from upstairs.

Marianne walked across the living room, pulling off her shawl and worn, gray coat. As she hung it on the carved oak hanger that had belonged to her Father, again she felt the hurt caused by his sudden death. Though it had been several years now, the memory was fresh in her mind. She ran her fingers over the grooves in the polished wood and saw him coming through the door again, slapping his hands together for her and Betty Lou to run into. "His little angels," he called them. What would he think now? She was almost glad that he wasn't here to witness Betty Lou's scandalous behavior.

"Marianne is that you? How was church, Dear?" Her Mother called out to her in a cheery voice.

"Fine, Mother," she answered walking into the large, cozy kitchen. A fire was burning in the fireplace, and the room smelled of sausages frying.

"Mother, you aren't fixing breakfast on that ankle!"

"I'm just fixing a few sausages and toast, Marianne. I haven't put any weight on my ankle. See, I'm leaning on the table here."

"Mother, I fixed breakfast for you before I left for that very reason. I didn't want you on your leg at all." She felt herself becoming more angry. "Mother, she can wait on herself!"

"Now, Marianne, don't start anything," her Mother said gently.

"Start anything! Of course not, Mother. If you want to wait on her for the rest of her life, why should I interfere?"

"Marianne, you know she's had a hard time of it with James running out on her and all. She needs our love right now. Who else does she have?"

"I wonder, Mother. I don't think she's lacking, for sure!"

Her Mother went on talking as if she hadn't heard those last words. Marianne knew that she refused to believe the things she'd heard.

"Did you talk with the little Barrett girl?"

"Yes, and I invited her over. I think she might come."

"Who might come?" Betty Lou yawned, wrapping her robe tightly around her slim waist as she entered the kitchen.

"A sweet, young lady from the church, Betty Lou. She might take over my class for a while. Her name is Emily Barrett. Sit down now and eat your breakfast. We must get this kitchen cleaned up."

Betty Lou sat down slowly. Emily Barrett! That *must* be Heath's wife, she thought, while helping herself to the plate of sausages. Well, how about that! This ought to be rather interesting.

EMILY AND ANNIE found Heath on the couch staring at the ceiling. Emily fixed him hot broth and potatoes. He didn't seem to even hear them when they told him about their plans to ride over to Weeping Hollow.

"I sho am worried 'bout that boy," Annie said as they drove off. "He's gotta git hold 'uv himself with a family to support an' all."

"More than he knows about," Emily half whispered.

"What do ya mean, Child?"

Emily burst into tears.

Annie pulled the wagon to a stop and put her arms around the frail shoulders as they shook with the sobs.

"Everythings gonna be alright, Honey. I'm sho sorry fer speakin' like I did, but you jest go 'head an git all them old tears out...be good fer ya."

Emily began to talk between sobs. "Annie, I'm...I'm pregnant again. I'm not crying because I don't want the baby. I *do*. It's just that I don't think Heath will. He's already down enough because he's got a family to support and can't get a decent job...I haven't even told him yet."

"Now, now Child. Everythings gonna work itself out. Don't go gettin' yourself all worked up. Remember what the good book say 'All things work t'gether fer good t'them that love God and t'them that a' called 'cording t'His purpose.' It mightn't look that'a way now, but He's got 't all planned."

Emily looked up through a film of tears. "He does,

doesn't He?"

"Why sho. You know, I always think 'uv that verse. It sort'a minds me 'uv makin' up my bread. I put in a li'l flour, a li'l baking powder, li'l soda, and a li'l lard. Now none 'uv them things are good by themselves. You ever tasted lard or flour? But when ya take them hot biscuits out 'uv the oven. M-m-m-m-m," she smiled her big, warm smile.

"I think I understand." Emily wiped her eyes with the blanket that covered their legs.

"That accident that Heath had an' him not being able t' find work an' now you being with child…all of them things…they be like tha flour an' lard an' sech. They be 'a heap 'uv trouble for sho an' they ain't good…but He (she waved her big hands upward)…He be working it all out fer good fer ya. He say so!"

"Oh, Annie, I needed that. Will I ever have your kind of faith?"

"Sho, Child. Jest trust Him…that's all." Annie patted her gently on the arm. "Now let's git on down tha road to tha Smiths."

They soon arrived at the farm house and were at the door knocking.

"Well, come in, please." Marianne's face lit up at the sight of them.

"Let me take your coats. Mother's in the kitchen." She led them back.

"I'm so glad you made it. Please sit down," Mrs. Smith greeted them, waving her arm toward two rocking chairs by the fireplace.

"This is my sister, Betty Lou," Marianne said, noticing the surprised look on Betty Lou's face.

"How do you do? I see the resemblance between you two." Emily smiled.

"Marianne, go get that bag on the secretary. It has most of the materials in it."

For the next hour, they went through the materials, sorting them out with Mrs. Smith explaining to Emily how to use them. Annie and Marianne carefully watched, and Betty Lou sat perched on a stool studying the whole lot. "Why, she isn't at all what I expected. In fact, she's just the opposite."

DAYS TURNED INTO WEEKS and still Heath found no work except for a few odd jobs that never lasted. He became more and more depressed, and Emily became more and more afraid to break the news to him. Spring came early, but even its new life and beauty couldn't lift Heath's spirits. He went back to staying out all hours of the night and coming in drunk. One of these nights, he stumbled in and fell down on the couch, thinking to himself even the liquor couldn't help him. He pounded the couch with his fist, wondering how Emily could be sleeping so peacefully. In doing so, he knocked a tablet off the arm of the couch. He picked it up. "Another one of her poems," he said with a sneer, but read anyway...

> Life is but a journey
> Made for me and you...
> Where valleys are plenty
> But mountains are few...
>
> 'Tis dark in the valley

No sun shining…
'Tis lonely in the valley
Only one crying…

But it's comforting to know
In the valley—we don't stay…
The 23rd Psalm tells us so
We only walk through on our way…

And there's joy beyond the highest mountain
While in that deepest valley…
Just call on Jesus, God's precious Son
He's the "Lily of the Valley!"

Tossing the tablet on the couch, he pulled himself up and went into the kitchen to fix a cup of coffee. This new side of Emily was confusing him. She must have something special if she could write words like that during all this trouble. With his cup in his hand, he went to the bedroom door. Emily lay sleeping peacefully , the twins also. He felt the desire to wrap her in his arms, but at the same time an even stronger desire to get away from her and the peace that stood between them. Suddenly he turned and left, left the room, left the cabin. Jumping into the wagon that he'd never unhitched, he set off down the road, leaving clouds of dust rolling up behind him into the darkness. His mind didn't have to tell his hands what to do. They automatically turned Old Nag onto the road leading to Tom's place.

The smoke-filled room looked the same. It was the first time he'd been back since the accident. It's nothing special, he thought, but I'm as much a success as the rest here. Suddenly he felt like laughing and did. Boy, you'd never catch brother Robert here! No, Robert was a real success...always doing what's right...no, you'd never catch Robert here. Oh well, all the Barretts were successes anyway, all but him, he was the black sheep of the family....

"Someone so young and handsome should never wear such a gloomy mask..." a familiar voice said.

"Well, hello, Betty Lou. Are you sure you're alone tonight?"

"Right now I am...but I don't hope to be later." Her inviting smile told him the rest.

The warm morning sun crept into the bedroom, awakening Emily from her peaceful sleep. Looking beside her, she felt her heart sink. Where is he? It was the first time in a long time that he'd stayed out all night. She suddenly felt like pulling the covers back over her head and escaping the problems of life, but realizing she had work to do and babies to care for, she pushed herself out of bed and onto the cold floor. Spring was here, but one would never know it early in the morning on this mountain, she thought to herself as she started to make the fire. Though the sun was shining, she couldn't shake the cloud that hung over her, pressing down upon her, imprisoning her with worries and fears. But then she remembered that today was the day she'd promised Annie to go with her to help with the spring cleaning of the church. Her spirits lifted. It would be a fun day being with Annie and the other members.

After starting the fire, she decided to make the

biscuits that she was going to take with her. Right in the middle of making up the dough, she had to run for the back door. She had been sick a lot lately, but she had managed to hide it from Heath. As she leaned against the door, trying to control the heaves, she felt an arm encircle her. So he was home! Without looking up she let him draw her to him.

"What is it?" he questioned.

"Nothing, just a little nausea."

What was that smell? It penetrated his sweater as her head pressed against it and overcame the strong smell of liquor.

Perfume!

She pulled away from him as if she had been slapped and turned back to her biscuits.

About an hour later, Annie pulled up. "The Smiths are going with us. Mrs. Smith is just gettin' along a little now...and she be d'termined to help with tha spring cleaning."

"Great...that's fine, Annie," Emily said absently as she handed Prudence up to her.

"You look a li'l pale, Honey. Are ya' ailin'?"

"No, I'm fine, Annie...just a little nauseous this morning." She turned to go back to the house for Patrick. Coming back out with him, she closed the door on Heath, who was asleep already.

"Heath not workin' t'day?" Annie asked, glancing at the wagon parked beside the cabin.

"He's not up to it after his night out, I guess," she answered, not looking up.

"Emily, Honey, are you sho you feel like cleanin' t'day?" Annie asked.

"Of course, Annie. Now let's be on our way," she answered with a forced smile. When they pulled up in front of the Smith's farmhouse, Mrs. Smith came out first, supporting herself on a big, black cane. Marianne followed, loaded down with cleaning tools, and then Betty Lou sauntered out.

"Why lo an' hold, we's got plenty'a help," Annie laughed.

"Annie, Betty Lou's gonna help, too" Mrs. Smith called out.

"Why sho…tha more—tha better. How you been doin', Child?"

"I *was* doing alright," Betty Lou answered with a touch of bitterness.

Emily climbed in the back with the twins. Annie helped Mrs. Smith up into the wagon, and Marianne and Betty Lou climbed into the back with Emily, one on either side. As the wagon bounced down the road with Annie and Mrs. Smith trying to outdo each other with suggestions on spring cleaning, and the twins squirming and playing, enjoying the ride, Emily sat puzzling over the fragrance that every now and then drifted over to her. Why did it seem so familiar? Without looking at the dark, pretty girl beside her, she felt Betty Lou's eyes on her. Feeling uneasy, she bounced Prudence on her knee and played with her. But that haunting feeling would not escape her. She sensed she was on the verge of something, something very disturbing…what was it? *The perfume! The perfume!* It was the same perfume! Instinctively she turned and looked into the coldest black eyes she'd ever seen. So cold and powerful were they that she turned away. What dark secrets were hidden behind those dark, treacherous eyes?

Emily wanted suddenly to be away, far away, from rubbing shoulders with this enemy. But what could she do? Certainly not run away. No, she would have to endure the day whatever came her way...she couldn't let Annie and Mrs. Smith down. She looked at Marianne and returned her smile. So gentle, so sweet...she hugged Patrick to her as if he were her own. How could the two be sisters?

As the wagon finally pulled up in front of the church, Annie spoke up, "Emily, why don't you an' Marianne an' Betty Lou take the cemetery. It sho has grown up with weeds."

The day turned out to be nice after all for most concerned. Emily and Marianne enjoyed each others' company immensely, creating a bond that would last through the years. The twins played on the big quilt spread out in front of the church, never lacking attention from somebody. About twenty people had shown up for the day and by noon, the place was taking on a different appearance. They all casually picnicked wherever they happened to be. Some had brought tablecloths they spread out and unpacked their baskets on. Others sat down on the front steps, eating off their laps. Betty Lou disappeared into the church as soon as she had the opportunity, enough was enough! She could still see those deep blue eyes revealing her innermost being...the hurt...the surprise...the sadness, all wrapped up together and being displayed through those sea blue mirrors.

How she let her Mother push her into this, she'd never know. Of course, what could she do? If only that darn cat hadn't knocked over those jars of molasses in the pantry, she wouldn't be here. She almost laughed at herself, remembering how startled she'd been. After creeping through the kitchen so silently with her shoes in her hand, she figured she was in fine without her Mother knowing the better until that loud crash. The cat shrieked and ran off through the house.

"Who's there?" Mother's frightened voice rang out.

Marianne appeared in the doorway with her hands on her hips.

"It's alright, Mother. It's just your prodigal Daughter," Marianne answered reproachfully. Her Mother had come down also, and for the next hour she was lectured by the two of them and during the process had somehow agreed to this...this cleanup day.

She lay down on one of the pews, suddenly feeling awful sleepy, hardly able to keep her eyes open.

Outside under an old, oak tree, Emily and Marianne were engaged in deep conversation.

"You know, Marianne, I've had a great time talking with you today. I do wish you'd consider visiting me sometime."

"I'd love to. It's so good to find someone close to my own age that feels the same way I do about the Lord. I'm sure you've gathered from today that my Sister doesn't."

"Yes, but it seems strange that you and your Mother are such fine Christians and she...well...."

"I know. Betty Lou's always been different, even as a child. I remember her delightfully fooling Mother time after time. She played hooky from school and sometimes bribed me to cover for her. She never seemed sorry for what she did...instead she actually seemed to get enjoyment from it. After we grew up, she rebelled against any authority that threatened her plans, including Mother's firm resistance to her marriage to James Whitehouse. She married him against everybody's warnings, and it ended in disaster."

"What happened?"

"He just up and ran off...she's really been hard to live with since then. She came back home for a while, but couldn't take our quiet, peaceful way of life. So she moved out and fixed up the cottage that belonged to Grandfather. She stayed there for a while, but soon it became too much for her, being alone and all. Mother pleaded with her to come back with us...and she's back...worse than ever I'm sorry to say. I wish you'd pray for her. She really needs the Lord. By the way, how's your class?" Marianne asked, changing the subject as if it were too painful to continue.

"Fine, just fine," Emily answered with relief, glad to change the subject. "But whenever your Mother wants to come back, just let me know."

"Oh, she's enjoying the rest. She's been teaching for so long, you know...and I think she's enjoying watching you transform into a wonderful teacher."

"Well, I don't know about that," Emily laughed, a little embarrassed, "but I just love to teach God's word to those little children. You know, when I'm up there in front of them, I don't feel like myself at all but...well...just a container for God to work through and live through and love through...it's wonderful."

"A container...I never thought about it like that...."

"Well, just the other day I got to thinking about it so much and was so thrilled by the thought that I wrote a little poem about it."

"A poem? I would love to see it."

"Well, I don't have it with me, but I know it by heart."

"Please recite it for me," Marianne begged.

Emily cleared her voice a little nervously. She wasn't used to anyone else's opinion of her rhyme-making. She shut her eyes and spoke so softly that Marianne had to lean close to hear.

> Just a container, oh Lord, for thee
> To live through and to love through,
> A vessel through which the world may see
> Not me, Oh God, but you...
>
> Just a container, I've always been
> Though even I was fooled,
> Controlled by a Master—the Prince of Sin
> My heart, my mind, he ruled...
>
> But Praise the Lord, I was born again
> And Masters changed within,
> Satan was gone, no longer to reign
> And Jesus Christ moved in...
>
> Just a container, you are too
> Do you know your Master?
> Whoever he is—is most important to you
> And where you spend hereafter!

"Why, that's beautiful, Emily. If I can round up some paper, would you write it down for me? I sure would like someone to see this, and I think you know who."

Emily knew who and remembered what Annie said—*God works in mysterious ways.*

A couple of weeks later, Emily sat at the kitchen table planning how to break the news about the baby to Heath. She had rehearsed the words over and over but still was nervous about telling him. She had begun to gain weight and wondered how he hadn't noticed anyhow, but he was so preoccupied these days, hardly noticing her at all. Suddenly she heard him drive up and then she heard his feet hit the porch with a bounce. Why, he hadn't jumped the porch railing for a long time now. He came in hurriedly, slamming the door behind him. "Emily, Honey, are you ready for this?" His face was lit up with a broad smile, and she could tell he was having a hard time concealing his news. "We're going to move," he finally blurted out.

"Move." She repeated after him, unable to quite comprehend what he'd said.

He pulled up a chair beside her. "Yeah, move, Honey. Uncle Raymond has asked me to go into partnership with him at his mill...."

"Uncle Raymond? But, Heath, he lives in South Dakota!"

"I know, Honey, and so will we soon!"

'Oh Heath, that's so far...how will we...I mean...how can we...."

"Don't worry about a thing, Honey. I've taken care of everything. We will just take the most necessary things with us. We'll close the cabin up. Dad said he'd look in on it occasionally, and Uncle Raymond already has a small cottage waiting for us very close to the mill." He stopped for a moment, pausing for breath.

"Aren't you excited, Honey? He asked, grabbing hold of her hands and squeezing them.

"I...I don't know, Heath...it's so sudden and...South Dakota is so far and...."

The enthusiasm began to drain from him and he lowered his head. "Emily, I'm tired of feeling like I can't take care of my family, and it's true, I can't...not here anyway. All I know is lumber and there's no work for me with this!" He frowned at his arm still hanging in the worn sling.

"But that's a lumber mill, too?" she questioned.

"True, but you don't understand, Honey. I won't be working with the wood but with the papers. I'm to be Uncle Raymond's partner. He's getting old, you know, and will be retiring before long. He needs a young man that knows lumber and knows the business, and I'm that young man," he smiled once again.

"How did you find out...when?"

"Last week when I went by the house. Dad told me about it then and said he wanted me to think about it. I didn't tell you then because I wasn't sure what I was going to do, but I've thought about it...I've thought about it all week. I want to try it. Don't you see, Emily? It's a chance in a million for me to really make good. I know now I should have gone to college. It's too late for that, but it's not too late for this."

She smiled at him. "When are we supposed to leave?"

"As soon as possible. There's nothing holding us here. You can start packing right now."

"How will we get there?" she questioned with disbelief.

"By train. I've always wanted to ride on one and now I'll get the chance."

"It all seems like a dream. I thought your Father and your Uncle Raymond didn't get along?"

"They don't, at least they didn't, but I think maybe this is Uncle Raymond's way of making amends. You see, he wronged Father many years ago and Father never quite got over it. It's a long story. But now, not only do I have a fantastic future ahead of me, but I'll be bringing the family back together, too."

Chapter IV
New Horizons

Trees and bushes raced by, blurred together as Emily glared out the window of the fast-moving train. It wove its way through the dense forests and shot across the miles of barren, dusty plains only to be immersed in more thick forest. She watched the trees grow farther apart, realizing the train was slowing down. She figured it must be refueling or taking on water when it actually came to a stop.

Suddenly there was a shrill, whistling sound piercing the air, and the train lurched forward. Emily caught hold of the seat. Her head was spinning. She could hear the steam hissing. Glancing out the window again, she could see the great locomotive as it rounded a curve way up ahead. Smoke billowed as it picked up speed. Riding behind that black, fire-eating, smoke plumed monstrosity, she felt weak and afraid. Was she dreaming? Ever since Heath had told her, she had been waiting to awaken from this dream. The train rolled on. The rail joints clicked off the miles, taking her farther and farther from her home, all she knew, the comforting mountains.

"You alright, Hon?" She was almost startled by Heath as he sat down beside her with Patrick on one knee and Prudence on the other.

"Yes, yes. Just a little excited, I guess."

"Well, you look very white to me. You sure you're fine?" he asked again.

"Yes, Heath. Here, let me have Prudence. She looks very sleepy." She nestled her against her bosom, and the tiny, blue-eyed girl was soon fast asleep.

"Isn't this something!" Heath exclaimed. "You should see the dining car! That's where I took Patrick and Prudence. All kinds of fancy-looking ladies and gents up there. A couple of guys were playing a game of cards, smoking these here long expensive lookin' cigars. One lady had on a big ring that glistened like the sun shining on Spears Mountain after a new fallen snow."

"Heath, this trip must be costing a fortune."

"Now, Honey, I explained all that to you before we left. Uncle Raymond's paying for it, and I'm gonna pay him back as soon as I start earning my keep." He laughed. "You little worry-wart, stop worrying and enjoy the ride. Isn't it great?"

She smiled up at him, then turned to look out the window again. How could she tell him that every time this gigantic piece of iron came to a stop and then lurched forward again, she had to fight to keep her breakfast down. Why did it have to stop so often? As if Heath was reading her mind as the train slowed down once again, he said, "You know, these big steam engines require a lot of water, that's why they have to stop so often. But it's better than it used to be. They say the first trains had to stop every twenty miles to take on more water."

"It's all very interesting," Emily began to feel dizzy again. She hoped Heath wouldn't notice.

"Honey, Patrick's asleep, too. Suppose I lay him down here beside you. I think I'd like to walk back up to the dining car. Maybe they'll let me get a first-hand glimpse of the engine."

Emily nodded, glad to see him go. Her hand flew to her mouth as the train started up again. She didn't know how long she would be able to keep her secret from him. He would have noticed by now if he hadn't been so keyed up by this trip. She felt a little better now and smiled to herself. Yes, he was just like a little boy, thrilled by it all.

"You all right, Ma'am?" A kind voice in front of her spoke. She looked up to see a small, graying man looking at her with concern.

"Yes sir, I'm fine," she answered with a smile.

He smiled back. "Well, I just thought you looked awful pale. You folks headed to take part in the lotteries?"

"The lotteries?" Emily repeated, realizing how dumb she must sound.

"Oh, you're not one of us then." He laughed at the puzzled look on her face. "I'm sorry, I must be totally confusing you. You see, most everybody on this train is headed for South Dakota to register for land. If we're lucky, we'll receive claims when they have the lottery drawings."

"You mean claims to land?" she asked, trying to understand.

"I sure do. The best darn land for farming I've heard tell of."

"Are you going alone?"

He laughed. "No, I'm a bit old for cuttin' out a new life for myself. I'm going along with my son and his family." He nodded in the direction of a couple in their thirties, seated in front of him. The father held a small boy of about six in his arms and the mother a toddler. Emily couldn't tell if it was a boy or a girl.

"Maybe you folks ought to look into it. That is, if you're planning on staying out here."

Emily nodded with a smile as the old man turned back around. Maybe she should tell Heath about this, but did she really want something to tie them to this far off place? She looked again out the window. The thick, sweeping forests had now been left far behind, the familiar but awesome mountains had vanished. Her eyes were open to the vastness of the country, the boundless plains.

As day grew into evening, lamps were lit and several people around her started a game of cards. Others were reading and still others joined in light-hearted conversation. Emily thought it strange that this little slice of civilization should go on as always, ignoring that they were rushing across a darkened, unfamiliar prairie.

After several days, all repeats of the first, the train

neared its destination. On a rainswept afternoon, it rolled into South Dakota territory. Most of the people in the car with them got off at the first town, including the old man in front of them and his family. Before leaving, he gave them both a warm handshake. Emily hated to see him leave. He was the nearest thing to a friend they had out here in this land of unfulfilled promises, unknown things, and unknown people.

While still waving goodbye to those who had exited, Emily turned to see a strange-looking man headed for the seat in front of them. His eyes were riveted on the floor, and he never looked up as he made his way back. He was clothed in soiled, heavy burlap and had what looked like some sort of animal skin flung over one shoulder. His sand-colored hair was mixed with gray, bushed out from under a strange-looking cap, and mingled with a wiry beard of the same color. In fact, he was more hair than anything else, Emily thought, wondering if this was a foretaste of the Dakota people. She had seen a lot of sights in the mountains of Virginia, but this was something different. There was a certain quality about him that frightened her, and she decided to avoid any contact with him. What a difference in him and the nice old man from the East who had been sitting there.

The train glided across the barren plains, miles and miles of all the same color, without a tree, much less a mountain, to break its pattern. Emily marveled at its scope. Never would she have imagined that there was so much land out here, or anywhere for that matter. They had left the rain and now the brilliant sun shone down upon the land, baking it to a hard crust.

"Look at all the tall grass up ahead. I'm sure glad to see that." Heath pointed toward vast stretches of grassy plains.

"Yes, that's comforting," Emily answered, rocking Prudence in her arms. "You know, the twins have really done wonderfully. This old train just lulls them to sleep. I think maybe we'd better stay on it," she laughed.

"I thought you were dying to get out and stretch your legs," Heath kidded.

"I am! That was just a joke. How much longer do you think it will be?"

"Well, I'm told...."

Suddenly the train lurched, throwing them forward.

"What is it?" Emily cried, holding Patrick and Prudence firmly.

"I don't know," Heath answered.

Everyone was talking at the same time in loud voices when the strange, hairy man in front of them turned around. "Don't worry, folks. We've just hit the grazing grounds of the bison." He pointed ahead to a large herd of buffalo, which were completely unaware that they were blocking the path of this iron monster that was out to destroy them. The hairy man began to laugh, first a low, uttering laugh, then increasing, shaking his whole body, furs and all. Heath and Emily stared first at the phenomenal sight of the hundreds of buffalo blocking them and then at this unusual man who found it funny to be stalled in the middle of nowhere.

"That's right, fellows, you show 'em!" he said, still shaking with laughter.

Emily and Heath looked at one another and then back at him.

"I'm sorry, folks," he finally said. "But it just pleases the possum out'a me to see 'em do this. It's just like they're standing there resisting this big, old piece of iron—showing 'em for the last time that they're still king of the prairie." He stopped laughing almost as suddenly as he'd started, as if a dark cloud had over-shadowed his face. He was silent for a long time. Heath and Emily were silent too, as if witnessing a sacred ritual. The silence was finally broken by a much sub-dued voice as the old man spoke once again, "Used to be 'bout sixty million of'em roaming these'ere plains...now hardly more'n you see right there now left."

"What happened to them?" Emily asked.

"Government mostly...and the cattlemen...and the railroad...they didn't stand a chance!"

"I don't understand what you mean, Mister," Heath said reluctantly, not knowing whether he wanted to pursue the subject with this weird fellow.

"The government, Son...it wanted to get rid 'a the Indians...get 'em off the prairie and onto the reserva-tions. Gettin' rid of the buffalo, their main source of food, was the best way. It worked, too. The cattlemen wanted this (he pointed to the land all around the train) for their herds. And the railroad men figured the buffalo were a hindrance to settlement."

"But how did they get rid of them?" Emily asked.

"By lettin' them low-down hunters in. They wiped 'em out in a hurry, killed hundreds in a day just for the sport of it, then would leave 'em to rot in the sun. No good for anybody!"

"Why, that's terrible!" Emily exclaimed.

"Look, we're moving again," Heath said.

They all watched as the train inched along beside the herd of buffalo. The big, powerful creatures went on grazing, never looking up.

"They're so big!" Emily said with awe.

"Yes, Ma'am, they sho' are." The old man smiled as he watched them tenderly. "And they're as strong as they are big. It's the times, Ma'am, the times. Everything's changing. A body don't know what to expect no more."

"Where are you headed?" Heath asked, trying to change the subject.

"Nowhere much, got nowhere to go. My Pa was a trapper and his Pa afore him. I was trappin' before I was knee high to a grasshopper." He smiled, showing his snaggled teeth. "We had some times, we did."

Again, his countenance changed suddenly. "Ain't hardly nowhere to trap no more...people crowdin' in everywhere making all kinds of rules.... No, Ma'am, I ain't going nowhere. Nowhere to go, but you see, my Son is an engineer on one of these smoke puffin' things and I can ride fer free as I see fit."

"Why, that's really nice," Emily answered, with a little too much enthusiasm.

"No Ma'am, it ain't. Nothing's nice no more. You should 'ave been here in the good ol' days...where you folk from, anyway?"

"From the mountains of Virginia," Heath answered.

"East folks, huh. What ya' think of these 'ere plains?"

"Big and flat, Sir...a lot different from the mountains we're used to," Heath answered.

"You betcha! Takes a tough man to survive this land. If you can stand the blizzards with their furious winds that pile up snowdrifts that'd bury an army, and the droughts that leave these 'ere plains parched and dry, wiping out the hopes of the farmers, and the dust that seeps through everything, parching your throat, crackin' your lips and burnin' your eyes, the hailstorms that destroy hundreds of crops with stones big as apples, not to mention the temperatures that drop forty below, cold enough to freeze an Eskimo."

"Well, if it's all that bad, why are all these people flooding into this land?" Heath asked, a bit irritated with the old man's description of their new home.

"They don't know the plains. Give 'em a year, maybe not that long, the strong will be sifted from the weak soon enough."

"Why do you stay here?" Emily asked, trying to understand the old man.

"Why do I stay here? Ma'am, this 'ere is my home...these 'ere plains are part of me. The wailing winds that never stop blowing are part of me, this wide open land (he stretched forth his arms) that was made for giants instead of man is part of me, even the loneliness that you can't get away from is part of me. I love it, Ma'am."

"I understand," Emily said, smiling. "I feel the same about the mountains we're from. Have you ever been east?"

"Once. That was enough, too hemmed in by your mountains. Here in the plains, a man stands open to nature with its wild and crazy ways. We don't have the shelter of forests that you have. A man is sho' aware of his smallness as he walks this 'ere land. He either shrinks from it an' cries out in his loneliness or rises up and becomes more man than he could be somewheres else."

"That's beautiful!" Emily exclaimed. "I can see you really know this land and love it."

"Thank you, Ma'am." With that he turned around and within minutes was snoring.

THE TRAIN SPED ON across the prairie. The twins awoke and Heath took them for a walk back to the dining car. Emily sat staring out at the silent plains that glided by, thinking on all the things that the old trapper had said. Would Heath rise to its expectations? Would he become more man here than back in the Virginia mountains? She remembered the many nights she'd lain alone and cried herself to sleep. Would she rise to its expectations? "He either shrinks from it and cries out in his loneliness." She recalled the old man's words. Would she cry out in loneliness?

As the day faded into dusk, the passengers settled down, what was left of them, that is. Most had left already, and the remaining ones seemed tired from the journey and ceased to chatter or play cards. Only one lamp was lit so far. The twins were retired for the night. Heath rested with his eyes closed and his head against the back of the seat, but Emily still gazed out the window. All day she'd seen the same stretches of land sprawled out before her, miles and miles and miles of it. Was there any end to it? What was there to stop this endless procession of land if there were no mountains or no sea to fall into?

Suddenly rising up from this monotony was a *mountain*...no, not *a* mountain, but mountains. Emily rubbed her eyes, wondering if she were seeing things. But no, there it was. Where did it come from? They seemed to have risen abruptly from nowhere, towering above the level plains all around them. It was almost eerie! She stared in disbelief.

"Heath, Heath." Without taking her eyes from the sight, she shook him.

"What is it?" he asked loudly, waking suddenly.

Emily simply pointed in the direction of the black, ominous mountains. As they both stared toward the window, a familiar voice spoke.

"We got us a mountain, don't we, Ma'am?" The old trapper came alive again. He'd been sleeping all day.

"It's the strangest sight I've ever seen. What is it?" Emily was glad to have someone to ask.

"It's the mountains, Ma'am, not like your'n. They're pure granite, they are...full of rugged cliffs and jagged peaks."

"They're gigantic. How high are they?" Heath questioned.

"'Bout a couple thousand feet to the top."

Heath whistled.

"What are they called?" Emily asked.

"Called the Black Hills, Ma'am, but they're neither black nor hills. As you can see, they're mountains and they're covered with green pines so thick that from a distance, they look black. That's why they're called that."

"Does anyone live there?" Emily asked.

"No, Ma'am, haven't you heard of the great gold rush in these 'ere parts?"

"Yes, we have," Heath answered.

"Well, that's where it was. The Black Hills are full 'uv gold. When I was a young fellow, people from everywhere came floodin' in to get rich. Some did...some didn't...some never lived to spend it."

"What happened?" Emily asked again.

"The gold rush triggered many Indian wars. You see, the Black Hills was sacred Indian land—guaranteed by a government treaty, the United States government, but like all 'uv them government treaties, it was broken. The Indians' claim was just ignored. They fought to protect what was theirs and what they believed was sacred, but in the end, they lost—just like always."

"Are there many Indians here now?" Emily asked the question she'd been waiting to ask.

"Not like it used to be, Ma'am. I heard my Pa tell 'uv how the Sioux would send out as many as 10,000 warriors into battle anytime. They were the best warriors, you know, Ma'am...the Sioux. This 'ere is Sioux country, least it was, before they were herded onto reservations like cattle. Yep, Pa said them wars went on for years before the great massacre at Wounded Knee. After that all the survivors were forced onto reservations, as wards of the state, no longer free to roam and hunt. 'Course there wasn't anything to hunt anymore anyway. The government had taken care of that."

"So the Indians are all on reservations then?"

Emily asked.

"Yes Ma'am, they are." The old trapper answered and turned around abruptly as if he wasn't interested in talking about it any further.

For the rest of the trip, the twins slept and Emily herself finally gave in to a restful doze. She fought it at first, not wanting to miss a thing, but fatigue won and her eyes closed.

Heath looked at the three of them with tenderness. How could he ask for more? And with his future looking bright, he was happy for the first time in a long, long time. He thought of his Father's strong handclasp before they left. He was behind him in spite of his Mother's behavior. Why did she have to carry on so? He could still see her throwing one of her little temper tantrums and running off upstairs crying. Finally she had come back downstairs with swollen eyes and a stubborn front that refused to accept the whole idea. Robert said openly that he thought the whole thing absurd. Elizabeth had discreetly let everyone know what she thought—it was Emily's fault, of course! He wondered why Elizabeth found it so hard to accept Emily. Looking at her asleep beside him, he guessed it would be hard for this dominant, arrogant Sister of his to accept her...she would be jealous, of course. Only Karen was quiet about the whole matter. A little sad, if anything. With all these hostile and disagreeable, hidden attitudes, the parting was not the happiest. He did remember Annie, though, standing in the background, quietly, with tears on her wrinkled cheeks. He'd asked her, "Annie, do you think I'm crazy, too?"

"Now, you know better'n t' ask that 'uv your Annie!

I jest hate t'see ya go, some'in tells me I mightn't ever see ya agin." With that she'd hugged him to her the way she'd done so many times when he was small. Yes, he'd miss her for sure. He could still see her watching as they drove off. He remembered thinking at the time that he hadn't noticed all those white hairs before. It dawned on him for the first time that Annie was old, really old. Somehow colored folk had a way of hiding their age from you, they just didn't seem to age. He glanced out the window and saw his image, only now against the blackened night.

Yes, Annie had loved him as her own all those years, like a second mother. She was different. She had always been different from anyone else he'd known, until recently, and strangely enough, he somehow sensed the same difference in Emily. He figured it must be what she'd told him about her faith. Annie had spoken to him frequently of it through the years. It wasn't just religion, he knew that! His folks had plenty of that. He remembered all the Sundays he'd spent squirming in the hard seat beside his Mother and wishing church would soon be over. It had always been awfully dull for him, but not only for *him*. Even as a young boy, he had realized it was dull for his Father, too. His Mother endured the sermons with grace and anxiously awaited the final amen so she and her friends could socialize. His Father was a deacon, his Mother chairman of the ladies' missionary circle, and Elizabeth taught Sunday school...but it was all a farce. He never could remember his Mother even going next door to evangelize. How could they be missionaries? His Father spent Sunday dinners criticizing the preacher's sermon...and Elizabeth, *that* was a joke! When he grew older, he wondered why they wasted their time going to church at all, and as soon as he reached the age where he thought he could do as he pleased, he quit going all together.

But Annie, yes, she was different. Of course, she'd never gone with them to Mount Moriah. She'd always insisted on attending Mountain Creek Baptist, which was really out of the way, but his folks had always humored her and let her drive there on one of the surreys. He wondered what she would have done if they hadn't. Something told him that she would have gotten there one way or the other. He remembered asking her one day, "Annie, how come you go to Mountain Creek? I heard Elizabeth say that *it's* a white church, too?"

"It sho' be that, Son. But don't you know that God be color blind. He don't know the black from the white. He jest loves us all! But ya' see...it happened like this. I was a young girl, tall, not humped like now. An' mighty pretty, some folk say. I'd been runnin' through tha woods on a day maybe like this'n. Early November, I believe. There was'a briskness in tha air and I was feeling my oats...ya might say." She laughed aloud.

"Ya Mother was a young girl too, then. Sometimes we'd run through tha woods together...but that day I happen to be all alone. Well'sa all 'uv a sudden, I heard this 'ere screaming. It plum'nelly scared the wits out'a me. I took off 'ta runnin' as fast as my skinny l'il legs would carry me. But then I hear tha words H-E-L-P. Yes'm, somebody was calling H-E-L-P fer sho...over an over they call. I feel like gettin' out'a them woods fast, but somethin' tells me ta go help whoever that be'a hollerin'. So's I make my way back, tremblin' all tha time, to that awful screamin'...and 'lo it be jest a li'l girl 'bout six years old a'lyin' on the cold ground. She done been caught by one'a them ol' rabbit traps. It was awful. Her leg was'a swollen an' bleedin' somethin' terrible.

"Well'sa, I remembered seein' my Pa break one'a them things a'fore. I found two big rocks and commenced ta hittin' that thing in tha right place...first thing ya know...I done broke it. I picked her up and headed fer home, but as I was a'crossing the road, a wagon pulled up aside 'uv me. A big, heavyset man jumped down out'a that wagon and took her out'a my arms. He say, 'What happened?' I told 'em and he say, 'Get in!' He lay tha child in tha back 'uv tha wagon an' asked me to sit a'side 'uv her. I did jest that. Well'sa, it turned out that he be tha child's father an' not only that, but he be tha new preacher of Mountain Creek Baptist Church. From that day on, he or one'a tha members would drive over tha mountain every Sunday morning an' pick me up. That's how come I be tha only colored folk in tha white Baptist church, Son. 'Course, Mr. Kinderly done long since gone ta Heaven. An' Jennifer, she growed up an' moved away up North somewhere, ain't seen'er since I was'a married long time ago. Mr. Brown an' me, you know. We was'a married in tha church...an' Jennifer sang tha prettiest song fer us. Yes'm I sho like ta see'er agin. Don't reckon I ever will though...."

Heath remembered her rocking back and forth, her eyes closed, in the kitchen chair. He had left her that way, with thoughts of the past. Those people there at that little church must have been good people.

There's no way they would have accepted Annie other-
wise. He was glad that Emily was like them. He looked
at her and gently smoothed her hair back. The train
slowed down and stopped.

"IT'S SO WIDE," Emily said out loud while standing at the door looking out at the sky. Would she ever
get used to it? She turned around to see her pot of beans
about to boil over and quickly strode across the room to
remedy the situation. Pulling the pot over to the side,
she heard a few sounds coming from the adjoining
room. She hastened to the crib and picked him up.
"Jonathon...Jonathon...you be quiet...you don't want
to wake up your Brother and Sister."

She took him back into the kitchen to feed him. I
sure wish I had my rocking chair here, she thought.
There were only a few things she missed...the rocking
chair...the porch swing. Overall though, this was
much better than the mountain cabin. Someone had
taken very good care of the little house. She remembered asking Heath when they first arrived, "Who lived
here?"

"Uncle Raymond says a young farmer and his
wife, but they didn't stay too long."

"Why?"

"The wife couldn't take the prairie life. Soon after
they arrived, there was a mighty windstorm. It lasted
for weeks, and they say it was followed by a drought, one
of the worst. She just couldn't take it, being from the
East and all."

"But we're from the east, Heath."

"True, Honey, but we're from the mountains!"

She'd smiled at him. "What happened to her?"

"Uncle Raymond says her mind got bad, started talking out'a her head and all. Her husband had to take her back east."

She shuddered from a cold chill just thinking about it all again. The poor girl, whoever she was. She could understand, listening to the whistling wind as it moaned and wailed. Jonathon jerked within her arms and cried out.

"Poor baby, is it your tummy again?" She put him up on her shoulder, gently patting his back. Colic. She wondered if he really did have colic. Well, that's what Uncle Raymond said, anyway, although Heath disagreed. This son was too much of a man already for that stuff, he'd told her with pride. Yes, he seemed overjoyed with this son. Of course, she knew he loved Patrick as much but when the twins came, he was still getting over Little David. They both were.

Suddenly her thoughts went back to that little grave on the mountainside. She'd hated to leave it behind. She forced her thoughts back to Heath's pride in Jonathon. "It's probably because you look so much like him and act so much like him already, little fellow," she said aloud.   She remembered Heath's reaction when she finally broke the news to him that she was pregnant again. "But why didn't you tell me?" he'd asked, puzzled and somewhat irritated.

"I didn't want to spoil everything for you. I figured you'd turn down Uncle Raymond's offer if you knew, and I just couldn't bring myself to tell you. I tried."

He had accepted it with little to say, but was withdrawn for days. She knew he was worried. But the day that little, squalling piece of flesh and blood fought its way into the world, Heath changed. He laughed and joked and couldn't see enough of his new son. He seemed to be happier with his new job and with everything in general. He was the one who insisted on calling the baby after himself: Heath Jonathon Barrett, Jr. Before he'd refused, saying he didn't want any son of his to be saddled with his misfortune. It had to be because he felt so good about himself, Emily figured.

"Yes, Heath Jonathon Barrett, Jr., I do believe you're going to be a carbon copy of your Father."

The child squirmed against her breast as if satisfied with her proclamation. Suddenly she remembered what today was...the mission meeting. She rose to put Jonathon back in his crib and proceeded to busy herself for the day.

Mrs. Bertram would be knocking at the door promptly at nine, she was sure. Tardiness was not one of her shortcomings. Frankly, Emily couldn't think of any shortcoming that she had. Well, she was a godly woman for sure, and all who knew her agreed. As Emily cleaned up the kitchen, she recalled her first encounter with this old saint. They had only been here a week when she heard a soft knock at the door and opened it to a dear, old lady with snow white hair and a smile that lit up the whole room. She had hardly taken her coat off before she asked, "Isn't it wonderful to serve such a wonderful Saviour?"

"Yes Ma'am, it is," Emily had answered, a little surprised.

"Are you a Christian?" the old lady asked.

"Why yes Ma'am, I am," Emily answered.

"I thought so," the old lady smiled. "I can pick'em out pretty good in my old age." She patted Emily on the shoulder and thus began a close friendship. Mrs. Bertram introduced her to the mission—a small building which housed a handful of dedicated Christians each week as they taught a group of children from the nearby Sioux reservation. Emily looked forward each week to this. Although she had fulfillment with her own family, this was different—a real way to serve the Lord. Heath had balked a little at first about her dragging the children out and after Jonathon came, he simply refused. But Mrs. Bertram came up with an idea. She had an old spinster sister, Mae-Mae she was called, who loved children and would be delighted to come over and sit with the children every Tuesday while they went to the mission. Heath had given in then, realizing how much it meant to Emily.

After waving goodbye to Mae-Mae as she stood in the doorway holding both the twins in her arms, Emily climbed up into the wagon beside Mrs. Bertram.

"Let's go, Suzy," the old lady coached as she slapped the reins and the big, well-built wagon lurched forward. The snow that had fallen through the night still clung to the trees and bushes, creating a white wonderland that made one wonder whether or not they lived in reality or had just stepped over the border to dream land. As the big wagon quietly rolled down the snow-packed road, Mrs. Bertram hummed a catchy tune unfamiliar to Emily, thus adding to the dream-like effect. She looked at the old woman who seemed to be lost in her thoughts. Emily admired her tremendously.

She had learned enough from Mae-Mae to know that Mrs. Bertram had had a very hard life, but it hadn't seemed to hurt her at all. Instead, she seemed to thrive on it.

"How do you stay so happy all the time?" Emily asked, wanting to be included in her thoughts.

"I love life," Mrs. Bertram answered quickly.

"Even with all the troubles you have been called upon to bear throughout the years?"

"I kind'a look at life as a journey, Emily, and I'm just a pilgrim passing through. I don't see my home being here. It's way up yonder waiting for me." She waved her arms toward heaven with a big smile on her face. "And this journey has had a lot of valleys...but it's had its mountain tops too. Those mountain tops, they can be so exhilarating, so happy, but they fool you, you know. It's the valleys that bring you really close to God. That's when you're really happy because we're the happiest when we're the closest to Him. So you see, if I'm happy on the mountain tops and happier in the valleys...why then...I'm just happy all the time!" She ended her philosophy of life with one of her frequent laughs.

Emily thought about this for a while as the wagon rolled on. She knew there was much to learn from one whose hair was turning gray from the years and yet had found the secret of happiness.

"Just look at that!" Mrs. Bertram interrupted her thoughts, pointing toward a clump of trees in the distance. They glistened in the sunlight as each and every twig was clothed in ice that refused to melt under the increasing warm rays.

"Ah, such beauty!" Mrs. Bertram whispered almost reverently as she pulled the reins causing the old mare to slow its pace. "Emily, here is your answer! How to stay happy all the time, though your life will at times seem bustling, busy and full of confusion. Take time to see the beauty around you...it's everywhere. Every time a snowflake falls, every time a tiny flower buds and opens its face to the sun, every time the sun casts its rays of fiery red over the earth as it sinks beneath the open plains, every time the moon full and bright lights up the night in a majestic way, God's creation is reaching out to us. We must take time to enjoy it...to see it."

Emily hid those words away in her heart.

When they reached the mission, they were greeted by small upturned faces with wide grins spreading from ear to ear. Emily had quickly learned to love these little, dark-skinned children with their high cheek bones and black eyes that responded to attention with such love.

"Hi, Miss Emily!" said a little fellow, lean and tall for his age. "I got present, see!"

"Hi, Joe," she answered, wondering what he'd brought this time. Little Joe Stranger Horse had been known to bring some rather unwanted gifts. She went over to him reluctantly, remembering the live snake story she'd heard from Mrs. Bertram. Of course, he had thought it was a wonderful gift and was saddened when he was sternly told to get rid of the snake. Even though Emily realized they didn't have snakes here like in Virginia—only small, harmless ones—she still approached him cautiously.

"What do you have in your bag this time, Joe?"

"Present...for...you." He carefully formed the words that had been so hard for him in the beginning and handed the bag to her.

She held her breath and took it from him, opening it slowly. She jumped when something furry protruded from the bag. But she breathed a sigh of relief when she saw it was only a coyote tail, and turning to little Joe, saw a look of pride on his boyish features. She knew she must not spoil it for him.

"Why Joe, it's so beautiful! Where did you get it?"

"I shoot...I shoot...with White Hawk's gun," he replied, smiling.

"Well, you must be some shot. Who is White Hawk?"

"White Hawk best hunter on reservation...he teach me."

"Well, that is nice, and we are here to teach you other things today. Are you ready?"

He nodded his head and grabbed hold of her hand. She led him to the table beside the big window where already several others were waiting. Mrs. Bertram opened the teaching session with prayer and began the exercises. They had been working for about twenty minutes when Mrs. Bertram leaned over her shoulder. "Emily, would you mind working with the smaller ones today? We have a new pupil and I can't seem to get her to warm up at all. You're so good with them...I thought maybe you could. I'll take over here."

"Sure."

Emily exchanged places with Mrs. Bertram and found herself staring into the biggest, blackest, saddest eyes she'd ever seen. She was not more than three years old at the most but already wore a look of disillusion-ment that no child should know.

"Hi, I'm Miss Emily. What's your name?" she asked gently.

The child looked away and never spoke. Emily proceeded to teach the others all the while watching for some response in the new pupil but received none. Instead, the child sat very still looking over the others' heads beyond the small classroom and on out into the big world that lay beyond the small window. What was she thinking? What could be going on in the mind of one so young but yet not so young?

The next three weeks continued the same way. Each time Emily tried a little harder to make friends with the child, but to no avail. She came home frus-trated. Watching her own three happy and loved babies, she couldn't forget those haunting, black eyes. She talked to Heath about her, but not knowing the child, he couldn't understand Emily's obsession with an Indian child.

"My goodness, Honey, you act like she's one of your own."

Emily smiled at him and said no more. How could he understand? She anxiously awaited the next meet-ing. The week seemed to drag by, but when Tuesday did arrive and once again she found herself opening the big pine door, her eyes darted from one child to another. Where was she?

The day was a real success, with all of the children responding and learning their lessons, but Emily couldn't join in the enthusiasm. Where was the little girl with the big, black eyes?

The next week was the same. Again Emily waited anxiously, only to find the little girl missing. Emily tried to get her mind off her, losing herself in her work. They read the whole first chapter of Genesis together.

"We have a b-i-g God." Little Joe Stranger Horse said, his eyes beaming. "He make me!" He patted his tiny chest, which was covered with a worn and faded shirt two sizes too big. Emily felt the tears well up in her eyes. She loved those little children.

Regaining her composure, she asked, "And how did God make the first man?"

All the little hands flew up at the same time.

"John?"

John Waln was a gifted boy who learned quickly.

"God made 'em out'a dirt, and then, he breath life into 'em," he smiled. "Only real God can do that."

"You're right, John. Let's back up a bit and go through the creation. Who can tell me what did God make on the very first day of creation?"

A flurry of hands responded.

"Sandra?"

"Light!" a tall, thin girl of about nine spoke out. Her complete name was Sandra White Hawk and her family was well-respected within the reservation. Her great-grandfather had once been an honorable chief and though he was dead and his sons did not follow in his footsteps, the family was still held in high regard. Sandra was a child of faith already.

"And how did He make light?"

The children squirmed in their chairs, each wanting a chance to answer.

"Jacob?"

Jacob Waugh jumped up, but his feet were faster than his English. "He...He...He...s-p—ok-e!"

"That's right, Jacob. All God had to do was to speak. He said, 'Let there be light,' and there was light, just like that! What did God do on the second day of creation, George Kills-In-Sight?" George insisted on being called by his complete name.

"He...divide the water."

"Right. And what is the water in the sky, Green Leaf?"

"Clouds. But, Teacher, they don't look like water." Green Leaf was another promising student, always full of questions.

"You're right, Green Leaf. They sure don't. When I was a little girl, I thought clouds were made out of cotton. I used to daydream about jumping up and down on them and falling into the soft, puffy stuff. You know, this just goes to show us that our eyes deceive us often. Everything is not what it always appears to be. It is good to question, Green Leaf. We want to be sure about what we believe. But the clouds are water, a misty water like fog. We can't jump up and down on them. We can't even stand on them, but we can enjoy watching them glide silently across the big sky."

"I wish they *were* cotton," Green Leaf said.

"Well, let's get on with our lesson. What did God make on the third day? Running Fox?"

"Mountains, and trees, and tall grass, and everything," he answered, grinning.

"Right, Running Fox, God made the land and everything that grows on the land. What about the fourth day, Joe?"

"Big light!" His little hand shot upwards towards the sky, pointing to the sun.

"The sun, Joe. What else?"

"Silver moon that lights path for warriors...war paint shine in't...warriors ride ponies...s-s-s-h...big fight with pale faces."

"Joe, there are no more big fights between the warriors and the white man. Why do you talk that way?"

He grinned at her in his usually sly way. She really didn't need an answer, knowing that the reservation was filled with this kind of talk of the old days. Mrs. Bertram had explained this to her.

"Well, what about the fifth day?"

Again the little hands flew up.

"Birds an' fish." A small boy who usually never spoke up said quickly.

Emily didn't have the heart to discipline him for not waiting to be called on. "That's right, Spot." She smiled at him.

"His name not Spot...Spotted Tail his name," Green Leaf said authoritatively.

"Well, I happen to like Spot," Emily replied, still smiling. She wished they would all use Indian names or English names. Some having one and some the other was confusing.

"Well, we come to the last day of creation but the most important day. Who can tell me, what did God create on the sixth day?

"George Kills-In-Sight?"

"He make man...most import—ant."

"Right, God made man on the sixth day. But what else did He make on the sixth day?

"Running Fox?"

"Buffalo...ponies...wolves...all the animals...fox too!"

"Exactly, Running Fox. I'm proud of you all. What do you say we play a game now?"

The organized class was disrupted as they all ran, playfully pushing one another, to the floor and seated themselves, giggling and laughing.

That evening Emily sat rocking Jonathon in her arms and going over the morning in her mind. She felt good to be teaching the class. But what about the little girl with the dark eyes? Why didn't she come? Heath was reading a letter from his Mother. It was a long letter, as usual. Emily could see several pages. Mrs. Barrett always addressed her letters to Heath, but he handed them over to her as soon as he'd read them. Her letters were always newsy—full of the latest scoop on everybody. Emily wondered what she had to say this time. She wasn't usually that interested, but anything to get her mind off the little girl.

Finally, Heath handed her the letter and went back to his figuring. He had been bringing home lots of paperwork these days but didn't seem to mind. He didn't seem to mind all the long hours he was putting in at the mill, either. In fact, he seemed happier than she'd seen him in a long, long, time. Emily read: Pop was ailing with the flu but had perked up some. Good, she thought, feeling much warmer towards him than Mrs. Barrett. Karen's twins had both had chicken pox and Mrs. Barrett was worried that Karen might catch it since she'd never had it as a child. John was in Georgia on a business trip and Constance and the six boys were staying with them. Those six boys! Emily was sure glad she wasn't there. Of course, they wouldn't be so bad if they were taken out behind the barn more often, she thought. Elizabeth was busy working on the special design for her quilt that she was entering in the county fair in the spring. Mrs. Barrett used up two-thirds of a page describing it! Annie was baking a big birthday cake for Robert Jr. who would turn eight on Sunday—they had a surprise party planned for him. Annie sent word that the whole church missed her.

The next sentence stood out from the rest: "Remember Betty Lou Smith? Well, she up and ran off and married that no-account Buck Bryant. Her poor Mother is just grieved sick over it." Emily glanced over at Heath who seemed lost in his paperwork. Realizing he'd read those same words only a few minutes ago without so much as a change in expression, she suddenly felt a weight slide from her shoulders. Could she have imagined it all? Was he really innocent? She watched his brow wrinkle over some mathematical problem. He scratched his head with his pencil and sighed. How she loved him! *But the perfume!* That disgusting scent that she could smell whenever she thought about it. It was the same! Well, if he did, if he had (she couldn't say it…she couldn't even think it) then surely he didn't care for Betty Lou. Or how could he show no obvious signs of concern? Suddenly she was glad they were hundreds of miles away from those mountains she loved but which held heartbreaking memories. She stepped over softly to him and embracing him said, "I love you." He looked a little surprised and smiled at her, "I love you, too."

"Would you like some hot tea and rolls?"

"Sounds great," he answered a bit absently, going back to his work.

While pouring the tea, Emily decided to tell Heath about the little Indian girl. As she came back into the room, he broke away from his work and relaxed in the old, overstuffed chair. While they ate, Emily described the child to him in such a vivid and desperate way that he found himself admiring and loving this strong but tender girl he'd married. Who else, he thought, would have the time to think of another child with three babies of her own demanding all of her attention.

"You know, I have to go over to the north mill tomorrow, and I pass right by the Rosebud Reservation. You did say she lives there, didn't you?"

"Oh yes, that's what Mrs. Bertram told me."

"How would you like to come along? That is, if you could get Mae-Mae to come and stay with the children."

"Oh Heath, would you?" She jumped up and ran over to him, hugging him so hard that he spilled his tea. They both laughed.

Saturday morning dawned bright and sunny. Emily was up early preparing for the day. One hour later and they would be on their way. Mae-Mae should be arriving any minute now. She hated leaving the children twice in one week, but it wasn't far to the North Mill, and they would be back soon.

As they pulled off, Heath seemed pleased having her with him, and pulled her close to him.

"Heath, people will see us here in broad daylight all hugged up together." She laughed, sliding closer to him across the rugged seat.

"Who cares? We're in love!" he yelled out.

"Heath!" She smacked him on the knee.

"Isn't it beautiful, Heath?"

"It sure is," he answered, brushing from her face a curl that had blown down from where she'd had it neatly pinned.

"I don't mean me, silly. I mean all of this!" She threw her arms out as if to embrace it all.

Heath wasn't one to notice his surroundings, but he looked about now to satisfy Emily. The sun was shining so brilliantly, illuminating wide open stretches of gleaming white fields so that it nearly hurt his eyes. Each and every fir was covered with glistening ice. The millions and millions of needles laden with ice forced the tall, straight trees to bend, yielding to its power.

As the bright sun's rays streamed through the icy branches, the effect was that of a fairyland and its beauty was intoxicating. Even Heath sat still in awe.

"It makes me feel like I could jump off this here wagon and dance all over these icy fields. It makes me feel like I just have to do something," Emily said excitedly.

"How about this." Heath laid his cold lips upon hers. The mare seemed to sense the seriousness of the occasion and slowed her gait somewhat.

They soon arrived at the Indian reservation, and Emily tried to fight off the fears that suddenly engulfed her. Teaching those sweet, little children at the mission was one thing but this was something else. It was all so alien! Smoke circled upward from the cluster of tents that were surrounded by children of all ages. They sat in the wagon witnessing it all and waiting to soon be noticed, but everyone was bustling about, seemingly busy preparing for something.

Heath and Emily really didn't know whether they had not been noticed or whether they were being ignored. Suddenly everyone started moving toward a clearing on the south side of the tents. It appeared to have been recently swept clean. Though Emily and Heath were a short distance away, they sensed the excitement in the air. The Indian squaws filed out of the tents following the men and children. Emily wondered how so many people could fit into such tiny tents. They just kept crawling out like bees from a hive. Soon they were all gathered, and Emily noticed two men advance to the center of the clearing.

"What are they going to do?" she whispered to Heath.

"I'm really not sure," he answered absently.

Everyone was standing close to the clearing now, and it was difficult to see the two men. But then they began to seat themselves on the ground as if awaiting some kind of entertainment. The two men stood out clearly now. They both had on decorative headgear but other than that, there was very little to shield them from the cold. Their strong, lithe bodies were painted with weird designs in deep crimsons, black and green.

"It makes me shiver to see them," Emily remarked, moving closer to Heath. She could tell now that one was very young and the other much older and much larger.

Suddenly the older one began blowing a whistle.

"That's an eagle bone!" Heath said in a low voice. "I've seen some over at Grizzim's Store.

"Oh no, Heath. Look, the younger one has feathers stuck in his arms and shoulders!"

"I didn't notice them at first, either. It's all part of their Sun Dance. I've heard tell of them. It's some sort of spiritual rite they have."

"It seems so gruesome!"

"To us it does. But you have to remember they didn't grow up like us. They don't see things like us."

"Well, it still seems ridiculous to me!"

"It's their way of proving themselves. When a young boy is to become a man among them, he has to prove his strength, his endurance of pain. It's not nearly as bad as it was, I hear. When they were to become warriors, the torture used to be almost inhuman. They would actually hang for hours with feathers and sticks stuck in their bodies, ripping the flesh. They were usually not taken down until they passed out from the pain, and they would sometimes be talking out of their heads with a high fever. Sometimes they would even die from this, but most of the time they survived to become the great warriors they hoped to be. For a Sioux, to be able to endure pain and be a strong warrior is everything."

"But they don't need warriors anymore. They don't fight anymore. They can live peacefully on the reservations."

"True. But they still dream...."

They were so engrossed in watching the two Indians dance around and listening to the foreboding beat of the drums that they didn't notice a very tall, young Indian come up to the wagon. He stood there silently, resembling a statue. The only visible sign that he wasn't was the slight movement of his broad chest and shoulders as he breathed in the cold air. He, too, was painted with the bright greens, deep crimsons, and blacks, and wore the decorative headgear. He had a long, sleek knife strapped to his right side, and his dark eyes gazed unwaveringly at the couple before him. Suddenly, Heath, feeling the presence of someone close, turned and peered into the cold, dark eyes.

The silence was finally broken when the Indian spoke, "What you want?"

Heath began to explain, very slowly, their reason for being there. He described the little girl who had come to the mission and asked if she might be ill.

A light of recognition clouded over the Indian's eyes. "She not here."

"Well, where is she?" Emily spoke up anxiously.

The Indian stared at her strangely. She didn't realize that he wasn't used to women speaking out so forthrightly.

"Do you know where she is?" she repeated.

He continued to stare at her and then abruptly turned back to Heath. "Little one get white man's sickness, she cry and cry and cry. Witch doctor work for her three moons. He give up. White man's doctor come and take little one away."

"Where did he take her?" Heath asked.

"To white man's village...north."

"That would probably be White Plains," he said to Emily.

White Plains was bustling with early morning activity as they drove up. Heath pulled up in front of a blacksmith's building and went inside to inquire about the whereabouts of the Indian Reservation office.

"Last building on your right, headin' out'a town," the old gent answered without looking up, still forging the black metal.

They found it easily enough, a small, non-descript building. A heavy-set, robust woman probably in her early fifties asked them in. After Heath stated their business, the woman squinted at them suspiciously.

"Why are you so interested in an Indian kid?" she asked, still eying them in that uncomfortable way.

"She was one of my pupils at the Indian Mission. I understand she's ill, and I would like to see her. Is she here?"

"Yes'm, she's here all right. Back yonder." She waved toward a back room with a closed door. "Don't reckon it'll do no good, though. Every time we try to talk with her, she cries loud 'nough to bust your eardrums. The doc didn't find nothing wrong with her, said to leave her here for a few days, though. I'll be glad when they take her back to the reservation."

Emily wondered how this cold, heartless woman ever happened to be part of the Reservation Office. How could she relate to these people? It was clear she had no sympathy for them or probably anyone. "Do you mind if I try anyway?" she asked.

"Go 'head, Ma'am."

Emily found the child curled up under some soiled blankets, apparently asleep. But when Emily moved closer, the big, haunting eyes that she'd seen so often in her mind now stared up at her. Emily began to talk very softly to her as Heath and the woman watched from the doorway. They saw Emily gently wipe the little girl's forehead with the palm of her hand. Still, no cries.

When Emily came out a little later, the woman said to her, "You must have a way with children. You're the first one's been able to talk to her without her bellowing."

"What will happen to her?" Emily asked.

"I done told the Doc I ain't able to keep her here much longer. I've got more'n I can take care of now with my man gone for three weeks way out to the big Sioux reservation. And my son and his family 'spose to arrive here Monday or Tuesday. They gonna move in with us, help us, you know. Don't know where I'm gonna put 'em, much less some Indian orphan. She gotta be going back to the reservation soon. That's all it is to it."

"What do you mean—orphan? Is she an orphan?" Emily asked.

"Yes'm, that's what they tell me anyhow. Seems her folk were up and killed somehow."

"Doesn't she have anyone?"

"Sure, the whole reservation. You know how Indians do. When somethin' happens to the parents, the chillun belong to the camp."

"But she doesn't have a mother or anyone of her own?"

"Guess that's what's bothering her, maybe. Doc says ain't nothing wrong with her, less it be a broken heart. You know, grieving for her family. 'Course that's been a good while now—they say, 'bout eight months or so. Still, she don't stop crying and makin' herself sick and all."

"Suppose we took her home with us!" Emily blurted out, looking first at Heath and then at the woman.

"Emily!" Heath looked at her, bewildered.

"Just till she gets better," she added quickly.

"I don't know, Ma'am. It'd be fine by me but I don't figure on her going with you. And when she starts up that bellowing, you'd be most likely dragging her back here."

Emily looked at Heath with pleading eyes. He thought to himself that he could never love her more than he did right now.

"Alright…until she gets better."

The two of them stood there smiling, understanding and loving each other. The woman interrupted. "They call her Spring Leaf."

WHEN HEATH WALKED into the house, he could hear Emily humming softly, rocking Jonathon. He walked over and sat down across from her. Spring Leaf was sitting at her feet, painting a picture.

"They're up kind'a late, aren't they?" Heath asked.

"Yes, Jonathon doesn't feel very good. The twins are asleep and Spring Leaf had another nightmare, so I'm letting her stay up till I put Jonathon down."

Heath looked at the small, frail child carefully painting her picture. She never looked up. She was a solemn little thing. Even after three weeks, she hardly ever smiled or displayed any emotion, but still she seemed content.

Emily arose with Jonathon, still humming the tune. "Come along, Spring Leaf," she said softly. Spring Leaf picked up her paper and paints and followed obediently. When Emily came back out of the bedroom, Heath asked her, "What was that tune you were humming?"

"It's an old Indian lullaby. Mrs. Bertram taught it to me. I thought Spring Leaf would like it."

"Does she?"

"I think so. You know how quiet she is."

"Are Patrick and Prudence still captivated by her?"

"Yes, sort of, they still follow her around. Of course, she doesn't seem to mind. In fact, I think maybe she rather likes it—the attention, you know."

"We had a rough day today. That's why I'm so late...but I think we got things straightened out somewhat, though."

"Would you like your supper now? I know you must be starved."

"Sure would."

"Come on to the table. I have it warm on the stove."

Heath noticed the two plates on the table. "Haven't you eaten yet? It's nine o'clock!"

"I thought I'd wait for you."

"That's good. I never liked eating alone, really. I guess it comes from growing up in a big family."

"Oh, that reminds me. You got a letter from your Mother today."

"I'll read it after supper."

Emily sat down across from him and bowed her head. Heath followed as she prayed, thanking God for the food. He marveled at how she never forgot. He grew up with Grace only being said on Sunday or when they had a special dinner like Thanksgiving or something. And then, of course, his Father had always done it. He could never remember his Mother saying it. When he and Emily were first married, he had started off saying it on Sundays too, like his Father, but after listening to Emily all during the week, his prayers came out flat and cold compared to hers. So he let her take over the duty completely.

They enjoyed a leisurely supper, talking about the lumber mill, mostly. The business was growing and Uncle Raymond seemed to be giving Heath most of the credit for it.

"I don't want to take all the credit," Heath said, getting up from the table, "but I have seen a big change in a lot of things lately."

"I always knew you could do anything you set your mind to, Honey."

He gave her a squeeze as he walked by. "That's because I've got a good woman behind me." Picking up the letter off the icebox, he made himself comfortable on the couch while lighting his pipe. Emily began to clear the dishes off the table as he opened the letter and began to read.

"Oh, no..." he gasped.

"What is it?"

Without speaking, he handed the letter to her. Emily read, "It happened on Sunday morning. We were all getting ready for church and we noticed Annie hadn't come down. You know, she was always the first to be ready. Elizabeth went up to check on her. She had died in her sleep. We are all grieving, Heath, as we know you will when you receive this letter, and you, most of all. The place will not be the same without her, that's for sure. But, Heath, if it's any comfort to you, she had the prettiest smile on her face. We know she's happy. We know she's in Heaven, her home that she so often spoke about."

After a long silence with his head down, he looked up with tears in his eyes. "She was a Mother to me."

"I know."

"I won't even be able to go to her funeral."

"I'm sure she understands."

"Understands?" He questioned with despair and bitterness all wrapped up in the tone of his voice. "What do you mean? Annie's dead!"

"Her body is dead, Heath, and it's being buried. But not Annie. *She* lives."

"You really believe that, don't you?"

"I sure do. Annie believed in Jesus as her Saviour. She told me about it—she gave her life to Him many years ago."

"Yes, she's told me about that, too." He remembered her face as she told the story to him."

"And the Bible says, Heath, that if we'll confess with our mouths the Lord Jesus and believe in our hearts that God has raised Him from the dead, then we shall be saved...and being saved means living forever in Heaven. So, you see, Annie is not dead—she lives!"

Heath was silent. Then he stood up and walked toward the bedroom. "I think I'll turn in early tonight." Emily knew he was suppressing the grief that raged through his body and wanted to be alone.

THREE YEARS PASSED, the best three years Emily could remember. Sitting at the kitchen table watching the children out in the yard, she couldn't believe that it had actually been that long since Spring had come to live with them. They had dropped the Leaf soon after—she had become just little Spring, and the name fit. She was always so fresh and full of ideas. Patrick and Prudence still followed her around, and she mothered them like an old hen. She didn't quite get the same respect from Jonathon, already proving himself a handful at the age of three. Emily watched as Spring tried to push him in the swing, while he kept trying to push her away, wanting to do it himself.

Patrick and Prudence stood by, arguing over whose turn was next. Suddenly, Jonathon jumped out, turned a flip, and awkwardly pulled himself back up. He toddled off on his fat, stubby legs. Patrick jumped into the swing and Spring tactfully explained to him that it was Prudence's turn. What a little peacemaker! How could they give her up? She remembered the words of the new reservation manager: "She needs to be with her own people. It is time she went back to the reservation."

Emily had cried a lot that night and Heath had tried to console her, but she could tell that he, too, was upset. Little Spring had also touched *his* heart deeply, and he looked on her as one of his own. But today was the day! She must be strong…she *had* to be strong for Spring. She realized it was her own fault. If she had never brought her home in the first place, it would have been better. They wouldn't be facing this now.

But it was too late for those kinds of thoughts. Going to the door, she called, "Spring…it's time for you to come in now and get ready. Come along children, bring Jonathon with you."

The five of them waited, dressed in their Sunday best. The children took turns peering out the window, looking for their Daddy. All except Spring, that is. She sat quietly, rather subdued, as if awaiting her sentence. All too soon for Emily, Heath and Mr. Geiser arrived. Mr. Geiser had suggested earlier not to tell Spring the reason for all of this, but rather just to take her out to the reservation to spend the day and see her reaction. At the end of the day, they would make their decision on what to do.

"Good morning, Mrs. Barrett. Fine day, isn't it?" Mr. Geiser said in his usual tactless way. Emily had taken an immediate dislike to him from the start. He was a short, surly man in his late fifties who seemed to delight in making other people miserable.

"She's Sioux all the way," he commented as Spring quietly walked across the room to get her shawl.

"She's a beautiful Sioux princess!" Emily retorted.

"Well, we'd best get on our way," he declared, unaware of the tension in the room.

They had not been back to the reservation since the day they were looking for Spring. In just three years, the situation had deteriorated. Many of the tents were badly in need of repair. The people seemed tattered and some were obviously suffering from malnutrition. How could they leave Spring here? Emily and Heath looked at each other silently and then turned back to the dismal picture.

"Why is this?" Heath asked, turning to Mr. Geiser.

Mr. Geiser saw the look of questioning disbelief in Heath's eyes. "It's been a hard winter," was his only answer.

Heath and Emily exchanged worried looks over his head.

As soon as they entered the reservation, Spring seemed to withdraw into the shell that had taken them three years to help her emerge from. It was obvious she remembered the reservation, but didn't seem to really recognize anyone. Chief Wild River and his wife were very kind and helpful. They tried their best to welcome Spring in the customary Indian way, but Spring would not respond. She clung to Emily as if she had some premonition of what was to happen.

Most of the day was spent in the chief's tent or just outside it. Patrick and Prudence and even little Jonathon seemed to be enjoying the day, playing with some of the Indian children and taking turns riding a small pony that Chief Wild River's son guided around in a large circle. This was how even the smallest of the children in the camp learned to ride. Jonathan's squeals of delight could be heard throughout the day, but still Spring sat quietly beside Emily, never moving from her side. Chief Wild River gave them Spring's background in bits and pieces as the day wore on. If Spring listened, it was not apparent. She showed no signs of interest, sitting there as if her soul had escaped her and roamed somewhere off in the distant prairie.

"I not surprised," Chief Wild River began, "she take to you people. Her Great, Great Grandfather was white man from St. Louis. Trapper he was, brave man—man to be trusted."

"What happened to him?" Emily asked.

"Killed by Commanche arrow, trapping in Commanche territory. His squaw with child when he killed. A son was born to her...Lost Son, named this because he had no father. Lost Son toughest warrior of all Sioux. He lead many war parties to victory. But one day Pawnee war party caught him and his warriors by surprise. They sleeping, have no chance. Most all die sleeping, also Lost Son. Lost Son's scalp great honor for Pawnee. His body brought back to camp. Lost Son's Daughter, Spring Leaf's Mother, small child when this happen. She never forget what happen to her Father. One day she remember it over and over, and it drive her to do what she do." He paused as if remembering himself.

"What did she do?" Heath asked impatiently.

"She never content with squaw's position. Some say great White God make mistake. This squaw should be warrior like Father. She marry son of Grey Fox. One day, this little one (nodding in Spring's direction) just a papoose sleeping from tree and she lose both parents."

"How?" Emily questioned rather quickly, caught up in this unbelievable story.

"Group of rough riders come onto reservation that day and demand Father's arrest. He was called thief. They plan to hang him."

"Why?" Emily asked again.

"They say he thief." The Chief hesitated for a long pause, looking out over the vast prairie. "They say he thief because he lead Sioux party to distant farm and take most harvest...to feed our hungry families."

"Was anyone hurt?" Heath asked.

"No. Family not home."

"Why were your families hungry?" Emily asked, becoming more and more involved.

"Long story, my Child. Our people suffer this hunger since white man kill buffalo." His eyes suddenly gleamed as he continued. "My Grandfather tell me of great herds of buffalo. They roam these prairies, thousands of them. He hunt them. Plenty for Sioux, Commanche, Pawnee, Arapoho, plenty for all, until white man come and kill like one kills lice...leave them to die, rot in blazing sun...hundreds at one time from white man's guns. They not kill to eat, they not kill for skins, they kill to kill. Now there no buffalo. We wait on white man's food, sometimes it comes, sometimes no food!"

"Why, that's terrible!" Emily exclaimed, with a sudden awareness of the truth.

"But what happened to Spring's parents?" Heath asked, trying to bring the old chief back to the subject and out of the despondency he had fallen into.

The chief looked up at Heath as if seeing him for the first time. His eyes were filled with water and a sadness beyond description. Heath was quiet. The old chief sat there for a long time in silence before speaking again. When he finally spoke, his voice cracked with emotion.

"That day, white men ride in. They grab son of Grey Fox to take him away. Bright Star, little one's Mother (again he nodded in Spring's direction) run to his side, throw herself between he and white men. I not see, I told later...gover'ment men and me...we talk peace at reservation office...all time I talk peace with gover'ment men...their brothers murder my people."

"What do you mean?" Heath asked.

"When Bright Star throw herself between...white

man hit her with barrel of gun. She fall to ground. Son of Grey Fox attack white man. Then, loud blast, and Son of Grey Fox dead. Many people say, Bright Star stood, she have look of one who crazy. She spring on white man that hold gun like...like lioness spring on prey while protecting cubs. She stab him with own knife. While blood spurted from white man's chest, sound of thunder from sky...three blasts sound together...Bright Star fall at feet of Son of Grey Fox."

All were quiet. Only the yells and squeals from the children playing beyond the tent broke the silence.

As the day drew to a close, the chief and his wife sat down with Spring, explaining to her what they proposed to do. The kind, old woman patted her on the shoulder and told her the duties and joys of an Indian squaw. The chief even invited her to come and live with them in their tent, and be their daughter. Very tenderly and patiently, they strove for her acceptance, but still she resisted and in her proud, stubborn, silent way, she gave them her answer. The chief sent for Emily, Heath and the reservation manager. They appeared in the doorway.

"She not live here," the chief announced, "her place with *these* people where her heart is."

The manager kicked at the ground, sending a spray of dust upward as he strode off. He would never understand these Indians! Oh well, he had done his part.

Before they departed, the chief insisted on a ceremony for Spring. He wanted to adopt her, giving her the title of "princess." Though it was late, they all walked out beyond the camp to a hillside where it was performed, short but very meaningful. Heath and Emily did not understand most of it, but each part was carefully explained to Spring. It did not come as a surprise that she seemed to understand. No, it was already plain to see there were deep thoughts behind those big, black eyes.

Riding back home, Jonathon asleep on her lap, the twins and Spring curled up in the back of the wagon, Emily said softly, "We came with broken hearts. But God has intervened and we leave with a princess!"

Heath smiled.

Chapter V
The Treasure

"Spring is here!" Emily exclaimed one morning as she looked out the mist-clouded window. The sun was already doing its job as each tiny drop of water evaporated before her eyes. She turned and saw Spring staring questioningly.

"Oh, not you, Honey. I mean Spring, the season, a special time of year. Come and look—see those little buds on the trees. It's a beautiful time of year."

Spring looked up at her and smiled.

"The name fits you, too, Spring. *You* are beautiful, too."

This year had made a big difference in her. It was as if she realized now that she really belonged to them and had taken her place rightfully among the family, asserting herself in a motherly fashion over the others. Still, she was a deep thinker and was often quiet in her own little world. By now, the other children were pushing and shoving to get a glimpse out the window and discover this other spring their Mother was talking about.

"Why don't we go for a picnic, children?"

It was as if she'd taken the lid off a barrel of confusion. All their little voices squealing and exclaiming, "Let's go...let's go...me want'a go," jumping up and down and stomping their feet.

"Calm down now, we can't go far, just out beyond that thicket of trees in the distance."

Emily packed a basket with apple butter sandwiches, buttermilk and slices of chocolate cake she'd baked the day before. She instructed them to wrap up with their warm sweaters. The air was still chilly. They set out walking, Emily carrying Jonathon on her hip and Spring carrying the basket. She wished they were back in Virginia. It would be really warm now and instead of the few daring signs of spring that had cropped up here, the whole mountain would be bursting forth with life under every rock and crevice. She could see it all again as if she'd been transported back there— the dogwoods spotting the dark forest, the wild roses climbing old and rotted fences, deep purple violets hugging the rich forest floor partially covered with the green, velvet carpet of moss, the buzzing of the many varieties of bees out to plunder nature's gifts, and the birds—she could hear them—singing in the treetops. Was she homesick?

Jonathon was getting heavier and she shifted him to the other side. They had been walking for some time now, and still the thicket of trees seemed no closer.

There was something deceiving about these plains. After what seemed like an hour, the thicket loomed in front of them. The children ran ahead, skipping and twirling themselves around the slender trees. Emily walked through the trees, peeling the loose white bark off as she thought, this is the closest we'll come to a Virginia picnic.

"Hey Mama, look," Spring called from the top of a nearby tree.

"Be careful."

"See me, Mama!" Patrick was halfway up the same tree, trying not to let Spring get anything on him.

"Hold on, Patrick. Those trees are slippery."

Prudence and Jonathon stood at the bottom looking up, one too afraid to try, the other too small.

Emily sat down nearby. The bright, piercing sun seeped down through the trees, throwing a warm blanket over her legs. A gentle breeze was causing the tall, slender blades of grass that stretched out over the plains between them and home to yield and bend toward the rich earth. So green was the grass. Yes, this was a beautiful land too, in its way, she thought. The snow, lying heavy from November until April, does its job of preparing this. This greenery! She remembered when the last drop of snow melted, revealing the breathtaking lush, green carpet beneath it. She had to admit that not even in Virginia was there a green to surpass it. But Virginia—ah Virginia—April in Virginia would now be bursting forth with new life. She remembered how she always waited patiently through those long dull months of January, February and March for April. That was the turning point from the lifeless winter to the fascinating signs of spring. She almost dozed in the warmth of the sun with the pleasant memories of home.

The children enjoyed romping and playing and eating on the faded cloth thrown on the green grass. Emily delighted in watching them. As the day came to a close and the bright sun made its path downward across those straight stretches of flat land, five tired but happy figures made their way home. As they leisurely walked, Emily watched the slow descent of the sun. It took so much longer to disappear here, since it had to bow down completely to the earth, not like back home where it dipped suddenly behind the mountains without giving one proper notice.

Carrying Jonathon, who had fallen asleep on her hip, she began to sing...

"I'm tired and I want'a go home."

The children laughed and joined in. When home became clearly visible in the distance, Emily experienced a foreboding of trouble, and when she saw Heath's figure pacing the yard, she knew she wasn't just imagining it. Quickening her pace, she urged the children to follow. Spring, who had been aimlessly swinging the empty basket, caught hold of Prudence's hand, pulling her along faster. Emily noticed the carefree little face stiffen with purpose. Had she experienced such heartbreak as a child, that she was now quick to sense trouble, like one beyond her years?

As they neared the house, Heath walked towards them, his shoulders drooped.

"What is it?" she called.

He just looked at her with a hopelessness in his

usually happy eyes.

"What is it?" she repeated.

"Today...President Wilson declared war on Germany!"

Emily whispered, "Oh, no."

"We're at war now," Heath went on. "We're now part of that monster that has been destroying all the nations—a real world war."

"But I thought the President declared that we would be neutral three years ago?"

"He did. But you know what's been going on, how Germany has destroyed several of our ships. How about the Lusitania? I don't blame the President. He had no choice."

"But what will happen now?"

"I don't know," he answered, but deep down in his heart he did know.

EXACTLY THREE MONTHS later, Heath was in the middle of the big Atlantic, heading to war along with hundreds of other young, scared men. As he held onto the cramped cot with one hand, keeping the other over his mouth, he wondered how he would ever be any good in a war when he couldn't even fight off this blasted seasickness.

At the same time, Emily and the children sped across the vast prairies, leaving the wide open country behind. The train seemed to move much faster leaving this big land than it had when they'd come. As the tall, green grass whipped by, Emily prayed. She prayed for Heath. She prayed for the children. She prayed for herself. She prayed for the unknown. When they

crossed the wide Missouri for the last time, she looked
at Spring, who was staring out the window with her big,
alert eyes. She was leaving her home, the home of her
people. Would she ever return? Would she love the
Virginia mountains as her own? Patrick and Prudence
had fallen asleep again and Jonathon was well on his
way in her arms. The train had a soothing effect on
them as it rocked its way down the long tracks. Emily
watched them lovingly, taking in each minute aspect of
their tiny faces, trying to keep her mind off Heath.
Where was he? What was he doing right now? Would
he come.... No, she would not think of it. She prayed
some more. The trip did not seem as long as the first
one and after a while, the majestic Blue Ridge Mountains rose up before them. It was like seeing an old
friend; Emily couldn't take her eyes off them. She had
almost forgotten the sense of power and wonder those
gigantic mounds of earth created within her. It was
good to be home. She felt a resignation come over her,
a resignation to God's will, whatever it might be. But
it would be good to be a part of the mountains again.
They would comfort her, too. Not like the prairies
where one was left alone and barren, so tiny and
helpless without even the haven of forest and hills to
lose oneself. But here among the many folds and crev-
ices, one could escape and hide from life's devastating
dreams and just be alone with God.

"That's home, Children. Those big, beautiful
mountains!"

They all strained their necks, trying to see them
better.

"How did they get so big?" Patrick questioned.

"It took many, many years, Patrick."

"Betcha I can climb 'em," he added confidently.

"Bet Spring could beat you," Prudence piped in.

"No, she couldn't!" he retorted.

"We'll all get to climb them," Emily said, noticing Spring sitting so still, absorbing it all with those big, black eyes.

Their future had been well laid out for them when they arrived. Mrs. Barrett had everything planned in her matter of fact way. They were to stay at the Barrett house temporarily, until Heath came home.

This sudden surge of hospitality surprised Emily until she realized it was a show. It was what everybody would expect, the least they could do for the cause, and of course, it was what Heath would want. The home-coming was not a typical hugging and crying episode. Rather, the meeting was stilted and forced with each member of the family in turn expressing false concern for her and the children. How could intelligent people all take their parts in this live play of pretension, she thought to herself as they were all seated in the formal parlor. The children were little strangers to them. Patrick and Prudence kept their distance and Spring was totally ignored except for curious stares when she wasn't looking. Only Jonathon was his usual bouncing self, chattering away to everyone.

"Doesn't he look like Heath, Mother?" Elizabeth asked, nodding at Jonathon.

"His eyes are not as blue and there is a difference in the shape of their faces, but overall, yes, he does." Mrs. Barrett smiled, acknowledging her approval.

"I don't know about the looks, but he acts just like

him," Karen laughed.

Suddenly there was a ruckus in the hallway and all eyes turned in that direction in time to see a big, brown dog stumble into the parlor.

"Oh my!" Mrs. Barrett gasped. "Robert, please get Doggy out of here."

Robert was already on his feet leading the harmless creature back the way he'd come, but Jonathon ran after them excitedly calling, "Dog...Dog...Dog...."

Emily gripped the arms of the chair as the past rolled before her, the pictures flashing vividly...Doggy, but not a big Doggy then, a much smaller one, Little David...Jonathon...it all ran together in her mind as her heart pounded.

"Emily, are you all right?" Karen asked.

"Yes, yes, I'm alright," she answered.

DAYS PASSED INTO weeks and still no word from Heath. Emily tried frantically to keep her mind off the war and not to worry, but to no avail. She was too idle, for the first time in her life. If there was just something I could do, she would often say to herself. But here in the Barrett household, there was nothing for her to do. If only Annie were still here! She had tried to get into the kitchen but was rudely informed that it belonged solely to Mrs. Harding. She was a cantankerous, elderly woman who was trying to take Annie's place. Emily tried a little housecleaning but was tactlessly informed, this time by Mrs. Barrett herself, that it would be best if she left these things to Mrs. Harding, who was quite capable of their complete undertaking.

She played with the children most of the time, but

still found herself yearning for something to do. One morning as she lay in bed facing another idle day trying to keep out of the Barretts' way, she decided to do something. The bright rays of sun fell on her bed, warming her feet, sending surges of energy through her small body.

"I'm going home!" she said aloud as the rapid flow of energy raced up her body, up her spine, her neck, her brain, forcing the thoughts that had been dormant out into the wide and waiting world. "I'm going home—home to the cabin—home to Little David." Suddenly she couldn't lie in bed a second longer. Springing from the sunken, feathery mattress, throwing the heavy quilt aside, she placed her feet solidly on the cold floor with purpose in mind.

It was a long ride, but she was enjoying every minute of it. She was alone, due to Mrs. Barrett's insistence. But this time, she was glad for her domineering way. She *wanted* to be alone. Nothing had changed much. Life seemed to stay the same here in the mountains, she thought, except for a little more traffic along the way and the new parson of the Barretts' church she met on the way. He tipped his hat at her when they passed, and, of course, she knew who he was, driving the new Dodge. She had heard about that already. He was one of the first to have a motor vehicle. Of course, the Barretts were talking about buying one after the war.

Finally, as she approached the familiar curve, she slowed the horse's gait as if afraid of what she might find. There was a mixture of feelings reeling around within her, happiness, reservations, excitement, fear.

As she rounded the curve, there it was. Tears welled up in her eyes and she blinked to see more. It was the same. A few boards had fallen off the windows and weeds and brush were fast concealing it, but it was still beautiful to her. It was home. She glanced toward the hill beside the cabin for that familiar sight, but it too was obscured by the entanglement of weeds and overgrown brush. A gentle breeze caused the porch swing to sway to and fro, beckoning her with its rhythmic creaking sound, and she responded. Climbing down from the wagon, she walked cautiously through the weeds aware that she was no longer in South Dakota. She remembered the rattler that Heath killed the summer before they left. She eased up the steps and across the porch and sat down in the swing. A sense of contentment descended upon her and her drooping shoulders straightened. Pushing back and forth slowly, she prayed, "Please God, let us come back home."

After soaking up the sun and sense of freedom she was experiencing away from the Barrett household, she decided to examine things more closely. Walking around, she kept finding things to do, picking up trash, pulling up tall weeds, all the time putting off what she had longed to do, but now found difficult. Finally she ascended the hill, pushing the brush aside. There it was, just as she'd left it. The weeds were everywhere and the earth was somewhat sunken from the heavy rains, but the name was still clear—David Edward Barrett! The tears she expected did not come. Instead, the contentment deepened.

"We're back home, Little David. Mama's back! And, you have another brother now, Jonathon, and a real little Indian princess for a sister, too. How about that? But I suppose you already knew that. No, I don't suppose it, Son—I know it. I know you're watching. That's why I'm here—to let you know I haven't forgotten you. I will never forget you, Son. You are my first born, and Son, that is special...you're special. One day we'll be together again."

She picked some wildflowers nearby and placed them on the small grave. "I'm going now, Son, but I'll be back, and soon."

Although cautiously walking down the hill, she stumbled over something hidden in the tall weeds, and jumped back, frightened—something black was shining in the sun. Taking a closer look, she saw it was a black purse, and a very nice one at that. She picked it up and opened it. There was a change purse within that she didn't touch, a delicate handkerchief with tiny, pink roses embroidered on its edges, a deep scarlet pin, and several neatly folded papers. A name stood out on one of the papers, Miss Gertrude Blanche. Blanche... Blanche...where had she heard that name? Oh yes, the Blanches—they lived several miles up the road. But how on earth did this purse get all the way over here? She held it up, wondering what to do with it. Well, there was only one thing to do—she would drop it off on the way. She really didn't know the Blanches very well. They had always been sort of uppity folk with more money than most and she'd heard tell that they didn't cotton to strangers—and she would be a stranger to them.

She had planned to drop the purse off quickly and be on her way, but they lived farther off the main road

than she remembered. The long drive leading up to the
the house was lined with rows of huge boxwoods that
towered above her, increasing her feeling of intimida-
tion. She drove on, with a certain amount of reluctance
now as she recalled a childhood memory of visiting the
old mansion with several other children. Let's see,
there was Billy Jackson, Grace Martin, and Franklin.... What was his name? Oh well, time has a way
of clouding one's memory.

They had meant no harm, only looking for some
fun when they decided to snoop around the place one
day. Yes, she remembered it was right after Billy had
started delivering milk for his Father. He had invited
them all that day for the ride. They were jostling down
the road when the idea hit them. Billy parked the
wagon at the end of the drive, and they ran down it,
darting in and out of the boxwoods, laughing and daring
each other to venture farther.

The elegant, Victorian style house had loomed up
before them in enlarged dimensions to their young eyes.
They hesitated, taking in the foggy mist that encircled
it and the masses of dark green ivy that practically
covered it. But their youthful curiosity overcame
their fear, and they proceeded up to the porch. They
were about to peer in one of the wide windows when it
happened. A deafening blow vibrated from the eaves,
rattling the windows and when she looked about, she
was alone. Billy, Grace and Franklin had suddenly
disappeared; she caught sight of their clothing vanishing through the thick shrubbery. Taking flight and
following, she heard a shrill voice yelling, "The next
time it will be *you* that gets the buckshot!"

Now, approaching the house once again, she could almost hear the shot ring out. Pushing these childhood memories out of her head, she viewed the place now from adult eyes. Its size diminished with the years, and it had lost the ghostly aura that held them in awe so many years ago. Even the ivy had spent itself and now dangled brown and listless from the brooding eaves. Certainly the old place had seen better days. She stepped down from the wagon and climbed the steps, noticing the crumbling concrete.

Her knock was answered by an old, bent-over man with a bushy head of thick, gray hair. He squinted at the piercing sun and asked with his aging voice, "Who calls?"

"My name is Emily Barrett. I live over the way, and I brought something that I think belongs here—I found it." She held up the purse.

The old man peered at it unbelievingly. "Well, bless my bones! Come here, Kathryn, look what this here child has."

A tall, thin, but elegant lady appeared in the doorway beside him.

"Well, Wilton, do ask the young lady in," she scolded.

As Emily protested, she was seized by the old man. His long, bony fingers clasped her arm and lead her into the foyer. She could not see into the parlor off to the right. It was gloomy with heavy draperies shutting out the sun.

"Where did you find it, Child?" asked the elegant lady.

"A few miles from here—it was lying in the woods,"

Emily stammered.

"What did you say your name was again?" the old man inquired as he stared at her.

"Emily, Emily Barrett."

"Barrett...Barrett.... Oh yes, you must be one of Charles Barrett's children."

"Not exactly. I'm married to Heath, his son, and we used to live just over the hollow. That's where I found the purse."

"The purse, the purse...oh yes."

The elegant lady spoke to the old man who Emily had figured out by now to be her husband, Mr. Blanche. "Wilton, she couldn't have gotten that far. The dogs must have carried it there."

"I wouldn't be surprised if she didn't get there by herself. You underestimate her. She's mad, I told you."

"Wilton!" she exclaimed. Turning to Emily somewhat embarrassed, "Dear Child, do come and sit a spell. We must explain about Gertrude."

Emily felt as if she were being drawn into a net and couldn't escape, although she didn't want to. Her curiosity had been stirred, and she must find out about Gertrude. She was led into the formal parlor with its heavy, midnight blue drapes and elegant furniture of another period. She sat down in one of the highback chairs, still holding the purse since no one had made an effort to retrieve it.

"You see, Child," the old lady began, "Gertrude is my cousin. She lives with us and has for some fifteen years. She and I were like sisters growing up," Mrs. Blanche smiled. "There's really not much difference in our ages, but Gertrude has become rather senile lately, you know. She sometimes does strange things...."

"What she does is crazy things!" Mr. Blanche interrupted. "She up and disappeared last Wednesday—was gone all day. We called Sheriff Rhodes. He and his deputy found her just walking up the road not too awfully far from here. That was when she lost her purse."

"You see, Child, it isn't the first time she's done this. But she usually turns up before we have to call the authorities. I just don't know what we're going to do with her," Mrs. Blanche confided worriedly.

"Claims to be out looking for some treasure." Mr. Blanche shook his head. "Can you believe that?"

"And in the meantime she loses a *real* treasure," Mrs. Blanche added.

At that time, a little, old lady bounced into the parlor, stopped, looked around from face to face and spotted the purse.

"There it be! Who found my purse?" she asked with a broad smile.

"Gertrude, this here's Mrs. Barrett. She found it...she found it way over the hollow...in the woods!"

The old lady looked at Emily with a twinkle in her eye. "Well, how about that!" Then she opened the purse as if she were looking for something. Pulling out a roll of bills, she smiled at Emily. "You have made my day, Honey. I must repay you for your honesty." She handed some of the bills to Emily.

"Oh no, I'm sorry but I couldn't take that." Emily started to go.

Mrs. Blanche stood quickly and began to lead her from the room. Mr. Blanche followed, but Gertrude remained and smiled at Emily as she glanced over her shoulder.

When they reached the door, Mr. Blanche leaned close to Emily and half-whispered, "If you know of anyone who would like to care for an old lady, please let us know."

"You mean Gertrude?"

"My wife isn't able to look after her any longer. She's been ailing a lot herself here lately, and Gertrude is a handful. We're willing to pay quite reasonably."

"Well, if I hear of anyone, I certainly will let you know."

She climbed into the wagon and looked back at the old house. It did look rather forlorn and sad. The Blanches had closed the door, shutting out the warm sunlight, but she noticed the heavy parlor drapes at one of the windows begin to part and there was Gertrude waving at her. She waved back and left. As she approached the bend in the drive, she looked back for the last time, and still the old lady stood in the archway of the heavy drapes—watching.

All during the next week, that lonesome figure haunted her although she couldn't figure why—someone she didn't even know. But there was something about that scene—something eerie—as if the old lady were a helpless fly caught in a spider's web awaiting its doom.

She was thinking of Gertrude when her thoughts were interrupted by a scream. She flew to a window just in time to see Ramona, Elizabeth's eight-year-old, running to the house. Spring was standing in the sand pile, covered with sand from head to foot but not uttering a sound. She looked frightened. When Emily reached the foot of the stairs, she saw Mrs. Barrett and Elizabeth soothing Ramona, trying to stop her cries. She ran past them out to Spring.

"What happened, Honey?"

Before she could speak, Patrick blurted out, "Ramona dumped her sand bucket on Spring's head, and Spring hit her!"

"Is that what happened, Spring?"

Spring nodded her head in agreement, and Emily's heart went out to her just as it had the first time she'd seen that frightened look in those big, black eyes.

"Why did Ramona do that?" she asked, already knowing why. The Barrett children delighted in picking on Spring and poking fun at her.

"Why did Ramona do *what*?" Elizabeth was practically screaming as she stormed across the yard, with Ramona by the hand. Ramona was pouting.

"Look at what your little heathen did!" she exclaimed, pointing to a dark, swollen area around one of the child's eyes.

"Just a minute, Elizabeth! You can't call my child names." Emily tried to control her temper.

"Your child! Is that what she is...I thought...."

"Elizabeth!" Mrs. Barrett interrupted as she ran up, out of breath.

Emily grabbed Spring and Patrick by their dirty, little hands and practically dragged them up to the house and to their rooms. Once in, with the door shut behind them, she collapsed in the nearest chair and breathed in and out deeply, trying hard to suppress the cries that wanted to come. The children stood around her, watching with frightened eyes. Jonathon was still napping, but Prudence had left her dolls in the adjoining room to come and see what was happening. She had never heard her Mother mount the steps with such speed or firmness.

"Run along and play now...Mother's all right," she said with difficulty as she gently patted Spring's head. The three of them dutifully walked into the next room and were soon playing as if nothing had happened. Emily continued to sit, part of her beginning to calm down, and part of her building up to action. The sweet fragrance of lilacs drifted in the window. She looked out at the many different trees and shrubs, the peach trees, the English boxwoods, the willows. It was all so lovely, but it wasn't home. We're going home!

The next morning, she rose early to put her plan into action. The children were still sleeping when she approached Mrs. Barrett.

"I would very much like to go over to the cabin and clean up around it some. Do you think Mrs. Harding would mind watching the children today?"

Mrs. Barrett looked at her, rather surprised, but remembering the incident of the day before, she answered almost gently, "I'm sure that will be alright, but I don't see why you would want to do that."

"It is so grown up and all. I want to cut some of the weeds and just clean it up some."

"Well, take whatever you need. The garden tools are out in the shed next to the smoke house." Mrs. Barrett watched Emily turn excitedly away to fetch the tools. It must be, she thought to herself, that she wants to take care of the child's grave. Why else would she want to go over there?

Traveling down the dusty road alone, Emily wondered if she was doing the right thing. But it must be! It wasn't fair to the children to be cramped up in the Barrett household where they really weren't wanted, especially Spring. She couldn't allow her to be ridiculed. Once again she turned the wagon onto the Blanche driveway and summoned up all her courage. She stepped down and walked directly to the door, knocking firmly and quickly. Mr. Blanche answered, looking older and more tired than before. He seemed glad enough to see her and invited her into the parlor.

"I'm sorry, Mrs. Barrett, my wife is very ill today. She will not be able to come down."

"Is there anything I can do?"

"No, thank you. Mrs. Christian came by earlier and did a few things for us. She lives up the road and is very good to us."

"Mr. Blanche, today I have come on business. You asked me to let you know if I heard of anyone that would be interested in taking care of Gertrude."

Yes, that is correct, my Dear, and...."

"Well, I would like to offer my services. I am going to move back to the cabin, the children and I. As you know, it's not far from here."

"My Dear, how would you manage Gertrude along with your children?"

"I can do it, Mr. Blanche, I'm sure. I would like to have the chance."

The old man shook his head, a little confused. "Well, I don't know. I will talk to Mrs. Blanche about it as soon as she's feeling better, and I will talk with

Gertrude also."

"I'll stop by here day after tomorrow. You can let me know then if it's alright."

"Yes, yes, that will be fine."

Emily spent most of the day cutting the tall weeds with a sickle. Her arms ached as she drove back that evening, but she felt good and could hardly wait to find out the Blanches' answer. What if they wouldn't let her? What would she do then? The reins were difficult to hold with her blistered hands, and she kept changing them. But it *had* to work out! She looked up at the giant, blazing, fiery ball that was about to descend behind the mountains. It cast its fiery rays out over the sky, creating an awesome effect. She sped up, wanting to make it back before the sun made its final dip.

Two weeks later, the place once again looked like home as Emily brushed on the last of the whitewash Mr. Barrett had brought over. She stepped back, admiring her work, and tried to hold back the excitement as she thought, "Tomorrow we'll move!"

Everybody seemed excited except Mrs. Barrett, who refused to believe that she would actually do such a thing—move back in *that* cabin alone! But she would not be alone, Emily had answered. Not hardly, with four children, and Gertrude.

"Why in the world would Miss Gertrude Blanche consider leaving that beautiful, old home of theirs to go and live in a mountain cabin?" Mrs. Barrett had questioned.

"I don't know, but she wants to," Emily answered, remembering the look in her eyes when the old couple gave her the option.

"The only thing that really concerns me is the fact that you have no man there with you—just two women and a bunch of children," Mr. Barrett added worriedly.

"Don't be concerned, Mr. Barrett. I have Heath's shotgun, and I know how to use it." She remembered those words now. However, she didn't feel as confident as she had appeared to him, but she could do it. She must.

"WHEN IS DADDY coming home?" Patrick asked, lugging in the last armful of wood. He was really becoming a little man.

"It shouldn't be too much longer, Honey."

"How about a story after you finish with that there wood, Son?" Gertrude asked, knowing in her wise, old way that this would surely cheer him up.

"Would ya, Gertrude?" he asked excitedly.

Soon she was surrounded with four pairs of eyes waiting for another one of her tall tales. Emily never could figure how much of them were truth and how much fairy tale, but they certainly captured the children's interest and gave them something to look forward to every day. She had found that Gertrude wasn't at all like the Blanches had said. Her keen mind was stimulating and often challenged Emily.

Certainly, she was a bit out of step with the rest of the world, but not due to any deterioration of her mind. Instead, it was a stubborn refusal to grow old. She didn't *act* old! It was as if someone had placed the mind and soul of an eighteen-year-old inside that decrepit, old body.

As the story neared its end, only two pairs of eyes

were on her. Jonathon and Prudence had fallen asleep. Patrick fought to stay awake, but Spring hung on every word, as usual.

Once the children were in bed, Emily sat down beside Gertrude. "I don't know where you get all those stories," she laughed.

"Well, Child, after you've lived as long as me, you'll have a storehouse full of them, too. 'Course, my best you haven't heard yet. There was the time of the Apple Blossom Ball! Now that was a time...I recall I was dressed all in pink, soft pale pink—just like a baby's cheeks. My hair was the color of fresh made butter, yellow as could be. I was the belle of the ball, at least *I* thought I was. There were two gentlemen seeking my favor at the time, and I couldn't figure out which I liked best, so I was just nice to both of them. I would dance first with the one and then with the other." She laughed.

"But you know, those two fellows hated each other with a passion." Suddenly her old face changed and Emily thought she could see the flicker of youth appear and quickly vanish. Gertrude was silent. Emily watched.

"It was that night...the night of the Apple Blossom Ball...that I first saw Charles. He was standing over by the bandstand with his arm resting on the platform. He was staring right at me with a little grin on his handsome face. When my eyes rested on his, I knew *he* was the one—the one for me. I kept dancing with the other two fellows, but my eyes were drawn to him. There was something about his eyes, anyway...they were special. My friends said he wasn't nearly as handsome as those other two fellows—but he was to me."

"What happened?" Emily asked, with increasing interest.

"Well, before the ball was over, he finally came over to me. We danced…oh, I thought I was in heaven. He was some dancer, too. I wasn't bad either. We became quite a pair…never missed a dance after that. We fit together just like we were made for each other, always in step—folks would often stop just to watch us."

Emily wanted to ask again, "What happened," but she refrained, sensing this was a special moment for Gertrude as she sat there with a mixture of happiness and sadness on her aged face.

Suddenly she spoke very softly, "I loved him so. We were going to be married, you know, had everything arranged. I still have my wedding dress. 'Course, it's all yellow with age now. I didn't bring it with me this time—left it back at the house. No need of still carrying it around with me."

A smile crept over her face. "It was through Charles that I found out about the treasure."

"The treasure?" Emily blurted, remembering her first visit to the Blanches'.

"It was Charles' Grandfather's money. They were quite wealthy, you see, before the Civil War. Yes, they owned a huge plantation with more slaves than you could count. But like most folk, the war struck them and Charles' Father had to go off, leaving only Charles, his Mother, his Grandfather, and little Sister. He never came back—was killed in the first battle. After the war, his Mother tried to keep things together the best she could, but those blasted carpetbaggers moved in and the impossible high taxes! They finally lost everything, the plantation and all—all except for the money his Grandfather had been saving for his education. You see, the old man had hidden it when things got bad and the Union soldiers began looting the plantations."

"Well, what happened to it?"

"His Grandfather was shot one night by some deserters while he was trying to defend their home. Charles found him stretched out on the dining room floor in a puddle of blood. He was still breathing, but Charles knew he was dying. He kept trying to tell Charles something, but all he could make out was something about hidden money and Lover's Leap. The old man died of course, and the family spent many a day searching for that money, but to no avail. Never 'twas found!"

"What happened to Charles?" Emily asked reluctantly.

The gleam vanished. "Charles was tall, tall and strong, and he loved horses. There was quite a number of them on the place next to theirs, Mrs. Jeb Stinsons'. This is where they had moved. Charles broke in the high-spirited ones—nobody could match him. They used to say there wasn't a horse he couldn't break—that his spirit was stronger than any stallion's, but...one day they brought this here grey stallion in. There was something wrong about that horse—I sensed it right off, and I asked Charles not to break him—to let someone else have a try at it, but he wouldn't hear of it. You see, it was a challenge, always a challenge for him. But the stallion won. Charles was killed—his neck broken in the fall."

"I'm sorry, Gertrude."

The old woman sat silently for a while as her spirit walked the corridors of the past, but suddenly a smile broke out over her wrinkled face. "Yes, he was a handsome one, the most dashing in the countryside. Most of the girls far and wide were seeking his favors, but he had eyes only for me. Yes, he loved me, and I loved him. Never found anyone else to take his place."

"That's why you never married?"

"That's right."

"But what about the treasure, Gertrude?"

"Well, you know, all of Charles' family is gone now. His sister passed away three years ago. I started looking for the treasure again. Oh, I don't know why. I really don't need the money, but just because it belonged to Charles—I just thought I might like to have it. That's why I was up at Lover's Leap when I lost my purse."

The pieces began to fall into place. No, this old woman wasn't the least bit crazy. Emily was glad now that she had gambled on Gertrude's sanity, and she wanted to make the old woman happy.

"Lover's Leap isn't too far from here," Emily said with a certain amount of excitement in her voice.

The old woman looked at her with that familiar twinkle in her eyes. "Mightn't you want to go with me sometimes?"

"Sounds like fun. Maybe we could make a picnic of it for the children."

"Don't get your hopes up, though, Child. I've been looking for a long time."

"If only you had some clue. You know, Lover's Leap is a pretty big place."

"I do—at least I thought I did at one time. Charles' Grandfather did mention one more thing just before he died. Charles told me that he uttered something about dogwoods."

"Dogwoods?"

"That's right, but you know, there are dogwoods all over these mountains."

"When the dogwoods bloom, maybe we'll picnic over at Lover's Leap, Gertrude. I think we'd better turn in now, what do you think?"

"Guess you're right, Child. Morning comes mighty soon for tired eyes."

As the old woman hobbled off to her room, Emily breathed a sigh of relief. Not that she hadn't enjoyed the conversation, but her mind kept straying to that letter on her bureau. Though she had read it several times already, she wanted to again. His letters were so few. After undressing and pulling on her worn, flannel nightgown, she settled down on the big bed, acknowledging again how big it was without him. Quietly she unfolded the pages and read:

My Dearest Darling,

My heart aches to see you again! Just to hold you in my arms and smooth those sandy curls away from your forehead, just to touch your soft skin and kiss your warm lips. I don't know how much longer this cruel and cold war will continue, but the thought of you keeps me going. I know I wasn't always good to you, Emily. How I wish I could relive those days, but when I get back to you, I'll never leave you again, not for any old war, not for one night....

She laid the letter down, unfinished, and wiped the tears from her eyes. Soon darkness filled the little cabin as it, too, slept midst the forest. Only an occasional whistle from the wind was to be heard, the screeching of an owl and a muffled sob, if one were to listen.

SPRING HAD ARRIVED. Emily could see the sprays of white spotting the dark forest. Dogwoods! She recalled her conversation with Gertrude a few months earlier. Now was the time.

Gertrude shuffled into the kitchen without her usual pep. Her spirits seemed to be sagging a bit lately. Was the old enemy of age catching up with her finally? She sat down at the table with her cup of coffee.

"The dogwoods are blooming, Gertrude."

"That so, Child?" she answered absently.

"Looks like today might just be a good day for a picnic?"

Gertrude looked up at her with understanding.

"Do you think so, Child?" She rose from the table and went to the window. "I do believe you're right. Today would be a fine day for a picnic." She smiled now with a touch of the old gleam.

"Picnic! Picnic! Picnic!" Jonathon screamed as he ran from the kitchen where he had overheard the conversation. Soon the others were chiming in as they crowded into the kitchen.

The walk turned out to be longer than they had anticipated. Emily wondered if maybe it had been such a good idea after all. Would it be too much for Gertrude?

But her fears vanished as she watched the old lady pushing ahead with new vigor as excited as the children, or more so. The children ran along ahead of them, each one trying to outdo the other with their discoveries: wild flowers, odd shaped rocks, and every now and then some creature of the forest.

"Look Mommy!" Jonathon held a small toad in his hands.

"Oh, put that down, Jonathon—it's dirty," Prudence said with disgust.

"Leave him alone. It's just a little toad," Spring retorted with her hands on her hips. The rivalry was sparked again. Emily observed the two girls. How different they are, she thought.

"Look yonder, there it be," Gertrude said, gasping for breath. Sure enough, Lover's Leap rose before them, beautiful but sinister, as the legend of old had clothed it. There were the dogwoods, a great deal more than elsewhere in the forest.

"Here's a good spot." Gertrude began throwing out her blanket already and resting her tired body on it. Emily and the children followed. After the cool, fresh mountain air had done its rejuvenating work, Gertrude rose and began to amble around, examining the familiar surroundings. How many times had she been here? She remembered the first time with Charles, when he told her about the legend. Whether it was true or not, nobody really knew—but the story was told that a beautiful, young girl had leaped to her death from that very spot because of her lover's rejection. A shudder ran over her wrinkled brow again as she thought of it. She looked back at Emily and the children stretched out on the cool ground—her new family. Suddenly she felt closer to the treasure than ever. It was as if she had come to this time in her life for a purpose.

The children played. Gertrude still ambled, and Emily sat watching the piercing sun rays push their way past the tallest trees and seep through the intricate pattern of leaves down to the earth, creating a beautiful contrast of dark shaded areas spotted with bright, illuminated designs. Whenever the light fell on a dogwood, it would suddenly become vibrant with life. She remembered what her Grandmother had told her about the dogwood. Was it true? She gently rubbed the bark of a nearby tree...

'Tis it true, oh Dogwood Tree?
That once you were a rugged one
Big and strong—a sight to see
Tall and reaching for the sun

'Tis it true, oh Dogwood Tree?
My Savior, Jesus, hung on you
And died for me at Calvary
'Twas it you? What could you do?

She rose and plucked a dogwood blossom, running her fingers around its familiar contours.

'Tis it true, oh Dogwood Tree?
That is why you're twisted and frail
That is why your flower to me
Is like the cross where He was nailed....

'Tis it true, oh Dogwood Tree?
If it be or not, no matter
For every spring, you still remind me
Of the Cross, the blood, the Master!

"You know there are twice as many dogwoods here now, Emily!" Gertrude yelled.

"There sure is a sight of them. It would be impossible to know where the exact spot is among all these dogwoods," Emily answered.

"Afraid you're right." Gertrude's spirits began sinking. Emily noticed immediately and tried to change the subject.

"You know, I can't see how anyone could take their own life!" She walked over close to the edge of the cliff and looked over. "No matter how tough life gets, there's always the beauty of life in the little things. Why, just *look* at this!"

The cliff dropped off suddenly but was covered with such a variety of flowers, including tiny purple violets and delicate golden buds. At the bottom of the cliff flowed a winding mountain stream. Its rushing sound reached up to her as it pushed its way over and through the boulders that blocked its path.

"You know, Gertrude, heaven must be simply *fantastic!*"

Gertrude, standing beside her now, asked, "Why do you say that?"

"Because the Bible says that 'eyes have never seen and ears have never heard how wonderful heaven is.' So it must be much better than all this. I don't know whether or not I'll be able to *stand* it if it's much more beautiful than this."

"I see what you mean, and you don't seem to have the slightest doubt that you'll see it."

"I don't, Gertrude. Do you?"

"Well, Child, when one gets as old as I am, he starts to thinkin' about where his old body will rest or whether it will rest at all. Death is a lot more real to us, you know."

"But Gertrude, you don't *have* to wonder. You can *know*. God tells us in 1st John, 'that we may know that we have eternal life.' "

"Look out!" Gertrude screamed as Emily slipped on the loose soil and toppled over. But just as quickly as she'd fallen, she caught hold of a protruding branch and managed to get a footing on a jutting ledge. Standing still for a moment, examining her position, she caught her breath. "Wow!" she practically whispered. Just in front of her was a hidden fairyland, clusters of dogwoods fused together, giving the appearance of a heavily embroidered lace garment. The gigantic boulder above it sheltered it and concealed it from all eyes.

"Emily! Are you alright?" Gertrude screamed.

"Yes, Gertrude, I'm fine," she called and proceeded to climb back up the cliff.

"You be careful Child, you could break your neck."

As she pulled herself up to the top, she smiled at Gertrude. "Don't worry—I've climbed up worse mountains than this in my time."

"I didn't know you to be a regular mountain goat." Gertrude laughed with relief as she extended a helping hand.

"Gertrude, I'm going to find your money for you!"

"What are you talking about, Child?"

"I've found the place, or rather it found me. The dogwoods!"

"Down there?"

"Yes, beneath the huge boulder I slipped from. Right there. We were standing on them all the time."

"How do you know, Child?"

"It has to be, Gertrude. If only you could see it! I've never seen anything like it before. More dogwoods in that one small spot than all the rest in the forest put together, or at least it seems so."

Gertrude glowed.

"We'll go ahead with our picnic. But we'll come back tomorrow, Gertrude. We'll bring a pick and shovel."

The next day, they were back. The children were excited to be going on another picnic so soon. Once there, Emily sat them down and explained to them about the hidden treasure. They were even more excited now as they sat in a circle watching their Mother climb back down the mountainside.

"It's a good thing this side of the cliff slopes off the way it does, or else we could never get down to it," Emily called back to Gertrude.

"Or you might still be down there, too."

"Throw the pick down when I call."

Gertrude obeyed and sat back, waiting between the cliff and the children. It seemed a long time before Emily finally climbed back up, dirty and tired. But no treasure!

"We'll come back. I know it's there."

So they did. Four different times, they made the

long hike, had their picnic, and Emily climbed back up the mountainside, dirty and tired with no treasure. On the way back home that last day, Emily was feeling frustrated and beginning to doubt the whole business when the thought occurred to her, "I've been digging under the dogwoods all this time. Maybe it's not there—maybe it's on top of the dogwoods." She tried to picture in her mind that huge ledge that jutted out over the dogwoods. "It must be solid stone," she thought. "I'll find out next week."

The week passed by slower than ever as Emily's anticipation mounted. She felt she was on the right track but kept it to herself. No use in building high hopes in Gertrude, who had already had them shattered over and over.

Wednesday morning dawned bright and beautiful. Was this an omen? The hike up the mountainside seemed to take forever, but they finally reached their destination, and Gertrude took her post between the children and cliff once again as Emily made her familiar descent. Once below, she viewed the edge overhead. It was solid stone. She walked around, weaving in and out of the twisted, aging dogwoods, examining it closely. Her spirits fell, and just as she was about to give up, she noticed a slight opening just overhead, but dangerously near the edge of the ledge. She could never reach it! The pick. She grabbed for it—just maybe. Very gently, she tapped away at the opening and slowly it became larger. Dirt and small stones fell out and rolled down the cliff. The opening, which now looked more like a secret hiding place, became larger and larger. Emily forced back her excitement and concentrated on the opening, tapping gently with the pick.

Suddenly, something dark and wet fell at her feet, causing her to jump back. A sack!

"This must be *it*!" she shouted as she reached for it. It was molded and smelled pungently earthy—but it was heavy. She wanted to open it right away but decided against it. Instead, she climbed back up the cliff, holding onto the aged and gnarled dogwoods, and dragged the sack behind her. As she stepped back on the solid ground, pulling the sack with her, the children began to squeal, "We found it! We found it!" Gertrude just sat there, not moving, as if in a trance.

"Gertrude?"

"After all these years," the old woman spoke softly.

"It's *got* to be it—don't you think, Gertrude? Why don't you open it?"

"You open it, Child."

Emily began pulling at the snaps that were dirt encrusted and forever stuck. As she tugged and tugged, the material began to rip.

"It's rotted." Emily wondered about its contents.

"It's been here a long time," Gertrude sighed.

As the wet, earthy sack tore away, a small metal box fell out. Gertrude smiled.

Emily sat there staring at it, almost afraid to open it. The children were silent.

"Go ahead, Child," Gertrude urged.

Emily slowly pushed the lock and the lid fell open. The bright rays of sun fell upon the silver coins.

"Wow!" Spring and Patrick exclaimed jointly.

"That's more money than I've ever seen at one time," Emily whispered in disbelief.

Gertrude, who had moved closer, commented, "It's not as much as I'd expected...knowing it was put away for Charles' education, but then an education didn't take so much back then."

As they left Lover's Leap and made their way back home, Emily was pleased to see a wide smile on Gertrude's face. It gave her such satisfaction knowing that she had given the old woman this happiness. How much happiness had she had in her life?

But Gertrude had other thoughts on her mind. "Thank you, Charles—I knew you would come through, but you waited until just the right time—didn't you? What would I have done with that money a year ago, or five years ago. I surely didn't need it. Wilton and Kathryn had no use for it, although I'm sure they would have found some excuse to weedle it out of me. But you knew all the time—didn't you?"

The old woman smiled to herself, feeling closer than ever to Charles.

When they reached the cabin, Gertrude walked in ahead of the others and sat the box down on the kitchen table. "The money is yours," she said to Emily and the children.

"What?" Emily looked confused.

"The money is yours," she repeated.

"Gertrude, what are you saying? That is your money...Charles' money!"

"Now, you listen to me, Child. You and these here young'uns have made me happier than I've been in my whole life except...except for Charles, and I don't have any use for it. My days are numbered, and I have enough to take care of me until then. I want you and the children to have it. It's a gift from me."

"But Gertrude, we couldn't accept it. Why, it's just too much."

"What do you mean—you can't accept it? You must! You're not going to deprive me of the only happiness I have left in this world."

Emily was silent.

The money was hidden again under the kitchen floor. They decided that it would not be touched until Heath got home, unless there was an emergency. As the days wore on, Emily referred to the treasure as Gertrude's and Gertrude referred to it as theirs; but each time Emily walked over the creaking planks that shielded the treasure, she felt good just knowing about the nest egg lying beneath her feet. It gave her security and courage.

However, she continued to take in the wash from the Blanches and the Donalds in spite of Gertrude's nagging. "You don't have to do that now, Child." But she did and she continued to carefully administer the funds from the washing and from Gertrude. She would not touch the treasure—not until Heath came home.

IT WAS A HOT July morning about dawn, and Emily lay tossing on her bed. The seventh day of the heat wave, with no sign of it letting up. Seldom had it ever been as hot as this in the mountains, except maybe for that August that now seemed so long ago. She remembered it being so humid that her hair wouldn't stay curled. Heath was coming to see her, and she had been just terribly upset. But she remembered that he didn't even seem to notice. It had been so long now. Would he think she looked haggard? She felt it. She looked at her hands on the pillow beside her, rough and cracked from the washing she'd been doing. Would he notice?

Raising herself on one elbow, she peered into the mirror above the bureau, and a tired and drawn face stared back at her. Would he still love her? Surely she was not the girl he'd left behind. Where had she gone? The hardships of survival had driven her off—maybe never to return. Who was she now? She wondered, staring at the fixed gaze upon her, a woman hardening with the years, bracing herself for the next attack. What would it be next? Harder times, heartbreak, sickness…. She suddenly remembered what her Grandmother used to quote from the scriptures. Something about this life being short and full of sorrows. How true! But in spite of it, she loved living.

What would this day hold? The sun was steadily making its dreaded climb now. She sat up on the bed and stretched. Would this be the day that he would come home? The war had ended and the soldiers were returning. Each day she looked for him. But would she know him? Though she loved him as much as ever, she found it hard to visualize his face anymore. She strained her memory trying to see him again, but it remained vague, clouded with time. But how well she remembered his touch and how she felt within his arms and wished for the thousandth time that he were here with her.

Once begun, the day was a busy one as usual, with Gertrude in the rocking chair on the porch mending some clothes, and Patrick and Spring off on their fishing trip down at the creek. Mr. Jorden came by once a week to buy all the minnows that they could catch for his store. Emily herself was amazed at how successful those two were with this project. Prudence was sweeping the porch—one of her daily chores. She seemed to enjoy all the housekeeping, the little domestic lady that she was. But not Spring. She considered it punishment and could think of a million ways to get out of her chores. This new project was one of them, although she had to admit it was a success. They were making a little money and occasionally brought home a few small fish for supper. She watched them laughingly disappear into the woods and turned back to her scrub board. How could one family have so many clothes, she thought to herself. The Donalds weren't wealthy, but had somewhat more than most folks here in the mountains.

"Mama, look!" Jonathon ran up, holding a gold and black butterfly in his fat, little hands.

"Oh, how beautiful, Jonathon, but be careful—don't crush it."

"I want'a keep it," he announced stubbornly.

"But, Jonathon, that wouldn't be fair to the butterfly. God made him to fly, and he would be very unhappy if he couldn't."

Jonathon thought for a minute and then slowly flattened out the palms of his stubby, little hands. The butterfly hesitated for a second, and then fluttered upward and off.

As Emily watched it disappear in the distance, she saw a figure coming up the road. It seemed to be moving slowly. Suddenly a lump caught in her throat. It *couldn't* be. She blinked. Was the sun playing tricks on her? No, it was *him*! How many times she'd imagined this moment, but now that it was here, she didn't know what to do. She felt like running to him, and yet she felt restrained. She slowly laid the washboard to one side, stood up, wiped her hands on her apron and waited. She could see him now. He looked thin. He was smiling and that hadn't changed...the same old smile. She walked toward him. Soon they were running. Gertrude watched with tears in her eyes as the two figures embraced with love and longing. She felt as if it were she and Charles as she was once again lost in her fantasy world.

"Aunt Gertrude, Aunt Gertrude," Jonathon was pulling on her sleeve, forcing her back to reality. "Who is it?"

"Why bless you, Honey, that yonder is your Daddy!"

Chapter VI
Charity

Once again summer had faded into a crisp and colorful fall, and once again Emily found herself marveling in God's creation. She sat in the porch swing inhaling the fresh air and studied the many varieties of colors that towered above her. Never had she been so happy. Heath had gone fishing with the children, and Gertrude was resting. For the first time since Heath had come home, she was totally alone and now she could just sit and bask in her happiness.

It had surely been a wonderful honeymoon—one that she'd always cherish. It seemed that the war had smoothed out his rough spots and highlighted his good points. More patient and understanding than ever before, his gentleness touched her beyond anything else. The only tell-tale sign of the war was a deep, brooding look in the depths of those sea blue eyes every now and then when he was caught off guard.

What had gone on in the lands across the vast ocean? He didn't speak of it, but Emily knew that behind that happy expression he most often wore, behind those blue eyes, tucked away beyond reach was a closet filled with memories—all jumbled and pushed in behind the closed door. If one could open the door, she felt as if they would come tumbling out like boxes stored in disorder. What was in those boxes? Did she really want to know? Or was this the cross that all soldiers had to bear alone?

Suddenly Doggy began to bark, and she watched him chase a rabbit out of sight. Well, he wasn't too old after all. She laughed, remembering Heath kidding him about being too old to catch a rabbit now. How many times a day, every day, did she watch Doggy eating, sleeping, playing—without so much as giving him a thought—but now, all alone in her meditating mood, he stood for something, another time...another time of happiness. She remembered that Christmas that seemed so long ago. "Doggy, Doggy," Little David had squealed with delight. The name stuck—at least the Barretts allowed it to. Her eyes almost began to tear, but time had done its work—the hurt was almost gone now, replaced by a beautiful memory. Even Doggy was proof of that. There was a time when she couldn't bear to look at him...much less keep him.

The Barretts had kept him until the time was right, which wasn't until she and the children moved back from South Dakota. Jonathon had fallen in love with him and wanted to take him with them to the cabin, and she *did* feel much safer with him lying there

on the front porch. He had been lying there the day
Heath came home, and springing to his gangly legs, he
had given Heath much more of a welcome than the
children, who were a little subdued at first. It had
taken them a few days to get used to him all over
again...all but Jonathon, that is, who had jumped into
his arms immediately, much to Heath's delight.

With sadness, Emily watched a nervous side of
Heath that never was before. When one of the children
would yell suddenly while playing, he would flinch.
Occasionally, he had nightmares which he never revealed afterward. One such night, Emily watched him
get up out of bed, rush out of the house, out to the
chicken house and begin yelling, "Look out, I'll get him.
No, no, no, shoot him!" He was swatting at the chickens
with his clenched fists while they darted this way and
that, flapping their wings and clucking loudly. Emily
screamed, "Heath, Heath, no, wake up!"

He stood still, suddenly coming back to reality.
Realizing where he was, with the chickens settling
down now except for a few feathers still floating in the
air, he looked at her sadly.

But the days passed and with them, his fears and
anxieties as he became more his old self. Fall faded into
winter, and Heath was busy chopping wood and fighting against the elements of nature that beat down upon
the cabin, piling snow around it and making it nearly
impossible at times to get out.

Heath had returned to his old job, thanks to his
Uncle's influence in the lumber business. Though it did
not have the glory and prestige of the position in South
Dakota—it was a job. At first he was content with it and

even happy that he was able to use both hands again, which was still a mystery to old Dr. Harris.

"A miracle it is, my Son, a miracle," he had repeated just the other day. But it was a miracle that Heath had disregarded and began to look on as just another obstacle in his path to success.

"That depends on how you look at it, Doc," he'd answered. "If it hadn't healed, then I wouldn't have found myself in the middle of a war. I wouldn't have lost the only chance I've ever had for success."

"You mean...in South Dakota."

"That's right."

"Why didn't you go back to it?"

"It's gone, thanks to the war. It was hanging on by a string anyway, but I could've saved it. I *know* I could've."

The old doctor looked at the young man with a sadness in his heart. He had a lot to learn yet...still fighting against his fate in life, unwilling to make the best of it, to be content with what life handed him.

As the temperatures rose a little toward the end of March, Heath's spirits rose with them. He had received a promotion already, due to the knowledge he'd picked up in South Dakota, plus hard, dedicated work. Things were really beginning to look up. He burst into the house one evening and grabbed Emily, swinging her off her feet. "Guess what, Sweetheart, we're going to have a new home!"

Remembering a similar time, she suppressed her fear. "What are you talking about, Heath?"

"You know that beautiful valley that sits down below Crag Mountain, where we stop every time on the way to Mother's?"

"Yes," Emily answered, puzzled.

"Well, you remember Father owns it, and he just gave us a nice section of it. Just this evening, he stopped by the mill to tell me. I knew he was going to give me some land some day, but it sure came as a surprise today. Guess he was waiting for me to prove myself— the promotion must have convinced him. He always knew I had my eye on that piece of land, too. The way I figure it, Emily...we'll build us a house, a big house for our big family," he laughed, "right at the foot of Crag Mountain facing Blind Man's Mountain. I can get the lumber for just about nothing from the mill—all the guys do it."

Emily stood amazed, trying to take it all in at once. "It's wonderful, Heath...it seems too good to be true. A big house, plenty big, and in that beautiful place, but you will pay for the wood, Heath?"

"Of course," he answered, a little irritated. "We'll have a white picket fence, you'd like that. And a porch all the way across the front with a railing, and an upstairs. We'll have a big, flat yard, and Beaver Creek runs just behind the place, for the kids to fish in."

"It's just too good to be true," Emily answered while he hugged her to him.

Gertrude had come in unnoticed but now spoke up. "Now is the time for the money!"

Heath had been told about the treasure money soon after his arrival but insisted that it belonged to Gertrude and wouldn't have any part of it.

"Now Gertrude, don't start that again," he said gently. He had come to love the old lady, along with the rest of them.

"You young folks will have no peace until you let me have my way. You know you should let old folks like us have our way anyway...it's showing respect, and it's not as if I'm giving it all to you. I plan on living in that big fine house with the white picket fence, too," she grinned.

Emily and Heath smiled at each other, not knowing how long Gertrude had been standing there. She *was* part of the family, and it certainly would make building the house a lot easier.

"Is it a deal?" Gertrude advanced, extending her wrinkled, old hand.

Heath grabbed her hand and conceded, "It's a deal."

For several weeks after that, Heath spent each night huddled over his plans for the house. He would draw them up excitedly, and then find himself dissatisfied and spend the next night changing them. Finally he had the right house—just the one. After that Emily didn't see much of him anymore. Each night he would leave work and go straight to the valley and work on the house until dark. William, Karen's husband, helped him a lot and occasionally his brother, Robert, or John, Elizabeth's husband, would come over and help out. The house went up slowly. Emily didn't get over to see it until the framework was finished. It was late evening, and the sun was just beginning to set behind Crag Mountain, casting its weakened, fiery rays through the skeleton of a house. Suddenly Emily had an eerie and foreboding feeling.

"Well, what do you think?" Heath asked proudly.

She quickly brushed the feeling aside. "It's beautiful already, Heath. It's so...so large."

"Not really, Honey. It's just that you're so used to living in a mountain cabin. Come on, little ones." He jumped down from the wagon and the children followed excitedly.

Emily remained in the wagon, staring at the skeleton. What was that feeling? Oh, it was probably because of the reluctance she felt at leaving the cabin, and wasn't that ridiculous? Who would think twice about leaving a mountain cabin for this? But *she* was! The cabin was her home. Oak Mountain was her home. Would she really be happy leaving it—and Little David? Yes, he was part of the cabin and Oak Mountain. But she must be reasonable. The cabin was too small for them with Heath back, and Gertrude too. She had sort of figured that they would add on to it, though. Who would have guessed all this?

IT TOOK ALMOST a year before the house was finally completed. In the early part of June, it stood gleaming in the sun. All the Barrett family had come out to help with the painting and now the last bucket was empty. Heath and Emily swelled with pride as they stood in silence, gazing upon their new home. She reached for his hand. She was so proud of him. He'd worked so hard, not only on the house itself but at night at the cabin—he still worked, hewing the long kitchen table and benches and other pieces of furniture. She looked down at her feet...even the earth she stood on had been placed there by him. He was such a perfectionist! She had thought him crazy when she saw him digging up large squares of grass and earth on Oak Mountain and hauling them down here to fit together as a puzzle for their front lawn.

"Why?" she'd asked.

"It will have the best, and there's no better grass anywhere than up on Oak Mountain," he answered proudly.

She walked across the grass clumps that were oozing together now after the rain last night and up to the wide steps of the front porch. Her eyes focused on the freshly painted white swing swaying in front of her. A lump formed in her throat. It was the only thing they'd brought from the cabin. She couldn't leave it behind. She walked over to it and sat down, gently swinging. "You will always belong to the mountain cabin," she patted the seat beside her. "You and I, but we will not look back. No, we will not look back to those mountains to the east, but we will look forward to a brighter and happier future here in this beautiful valley."

"Who you talking to, Mommy?" Jonathon asked, coming up from behind.

"Oh, just to this old swing, I guess," she laughed. "How do you like your new home?"

"Good!" he exclaimed and ran off again. All the children were so excited.

"Emily, come help me with this here curtain, it just don't want'a do right," Gertrude called from within. She was just as tickled as the rest of them. She and Emily had made all the curtains, working together on them each night while sitting in front of the fire at the cabin during those long, cold winter nights.

Several weeks later, the cabin was all boarded up and the Barrett family was comfortably settled in their new home. Before the excitement of the new house had time to wear, a new excitement filled the house. Emily was pregnant again! She had been so busy getting the house ready that she had simply overlooked it. This was one pregnancy that was received with a joyous response from the whole household...from Gertrude down to Jonathon.

"I hope it's a boy!" he shouted, "and I won't be the baby no more."

"You won't be the baby no more whether it be a boy *or* a girl, Silly," Prudence said.

The days flew by, the weeks, the months, as they all anticipated with joy the coming event. Prudence and Spring tried to outdo each other helping Emily as she grew larger and larger.

Gertrude seemed to have aged and grown weaker since the move, and she mostly sat these days but was never idle. Already, she had knitted several things for the new baby. Patrick, the compassionate one, though just as excited as the others, seemed to feel sorry for Emily in her awkward state and sometimes couldn't bear to be around her, staying outside much of the time. Jonathon grew more excited with every passing day, but none equaled Heath.

Emily had never seen him so happy. The house stood as a silent reminder of all his accomplishments, boosting his pride each day. His job looked as if it had real future now, and then this! The coming baby was a real joy for him, and he looked forward to it more than he had the others. Of course, Emily understood this.

For the first time, he was in a position to be happy, *really* happy about a new baby. Emily herself felt better than ever before and was busy all the time, full of energy.

In her seventh month, she was still active and happened to be upstairs scrubbing the boys' floor one morning when she heard a crash down below. Getting up as quickly as she could, she made her way downstairs, calling for Gertrude. The children were all at school, and Heath was at work. When she got to the kitchen, she found Gertrude stretched out on the bare floor with one end of the checked tablecloth still in her hand. Broken dishes were scattered on the floor surrounding her. Was she dead? Emily knelt beside her. She was still breathing. What should she do, she wondered frantically. She must get help!

She grabbed her coat from the nail behind the door and pulled it on, trying to button it. It was no use, so she pulled it tight around her middle and held it. But as soon as she opened the door and started for the old wagon, her coat blew open again. The bitter cold penetrated through her cotton dress as she hitched Poky to the wagon. Making her way toward Doc Harris', she tried to control the panic she felt. Poky trotted with a steady gait, seeming to sense her dilemma.

She recalled the day Heath had named him. The Barretts had given him to them to work their garden. She remembered the first time she'd seen him, a sad lookin' lot for sure, always looking half-starved, although he sure ate his share. Gertrude had said that it made him poor to carry it. They had all stood by and watched Heath the first time he hitched him to the plow, wondering if he had enough energy to plow a field. He did it, to their surprise, but he certainly didn't break any speed records.

"He's a might poky, but he sure gets the job done," Gertrude remarked.

"Let's go, Poky, let's show them," Heath kidded and the name had stuck.

"Oh, why am I thinking about things that don't matter in the least when Gertrude is probably dying right this minute." She slapped the reins, but Poky still kept his steady gait. Well, she ought to be glad that he was at least moving as fast as he was. It sure would be nice to have one of those automobiles right now. She thought of the Barretts' nice, new Dodge. The cold wind was whipping through her open coat, and she tried holding it together with one hand, driving with the other. She did make it to the doctor's, and had him back at the house sooner than she thought she could.

After looking Gertrude over, he shook his head.

"She's had a stroke, a very severe one. If you'll help me, we'll get her to bed."

After getting Gertrude comfortably settled into her bed, Dr. Harris and Emily walked out into the hall.

"Her whole right side is paralyzed. She will most likely be bedridden from now on, unable to do for herself, unable to talk much either."

Emily looked down at the floor.

"Emily, I think it would be best for you folks to consider the Shady Rest Home over in Spottswood. There's no way you'll be able to care for her now with all your other chores, and in your condition."

Emily looked up. "Doctor, this is Gertrude's home,

as much as it is ours. I appreciate your concern, but we'll make out. Spring and Prudence are a lot of help to me now."

"Well, it's your decision, although I think you're making a mistake. What about her folks, Mr. and Mrs. Blanche?"

"I'm going to send Patrick over with the news as soon as he gets home. But they are in bad health themselves. I'm sure they wouldn't be able to care for her."

She was thinking to herself that Gertrude would not want to go back there anyway.

"Well, I hate to say this, but I don't think you'll have to care for her too long. I don't think she'll linger so long."

"How much time, Doctor?"

"That's hard to say. She might go tomorrow, and then she might last a year."

A month later, Gertrude had not improved. She seemed to be wasting away gradually. It was difficult for her to eat and no matter how much Emily, Spring and Prudence coaxed her, she still ate very little. She mostly slept. Talking was a real effort for her, and she seldom tried. But one day Emily was straightening up her room, and she heard her utter something. She moved closer to her side.

"What is it, Gertrude?"

"Emily...I...I'm afraid"

"Afraid? Afraid of what, Gertrude?"

The old lady struggled to get each word out. "To... die...."

"Oh Gertrude, you musn't think about dying. You

must think...." She stopped. She couldn't give her false hope. She needed real help.

They looked at each other in silence, and then Gertrude began to weep. It was a pitiful sight as her left side shook with sobs while her right side lay rigid and her face twisted as she cried with half of it.

"Gertrude, you don't have to be afraid. Please don't cry. You don't have to face death alone. You have a Shepherd who has promised to walk that path with you. Remember what David said: 'Yea, though I walk through the valley of death, I will fear no evil, for thou art with me, thy rod and thy staff they comfort me...'"

The old lady struggled, "I've...tried...to live...good life...but...."

"Gertrude, have you ever believed in the Lord Jesus Christ as your Saviour? I mean, believed that He died for your sins...and accepted His death on the cross as your way to heaven?"

She stopped crying and just looked at Emily, somewhat puzzled.

"Gertrude, your good works cannot get you to heaven. If they could, you would have no problem. But they can't. Jesus said all of our best works are as filthy rags in his sight. He said, 'I am the way, the truth and the life, no man cometh unto the Father but by me.' You have to believe in the Lord and his death. He died for you so that you would be able to go to Heaven. The Bible says that 'whosoever shall call upon the name of the Lord shall be saved.' Gertrude, all you have to do is believe and...tell Him...call upon His name."

Gertrude's eyes closed.

Emily sat in silence, hoping and praying that she

wouldn't go off into one of her half-death-like naps right now. "Lord, please help her, please save her soul."

The room was still. It had begun to rain and Emily listened to the frantic raindrops that were being cast upon the window panes by the increasing wind, some large and loose that spread themselves immediately covering the windows with a wavering film...others small and intact, hitting the pane with a stinging blow. She thought of what she'd said to Gertrude. Were her words like these large drops, creating a wavering, a confusion? Or had they been like the small drops hitting the problem directly, opening the door of understanding? She waited.

After several minutes which seemed like hours, Gertrude opened her eyes, looked up, and smiled. Even though only half of her face smiled, she looked beautiful to Emily.

"I...ready...I...believe." The old lady forced the words out and then sank into a tranquil sleep with the half smile still on her face.

The next day, when Emily went up to her room, Gertrude pointed to the Bible on the table beside her bed and smiled again. Emily picked it up, deciding Gertrude must want her to read it. She would read to her that which would comfort her and turning to I John, chapter 5, she began to read, "He that believeth on the Son of God hath the witness in himself, he that believeth not God hath made Him a liar, because he believeth not the record that God gave His Son. And this is the record, that God hath given to us eternal life, and this life is in His Son. He that hath the Son hath life, and he that hath not the Son of God hath not life. These things have I written unto you that believe on the name of the Son of God, that ye may know that ye have eternal life, and that ye may believe on the name of the Son of God."

Gertrude smiled her half smile and tried to speak. "I...won't...die...I...live...I live...forever."

"That's right, Gertrude. You will only leave this world for a much, much better one."

And that is exactly what she did, only three days later.

"TO EVERY THING THERE Is a season, and a time to every purpose under the heaven: a time to be born, and a time to die." Emily thought on these words as she lay beside the crib of her newborn baby, Charity. They had named her Charity because she represented all the love that they had for each other. She remembered the night the whole family had sat in front of the fire trying to decide on a name. "It must have something to do with love," Gertrude had insisted, "because this one is surely loved."

"Charity!" Heath said suddenly. "Let's name her Charity."

"Who said it's going to be a girl?" Jonathon asked with a funny smirk on his round face.

They all laughed. But Charity she was! Emily looked down at the tiny face so pretty. She was the prettiest baby she had ever seen, each feature perfect. She heard dishes rattling down below. Prudence must be washing them. She could take it easier this time with Prudence and Spring both trying to outdo the other. Heath came into the room and sat down on the bed beside her, taking her hand in his and looking down into the crib with her.

"Well, little Mama, you've done it again."

"Well, I didn't do it all alone."

"You're right about that." He took her in his arms and kissed her.

"Now wait a minute, it's a little early for that," she kidded.

"I can't help it. You just look so irresistible. I don't know of anybody more beautiful than you, unless maybe...." He looked into the crib with a smile on his face.

Emily smiled back at him. "Heath, I would like to go to church this Sunday. I think Charity would be just fine. I would love for you to go, too."

He thought for a second. "If it will make you happy, I'll go. I wouldn't mind showing this one off myself."

Emily squeezed his hand.

That Sunday was one of those days full of rich ingredients to store up for memories. It was a beautiful sight, seeing the whole family walk into that little, country church and fill up one pew. They all lifted their voices loud and clear to the tune of *The Old Rugged Cross*.

Once they were seated, the preacher began to deliver his sermon, and everyone settled back prepared to take their own private dose. So happy was Emily to have her whole family in church, she couldn't keep her mind on what he was saying. She held Heath's hand still between them. Was he as happy as she? She glanced up at him and caught his intent gaze on the preacher. Charity slept in his right arm. So beautiful a child!

She couldn't help filling up with pride every time she looked at her. Of course, all her children had been lovely babies and Spring certainly was growing up to be a beauty, but there was something—something almost angelic about this little one with the silky, golden curls framing her tiny face with its upturned nose and rose-colored lips, and the skin that looked almost transparent at times—but those eyes, *that* was it! There was something about her eyes, though she was but an infant. When she looked at you with those deep blue eyes, it was as if...as if she understood what you were thinking.

Jonathon patted her suddenly, leaning over Heath's arm. He smiled that mischievous smile of his up at Heath. They were buddies for sure. So alike were they that it was hard for Heath to scold him. He understood just how hard it was for the little tyke to behave himself. Prudence pulled him back around with a reprimanding look. What a bossy, little mother she was. Emily smiled to herself. Prudence reminded her of herself when she was about that age, always wanting everything to be just right. At ten years old, she was very mature for her age and a great help to Emily. Spring sat tall and straight beside her with her long, dark hair falling over her shoulders and her dark eyes glued on the preacher, but there was an air about her that bothered Emily, not a receptive one—no—but rather a cold, unpenetrating air. True, she was growing up to be a striking beauty, and she was very warm and tender toward them, her family, but towards the rest of the world, it was as if they didn't exist. Oh, well, it was probably just a stage that she would pass through. Lastly, seated beside her was Patrick, her serious son, her scholar who'd rather read or spend his time alone building something. He was already a blessing to her, even at the age of ten.

Suddenly, the preacher slammed his fist down on the pulpit, jerking Emily's head toward him. For the rest of the sermon, he kept her attention. After the service, Heath seemed to enjoy the fellowship, mingling with the crowd. Everyone was so friendly. Finally they were all piled into the surrey, ready to leave, and as they waved to the surrounding folk, Emily noticed a shadowy figure standing beneath one of the old oaks. She was staring at them intently. There was something familiar about her. It couldn't be? But it was. She hadn't seen her in church, though. Where had she been? Then she noticed Mrs. Smith approach the figure, and as the two of them walked from under the heavy boughs out into the bright sun, Emily's fears were confirmed.

SPRING WAS FIGHTING to make its splashing entrance once again, but old man winter was stubborn. The sun would shine brightly, and a few brave birds would send forth their own personal tribute while the frost clung to each blade of grass and framed the window panes.

One of those mornings, Emily opened the door to Mrs. Barrett as she paid them one of her rare visits. She sort of inspected the house, giving obvious approval. She was so glad to see them living in this nice house instead of that mountain cabin. How her son could ever have been happy in that place, she'd never understand. She had to admit, Emily certainly had done a fine job with the house, though. Her limited knowledge of proper decor was a shame, but one must overlook this in the light of her background. Still the place was neat, clean, and rather cozy, one might say.

"I brought you something, Emily." She pointed to a large sack sitting beside the porch.

"What is it?"

"Spirea. You know, I have it growing out in front of our place as a hedge. You could do the same here. It grows very fast."

"Oh, thank you. I'll plant it right now."

"I believe I'd wait a bit. From the looks of the sun, I think we're going to have a real spring day today."

An hour or so later, sure enough, had brought the sun rays to the earth, warming each and every rock that Emily picked up to clear a path for the spirea. Mrs. Barrett sat on the porch in the swing, watching. "I sure am glad you brought this swing with you. It does add something."

Emily looked up. The old swing with its new coat of white paint did look good.

"Prudence, Darling. You should sit in a more lady-like manner. There now, that's better." Mrs. Barrett had begun her crusade on manners again.

Too bad she had to come on Saturday when the children were home. It certainly stifled their day.

Emily continued digging and planting, trying not to hear bits of critical advice which were directed at the children until each of them had disappeared.

Only Charity remained in her crib, a captive victim. Fortunately, she couldn't understand her Grandmother's well-meant criticism. Suddenly Mrs. Barrett called, "Emily, come here a minute."

Emily laid down her tools patiently and walked over to the porch. "What is it?"

"I don't know. But haven't you noticed anything sort of strange about...about this baby?"

Emily looked at Mrs. Barrett. "What do you mean?"

"Something isn't right. She doesn't respond the way she should, and look at the way she looks at things, or through things. Such a blank look."

"She's so tiny still—how can you expect her to." Emily tried to cover up her own feelings of doubt. She had already tried to erase them.

"I don't know, Emily," Mrs. Barrett interrupted, "but I think you should take her over to that new doctor in Spottswood. I hear he is very good."

Trying to hold back the tears, Emily said, "What about Doc..."

"Oh, of course, Doc Harris is a fine doctor, but he is just a country doctor, and maybe not up on all these things. I think you should get Heath to take you over to that new doctor. I believe his name is Doctor Frederick."

The next Tuesday, Heath and Emily drove over to Spottswood. They had borrowed the Barretts' new Dodge. It didn't take long in that. As a matter of fact, the whole trip didn't take long.

Dr. Frederick, efficient as he was, had them in and out within an hour. How could he be so brisk and businesslike with their baby, their life, their future. Now, as they bumped down the deep rutted roads with the clouds of dust rolling up behind them, Emily thought on those words, the doctor's words, words she would never be able to forget: "I'm afraid your fears were right. She seems to be responding slowly, and she has signs of retardation."

She shook her head trying to erase those words from her memory. No, she wouldn't believe it—she *couldn't*—she was too beautiful, even the doctor had said that. "She is such a beautiful child."

Suddenly she wanted to lay her head upon Heath's shoulder and let the tears flow, but she couldn't. He hadn't spoken since they'd gotten in the car and somehow she sensed that he wanted to be alone, as if he'd put up a barrier between them. How could he? She felt like screaming, but something restrained her, sealed her lips. What was going on in his mind? She was afraid to ask. She knew he loved all the children as she did, but Charity—there was something special about Charity for him. It was almost as if she were a symbol of his new life, his successful life, his happy life. She reached out and gently laid her hand upon his shoulder. He drove on.

The next few weeks went by with Emily in a daze while they waited for the next step, which Mr. Barrett had arranged.

There was a specialist in Richmond who had agreed to see her. The Barretts would drive them over. Each day, as Emily went about her chores mechanically, her thoughts centered on Charity. Could she accept this thing if it turned out…. "Lord, don't let it be.

Please let her be fine. Please make her alright." But it seemed as if her words were bouncing off the ceiling.

One week before the planned doctor's visit, Emily got the children dressed, including Charity in her pretty, little, white dress, and took them to church. She knew there was no use asking Heath. He had shut himself off from her and the children, staying at work long hours and coming home to bed. Once she tried to approach the subject with him, but he immediately turned away. "There's no use discussing it yet."

The service was unusually touching, and God's presence was so real that Emily felt drawn to talk to Him. "Lord, please speak to me today...I need your strength...I need your guidance."

As she lifted her head, the preacher's voice sounded strong and clear: "Our text today is found in Luke 22, beginning with verse 39, where Jesus is found in the Garden of Gethsemane talking with His Father. He sees the cup before him, such a bitter cup, but a cup that He must drink. This cup contained the sins of the whole world, past, present and future. We can't understand this, but the Bible says 'tis so. You see, Jesus was crushed beneath this load, and the Bible says He called out to His Father, 'Father, if thou be willing, remove this cup from me, nevertheless, not my will, but thine be done.' It goes on to say that His sweat was as great drops of blood falling to the ground."

The preacher continued, but Emily's mind had stopped at those words: "Nevertheless, not my will, but thine be done." She looked down upon Charity's tiny head with its golden curls, and she realized that God was speaking to her. She recalled her life verse, Romans 8:28, "All things work together for good to them that love God, to them who are called according to his purpose."

Could it be God's will? His ways are past our ways! How can we understand the mind of God? If it is His will, and all things work together for good, why then—why then I *must* trust Him, and...and accept His will. Though tears welled up and escaped her blinking, frightened eyes, she felt peace flood over her.

"Surrender!" the preacher concluded. "This is the secret, if we are to find happiness in this life and the peace that passeth all understanding, we must first learn to surrender our will to God's! It is when we are fighting our will against God's that we are most miserable creatures. But when we surrender, ah, then we find freedom—freedom from worry—freedom from fear. Jesus Christ wants to be Lord of your life, but how can He be if you have not surrendered your will and your life to Him?"

A small tear dropped upon the tiny, golden head in her lap. Such a beautiful child! Suddenly she knew that Charity did not belong to her...she belonged to God.

The next Monday turned out to be terribly rainy. Heath's nerves were taut as he strained to see through the flooded windshield. It was going to be a long drive to Richmond, he thought to himself. The wipers were doing their best but seemed to be fighting a losing battle against the gushing downpours. Mrs. Barrett rattled on unceasingly about one thing and then another. "I certainly wish Mr. Barrett could have come," she complained. "It's a shame he had to get ill at this time, but then, he hasn't been feeling well for some time now."

Heath wished his Father could have come too. He felt very insecure, sort of like when he was a boy facing a reprimand from old Miss Hostetter, his fifth grade teacher. He needed support. He needed strength to face the possibility...no, it just was *not* true! He refused to believe it. Emily sat quietly holding Charity and watching the rain hit the windshield. Mrs. Barrett's chattering seemed to keep rhythm with the steady beat of the rain drops. In fact, the two were muted after a while as Emily withdrew into her own world.

She was glad that Mrs. Barrett had taken a sincere interest in Charity. It was what she'd always wanted for the others. But it had taken all these years for the Barretts to come around. Actually, Jonathon had done it. There was no way they could ignore this replica of Heath, not only in looks but in behavior as well. So with Jonathon, it was understandable. But she really did not know what it was with Charity, except that everyone fell in love with her. Mrs. Barrett constantly bragged on her beauty to all of her friends. Of course, what grandmother could ask for a more beautiful grandchild.

And that was exactly what Mrs. Barrett was thinking now that she had ceased to talk, noticing that neither Heath nor Emily were listening. Yes, she was even prettier than Abigail Franklin's spoiled grand-daughter, who won the "most beautiful baby" contest last year. She smiled to herself, remembering the look on Abigail's face when she showed her Charity. What child in all these here parts could match her? Finally, she had a Grandchild that ceased all talking. Yes, she knew how they'd all talked—gossiped rather—about Spring. How she wished they'd listened to her and changed her name. Bad enough that she was an...an Indian, but did they have to advertise it with that name?

Preposterous! Sometimes she thought she'd never understand this son of hers. But she wondered now as she had so often—was it his idea or hers to bring the Indian child back with them? No one had ever said, and it was a question that even *she* thought better not to ask after all these years. What was the use anyway? The damage had been done!

The rain continued its steady beat as they neared Richmond, each of them quietly tossing their own thoughts around, trying to evade the inevitable question. Was it true?

The day seemed the longest of all days as they waited in the big hospital while the doctors performed the tests. It was late afternoon when the head doctor faced the trio with the final word—the verdict—Emily thought.

His voice was steady and cool.

"The child is severely retarded. It most likely occurred during pregnancy, but of course, we have no way of knowing how or why."

Heath turned away slowly and walked over to the window.

"Oh no, what will we do?" Mrs. Barrett nearly shouted.

"I'm sorry, Ma'am. There's nothing you or we can do. You can keep her with you. It will be difficult, I assure you, or you can place her in a hospital. There is a very good one not too far from here. They are given the best of care...."

"She will stay with us," Emily said calmly.

PATRICK WAS BEHIND the chicken house, completely absorbed in his latest experiment. Prudence wondered what it would be this time, but knew better than to snoop. She remembered the last time. How could he find that bunch of junk and gadgets so interesting? As for herself, she was downright bored. Yes, bored stiff. How come Patrick never got bored? Oh, this dumb in-between-age is for the birds, she thought. I want to hurry and grow up, and have beaux, and get married, and have babies. She went back to weeding the rose garden. Weed the garden for me please, Prudence...wash the dishes for me please, Prudence...fetch some water for me please, Prudence. Shucks, didn't anybody ever think that maybe there were other things she'd rather do? Why, if she were just a couple of years older, she'd maybe go to a dance, a real one like Julia Adamson went to the other week and came to Sunday School bragging about.

She forgot about her weeding and was lost in another one of her daydreams. I wonder what it would be like? Would the beaux flock around me like they did Julia? Maybe they wouldn't? Am I pretty, she wondered again, and then noticed Spring coming around the side of the house, leading Charity. They headed toward the north field where the many wild daisies grew that Charity loved so.

Prudence sat watching them. Spring was pretty. No, Spring was *beautiful* with her long, thick, black hair and big, black eyes, and she was sixteen now! But for the life of her, she couldn't understand her big sister. Why didn't she want to go to dances? Why wasn't she bored? Why didn't she want a beau? She had asked her these questions but really hadn't received any answers. Spring was like that. It was hard to understand her.

Emily dried the last dish and absently stored it in the cupboard while gazing out the window. She watched Charity clutching Spring's hand as she toddled along in her own fragile way. One would never know that she was three years old. Could it be three years since that awful day in Richmond? She saw Spring reach down, tenderly picking her up and carrying her through the tall weeds. How she loved Charity. Spring had certainly blossomed into a striking beauty, almost frightening at times. She still carried herself tall and proud with an air of, well, almost of hostility. She was like two different people—sweet and giving at home but cold and distant to outsiders. It was like a shell she enveloped herself in—a shell of protection. Beneath that shell was a loving, tender heart that had been bruised and battered from birth. Emily had tried to shelter her from the cruel and cutting remarks of the villagers, but she feared to think of the suffering she knew she'd experienced at the mercy of the children at school. Many a child would have refused to go back, but not Spring. There was a stubborn determination that drove her on.

Emily wondered now as she had so often—had she done the right thing in bringing her back with them? Could you take a lily out of its pond without it wilting, shriveling up, and dying? No, she would not believe that! Spring was happy enough at home, and she truly loved them all.

Suddenly Doggy began barking and Emily knew it was Heath, home for dinner. She proceeded to take out the leftover chicken and place it in the stove. She wiped her forehead with the corner of her apron. The kitchen was getting hot, between the woodstove and the hot summer sun beating through the windows. She heard Jonathon burst through the door at his usual speed and not stop until he hit the kitchen.

"Mama, what's for dinner?"

"Leftover chicken and dumplings."

"Whoopee!" he hollered, running out with the screen door slamming behind him.

Emily sighed and smiled to herself. So much like his Father. No wonder they got along so well. Heath encouraged him to go to the mill with him sometimes. Today was one of those times. As she set the table, she wondered what was keeping Heath so long. Looking out the window, she saw him walking toward the wagon with Charity in his arms. He stopped in front of the new mare he'd just purchased from Doc Harris and allowed Charity to pat her. No matter how tired he might be, he always had time for Charity.

"Mother, need any help?" Spring asked, coming through the door.

"Yes Dear, I could use some."

Dinner was delightful with the family gathered around the table, all trying to talk at once. Emily enjoyed this part of the day most.

"Pop, you ought'a see what Patrick is making."

"Jonathon, I told ya' it's a secret."

"I ain't gonna tell 'em. I just said he ought'a see it."

"Yeah, I bet."

"Children," Emily scolded.

"It ought'a be good. He's been working on it all day." Spring spoke authoritatively.

"Yeah, he was so busy, he couldn't even help me clean out the cellar this morning!" Prudence scorned.

"Patrick, wasn't it partly your job to clean the cellar?" Heath asked.

"Yes, Father, but I gave Spring my new writing tablet, and she did it for me."

Heath looked a little confused. "Well, I don't know whether it was the right thing to do or not."

"It's fine, Father. I was glad to do it for the tablet."

"That ain't fair!" Jonathon exclaimed. "I didn't get to...."

"Jonathon, please quit using ain't," Prudence said with a frown on her face.

"Well, it's not...."

"That's enough, Jonathon." Heath had only to speak and any disruption seemed to dissolve.

"Who knows, one day we just might have a famous inventor on our hands," Emily said, smiling at Patrick who looked up seriously. Everyone laughed.

"How was your morning at the mill, Jonathon?" Emily tried changing the subject.

"Great!"

"Yeah, he's getting to be *some* help now," Heath added, winking at Emily.

Suddenly Charity let out a scream. She had spilled milk all over her dress.

Emily jumped up. "Oh Honey, it's all right, don't cry." As she cuddled her frail body in her arms and carried her out of the room, Heath stopped eating. Again he had that faraway look in his eyes, mingled with pain and fear.

That night as Emily lay on the big bed that she and Heath had shared for so many years, she wondered, where could he be?

She knew he wasn't working late. He'd used that excuse too many times lately, and too many times he'd come home with liquor on his breath. Again, Mrs. Smith's words rang out in the still night, "How's Heath these days? Is he working a lot of overtime?"

What was the hidden meaning? Why did she look so strange when she'd asked? Could it be after all this time? Could it be...? "Lord," she pleaded, "must I lose him, too? Please, Lord," she whispered before falling asleep, "please don't let me lose him."

At that moment, the darkened sky merged with a touch of light as the moon slipped out from captive clouds. Betty Lou stood on the front porch of the old farmhouse. The moon sprayed its silver rays across the white banisters, across the potted ferns and across that ivory face set in fierce determination. As she turned the doorknob, she heard the last sounds of the wagon. He would be hers one day! One way or the other!

She walked in this time without removing her shoes, and boldly climbed the stairs. She had won again. What could Mother do? What would Marianne do? She smiled to herself. That last argument had done it. Her blatant threat to move out if they didn't leave her alone had done it.

As Betty Lou strode past her Mother's door, Mrs. Smith sighed and turned over. She never went to sleep until Betty Lou came home. She would lie listening for the familiar sound of that wagon. She would pray until she came home. She pictured her now behind her closed door carelessly throwing off the clothes that she had painstakingly made for her.

But what broke her heart was that she'd carelessly thrown off all the values she'd tried to teach her through the years. What had happened to her little girl? So cute, so full of laughter, so affectionate she was, whereas Marianne had always been the somber one, the serious one. But hadn't she seen it coming a long, long time ago? Though Betty Lou was the one always sought after, over Marianne, the one with the happy personality, there was always that rebellious spirit. She had noticed it from the time Betty Lou was about four years old. She had prayed for her and hoped that she would change. But change she did not. Instead, that rebellious spirit strengthened with the years.

The next morning when Mrs. Smith arose, she felt an urge to reach out a hand of kindness toward Emily Barrett, and decided to call on her and take her some old magazines. She remembered how she'd enjoyed the last ones. As she started breakfast, she watched the sun rise from behind those familiar, old mountains. How many times had she watched the sun rise in the same way? How many times had she gazed upon those solid, secure mountains? As so many times before, they eased her worry and lifted her spirits. "God is like that," she said aloud.

"God is like what?" Marianne asked, coming into

the kitchen.

"Like the mountains, solid and secure, never changing, always there."

"That's true, Mother, but the mountains do change. They're always changing. Look at them now with the sun shining on parts of them. In a few minutes, they will all be lit up. Tomorrow they will disappear if it rains, and if it happens to just be cloudy or misty, they will partly disappear, and...."

"But the mountains don't change, Marianne, they just appear to."

Marianne stopped what she was doing and walked over to the window. "You're right, Mother. I never thought about it before, but you're right. It just depends on where we are, as to how they look, whether or not there's a cloud between us, or sun rays."

"You see, they *are* like God. He never changes. It depends on where we are."

Marianne looked around at her Mother. "You know, Mother, I'm glad we live here, close to the mountains. It sort of makes one feel closer to God."

"I feel that way too, Marianne."

"Are you going to work in the garden this morning?"

"No, I thought I'd ride over to call on Emily Barrett instead."

Mrs. Smith couldn't have arrived on a better day. Emily was out in the garden picking pole beans. Spring and Patrick were helping.

"Well, looks like you could use another hand," Mrs. Smith called.

Emily looked surprised. She slowly straightened

up and wiped the sweat off her forehead with her apron. "Why, Mrs. Smith, what a nice surprise!"

As Mrs. Smith approached the threesome, she couldn't help but notice the dark circles under Emily's eyes. She bent down and began picking beans.

"Mrs. Smith, you shouldn't. You have enough garden to work yourself."

"No, I don't neither. Old Jim just about does it all for me these days. He's a working trick you know."

"That's what I've heard."

"Yes, wouldn't be a bad idea to have him help a bit here at your place."

"No thank you, Mrs. Smith, we've gotta have something for these growing young'uns to do."

"S'pose you're right. Where are the rest of the children?"

"Prudence is inside watching Charity, and Jonathon is gone with Heath."

"That one likes to follow his Daddy, doesn't he?"

"He sure does. But you know they're so much alike that every now and then they get on each other's nerves. I have to laugh."

"Yes, they sure are. I remember Heath when he was that age, an exact copy for sure. My, you sure do have some good help out here. Spring, I know your Mama's proud of you, the way you help so."

"She's my right hand."

"And such a beauty, too. You watch out for all those beaux, Spring—don't let 'um turn your head. You take your time and get the right one."

"I'm not a bit interested in beaux, Mrs. Smith."

Mrs. Smith laughed. "I've heard that one before."

"She plans to get an education first, Mrs. Smith." Emily added quickly before Spring could elaborate on her feelings for the opposite sex.

"You do say, now that's a fine thing, Child. I know you can do it."

"Speaking of beaux, Mrs. Smith, what's this I hear about Marianne?" Emily asked.

"Well, I think they're finally gonna tie the knot."

"That's really nice. Marianne is such a fine girl."

"Yes, and he's a fine young man, too. I was getting a little worried there for a while. I was afraid she might just jump up and marry the first thing that came along. You know how people are. They kept telling her that she was gonna be an old maid and all that such stuff. But then Howard came along."

"Well, I know it's a blessing."

" 'Tis that. Oh, before I forget by rattling on, I brought you some magazines over. I know how you like to read."

"Oh, thank you. That was very nice of you."

That night when all was still and the children were asleep, Emily sat down with the magazines. She felt very warm towards Mrs. Smith for bringing them. They had had a nice visit, and she stayed through dinner. But never once did they mention Betty Lou. It was as though they were both making an effort not to, Emily thought, as she flipped through the pages of the first magazine..."HAVE YOU WRITTEN A POEM?"

The words leaped from the page, bold and black.

Emily answered aloud, "I've written a poem, lots of them." She read on and then got up to get her old sewing box. There they were, all neatly folded and put away—exactly thirty-three.

"I wonder if any of these could really win—we could use the money," she whispered to herself as her excitement mounted. She sat down and read and reread each poem over and over. Finally, she removed one of the neatly folded papers from the others and stuck it in her apron pocket.

The next day, Emily slipped to the mailbox unnoticed. As she returned to the house, she heard fine tunes from the baby grand piano. They flowed out to meet her. She was so glad Mrs. Barrett had finally decided to give it to Prudence even though it had caused quite a stir within the family. It was a family relic, to be kept in the family, and of course, the rest of the grandchildren had pianos in their homes. But none of them could play like Prudence. Mrs. Barrett knew this and that was what helped her make this decision. Heath's sisters were furious for a while, though. Mrs. Barrett seemed to be softening in her old age, especially toward Prudence since she played so well.

Of course, Prudence would be the one that Mrs, Barrett would draw out from the rest to center her attention on. Spring was not included. Charity was now a subject to be hidden and the rest of her granddaughters just couldn't hold a candle to Prudence. She was developing into a fine specimen of southern delicacy—just what Mrs. Barrett appreciated.

As the soft melody caressed the crisp morning air, Emily sat down on the porch swing. "I wonder if the poem's good enough?"

She daydreamed for a while and then got up to start dinner.

For the next four weeks, Emily secretly, anxiously watched for the mailman, but each day—nothing.

She thought about telling Heath. She didn't like to keep anything from him, but then *she* did want to surprise him, if she happened to win. And for some reason, she felt it in her bones that she was going to win.

It happened on a Tuesday, several weeks later. Emily made her usual trip to the mailbox. It was there. A letter from *Our Heritage*. She held it tightly and walked back to the house, trying not to run. Not until she was safely locked in her room behind closed doors, did she open it.

Dear Mrs. Barrett:

We are happy to announce that your poem was chosen to be published in our August issue. We want to express our thanks for your interest in our magazine and our poetry contest. Your talent and interest is appreciated here at *Our Heritage*.

Enclosed is a check for $15.00. We will be sending you one year's free subscription of *Our Heritage*, starting with the August issue in which your Poem will be printed. Thank you.

Sincerely,
Mr. Carter Davis
President

Emily sat and read the letter over and over.

"Mother," Spring called as she came up the steps, "may I come in?"

"Of course." Emily got up and unlocked the door,

still holding the letter in her hand.

"Is everything all right?"

"Yes, Honey. Why?"

"Well, I just saw you get something from the mailbox and then come up here alone."

Emily smiled. "My little mother. I can't get anything by you, can I? Here!"

Spring scanned the letter quickly and then reached out to hug her Mother. "Oh, Mother, that's wonderful! Can I tell everyone?"

"Well, I was planning on using the money for a very special purpose. I thought I'd buy Mr. Peter's young stallion for your Father. You know his birthday is coming up soon, and he needs another horse for the surrey now. Old Poky needs to retire, I think." She laughed, unable to contain her happiness.

"Oh, that will be great. We won't tell him—we'll surprise him!"

"Yes, I had that in mind."

"Don't worry, I won't breathe a word."

THE SECRET WAS kept. Heath's birthday was a happy one. He was not one for celebrating birthdays, especially his. He'd just as soon forget he was another year older, but the family wouldn't let him. Prudence baked a beautiful cake. Patrick and Jonathon made peach ice cream and Spring had knitted him a new pair of socks. Indeed, it was a happy occasion, especially when Emily went out back and led the high spirited, young stallion around to the front yard. She called Heath out. He took one look at the young horse and recognized it at once.

"What's *he* doing here?"

"He's yours," Emily answered, bursting with pleasure.

"What do you mean?"

"I bought 'em. He's yours."

"But how...with what?"

After all the explaining, Heath hugged her to him. "What can a man do with a wife like you?"

The rest of the day was full of excitement and fun as Heath and the children took turns riding.

For the next few weeks, Heath was very attentive, never late from work. Emily was basking in her happiness. But the day came when he told her again that he would be late from work. She braced herself, fought off the tears, and hardened her heart.

The screen door slammed behind him, and she trembled. She listened to the stallion's clopping steps until they disappeared. He still doesn't have a name, she thought, remembering how they couldn't agree on one and just left him unnamed for the time being. The tears began to flow. She got up and climbed the steps very slowly. Once in the bedroom, she kneeled beside the bed and prayed.

IT WAS A HOT, humid day in August when the first issue of *Our Heritage* arrived in the mail. Emily was just as excited or more so than the children as they huddled over it.

"There it is!" Jonathon exclaimed.

"That's it." Emily repeated almost reverently. Her heart swelled with pride to see something of hers in print.

Patrick patted her on the shoulder. "We're really proud of you, Mama."

"I can't wait until Daddy gets home. Can I show it to him, Mother?" Prudence begged.

"I guess so, Prudence."

Prudence waited up until almost midnight for her Father. Spring sat beside her.

It was long after the two had drowsily climbed the stairway before their Father made his entrance. The house was dark except for the one oil lamp above the piano, and its flame flickered and died as he shut the front door. He stumbled through the darkness and made his way to the kitchen. After he finally got the kitchen lantern lit, he fixed himself a large glass of buttermilk, grabbed some fudge from the cabinet and sat down to eat. His eyes fell on the open magazine, and he read:

The Cloak of God

I gazed upon a lonely sight...
A winter's tree in nakedness!
It did not seem to be quite right
of Nature's clothing—it should miss

Then the heavens seemed to open
And the tiny flakes did softly fall,
The lonely tree—they did befriend
and covered its branches, trunk and all,

No more is there a lonely sight
But a creation of art within my yard,
To all beholders, it gives delight
For now it wears, "the cloak of God!"

He sat there with his head between his hands.

At last he stood up and slowly climbed the stairs. He stopped as always at Charity's door, and gently pushing it ajar, he eased into the room. She looked like an angel when asleep with her long, dark lashes curled upward as they lay upon her rosy cheeks, and her tiny head so delicately framed by those soft, golden curls. He leaned down and kissed her. "Why...why...why?" he whispered.

Chapter VII
Nightmare in the Valley

August slipped into September, September into October. The months flew by. Not much happened, not much changed. Heath continued coming home later and later. Two years passed and Emily watched her first child leave home.

Spring waved goodbye with tears in her big, dark eyes as Heath drove her to the train station. As she stood there watching the car disappear, Emily thought a silly thought, "I'm glad we finally got a car—it moves so much faster than the surrey or wagon, and I know that I couldn't have held these tears any longer." She turned back to the house, tears and all.

Spring didn't want to leave home, but she was determined to go to college. She fought off the homesickness along with her college mates. She pushed her fears and loneliness back into a corner and studied day and night. She declined the social life, and the other students soon pegged her as a loner. But this didn't bother her because she had been a loner all her life. Even among a big family, Spring was a loner.

Life went on as usual back home—the same everyday chores were done, the same meals were fixed, the same conversations took place as it had for years. Emily thought it sad how one so important to everyone could leave and her place would fade slowly into the past as the bustle of life pushed forward. But her presence was still there and ever would be. Emily worried about her more than the others at times. She was still so bitter and so independent. Patrick and Prudence had gone forward in the little Baptist church, but Spring seemed more bitter toward churches than anything.

Emily worried about Spring's future. Would she ever be happy? But life's responsibilities kept Emily from dwelling too much on these worries. The days passed, the months—life went on. There was one who didn't seem to accept this new change as well as the others—Charity. She truly missed Spring. One day Emily caught her holding on to Spring's graduation picture. When Emily tried to take it from her, she cried, "lost, lost, lost." Emily tried to explain to her but she continued crying, "lost, lost, lost."

Sometimes that was exactly how Spring felt. There were so many students that she actually felt lost in a maze at times. At least, they didn't stare at her as much as back home. There were too many other students, and she didn't stand out as much as she had back home. She actually felt more accepted here at college than she ever had in her own hometown. However, every now and then she was asked, "Where are you from?"

The question almost always was accompanied with that inquiring look to which she had become accustomed. When she noticed the first hint of suspicion or doubt, she had learned to answer quickly, "from Oak Mountain," with never a hint of her true origin. She wasn't exactly hiding the fact of her Indian background, but waiting for the right time to reveal it; and somehow, the right time just hadn't presented itself. She had never been treated differently from the other children at home, but she had always known she was different. Whether it was because of the remarks and stares she'd endured in her hometown from some rather cruel people, or whether it was because deep down inside she had always felt different—she really didn't know.

Among her studies, she took art and this made college much more exciting. She had always loved to paint since that first box of crayons her Father had bought her, and she possessed the rare talent of painting her feelings, hurts, joys and whatever mood she experienced at the time. She often recalled how proud her Father was of her painting. Her memory didn't go much beyond those first crayons, but sometimes she vaguely recalled a different way of painting at a different time in a different place. However, when she tried to focus her thoughts on these vague pictures, they quickly disappeared leaving only a vapor to haunt her. She had often thought of asking Mother about these thoughts, but couldn't get the courage to do so. Wasn't that a paradox? She, who was known to be the courageous one, lacked that quality when it came to herself. She didn't want to know. She would paint and paint and paint. She would become a great painter and then who would dare to ask her with that inquiring look?

AT HOME, things continued much the same except Emily noticed that Prudence was maturing more since Spring left. She'd taken over Spring's duties without a word of complaint. In fact, she seemed to be enjoying her new authority.

"Take off those muddy shoes!" she called out to Patrick as he was about to enter.

"Aw, good day Pru, even *Spring* wasn't this hard."

"Mother spent all morning scrubbing these floors, and you aren't about to mess them up."

"I wasn't going to. All I want is some milk from the ice box."

"Well, you can have some just as soon as you take off those muddy shoes."

"Oh, women. Where's Father?"

"Upstairs with Mother."

Emily stood holding back the lace curtain watching Jonathon swinging Charity, and she tried to hold back the tears as Heath dressed. You'd think, she thought to herself, that one would get used to this after so many years and the tears would stop coming.

"Will you be late again tonight?

"Yes, I think so."

"I better get downstairs and get dinner on."

"That's a good idea. I'm hungry as a bear."

She walked down the stairs wondering how it would end or if it ever would. "Lord, please give me my husband back," she prayed.

That night out under the moonlight, the forest echoed back angry words flung out into it. "You *will* go away with me...or else...or else...you will be sorry!"

"Just what do you mean by that?" Heath yelled back.

"Just what would your little prim and proper wife think if she knew that her darling husband was about to become a father again—but not by her!"

"You wouldn't!"

"Oh, wouldn't I?"

"Betty Lou, be sensible. I told you I'd take care of the baby...and you. I'll always do that."

"How?"

"Well, we gotta works things out, you know. Don't expect me to have all the answers just like that."

"Are you going away with me or not?"

"Betty Lou, how can I just leave my family, my children? Who would take care of them?"

"That's a ridiculous question. Your Father, of course—he's got the money to do it."

"Oh Betty Lou, you don't understand."

"I do understand, too. My baby needs a father, its own father. Are you going or not?" she demanded.

"I...I can't reason with you."

"You have until Sunday to decide."

"And then what?"

"And then I'm paying a visit to dear, little Emily." With that she slammed the car door and walked away.

Heath sat a long time, thinking. How did I get myself into such a mess? What am I gonna do? I can't leave my family. I don't want to. I wouldn't. But if she goes to Emily...Oh, No!   I won't have to leave them then—they'll leave me. The children will hate me...my folks will disown me...what am I gonna do? But the baby...it is my baby. I've been such a fool...a fool...a crazy fool!

The next day was a very special day, which Heath had forgotten: Charity's birthday. She was six years old but still looked about three. Emily and Prudence had planned a big birthday party for her. When Heath arrived home from work, the dining room was strung with popcorn and crepe paper. There was a large cake frosted white with pink decorations on the table.

"Emily," Heath called as he quickly took all of this in.

She hustled out of the kitchen, wiping her hands on her apron.

"Oh Heath, don't you think it's nice?"

"Yes, I'm sorry I forgot." His words revealed his true feelings.

"Come on in the kitchen. I have your dinner ready." Emily was determined not to let anything ruin this birthday party.

"Where is she?"

"Oh, Jonathon has her upstairs."

"You've gone to a lot of trouble. Do you think she'll...well...enjoy it all?"

"Of course she will, and I've invited your parents over for cake and ice cream too."

She looked out at the rain still pouring. "I hope they won't let the rain stop them."

"Did they say they were coming?"

"Patrick said they'd be here."

"Where is he?"

"Still out behind the chicken house working on his surprise for Charity. Heath, you *will* be home tonight for supper and the party, won't you?"

"Yeah, of course."

But when quitting time came at the mill, Heath was surprised to see someone waiting for him, all alone in a surrey parked beside his car. It was Mrs. Smith.

"Why, hello, Mrs. Smith. What brings you way out here?" he asked.

"Heath, I want to talk with you. Can you take a little ride with me?"

His face turned ashen, because he know what was behind those honest words. "Yes, of course, Mrs. Smith. I'll be with you in a minute."

They were both very quiet as she drove out towards Oak Mountain. She had insisted upon them using the surrey, even though that unrelenting rain still plagued them. At least it had subsided into a steady drizzle now. There was a strange sort of heaviness in the air. The unusually swollen and low hanging clouds were suffocating.

"It looks like there is a lot more of this stuff to come," Heath remarked, trying to break the unpleasant silence.

"It is strange weather we've havin'," Mrs. Smith added as she pulled the surrey to a stop.

She turned slowly to Heath. "Heath, I've known you since you were a small pint sitting on your Mama's knee on the first day of school. I've watched you grow up. I wish I didn't have to say what I've come to say."

Heath lowered his head and waited.

"I'm sure you know what I'm talking about."

"She told you?"

"Yes, she did. It was hard for me to believe at first. Why, with such a sweet wife and a beautiful family... why would you...I don't know."

Heath waited.

Mrs. Smith continued, "Emily doesn't know anything, does she?"

"I don't think so."

"May the good Lord spare her, may she never know." She suddenly changed her voice. "Heath, what do you plan to do?"

He looked at the tired, old woman with nothing but confusion on his still boyish face. "I don't know," he answered.

"Betty Lou told me the alternative that she gave you, and I'm afraid she means it."

"I know she does. But, Mrs. Smith, I can't leave my family. Though I know you think I'm crazy—I love Emily and the kids."

"No, Heath, I don't think you're crazy for that. It's an age-old story. I know you love your family...and you must not even *think* of leaving them."

"But, if Betty Lou goes to Emily—I won't have to. They will leave me."

"Maybe not. Emily is a wise and strong, little girl. If she knew you were sincerely repenitent of your wrong, she would probably forgive you."

"I can't do it. I can't tell her."

"It would be the best way, Heath."

They talked on and on, longer than they realized, and it was dusk before Heath got back to the mill.

Caught up in his problems, he headed for Tom's Place, never thinking about the birthday party.

That night after the Barretts left and the children were asleep, Emily lay on the sofa thinking over the evening, and waiting for Heath. Why, why, why did he have to stay away on Charity's birthday? Of course, she didn't understand anyway, and that was a blessing. His folks had made excuses for him as always, but she could tell that deep down even they were deeply hurt by his absence. They had been unusually nice to Charity and gave her some lovely gifts. Yes, they must be mellowing in their old age, especially Mrs. Barrett. She didn't spend the entire evening bragging on Elizabeth's offspring as she usually did. Instead, she seemed more interested in Prudence, Patrick, Jonathon and even Charity. Her eyes fell upon the little, red wagon that Patrick had made for Charity—his big surprise. She was certainly pleased with it, too. Still lying in the wagon was the little, white Bible that Prudence had bought for her. She had carried it around with her the entire evening and once stomped her foot, saying, "Jesus book ...Jesus lov' me." They were all very touched by this, and then she wanted to take it to bed with her, but Prudence had persuaded her not to.

Emily turned over on her side. It had been an exhausting day. She yawned...and fell asleep.

The moon climbed high into the sky, though concealed by heavy clouds as Emily slept on. Suddenly, she was startled by a scream and realizing instantly it was Charity, she rushed to sooth her. Bundling her up, Emily carried her back downstairs and held her tightly as she calmed down.

"Another one of those old, bad dreams, Darling. It's alright now, Mama is here."

Charity lay against her Mother's breast—her big, blue eyes rolling around the room until they rested on the little red wagon. She pointed to it.

"Yes, Sweetheart, isn't it nice? Patrick made it just for you."

But shaking her little finger over and over again, Emily understood that it wasn't the wagon but the little Bible Charity was pointing to.

"Oh, your Bible. Do you want it?"

She shook her head, yes.

Emily stood up with the small, frail child clinging to her, walked over and picked up the little Bible. She carried Charity and the Bible back to the rocking chair. Instead of holding onto the Bible as she had done all evening, Charity pushed it into Emily's hands.

Emily stared back into the child's blue eyes. What is she thinking? Emily opened the Bible and began to leaf through its pages. What should she read? A familiar passage stood out, and she felt inclined to read, "Let not your heart be troubled; ye believe in God, believe also in me. In my Father's house are many mansions; if it were not so, I would have told you. I go to prepare a place for you. And if I go and prepare a place for you, I will come again, and receive you unto myself, that where I am, ye may be also...." Emily stopped reading, seeing that Charity's eyes were closed. She rose with her in her arms and carried her back to bed.

The next morning Heath realized when he went down to breakfast that he had missed the birthday celebrations. No one mentioned it. He was glad that

Charity was still sleeping when he left for work, more down than he'd ever been. "I'm a real heel," and today's Saturday. Tomorrow's Sunday—what can I do? I must do something. I'll see Betty Lou tonight—I'll do something. I'll make her understand." He drove off toward the mill.

Emily decided to work the ground up around her flowerbeds when she finished the breakfast dishes. Work was the best cure for problems, and it had helped her many a time release her feelings of frustration and bitterness. So she worked hard, hoeing around the rosebushes, the spirea and the daffodils that were just poking their way up through the soft, red clay. In fact, the earth was so soft and muddy from the incessant rain that she couldn't do a lot, but she hoed on with determination that she would have a beautiful yard this spring.

"Mama, look at those clouds," Jonathon pointed out as he walked up. "They're the strangest lookin' clouds I've ever seen!"

Emily straightened up, holding her aching back. "I see what you mean, Jonathon. I've been so engrossed in this here hoeing that I hadn't even looked up. Why, they're rolling something terrible, almost in one big roll and they seem to come to a peak right in the top of the sky."

"Don't you think you've done enough of that gardening for today, Mama?" He was concerned about her, realizing something was wrong between her and his Father. Things weren't right.

"Yes, I guess I better get inside. By the looks of those clouds, who knows what it might do next."

By suppertime, the clouds were gradually building up and getting larger. Jonathon was glued to the window.

"Look at 'em now. Wow!" he exclaimed. "Mama, do you think Daddy will get caught out in this storm that's coming?"

"I hope not, Son." She worried as she peeled potatoes.

"Why did he have to go out tonight, anyway, Mama?" Prudence asked with a hint of bitterness in her voice.

"He had some business to attend to, Prudence. Do you have the biscuits ready yet?"

"Yes Ma'am." She rolled out the last biscuit with the heavy rolling pin.

When they all sat down to supper, Charity looked at Heath's empty chair and said in her baby utterance, "Une miss'ng."

Everyone looked at her. She had begun saying this lately whenever Heath was absent. Tears came to Emily's eyes as she quickly changed the subject. "Didn't you have a wonderful birthday party, Charity?"

That night as the lights went out and all was still, there was still one missing as the rolling clouds kept rolling and rolling and rolling.

But out on Oak Mountain, the clouds were visible even in the dark. The black, rolling, luminous clouds swirled around the mountain top where two lone figures stood facing each other. There was no audience to witness the anger and tempers. Their bitter words were flung out into the night, echoing back until he turned to walk away. But like a tigress caught in a net, she chased after him beating him with her fists and screaming words not to be heard.

He turned suddenly and there was a swift movement. She toppled and rolled and disappeared.

"Betty Lou...Betty Lou!" he yelled as the rain began to pour. All of a sudden it seemed like there was some giant up above pouring water out of a huge bucket. It poured and poured, drowning out those frightening yells.

Over the valley that rested in sleep, the furious storm swooped down like an eagle enveloping its prey within its outstretched wings. Lightning flashed and flashed, and the tiny valley lit up bright as day. With the sky ablaze, that main cloud looked like a black streak up above. The valley awoke afraid and confused. Emily made her way down the stairs to check the windows and suddenly felt something wet and cold at her feet. Again the house lit up. Quickly retracing her steps, she saw to her horror that the whole living room floor was submerged in several inches of water.

What must I do—she thought with panic squeezing out reasoning. No, I must not panic...get the children...I must get the children out of here! Oh, where is Heath?

She ran upstairs and almost collided with Patrick. "What is it, Mama?"

"The house is flooding. Get Jonathon!"

Prudence woke up and called out in the dark, "What's happening?"

"Prudence, get Charity quick. We're leaving. The house is flooding."

Soon they were all together wading through the living room where the water had already risen several more inches. Emily noticed Charity's little wagon floating across the room.

Patrick pulled open the front door with all his strength, letting in solid sheets of rain. They made their way out to the Barretts' old car. She was suddenly glad that Heath had bought it. They all piled in while Patrick started it and then jumped in with them. Emily couldn't believe what she saw when he turned on the lights. Black water was running swiftly across the yard, a foot or more deep.

The old Dodge chugged out the drive and down the road.

"I can't see where I'm going!" Patrick yelled above the pounding rain. It was falling so hard against the windshield that the road was hardly visible ahead of them.

They stopped for a few seconds and then tried to move on again. "We'll try to make it up to the Wilsons' place. It's higher ground there and...."

"But we have to go over Winding Creek!" Prudence was crying.

"Well, we have no choice. We can't go back and we have to get to higher ground."

There was a dreadful silence from then on. No one talked. The pounding rain drowned out any sobs that might have been heard. The farther they drove, the higher the water became. Emily was amazed that the old Dodge hadn't choked out. Then, the bridge appeared just ahead.

"Well, it looks fine to me," Patrick breathed a sigh of relief. But when they started over, fear seized them as they heard the powerful water flapping against the wooden boards of the bridge. It was eerie within the walls of the old covered bridge. While they had momentarily escaped the mounting waters, they knew what awaited them. Suddenly they emerged back into the nightmare, only worse than before. The water seemed to be even higher.

"Let's go back, let's go back!" Jonathon yelled.

"Patrick, something's awfully wrong," Emily whispered as she held tightly to Charity. "The water's rising too fast. Maybe we should try and get back."

Patrick began to turn around toward the old bridge again but quickly slammed on the brake.

"Oh, no!" Prudence cried loudly.

The old bridge was quivering and fighting to stand upright when several feet of higher water gushed toward it. It swayed and fell sideways into the black waters.

Patrick groaned. "Oh no—the car is choked out."

"We'll have to make it on foot as fast as possible," Emily instructed, opening her door. "We've gotta make a run for it."

They all climbed out into the cold, swirling waters.

"Hold hands! Hold hands!" Patrick yelled, "See that clump of trees? Run for them."

They pushed their way through the water and reached the trees by holding on to each other. The swirling, dirty water was practically waist deep now. Prudence and Jonathon scrambled up one tall, sturdy tree while Patrick held Charity up toward them.

"Mama!" Prudence screamed. Her eyes were frozen on what seemed to be a towering wall coming toward them.

"Oh, no," Patrick said almost calmly as the wall of water swooped down, tearing them away from the trees and carrying them off into the nightmare.

"No, no, no!" screamed Prudence as she watched them carried off into the dark.

Jonathon was about to leap into the rushing waters when Prudence yelled, "No, Jonathon, NO!"

He hung on—torn as to what to do.

THE BARRETT FAMILY was not alone in its horror. The entire valley was being washed away by the mighty waters that rushed down the mountain slopes carrying earth, trees, houses and whatever stood in its path. Families were being torn apart by the towering walls of water. Homes fell under its force, carrying their sleeping inhabitants with them, never allowing them to discover their fate. The screams of those unfortunate enough to witness their plight were hushed by the mighty thunder. The elements of nature were working together to destroy this peaceful valley. The incessant rains that had plagued the valley for weeks had secretly loosed the earth from the mountains and now when the raging storm hit, it created a catastrophe. The streams, lakes and rivers swelled and burst, flooding the valley, making history that horrible night.

Emily clung on to what seemed like part of a barn roof. Her hands ached. How long had it been? She tried to recall what happened. Slowly the dreadful picture emerged from her confused state of mind.

"Oh God," she cried out, "please save my babies."

She had been thrust onto the remains of an old

barn roof soon after that powerful wall of water hit them. She hung on to what appeared to be old rafters. They creaked and cracked as the roof was tossed to and fro by the rushing water that only hours before had been a shallow creek. She had a hard time seeing anything beyond her own reach, not only because of the black, black night, but also because of the tears in her eyes, mingled with the water that drenched her from the stinging rain plus the muddy water that continually splashed her. She hung on...and prayed.

But nearby Oak Mountain was spared most of this. Its inhabitants slept on through the peaceful night, and the rain lulled them into a tranquil rest as it beat a rhythm on the leaves of the forest. They didn't know of the nightmare their neighbors were hurled into. There was one that did not sleep, though. He climbed over the rugged, muddy mountainside looking frantically. Where was she? She couldn't have fallen this far!

"Betty Lou!"

The earth trembled under his tired feet. Suddenly it felt as if he was standing upon a trampoline. At the same time, he could hear an awful rumble. He wondered what it could be! It couldn't be thunder—it was different. Pulling himself up from where he'd stumbled, he continued searching.

"Betty Lou...Betty Lou..."

Still no answer.

What could have happened to her? There was no trace of her. As he descended the mountainside and approached one of its streams, he heard a mighty rushing sound. "What is that?" he said out loud. The night was so black he couldn't see, but it sounded to him like a swirling river. The storm had about subsided, but once again the lightning illuminated the foot of the mountain, revealing to Heath a monstrous mass of water.

Where was the gentle mountain stream that he'd spent so many hours fishing in? What had happened? Terror seized him. Had Betty Lou fallen into that ugly, muddy mass of water...was she swallowed up? Once again he heard that awful rumbling sound—once again the earth under his feet quivered like a leaf. But this time he could tell from what direction it was coming...Home!

Suddenly he sensed something very terrible was happening and he must get home. Torn between his guilt and worry over Betty Lou and his desire to get home, he set out back up the hillside to his wagon. The rain still poured. He seemed to slide back down more than he went forward. Then he realized this was useless. He would never get back up there and even if he could, there would be no way for him to make it in the wagon in all this. He'd just have to try and get home by foot.

PRUDENCE AND JONATHON witnessed the parade of horror that flowed past them as they hung onto the tree. Whether in shock or just resigned sadness, they watched in silence—as furniture, mattresses, dog houses, animals and parts of people's homes were being carried away by the swift, muddy water. Every now and then, they would hear a scream, and they'd know there must be somebody out there in the black night hanging onto something...hanging onto life.

Emily prayed, "Lord...please...please...take care of my Children...please keep them safe." Suddenly, her arms were wrenched away from the rafters, and she fell back into the swift water. She fought the muddy monster as it carried her under.

"I'm going to die," she thought as her lungs filled with water. But just as suddenly, she found herself once again out of the water, at least her head and arms. She struggled to stay up and finally managed to pull herself out. She held onto something big and solid. It looked to be white—the best she could tell in the darkness, and it wasn't swirling and moving anymore. Apparently the rafters she'd been holding onto had struck this thing, and she'd been thrown into the water by force. How close she'd come! Slowly and carefully, she managed to climb upon a higher ledge and soon another, even though her body was wracked with pain. Now she was completely out of the water and rested on what seemed to be part of a building. She cried out, "Oh God, help us. Help my Children!" She lost consciousness.

Heath reached the valley what seemed like hours later. He was met by several men trying to keep people from crossing the only bridge left standing.

"You can't get through there, Heath," one of the men called out.

"I have to. My family's in there!"

"Well, it's impossible to get through. This bridge is gonna go any minute now. Maybe if you go around and up to Cap's dock, you can get a boat, but I don't know that I'd trust gettin' in one in this here stuff."

Heath turned quickly and headed toward the dock.

He found total confusion there. People were crowded around arguing over who was going to go out in what boat and there were not enough boats, of course.

"Heath Boy, what're you doing here?" A rough voice called from behind.

"Jack, I've got to have a boat. I've got to find my family."

"Alright, Son, you can go with me."

Soon they were moving slowly through the black water, dodging all sorts of debris.

"What happened?" Heath finally asked the old man.

"Don't know. Happened so fast. We'll head for your place. You know I don't have no family nohow."

Dawn had begun to light their path, and they stifled their cries of shock and disbelief at what they saw. It took them a lot longer than they expected to reach Heath's place. As they came into view of the place, Heath moaned.

"Oh No!"

The stately, two-story house was no longer standing tall and erect. It had fallen completely. What was left lay tumbled in a heap with the roof half torn off, exposing part of the boys' room, submerged in mud and water.

"No, No, No!" Heath buried his head in his hands, shaking with uncontrollable sobs.

Mr. Matthews was silent at first, not knowing what to do or think. But then Heath's sobs began to shake him, too. "Now hold on there, Son. This don't mean your family's all gone. We gotta look for 'em. They might'a got away before it hit."

Heath looked up with hope.

They rowed around the house with Heath calling, "Emily, Emily, Patrick...."

The only sounds were the sloshing water and the creaking and cracking of the house settling beneath it. Just as he was about to climb out, Heath realized the car was gone.

"They left in the car! I forgot it was here when I left. I took the wagon."

"See thar, I told you, Son. Now all we gotta do is find the car."

"Let's go by the Wilsons' place. Maybe they're over there."

But when they reached the Wilsons' place, they found the same situation. The house was leveled and deserted. They kept going, dodging bales of hay, up-rooted trees, all kinds of debris floating atop the black water. The next house they reached was still standing, but they heard screams coming from it. They found the family trapped upstairs with the whole bottom floor flooded. Within thirty minutes, they'd rescued all four of them and were headed back to the dock.

When Mrs. Lee stepped into the boat, she saw Heath. "Why Heath Barrett, I'm so glad to see you. We were afraid you mightn't make it when we saw you go by in the Dodge."

"When?" Heath turned anxiously to her. "What are you talking about?"

"When you went by our house. We were sure it was you when that lightning lit up...you know it would light up just about the whole world."

"What time was it, Mrs. Lee?"

"I don't know as I know, Son. It's been such a horrible night...I don't reckon I'll ever be the same."

As the black skies slowly turned gray, bringing the first, faint, morning rays of light, Emily tried to turn her head. Her neck ached. She blinked and began to take in the devastating sights all around her. But her aching body did not allow time for grief. It was caught up in the racking pain, and she was sinking into a feverish sleep. Fortunately, she was being held secure, sandwiched between heavy boulders. Her eyes closed again. Several hours later, she was found, still unconscious, by a rescue party.

"I don't think there's much hope for her," someone said as they lifted her into the boat.

"I do believe that be Mrs. Barrett," a young, black boy said.

They carried her as quickly as possible to Mount Moriah Hospital, over in Spottswood.

Prudence and Jonathon had also been rescued from the tree that had saved their lives. They sat huddled together at the school house that was being used to house survivors. Silently they sat and shivered, not from the cold, because it was warm in the school house; but instead from the memories that still stood between them and the kind people who were trying to make them comfortable.

Each time the doors opened, they looked up quickly and hopefully. The hours crept on. Just before noon, they heard a familiar voice and looked up to see their Father coming toward them.

"Daddy!" Jonathon yelled and grabbed hold of him the way he used to do when he was much younger.

Prudence embraced him. The three clung together for several minutes before they could talk.

"Do you know where your Mother is?"

"No," Prudence answered. She began to tell him the story as they sat down together on one of the hard benches.

Soup and hot coffee were being served, but they couldn't eat.

"I'm going back to look. It's best for you two to stay here though; they're fixin' up some cots in the back room yonder."

"I'm goin' with you, Daddy," Jonathon spoke up with authority.

"No Son, I want you to stay here with Pru. She needs you here."

Jonathon didn't have his usual resistance. Overcome with fatigue, he gave in and Heath left.

Minutes later, Patrick walked in.

"Patrick!" they cried in unison.

He stood looking at them with a strange, blank expression on his face.

"He's in shock," one of the rescue workers said and gently led him to the back room to a cot. He was given a shot and soon he slept. Prudence sat by his side.

HEATH CONTINUED searching. He stopped everyone he could find to ask them. It was evening before he happened upon an old man who had some information.

"Why yes, Mr. Barrett, I do believe so. It was Mrs.

Barrett that was rescued this morning from over near Parson's Corner. She was taken to the new hospital over in Spottswood."

He felt like a mountain had been lifted off his back. She was alive! He set out for Spottswood. It took him two hours to get there with all the bridges out and a lot of roads impassable. On the way, he thought a lot and was haunted by fears. Where was Charity? Where was Patrick? Was Emily alright?

When he finally reached her bedside, she was still sleeping. Her tiny face, though badly bruised, was white as a ghost. What had she gone through?

A nurse ushered him out as the doctor came in. He waited outside the door for what seemed like hours.

The doctor walked out, but his face didn't hold much hope.

Heath stared at him, afraid to speak.

"Mr. Barrett, your wife has pnuemonia, and her chances don't look good, frankly. We're doing all we can for her. I have to be honest with you—all I can tell you to do now is pray."

With those words of doom, he patted Heath on the back gently and moved to the next victim of the horrible flood.

Heath still stood in the same spot. He felt like the world was tumbling down all around him. What could he do? He walked over to the window and looked out, seeing people moving around just as always. "How can they act like nothing has happened? My life is falling apart. She's gonna die."

He kept standing at the window repeating, "She's gonna die, she's gonna die." Suddenly he said aloud,

"She *can't* die!" He began hitting the wall with his fist. A nurse came over and led him to a nearby couch. As he sat there, he remembered the doctor's words, "All I can tell you to do now is pray."

"Pray—I don't know how. She's the one who knows how and she's dying."

He thought about how long it had been since he prayed. Had he ever really prayed? He remembered how Annie used to listen to him every night as he said his prayers. He wondered if God would listen to him as well as she did. Would God answer his prayers after the way he'd been living? But he thought, "I have no place to turn now...but to Him."

He knelt down beside the couch and began to talk earnestly.

"God, I know I'm not good enough to call on You just now, but I don't have anyone else to turn to. I do believe that You can make Emily well if You see fit to. 'Course, I know there's no reason for You to listen to me after all I've done and all, but Emily's good...You know that, God. And the children...they need her. And, Lord, I don't mean to be making any deal with You, but if You'll just let her live and be alright...I promise...I promise I'll do what You want me to do."

He pulled himself back up on the couch and sat there thinking about his life and what he'd done with it so far—how he'd messed it up. He kept thinking.

More than an hour later, the doctor came back in and told him to go and get some rest—that there was nothing he could do. Emily was still unconscious and probably would be for some time.

Again he was torn as to what to do. He was afraid

to leave Emily, in case she were to wake up...but he had to find Charity and Patrick! He decided to get back home.

Patrick had slept for hours with Prudence and Jonathon never leaving his side. Jonathon noticed Prudence praying a lot. She did so remind him of Mother. Tears began to fall from his big, blue eyes. Would he ever see her again? Where was she?

Patrick opened his eyes. He took in the room with one swift glance and then looked from Prudence to Jonathon.

"Patrick," Prudence began gently. "Patrick, do you know where Mother and Charity are?"

He remained silent, looking from one to the other.

"Are they alright?" Jonathon asked.

Big tears welled up in Patrick's eyes. He tried to fight them.

"They're gone," he finally blurted out.

"No, no, no!" Prudence screamed, running out of the room and nearly colliding with Heath, who had walked in just in time to hear. He walked over to the bed very slowly.

"What do you mean, Son?" His voice cracked and shook.

Patrick began to cry uncontrollably now, and Heath sat on the bed beside him and held onto him.

"I was holding onto Charity, Dad...but the wave came up so quick...and knocked us under. I tried to hold on to her, Dad, but...."

Heath laid his head on Patrick's chest.

THERE WAS MUCH weeping in the valley for the

next few weeks. Many had lost loved ones. Many had lost their homes, or at least partially so. But Emily didn't weep as she lay next to death. She didn't know all of her family was safe except for her baby. She didn't know that Charity was gone.

Heath stayed beside her day and night. He kept praying. Maybe God wouldn't punish him doubly. "Please God, don't take her, too. I couldn't bear it."

As she lay unconscious to the world, her spirit soared, very much alive.

She witnessed the most beautiful sight she had ever seen. The sky above her was a breathtaking blue, the grass beneath her bare feet felt like velvet, and it was the greenest green she'd ever seen. There was a crystal clear stream flowing beside her with soft, murmuring sounds. Out in the distance there seemed to be a city—an entire city slowly descending from the blue sky. It was a city of gold, glistening gold, and there was a light—an extremely bright and warm light that radiated from it and seemed to be drawing her to it.

She felt herself being lifted and drawn toward that light. It was so pleasant. She experienced such a tranquility as she yielded to the light. Suddenly she knew that if she yielded to it, she would never wake up to the world she'd left. She felt herself wanting to yield ever so much, but yet there was something left unfinished—something she must return to.

She opened her eyes and there was Heath.

The sun was shining brightly through the hospital window—so bright it caused her to close her eyes again.

"Emily, Emily," Heath cried.

Was she ready? She tried to piece together what

had just happened. That wonderful light had vanished—that beautiful warmth was gone. Although the sun's rays were falling upon her, they could not compare to that warmth she'd just experienced. God was there, and He had let her choose. "I've chosen…and I'm alive. I'm alive for a purpose."

"Emily, Emily," Heath continued calling her name.

A foreboding feeling came upon her. She began to remember…the flood…there was something all wrong. She had to be ready before she could face the world. What was it? The flood, the Children…. Suddenly the nightmare was before her.

"The Children!" she cried, opening her eyes wide with fear.

Heath wasn't ready for this. He had planned on how he would break the news.

"The Children…they're alright, but…." He began to cry.

"Lord, give me the strength. Please give me the strength to face whatever it is," Emily prayed silently.

"Except…" Heath managed to say before he broke down sobbing.

"Except Charity," Emily finished.

She began to feel strangely warm and strong. Charity was there in that beautiful place. She was home now.

"How did you know?" Heath managed to ask.

The tears streamed down her face, but she smiled through them.

"Heath, Charity is with God. She's in a wonderful place, and I know she's happier there than she ever was here."

Heath marveled at how calmly she was taking this and with what authority she spoke, as if she really knew.

"Heath, she and Little David are there together. They will be waiting for us."

Heath left the hospital later that evening and walked the streets of the unfamiliar town, not knowing anyone and not wanting to. He wanted to be alone—to think. "I told God that I'd do whatever He wants me to do, if He'd just let Emily live."

He remembered his promise and strangely enough, he wanted more than anything to keep it. He walked past the many stores, past the few shoppers on the streets and soon found himself on the outskirts of town, alone. He sat down on a crumbling stone wall beneath a tall oak tree and thought, "She was my baby...such a beautiful baby, even though she wasn't...she wasn't like everybody else...she was the prettiest, little girl in these here parts."

He choked back the ready sobs, not wanting anyone to see him if someone did happen by, and he looked up into the sky which was slowly darkening.

"God, are you really up there? I need to know. I need to know if she is with you and Little David—is he there too?" He sat very still as if waiting for an answer. He began to remember the times long ago when Annie would hold him on her knee and read her old, worn Bible to him. He wished he could remember what she'd read, but it was blurred in his memory. What was that one verse that he'd liked so much and Annie would read to him over and over again?

Wait a minute, it was coming. "I stand at the door and knock, and if anybody...and if any man will hear my voice and open the door...I will come into him...." That was it!

He remembered and was amazed. Whenever he saw that picture of Jesus standing at the door and knocking over at his folks' house, he'd thought of Annie. He wondered what had happened to it. He didn't remember seeing it for a while now. Annie had told him that door was the door to his heart, and he remembered thinking how strange for his heart to have such a big door. Now the full meaning hit him. Jesus wanted him to open up to Him...to let Him live within him and guide him.

"Lord"...He began in a whisper, "if you're knocking at my door, the door to my heart, and I believe you are—I want you to come in. I want to give my life or at least what's left of it to you if you'll have me."

SEVERAL DAYS LATER, Emily was released from the hospital. She and Heath had discussed what they were going to do. She remembered him saying, "Emily, I've been thinking. You know we can't go back home, at least not now, of course, and I don't know whether I'll ever be able to go back. What would you think of going back to the cabin? I mean fix it up and maybe add on and...."

"Oh Heath, that's just what I've been thinking. It will be wonderful—just like old times."

"Not exactly, Honey. It's going to be much better."

Emily understood what he meant. He had not told her of his decision and what he had done, but somehow she sensed it and was waiting for him to confide in her at the right time.

"Sunday will be the funeral, Emily. Do you think you'll be up to it?"

"I will."

"'Course, it doesn't seem much like a funeral without...."

"Heath, it's alright. We know where she is."

"I know. But it'd be nice to have somewhere here to go and...you know, like little David's grave."

"We will. After the mass funeral Sunday, we'll have our own. We will mark a grave beside Little David's." She looked at him and smiled, "He would like that, too."

That Sunday dawned bright and beautiful as if to say to all, "It is over." The whole valley, or at least what was left of it, seemed to bask in it, sprawling its wet remains open to dry and find new life again.

There was a lot of silent crying during the service. The sobs and tears had been exhausted during the last few weeks. The people crowded together as if to gain strength from one another. Emily noticed Spring sitting tall and erect—not shedding a tear...and she hadn't since she arrived. But the pain was there. Just about every family had been touched one way or the other. The service was short and over before Emily realized it.

"Are you all right, Honey?" Heath asked Emily as he supported her with his arm, working their way back to the car. The children followed quietly.

Before she could answer, she heard a familiar voice.

"Emily, Heath," Mrs. Smith called out as she made her way toward them.

"I'm so sorry," she cried, embracing Emily.

"So am I, Mrs. Smith. I heard about Betty Lou."

"Yes, they haven't been able to find her either." Tears rolled down her face.

Heath stood silently.

Just before they arrived at the cabin, Prudence uncovered her surprise. It was Charity's Bible—the little, white one she'd given her for her birthday.

"Where did you get it?" Patrick asked unbelievingly.

"I found it the other day when we were at the house looking for things. See—the sun has dried it all out."

"I'm surprised there's anything left of it," Jonathon said, trying not to look at it.

"What are you going to do with it?" Spring asked sharply.

"Well...I think we should dig a grave instead of just putting up a marker, and I think we...I think we could put it in the grave. You know how she loved it."

"I think that we should, too, Prudence," Emily smiled tenderly.

The tiny grave was dug beside Little David's. Before placing the Bible in the grave, Emily read from it: "Let not your heart be troubled; ye believe in God, believe also in me. In my Father's house are many mansions; if it were not so, I would have told you, I go to prepare a place for you. And if I go and prepare a place for you, I will come again...." She choked back a sob. "I will come again and receive you unto myself, that where I am, there ye may be also."

Part II

Second Generation

Chapter VIII

Second Generation

"Oh, Mother, I can't get this dressing the way I want it," Prudence complained with frustration.

"Just a minute, Dear. I'll do it. How about you finishing this icing?"

"No, Grandmother, I want to do that!" Mary Tom exclaimed, rushing in from the other room.

Prudence looked up at her youngest daughter with slight irritation. "Oh well, I'll just finish setting the table. Don't you think they should be here already, Mother?"

"They'll be here directly. Listen to Melony on that piano. She sure can play."

Prudence thought of how proud she was of her oldest daughter. Melony showed great promise at the piano, and they all took pride in her playing.

"She reminds me much of you, Dear, when you

were about her age."

"Oh, Mother, I was never *that* good."

"Maybe not, but I enjoyed listening to you play all the same."

"Well, I get sick of hearing that stupid piano all the time," Mary Tom interrupted.

"Mary Tom!" Prudence quickly reprimanded her. "Why, you shouldn't say things like that." Mary Tom kept piling the chocolate icing on the layer cake, ignoring her Mother's words.

Emily and Prudence exchanged worried looks. Mary Tom's jealousy was nothing new to them.

Ellen walked into the kitchen. "What can I do to help?"

"How about spreading some butter over these rolls? Then they'll be ready to go in the oven soon as they get here," Emily said as she finished the dressing.

"What's Patrick doing?" Prudence asked.

"Oh, he and Spring are still at it. I don't know why he keeps on trying to make her see the light. She's so stubborn," Ellen half-whispered.

"Ellen, you understand. Of all people, you, the preacher's wife, should understand," Prudence answered.

"I do really. She just makes me so angry the way she talks sometimes."

"We must pray for her," Emily said quietly.

Prudence glanced at her Mother as she placed the dressing in the oven. She's getting old, she thought to herself, noticing the gray in Emily's head and the wrinkles that weren't there before. She felt a flood of warmth spread over her. She remembered all those good times she had had with her Mother down through the years. She just hoped that she could be as good a mother to her two girls. Of course, that was easy with Melony, but Mary Tom was different. She always had been, and it was hard to get close to her.

"The baby's crying!" Mary Tom exclaimed. "Can I get him, Aunt Ellen, please?"

"Of course, Honey."

"Now Mary Tom, you be careful. He's still so little," her Mother added.

"I will, I will," she called, running out the door.

"Ellen, I do want to thank you for naming him David. It means a lot to us—to Heath and me."

"It was what we wanted, too, Mother."

Emily glanced out the window and up the little hill. She hadn't forgotten him—her firstborn. After all these years, the scar was healed, but not forgotten. I must not think back, she told herself. I have another David now. She turned and smiled as Mary Tom brought him into the kitchen.

"I wish my name was David."

"Mary Tom, how silly. You're a girl," her Mother scolded.

"That's the trouble. I wish I was a boy. Then I could do anything like Uncle Jonathon. I could go away and fight a war or something."

"Well, you're just about one anyway, at least you have half the name," Ellen added with a laugh.

Emily spoke more seriously. "Now, Mary Tom, war is a terrible thing. You wouldn't want to go to war. We are very fortunate to have Jonathon coming back to us. Many boys will never come home."

"I know, Grandma, but I mean going far away across the ocean to other countries is exciting, even if it had to take a war—I would like to go. I want to do something besides cook and clean and play piano. I want to do something different."

Prudence tried to change the subject. "Look at him yawn, Mama—he looks just like Patrick when he yawns. You remember how he used to yawn all the time at the breakfast table and you used to get after him for it?"

Emily smiled. He did look like his Father. She silently hoped that he would grow up to be just like him. Two preachers in the family would be great.

Melony walked in. "When are Uncle Jonathon and Grandpa going to get here?"

"Should be soon, Honey," Emily answered. She was rather nervous herself. She had waited a long time to see her son again. She strained her eyes up the road to see if she could see any sign of them. She remembered another time—another homecoming. Though she wasn't waiting all prepared, it was a wonderful homecoming. She could still see him coming down the dusty road. His hair was thick and dark then. She realized how much older he looked now.

But now, she had a son coming back from war. "Thank you, Lord, you're so good to me. Thank you for bringing my husband back to me and now my son."

Voices rose from the living room.

"Ellen, you better go and try to break it up," Prudence said, turning to her sister-in-law. "Calm Patrick down."

As she entered the living room, Ellen felt a chill in the air.

"I can't help what you say, Preacher Brother. I will not accept a God that allows a people to be robbed of their own land, their livelihood and their pride. You don't know what it's all about, living here in these mountains all your life with your little family and all the security you'll ever want. You don't know how other people live. How can you say God loves everybody, and He is no respecter of persons? What do you know about it? Sure, it appears to *you* that there is a loving God way up there watching over you, but what about the Indian that sits alone in his cold and windy hut with all his dreams shattered? Does he, too, feel that there is a great and loving God watching over him? How can he?"

"Spring, you cannot blame God for what man has done," Patrick answered calmly.

Ellen took advantage of the lull and broke in, "Spring, how was your trip?"

"It was fine, Ellen, though tiring. It's good to be back home again."

"Well, we've all missed you. Do you have any of your paintings with you? I would love to see them."

"No, I don't. But I *do* plan to do some painting while here. I've never been able to capture the real spirit of these Virginia mountains."

"Spring, you'll never be able to capture the spirit of these mountains until you meet their creator."

"Oh Ellen, how do you put up with this preacher of yours?" Spring smiled at Patrick. She couldn't really be mad at him. He was her little brother.

Mary Tom, who had been standing in the doorway listening, spoke up boldly. "Aunt Spring, why haven't you ever gotten married?"

Caught off guard, a faint expression of sadness escaped that strong and noble face. Patrick and Ellen both caught it before it vanished, and they exchanged concerned looks. This beautiful, high-spirited woman, talented but mysterious, was human after all. They shared a feeling of pity for her.

Spring brushed back her thick, black hair with both hands and answered rather nonchalantly, "Mary Tom, getting married is not the only thing in life!"

"That's the way I feel too, Aunt Spring. I'm gonna be just like you. I'm gonna take off and travel and go where I want and do what I want to do."

Spring smiled at her. She sure wasn't like her Mother.

"What's South Dakota like?" Mary Tom continued.

"Well, it's rather flat country, not like what you're used to at all. You can look as far as your eyes can see and just see the land spread out before you for miles and miles and miles until all of a sudden the land stops and the sky starts. And the sky—it's so big up there. Looking up into it, you feel so small—it's all around you, above you, on all sides of you."

"There aren't any mountains?"

"No, not like here."

"What are the people like?"

"They're the same, more or less."

"How about your people, Aunt Spring, what are they really like?"

Spring's face clouded over, and she was drawn from the mountains in an instant.

"They are good people, Mary Tom, really good

people. They are an honest people, a very giving people—so giving, in fact, that they gave away their land, their heritage...."

"They're here, they're here!" Melony shouted from the kitchen.

The shiny, new Ford pulled up close to the porch. Emily wrung her hands on her apron as she watched Heath step out, then Clarence, Prudence's husband, and then her baby boy.

But Jonathon wasn't a baby any more. He climbed out slowly and stood up straight and tall. He looked much thinner and older than when he left two years ago. She felt like running to him and hugging him to her as she had done when he was small. But instead, she moved slowly toward him with tears in her eyes. Jonathon met her halfway, and they embraced. Then he was overcome with everyone shaking his hand, kissing him, hugging him and asking questions all at once.

Once they were all seated for dinner, Patrick asked grace. Emily always swelled with pride when she heard him, this Preacher Son of hers, talk to the Lord. Everyone began talking again, each seeking Jonathon's attention. Once again, we're all united, Emily thought to herself. It had been a long time. She watched Spring eating very quietly, still sitting proud and tall. It was good to have her home. She had been gone for several years off and on now. It seemed she couldn't make up her mind where home was, whether with them here on the mountain or with her true ancestors on the plains of South Dakota. Emily wished she could find peace.

Prudence sat beside Spring, smiling now and

then. She was truly a blessing, and had developed into a very mature and sweet person. Clarence was beside her. He was a good enough son-in-law. He was good to Prudence and the girls, and that's all that mattered. He had wanted a son so much that when the last baby was born, he named her Mary Tom. The name fits very well, Emily thought, noting that Mary Tom swallowed every word from Jonathon's mouth. Mary Tom had seen to it that she was seated beside Jonathon. That child has more determination than all the rest put together.

Then there was Jonathon, her baby. He was home again! How many prayers she'd lifted up for him. He wasn't given to talk about the war, but didn't seem to mind answering the many questions about it. Every now and then, he would look up and half smile at her the way he did when he was a little boy. She was proud of him. She wondered what he would do now.

Seated beside him was Patrick, quiet and serious, her Preacher Son. My, how proud she was of him. They had been so surprised when he announced to them all several years ago that he was going to preach. He had been taking church and the things of God quite seriously for some time before that, but they were still surprised. Why, there had never been a preacher in the family—at least none as far back as she could recall. But he had made a good one so far, and the little church he'd taken over was growing every week.

Ellen was a good preacher's wife, so mild and submissive. Everyone was drawn to her by her compassionate ways.

Seated between her and Heath was Melony. She generally managed to be close to her Grandpa. Heath enjoyed her as much as she enjoyed him. As the first grandchild, she somehow held a special place with him. He often said that she resembled her Grandmother, but Emily still couldn't see it that much. And there in the little wooden cradle on the floor was David. What a blessing he was going to be to them all. Emily silently thanked God for uniting her family once again.

Though busy answering the many questions fired at him, Jonathon's thoughts were elsewhere. They kept going back to that face he had seen on the train. He couldn't erase it no matter what.

He remembered laying his book down and stretching and yawning—when he saw her for the first time. She was breathtaking, and she was looking straight at him with those big, blue eyes. He stopped in the middle of his yawn and sat straight up, pretending to look at the passing meadows from the window. Now that was dumb, he thought to himself. Why did I do that? But somehow she made him feel uncomfortable and rather awkward. It must be her beauty. Never before had he seen such a magnificent girl. During the rest of the train ride, he was conscious of her but couldn't bring himself to look at her except for stealing a glance when he thought she was preoccupied.

When the train finally rolled into the little Oak Mountain Depot, he was very surprised to see her getting ready to get off, too. He smiled to himself and thought—maybe things here in Oak Mountain have improved since I left. He lost sight of her as the train pulled away and his Father grabbed hold of him.

"Jonathon, do you think you'll ever get married?" Mary Tom's question shattered his thoughts and brought him abruptly back to the dinner table.

"I guess so, maybe one day, Tommy."

She smiled up at him. She loved it when he called her Tommy.

"He doesn't seem to be in any hurry," Patrick kidded.

"Well, I haven't had time for such things lately. I guess I'll have to make up for lost time."

"We know just the right one, don't we, Honey?" Ellen looked at Patrick with a twinkle in her eyes.

"Uh-oh, don't start fixing me up. I can do that for myself."

"Seriously, Jonathon, there is the sweetest, young lady in our church. The man who gets her will be one lucky man," Ellen continued.

"I bet she plays the piano, too," Jonathon teased.

"Well, as a matter of fact, she does and very beautifully, too."

"I bet she can't play as pretty as little Melony here." He winked at Melony.

"Jonathon, I'm serious. Her name is Mildred Dudley, and she really is a sweet girl."

"Are you kidding, Aunt Ellen? Uncle Jonathon wouldn't be interested in *her*," Mary Tom spoke up in his defense. "She's not his type."

Jonathon laughed out loud. "Well, what *is* my type, Miss Know-It-All?"

Mary Tom got that faraway, dreamy look again. "Someone more exciting and mysterious."

Everyone laughed now.

"That type might be interesting, but they usually don't make the best wives. You want someone sweet like your Mother here," Heath added.

"What's wrong with being exciting and mysterious?" Mary Tom continued. "And what about Aunt Spring—she's exciting and mysterious."

"And I'm not married, either," Spring added with a smile.

AS THE FAMILY basked in the warmth of each other's love and enjoyed the sumptuous meal, there was a lone figure sitting on the side of a bed several miles away, feeling very alone and bitter. She took a crumpled letter from her purse and reread it for the hundredth time. She heard footsteps approaching and quickly stuffed it back into her purse.

"Jessica, are you awake?" her Aunt called out. "Dinner's ready."

"I'll be right down," she answered, then mumbled to herself, "I don't know whether I'll be able to stand this stuffy, old house that smells of mothballs, and Aunt Marianne." She straightened her new, tweed skirt and smoothed back her thick, black hair.

As she glided down the steps with her usual feathery grace, she felt eyes upon her. Turning, she noticed a tall, robust man several years her senior. He was staring up at her with his mouth wide open.

"Jessica, this is Christopher Connelly. Christopher, my niece, Jessica Wilder."

"How do you do, Mr. Connelly?"

"Oh, please do call me Christopher," he blurted, almost falling over his feet as he moved forward to shake her hand.

"Very well, Christopher."

"Jessica, Christopher is new in the area too. He is staying with his brother, Aaron Connelly."

"Oh...."

"Looks like we have something in common," he added with an awkward smile. "How do you like these here mountains?"

"I love them."

The evening wore on with Christopher staying for dinner and making a fool of himself over and over again with Jessica, who seemed to all but ignore him. While choking down his second helping of dessert, he asked, "Did you come in on the six o'clock train?"

"Yes."

"Then I bet you saw Jonathon Barrett. I hear tell over at Johnson's store that he came in on that train just back from the war."

"Really? I don't know Mr. Barrett." Jessica answered absently, concealing the thoughts that began racing through her mind.

"Is that right, Christopher? Well, isn't that just great," Aunt Marianne spoke up sincerely. "I'm so glad that he's back home safe and sound. He has the sweetest Mother. She's been a friend of mine for years."

"Did you fight in the war?" Jessica asked sarcastically.

Christopher squirmed uncomfortably in his chair. "No, I had to stay home and take care of my Mother who was ill at the time...but she just passed away recently."

"I'm sorry," Jessica said, without any real compassion.

When the door finally closed behind their guest, both she and her Aunt breathed a sigh of relief.

"Aunt Marianne, please don't try and fix me up. I'm quite capable of taking care of myself."

"I'm sure you are, Honey. But I thought it would be nice for you to know someone closer to your own age. I really didn't expect him so soon, though."

"It's alright. I think I'll turn in. I'm rather exhausted."

"Wouldn't you like some hot chocolate first? I thought it would be nice to sit and chat a little. I'm anxious to hear about your Mother."

"There's really nothing to tell. She died a year ago, like I said."

"Well, I'm so glad you've come home.

She managed to escape the chat and hot chocolate both. She'd learned all the tricks of getting her own way many years ago. After undressing and slipping into her soft, blue nightie, she cut out the light and went to bed. But she lay there quite some time before going to sleep, retracing her steps and the evening as a whole, but skipping over the Christopher Connelly part. That wasn't worth remembering. She would have to make sure to avoid him in the future…what a jerk! Then she remembered again…Jonathon Barrett…now wasn't that interesting?

Her Aunt pulled the covers up close under her chin and lay very still in the next room. It was strange having someone else in the house again. It had been a long time. She only wished Mother could have lived to know this Grandchild of hers—what a beautiful child she was. But then something seemed to say to her—it is for the best. Somehow, this child didn't seem like the kind of child that would bring joy to the heart. She was

Betty Lou's daughter all right.

Of course, Jessica had more beauty and polish, but she seemed to have inherited Betty Lou's cold, bitter ways. A tear welled up and fell on her cheek. Though it had been many a year since she'd seen her sister, just knowing that she was alive somewhere had helped.

But now, Betty Lou dead...I wonder if she was ready to die?

She almost started to pray for her like she'd done for so many years, ever since the flood, but suddenly realized it was too late. Had Betty Lou ever found happiness in life? Jessica had mentioned that her Father traveled a lot, leaving them alone much of the time. She could not imagine Betty Lou liking that. I wonder if she and Mother are together now—I hope so. Marianne tried to go to sleep with that thought in mind.

But sleep wouldn't come. Instead, her Mother's face was before her. She had grieved over Betty Lou for so many years. After the flood, Mother had changed. She couldn't get Betty Lou off her mind. Of course, it was awful right after the flood when everyone believed her dead. But she'd never forget the day when almost eighteen months later, her Mother had come trembling into the house, holding a letter. Marianne remembered asking, "What is it, Mother?"

"Betty Lou" was all her mother managed to utter before collapsing in the nearest chair.

She remembered that letter so well. She and her Mother had read it over and over again.

> Dearest Mother and Sis,
> I guess you'll both be surprised by this. Well,

I'm not dead after all. In fact, I'm alive and well. The flood was a great opportunity for me. A new life. I know you'll understand, Mother—I had to do it. Life was a mess for me, and those closed-in mountains—I never did like them anyway.

I have a husband now named George, and a daughter. I named her Jessica. She's beautiful. Don't worry about us. Take care now.

Love,
Betty Lou

It was the last they ever heard from her. Mother looked for another letter up to the day she died. I'll never, never understand how Betty Lou could be so cruel. Of course, Betty Lou never cared about anybody or anything but herself. Jessica did say that she'd died of cancer. I wonder if she suffered much. It was hard to get much out of that child. Tomorrow, though, tomorrow I'll try again. She finally drifted off into sleep.

THE NEXT COUPLE of weeks were happy ones around the Barrett household. Jonathon rested and made plans for the future. Spring was in and out hiking up the mountainside with her easel and paints with Mary Tom at her side. The rest of the family were in and out also.

One morning, Emily awoke early as usual, but realized it was Sunday, and Heath didn't have to go to work. She could sleep a bit longer. She turned over, but couldn't go back to sleep. She pulled the covers up against the chill of the house and snuggled up close to

Heath. He responded and wrapped his arms around her, drawing her closer to him, though still asleep. She smiled. He was such a good husband. But then she remembered he hadn't always been such a good husband.

One shouldn't remember the unhappy parts of life, she thought, but dwell on the happy parts. "Thank you Lord, for saving my husband," she breathed silently. That was the difference, and she well knew it. She often wondered what really happened to him and wanted to ask him more, but somehow she felt it was best to leave the past behind them.

She knew it had something to do with the flood, for that was the turning point in his life. He had taken Charity's death very hard and believed that it was his punishment for his wicked ways. Those were such hard days—Charity's death and the flood. Things had never quite been the same for the mountain folk after the flood. So many deaths and some just never turned up— Betty Lou for one. What had happened to Betty Lou?

Why am I reaching back into the past? she asked herself. Heath was here beside her, and all her children were fine, and—oh well—she had so much to be thankful for. She snuggled closer to Heath and fell back asleep.

A couple of hours later, she awoke to the smell of bacon frying in the kitchen. Now, who could that be? She arose and hurriedly dressed. When she entered the kitchen, she found Spring busy fixing breakfast.

"Well, for goodness sake, this sure is a nice surprise."

"Oh Mother, I was hoping to have it all finished

before you got up."

"This here bacon wouldn't let me sleep."

"Is Jonathon going with you to church this morning?"

"Yes, he said so. We'll all be going this morning, Spring. I do wish you would come along with us."

"No thank you, Mother."

"Do you have plans today, being up so early?"

"Yes, matter of fact, I have special plans. I'm hiking up to Lover's Leap."

"Lover's Leap! Why?"

"I want to get on canvas the dogwoods, and the feeling I experienced as a child when we searched for the treasure."

"Spring, that's a wonderful idea, but are you going alone?"

"Of course," Spring answered impatiently.

"Well, do be careful."

"What's all this chatter about?" Heath asked with a smile as he entered.

"Look who's fixing breakfast, Honey."

"I don't believe it. She couldn't be turning domestic after all these years?"

"Now just what do you mean—after all these years? You make me sound ancient, Father," Spring laughed.

"Well, just remember, if you're ancient, we must be real antiques!"

"I don't feel like an antique," Emily added with a twinkle in her eye.

"Don't worry, Honey, you aren't," Heath reached out and hugged her.

"Now you two cut it out in front of this old maid."

"Look who's calling herself an old maid, but woe to anyone else who does," Heath teased.

"That's right," she smiled.

"Spring is going up to Lover's Leap today to paint, Honey."

"Alone?"

"Yes, alone," Spring answered, a little too quickly.

"I don't know if that's such a good idea, Spring. Things are not like they used to be, you know."

"Oh Daddy, I'll be all right. I'm not a little girl anymore—in fact, I'm ancient, remember?"

"Who's ancient?" Jonathon boomed with his happy, boisterous voice as he entered the kitchen.

"Good morning," everyone said in unison.

"I'm glad to see this big breakfast. I'll need it for Big Brother's preaching," he teased, not realizing he'd spoken the truth.

That morning in the little, country church, Patrick seemed so filled with the spirit of God as he preached to the small but attentive congregation that it was hard for Jonathon to remember that he was his brother. Before Patrick concluded, everyone was captivated except Mary Tom. Prudence noticed her squirming as usual, anxious to get out. As soon as the last prayer was said, she bolted for the door before Prudence could slow her down. Everyone else milled around talking and enjoying the fellowship. Jonathon had been captured by Ellen immediately and whisked over to meet Mildred Dudley, who he instantly disliked.

"Son, that was a wonderful sermon." Heath extended his weathered hand in a hearty handshake.

"Thank you, Dad." Patrick still seemed to be up in those heavenly clouds and was reluctant to come down.

Everyone was crowding around him, praising his sermon and shaking his hand. Heath backed off admiringly. He could see that this small congregation already loved Patrick dearly as their pastor. He's so much like his Mother, he thought. He had never been, nor could he ever be as spiritual as this son of his. Sometimes he didn't even feel like Patrick was his son, but he sure was proud of him.

"Father, wasn't that a great sermon?" Prudence asked, breaking into his private thoughts.

"It sure was, Prudence."

"By the way, have you seen Mary Tom?"

"She darted outside at the last amen."

"I know. If only she could be more like her sister," she said, looking in Melony's direction.

Melony sat very prim and proper on the piano bench, looking over the music Mildred Dudley had been playing and secretly dreaming of the day she would be able to play before the congregation. Surely Uncle Patrick would want her to! But she wasn't going to stop there as most did. No—she was going to go on to bigger and better things. She could see herself one day playing for large audiences in some big city far away, maybe a fine concert hall or something like that. It was going to be great, and she would be so happy—just playing all the time.

"Melony Dear, come along. Let's find your Sister," Prudence called.

Mary Tom caught her name as it floated out the open door, and she quickly scrambled out of the crooked, old oak, ripping her new dress in the process.

"Mary Tom, I don't believe you!" Prudence scolded as she came out the door.

"I'm sorry, Mother, really."

"Mary Tom, you're not sorry that you disobeyed again. You're just sorry that you got caught."

Mary Tom reflected on her Mother's words as she was pulled into the car. "She's right," she thought to herself, "I am sorry that she caught me." She was very quiet on the way home, speaking only once. "Mother, wasn't that what Uncle Patrick said in his sermon today?"

"Why, Mary Tom, I didn't think you heard anything your Uncle said."

"You know...about only being sorry when you get caught."

"That's right. As a matter of fact, that was the essence of his sermon. True repentance comes only when we realize that we have sinned against God, and that it was because of our sin that Jesus died. Of course, all sin is against God."

Mary Tom was quiet again.

THINGS WERE NOT SO quiet on the ride home with Heath, Emily and Jonathon.

"Oh, come on folks, you know I can do better than that," Jonathon teased.

"Why Honey, she's really a very nice girl," Emily said gently.

"Yeah, I know, but I kind'a like something to go along with the niceness part."

Heath laughed. "I know what you mean, Son. It

does help a potion if you plan on spending the rest of your life with someone. You need to find somebody beautiful like your Mother here."

"I wish I could," he answered with a wink at Emily.

"Oh, you two. What did you think of Patrick's sermon? Wasn't it just wonderful?"

"It sure was," Heath answered quickly.

Jonathon added, "It was alright, I guess. Sometimes, though, it seems hard for me to believe that we're brothers. I mean—we're so different."

"Of course you're different, Jonathon. All of you children are different," Emily answered.

Heath understood Jonathon's feelings. He silently hoped that Jonathon wouldn't have to experience the hurt and sorrow that he had before he found himself. He could see that he was searching for his place in life.

"WELL, I GUESS THEY'RE just about out of church by now," Spring said aloud as she glanced down at her watch. She sat back and examined her work. "It's going to be good," she said to herself with a determined spirit. She could feel it. She could feel the emotions fighting their way to surface. I love these woods. I love these mountains. I love these dogwoods. She smiled to herself and why not? But she would not admit it to anyone else because...because she still harbored those old, old fears that someone or something might take them from her. Somebody might say she didn't belong here, like that day in the sixth grade when Gail Louise Johnson had told the whole class that she didn't belong here.

Spring could still feel the hurt and almost taste the salt in her tears again as they flowed down her cheeks that day so many years ago. It seemed like yesterday to her. It was the reason she found herself running back to the Dakota plains. Where was her home? Did she really belong in those wide stretches of plains? Where did she belong? She leaned back against the rough bark of the old, oak tree and gazed into the sky— a beautiful, cloudless sky—and began to talk to herself.

"Spring...Spring Leaf...my people call me. My people who look the same as I, but don't think like I do. Spring, you're awfully mixed up. You have the body of an Indian, but the mind of a white man. But if my people could think like I do, they might be able to rise above their circumstances. It's disgusting the way they sit back and accept whatever the white man sees fit to give them. Why don't they stand up and speak up for what they believe—for what our fathers believed?"

A twig broke. She turned and looked into a pair of deep set eyes that were staring at her—full of emotion.

"Who are you?" she asked, a bit shaken. "Where did you come from?"

He continued to stare at her—speechless.

AUNT MARIANNE PUT down the church bulletin and called, "Jessica, come here a minute."

Jessica came slowly down the steps from her bedroom, where she had been reading. Irritated that she'd been disturbed, she frowned at her Aunt.

Marianne overlooked it. "Listen, Jessica, we're having a big, country hoedown over at the church next week. There will be dinner served on the grounds before, and then we'll have this group from over in Tadsbury to play and sing for us. They're very good; we had them last year. Everyone will be there— all the young folk in the county just about. I know you'll enjoy it."

"You say just about everyone will be there?"

"Why sure. You don't want to miss this."

"I think you're right, Aunty. I don't believe I will miss it."

She returned to her room and stretched out on the soft bed. "No, I wouldn't miss it for the world." She began to think of the upcoming event. "This could be very interesting. I wonder if Mr. Jonathan Barrett will be there. Maybe even the entire Barrett clan. We'll see. Now, what can I wear?" She jumped up and threw open the closet door. "Oh, I don't have *anything* to wear. I'll have to get something new."

Marianne felt very satisfied as she cleaned off the table. "I really didn't expect her to accept so easily. Maybe she's not so difficult after all. This outing will be good for her, and maybe she can meet some young friends."

That evening, just as the sun was going down, and Jessica still lay on her bed reading and contemplating the upcoming event, Jonathon was invited to the country hoedown.

"Come on, Uncle Jonathon, take me along with you," Mary Tom pleaded.

"Now look here, Dear Child, how am I to enter as a dashing, young prince just back from the war with *you* tagging along behind me?" How he loved to tease her. "Why, I cannot be bothered by a mere tomboy. I must be about important business, you know."

"Yeah, I know—monkey business," she said, giggling.

"Mother, if Mary Tom goes with Uncle Jonathon, can I go too?" Melony asked.

"Come, Girls. Let your Uncle off the hook. He doesn't want to escort two little nieces to the outing. You can go with me."

"Yes, Girls, that's why I asked him to go—so he can enter as a dashing, young prince. You know there are those who would prefer to see him so," Ellen added with a smile.

"I guess Mildred Dudley will be there."

"Why, I don't reckon that I know, Jonathon Dear. However, I suppose so, as most of the young people will be making an appearance." Ellen tried to hide her real thoughts, remembering Mildred's words.

"Just don't try and set me up with her, okay?"

"Of course not, Jonathon. But I don't see why you take such a strong dislike to her. She's really a very dear girl."

"I'm sure she is," he teased.

"Here comes Aunt Spring!" Mary Tom hollered out as she ran to get the door.

Spring entered, loaded down with her paints and canvas. "Whe-e-e," she sighed while unloading. "What's for supper? I've worked up a ravenous appetite."

Everyone stared, surprised at her sudden enthusiasm for food. Up until now, she'd hardly had an appetite at all.

"Chicken and dumplings, Dear," Emily answered with a puzzled look.

"Great!" she exclaimed and left the room.

"What's got into her?" Ellen asked.

"Who knows? Who ever knows with big Sis?" Jonathon concluded.

Chapter IX

Whatsoever A Man Soweth

The church hoedown was a great success for the congregation. Everyone turned out, and the offering for missions was the largest ever. But it was a success in other ways for Jessica Wilder. All eyes were on her as she arrived in her soft, white, cotton dress, trimmed in intricate, yellow lace. Her long dark curls rested on her tiny shoulders and framed her lovely face ever so gracefully, and the yellow ribbon in her hair drew a sharp contrast with her ebony curls. She moved with the grace of a princess, knowing everyone was watching.

"Who's *that?*" Jennifer Lawhorne exclaimed.

"I don't know," Mildred Dudley answered with a frown.

"I'd sure *like* to know," piped in Jennifer's younger brother.

"I don't think you're the only one." Jennifer nodded in the direction of a group of fellows under an oak tree. They all stood gaping as if Jessica was the only girl there. Jonathon Barrett was in the midst of them, and he, too, was staring with an interested look on his face.

"It's her," he thought to himself. Even amid all the activity of his homecoming, he hadn't forgotten her.

The band began playing *Give Me That Old Time Religion.* Everyone was milling around and talking, waiting for supper. Jessica was already engaged in a conversation with two rather anxious looking young men who had rushed to her side immediately, but her eyes were following someone else as he moved from one circle of people to another. Jonathon was enjoying himself as he renewed old acquaintances. After a while, he was standing quite close to her and her boring friends. She waited for just the right moment.

"I believe you dropped this?" Jonathon asked as he bent to pick up the lacy, white handkerchief. On the way up, he met her big, blue, piercing eyes.

"Yes, thank you," she radiated such feeling and expression that Jonathon just stood there looking at her.

"Jonathon, have you met Jessica?" A voice broke the silence. It was Aunt Marianne.

"No, Ma'am. I don't believe so."

"Well, this is my niece, Jessica Wilder. She just moved all the way from New York to be with me. Jessica, this is Jonathon Barrett...and Jonathon, I'm so happy to see you safely back home from that horrible war."

"Thank you, Ma'am. I'm sure glad to be back, too," he said, never taking his eyes off Jessica.

"Oh, there's Mrs. Stone, please do excuse me." Aunt Marianne moved off—her mission accomplished.

"Well, how do you like Virginia?" Jonathon finally asked.

"I love it!" She answered in her very delicate and sensual voice.

"What's New York like?"

"Oh, not nearly as pretty as Virginia...too busy and too many people."

"Yeah, that's what I figured. There's no place like Virginia. I sure have missed these mountains."

"Was the war really bad?" she asked in a girlish way.

"Yes. But we don't have to talk about that. Would you like some lemonade? We could go over and sit under that clump of trees."

"That sounds delightful."

"BOY, SHE DIDN'T waste any time—did she?" Jennifer Lawhorne said to Mildred Dudley as they watched the two sit down under the trees.

Mildred was quiet.

"Great balls of fire. Look what Jonathon's captured," Mary Tom exclaimed to Melony.

"Mary Tom, that's not a very nice way to put it. I wonder who she is?"

"Let's go find out." Mary Tom started across the lawn and Melony followed.

"Don't look now, but we're about to be invaded by

two very pesty nieces."

"Hello, Uncle Jonathon. We wondered what happened to you." Mary Tom spoke with curiosity while staring down at Jessica.

"Oh, I'm still here, girls. This here is Miss Jessica Wilder. Jessica, meet Melony and Mary Tom."

"Hello, Miss Wilder. I'm Melony."

"And I'm Mary Tom—how do you get your hair to look so beautiful with the ribbon and all?"

"Why, thank you Honey."

"Girls, why don't you go over and help your Mother out? It looks like she could use it."

"Come on, Melony, do you feel a bit unwanted?" Mary Tom teased as they scampered off.

That night as Jessica Wilder pulled the covers up close under her lovely chin, she smiled to herself. This was going to be fun. More fun than when she'd stolen Bud Harper from Charlene Rice. This will be even better because I didn't even like Bud, but I think I'm going to enjoy Jonathon quite a bit. Mother Dear, if you only knew. She reached and turned out the light.

Jonathon didn't go to sleep as quickly. He tossed and turned, thinking about those big, blue, piercing eyes and that thick, ebony hair and creamy white complexion. He kept remembering those long, dark lashes that turned up so gently on the ends and her little girlish ways. How could one girl have it all? He found himself wondering what it would be like to hold her in his arms and suddenly wanting to more than anything else in the world. "You're crazy!" he said out loud to himself. "You've only met the girl. You don't even know her. Who cares? I'm going to know her." He finally fell into a restless sleep and dreamed he was searching for Jessica Wilder in a deep, dark forest. He could hear her soft, pleading voice, but he could never find her.

When he awoke, he was dripping with perspiration. He got up and looked at the clock: 2:30 a.m. He decided to go to the kitchen and fix himself some cookies and milk, warm milk—that's what he needed. It always helped him to sleep when he was a boy.

He walked into the kitchen and found himself not alone.

"Spring, what are you doing up at this hour?"

"Couldn't sleep. Like you, I guess, little Brother."

"Yeah, I couldn't. Had a crazy dream."

"Same here. Well, how was the hoedown?"

"Turned out great."

"See any interesting girls?" she asked with a slight smile.

Jonathon hesitated for a moment and suddenly felt an urge to tell someone about Jessica.

"Matter of fact, I did."

"Oh, really? Who?"

"Her name is Jessica...Jessica Wilder. She's old maid Smith's niece, just arrived here from New York."

"Well, well. I do say. What's she like?"

Jonathon sat down with his cookies and milk, forgetting to warm it, and stared out the dark window with a faraway look in his eyes. "She's different. She's beautiful, and I think I'm falling in love."

"Jonathon Barrett, you've only met her!"

"Who cares?"

"You don't know anything about her and...."
Spring stopped, recalling her own day. She didn't
know anything about him, but she felt all warm inside
just thinking about him.

"Right now, that doesn't seem important. I just
want to see her again...soon. I think I'm going over to
see her first thing in the morning. I've got to see if
she's real or just a figment of my imagination."

Spring laughed. "This *is* serious, little Brother."

"Yes, I think so, Sis." Jonathon answered with
that faraway look still in his eyes.

"You know, Jonathon, this is strange."

"What's strange?"

"Well, I met someone today also, up at Lover's
Leap while I was painting."

"*You?*"

"Yes. I'd been painting there for quite a while
when he appeared like a shining knight out of nowhere. We talked for hours. And what's really crazy
is that after talking for hours, I don't even know his
name."

"Now that *is* crazy, and you're talking about me.
What did you talk about?"

"Life...death...nature...what's really meaningful in life, you know."

"H-m-m-m-m. Sounds like you've finally met
someone who thinks like you do, anyway."

"He does. He can almost read my thoughts, and
vice-versa. It's almost psychic."

"Are you going to tell the folks about him?"

"No. This is just between us for now. Like you,

I want to find out if he's real or whether he's the prince still looking for Snow White."

"When will you see him again?"

"Tomorrow morning. I haven't finished my painting, and he said he'd be there."

"Suppose he isn't?"

"Then I'll know he found Snow White," she forced a smile.

EMILY WAS JUST finishing up the scrambled eggs when both Jonathon and Spring appeared, all dressed and ready for the day.

"My, what's going on? You two look like you've got to catch the last train leaving town. Where are you going?"

"I'm going back up to Lover's Leap to finish my painting, Mother."

"Well, how about you, Jonathon?"

"Just thought I'd get out and around a little. Been closed in long enough. I'll probably be back for lunch, but don't wait for me."

After breakfast, they left. As soon as the door closed behind them, Emily set about the dishes, a bit confused. "Children," she thought, "I'll never understand them. One day they're pouting, the next they're floating on some cloud."

She laughed out loud in the empty house. "Children. What am I saying? They're not children anymore...but they will always be children to me."

She finished the dishes. Drying her hands on the dish towel that Ellen had made, she walked into the living room and knelt beside the couch. She looked up toward the ceiling, past it and upward: "Lord, thank you for my children. Thank you for my husband. You're so good to me. Thank you for the good times and thank you for the hard times—those were the times I really got to know you, Lord. Please be with all my children now. Guide them and help them the way you have me all these years. Patrick...Lord. What a blessing. Thank you for a preacher son. He is my joy. Prudence...she's also a blessing. Thank you for her and bless her as she tries to lead her family now. But Jonathon and Spring— they especially need a touch from you. Draw them to thee, Lord. Spring really needs you—she needs to get to know you, Lord. She's so mixed up and lonely. Of course, you know, Lord. And my grandchildren...I pray...Father...that they will all grow up to be giants for thee. And, Lord...thank you for Heath. I don't want to forget him. Thank you for what we have between us today. We wouldn't have it if it weren't for You. Now, Lord, be with me today. Make me thy channel and live through me and speak through me. Make me a blessing to someone today, Lord. In Jesus' name, amen."

She rose to her feet to face a new day.

JESSICA WAS LOUNGING on the couch in her nightgown when she noticed the truck pull up out front. She jumped to her feet and ran upstairs, calling to her aunt.

"Aunt Marianne, someone's coming!"

Land sakes, why couldn't that child get dressed at a decent hour, Aunt Marianne thought, and then I wouldn't have to stop what I'm doing to answer the door.

Jessica peered out her window and much to her surprise, saw Jonathon striding across the front lawn. "Well, I didn't expect such fast results," she whispered while pulling off her gown.

"Jonathon Barrett, how nice to see you again. It's been a long time since you've been in my house," Marianne said happily. "Let's see, it must have been when I had that gathering about five years ago for the Youth For Christ group, and I believe you came over with the Roberts boys, didn't you?"

"You have a good memory, Miss Smith. I sure did, and I still remember that good hot chocolate you fixed us."

"Why, thank you, Jonathon. Here, have a seat over here by the window. I always seat my guests here because of the lilac bush just outside the window. There's nothing sweeter than the scent of lilac drifting through a window. Well, how's your Mother today? I've been meaning to call on her. Must do it soon."

"Mother's fine."

"And your Brothers and Sisters?"

"All fine. You know Spring is back—for a while at least."

"Is that so? No, I didn't know. I didn't see her at the gathering, and I just figured she was still out west. How is she doing?"

"Alright, I guess."

"She's never married either. Guess she'll be like me." She smiled at Jonathon, who couldn't help but think, "No way!"

"Miss Smith, it's such a beautiful day out—I just thought your niece might like to go for a ride."

"Why Jonathon, that sounds like a lovely idea. She *does* get bored here all the time with nobody but me for company. Young folk need young folk. I remember those days."

She walked over to the foot of the stairs and called, "Jessica, you have company, Dear."

"I'm sure she'll be down directly. It might be a little too warm for hot chocolate, but would you like some iced tea, Jonathon?"

"No thank you, I'm still full from that good breakfast Mama cooked."

After what seemed like a long while, Jessica came down the steps, stepping ever so lightly, with her long hair flowing. Her soft, blue blouse blended with her eyes and the black skirt accentuated her long legs and matched her hair. The black heels showed off her small feet and ankles. She smiled at Jonathon, making him squirm in his chair.

"Why, what a nice surprise," she said softly.

"Just thought I'd drop by and see...see if maybe you'd like to go for a ride."

"That would be just dandy. I'd love to see more of the mountains."

Aunt Marianne spoke up suddenly. "Why don't I pack you two a lunch to take with you? I have some leftover chicken from the gathering, and I'll throw in some biscuits and maybe even some blueberry rolls."

"It's sounding better all the time," Jonathon kidded as he stood up, anxious to leave.

The old truck bounced along the rugged road, curving around and around the mountainside. Jessica was so excited with the first signs of spring, she couldn't keep still.

"Oh, look over there! It's all so beautiful!"

"You know, Jessica, I've always loved these mountains, but somehow they seem even more beautiful than I remember. I don't know whether it's because of the war, or because of...you."

She smiled that tantalizing smile.

"As soon as I find a good place, we'll stop and go for a walk. Of course, just a little walk because you're not dressed for a good hike."

"Oh, shucks. I'd love to go for a big hike," she pouted.

"Well, I started to suggest that you change clothes, but you looked so beautiful...."

Her pouting lips spread into another smile.

"You're cute," she teased.

"I *do* wish I'd been able to use the car today. It wouldn't be so bumpy and uncomfortable, but Dad had to use it."

"Oh silly, I like this old truck. It's so quaint."

"Well, I don't know about that, but Daddy seems to love it. He won't get rid of it."

"You speak of your Father with such love."

"He's pretty special. I never realized it much until I went off to war. You know, he was in World War I himself. Somehow war has a way of making you think like you've never thought before. It sort of cuts away all the little, unnecessary things and gets down to basics."

"Is he like you?"

Jonathon laughed. "Funny you'd ask. Everyone has always said I'm his carbon copy, but I can't see it myself. But then, Mother says Dad's changed a lot. She said he used to do things on impulse like I do— like deciding to see you this morning."

"I'm glad you did. I wonder what made your Father change?"

"Partly age, I guess, and Mother says it was mostly when he got right with the Lord. I suppose that was it. Hey, here's the perfect place."

He pulled over under a huge, shady oak. Once out on the carpeted hills, Jessica stretched and suddenly felt like running. She bolted toward a wide open field, kicking her shoes off in the process. Jonathon just stood and watched for a moment, captivated by her unusual beauty, then he followed.

Her thick hair bounced off her shoulders and her black skirt was caught in the wind. He suddenly caught up with her and grabbed her hand. They continued to run, laughing all the way until they fell down on the soft carpet of grass, exhausted.

"You sure can't run and laugh at the same time very well," he said, still laughing.

"It's fun...It's fun...I love it," she gasped.

"I haven't had this much fun since...I don't know when," he looked into her beautiful face. With her hair all tossed and her skirt all wrinkled and her face all red from the run, she reminded him of a little girl, and he reached down and gently kissed her on the lips. She didn't object.

"I'm sorry. I shouldn't have," he said, pulling

away.

"Don't be sorry. *You* wanted to and *I* wanted to," she said as she searched his face with those big, blue eyes.

Suddenly, she was in his arms, and he felt all light-headed as he kissed her again. Just as he was feeling like he never wanted to let go of her, she jumped up and out of his arms.

"Come, let's have our picnic, I'm hungry." She ran off toward the truck.

IN ANOTHER PART of the forest some miles away, Spring was painting those delicate dogwoods. She was concentrating so on the intricate detail of her work that she'd almost forgotten him until she heard that familiar voice.

"Why do you paint?"

Turning toward his tall, erect stature, she smiled. "*Why?*"

"Yes, you paint with such seriousness, and at times you even seem to struggle with yourself."

"How long have you been watching?"

"For a while."

"You have the foot of an Indian. You crept up on me so," she said, smiling.

His countenance changed, and he turned from her.

"What is it? Do you not like to be referred to as an Indian?" Spring asked, already afraid of his answer. She waited for what seemed like eternity before he turned toward her with a look of despair on his face.

"You told them. I thought we were keeping this a secret," he said, almost angrily.

"Told who? What are you talking about?" She was really confused now.

"Your people. They have been talking about me—about us."

"Us?"

"Me and my people. You know. Go ahead and say it."

"Told them about you? How could I? I don't even know your name!" she exclaimed.

Suddenly he began to laugh, and his strong, masculine voice echoed throughout the forest. Spring stared at him with disbelief. He finally sat down beside her and was quiet again. There was something fighting to come to the surface within him. Spring could feel it. She knew that feeling.

"You, my beautiful lady...a real Indian princess. I never thought I'd ever meet a real Indian princess," he almost whispered.

She continued to wait.

"You don't understand, my little Princess, but I too am an Indian. Not a real one hundred percent Indian, but an Indian, just the same." He waited for the shock on her face to fade.

"So, *that's* it!"

"What?"

"I *knew* there was something in that face. In fact, I almost wondered at first, but then thought better. There are no Indians in these Virginia hills. But I see it now...of course. Your people? Are they all Indian?" she asked with interest.

"We are descendants of an Indian tribe that once lived in these mountains, many years ago. Of course, our blood has been mixed. We are not like you, little Princess."

She smiled at him, hardly able to contain her happiness.

He smiled back. "Then you haven't been talking to anyone about me?"

"Of course not. Why would I? Your Indian blood ...what tribe is it?"

"How do I know? It was a long, long time ago."

"Haven't you ever wanted to find out?" she asked.

"I have been too busy with the present to search into the past. And sometimes it is best to leave the past *in* the past."

"But the past is part of you. You are part of it. How can you say that?"

"It is easy for you, little Princess, to feel that way. You are an Indian. But what am I really? Am I to be called an Indian or a white man? Who can say which blood has the highest percentage, the Indian blood or the white man's blood? I am me—that is all."

"Of course you are, but the blood of your many grandfathers is running through those veins." She grabbed hold of his arms as if to show him.

"Calm down, little Princess. If it will satisfy you, I've been told that we are the descendants of a remnant of Cherokee that passed through these mountains many years ago."

"Cherokee." She looked at him and said no more.

"What's the matter? You don't like the Cherokee?"

"I like all Indians."

"There weren't a lot of Cherokee here, like in other places. But, they said that Cherokee delegations passed through these mountains on their way back and forth to Washington, negotiating treaties. Some stayed—they must have liked it here."

"I still can't believe that you're Indian! It's just that I grew up in these mountains, and I've never met anyone that's Indian, or even part Indian. Where did you go to school?"

He searched her face, as if trying to decide whether she was being honest with him. "I went to the mission."

"The mission?"

"You've never heard of the mission? But you didn't grow up all that far from it."

"What is it?"

"Our own school. It isn't anything like the schools you're used to. It is still there."

"I would like to see it. Why didn't you go to a regular school like everyone else?" Spring was beginning to feel she was uncovering a great mystery.

"We couldn't. We still can't. We are not white."

"But you're Indian...I don't understand. And you look more white than you do Indian."

"Little Princess, it is time you get back to your painting. I must go."

As he turned to leave, he looked back at her with sadness. "I will be here tomorrow in case you're painting."

"I will be painting."

After he left, she still could not paint. Her mind

kept going back to their conversation. She wanted to know more—she was sure there was more. Packing up her things, she started home. The way seemed longer than usual as her anticipation mounted. Mother must know.

Emily was mending Heath's socks as Spring entered. "Why, Spring, you're home earlier than I expected." It was so good having her back. She had really missed her the past few years.

"Mother, I'm glad you're alone. There's something I want to talk to you about."

"Well, we better take advantage of the stillness before the storm. The others will be here soon."

Spring sat down at the kitchen table, across from her Mother.

"Mother, what is it about the 'mission' and the people that attend school there? Why can't they go to our schools?"

Emily looked up, unprepared for such a question. "Why Spring, how do you know about the mission and these people?"

"I've met one. He is my friend."

Emily was shocked, but held her composure. "Is he the reason you've been so happy lately?"

"I guess he is, but you haven't answered my questions."

Emily sighed. "It's a sad story, Dear—at least what I know about. These people who attend the mission...they sort of stay to themselves. They're different and most folk around here just don't have much to do with them."

"But why?"

"I don't know exactly. It goes back a long way, I understand. It is questionable what kind of people they are. Some folk say they're partly Indian, and others say they're partly colored. Myself—I think they look more white than anything, but because they are mixed, people just don't want to have much to do with them."

"Why would some people think they're part colored?"

"I don't know except there are some colored folk, I understand, that live in their part of the mountains. Most folk have always called them 'Issues'. I believe it means mixed white and colored or mixed white and Indian."

"This is confusing. But why can't they attend our schools?" Spring stood up and paced the floor.

"Calm down, Dear. It is the law. They're not white, and therefore, they are not allowed to."

"But what about me?" she exclaimed. "I was allowed to, and I'm totally Indian."

"You are our adopted Daughter, Dear. You are a Barrett."

"I see. So that makes it *different*. So many double standards. I don't understand all this." Spring's temperature was rising.

The back door opened. "Hey, Sis, how are you?" Patrick asked jovially.

She turned toward him with bitterness in her dark eyes. "I'm just simply horrible, how are you?"

"Maybe if you'd try to come to church with us, things might look better, Sis," Patrick answered, not realizing the fuel he'd just added.

"Do the Issues attend your church?" she demanded.

Startled, he looked up. "The Issues? What are you talking about?"

"Do they attend your church?" she persisted.

"No, they don't. They have their own."

"That's good. I don't imagine your white christian folk would cotton to them much, would they?"

He turned to Emily. "What's this all about?"

Spring ran from the room and grabbed her shawl. "I'm going for a walk," she hollered back.

That was the last time the subject was discussed. Once, Emily tried to bring it up again, but Spring quickly cut her off.

A couple of weeks later, Emily looked out the kitchen window. "The dogwoods are just about gone," she said with a sigh.

"Where are they going?" Heath teased.

"Oh, you know what I mean. Their magic is disappearing. They're almost all green now. I wonder if Spring has finished her paintings. She's gone again today."

"I'll be glad when she does. She seems to be in another world."

Emily wished again that she could tell him, but she knew that he would explode and demand that Spring not see the young man again. Spring had to find her own way. She needed to work these things out for herself. Emily knew she was troubled over all this Indian stuff. Why did she have to find out about 'those' people? Emily had always tried to keep it from her, not knowing how she'd accept it.

"You know, I'm beginning to think she and Jonathon are carrying on some secret love affairs behind our backs."

Emily looked at him.

"They both stay gone all the time and Jonathon acts like he's in his own little world, too. I remember how I was when I first met you." He winked at her.

"Well, you know how young folk are nowadays, Dear. When they're ready, I'm sure they'll both come forth and reveal their mysteries."

"Guess you're right. One thing for sure, we can't pick their friends for them. No one did our choosing for us, did they?" he reached out and grabbed her hand.

"No, and I think we did a pretty good job of it, too." They hugged each other.

"Well, we worried about Patrick and Prudence, too. And they sure have turned out well," Heath added as he poured himself another cup of coffee.

"Yes, but Patrick and Prudence always were level-headed, you know. Spring is another story. She's so complex. And Jonathon—I'm afraid I *do* understand him. He's a lot like his Father used to be." She smiled up at him.

"Yeah, I know what you mean. That part bothers me, too. I just hope he doesn't have to suffer the way I did before he comes to his senses."

"Well, I never stopped praying for you, Dear, and God answered. We must keep praying for Jonathon... and Spring."

"Hey, isn't today Melony's birthday?"

"It sure is, and I've got to get busy. I've got the

cake to bake, the hen to bake, and all the fixin's yet to prepare."

"You shouldn't go to so much trouble. You know you're not getting any younger."

"Now, watch it. But you know I enjoy doing it."

Heath laughed. "What time is everyone getting here?"

"I really don't know. Why?"

"Oh, I thought if Patrick got here a little early, we might be able to walk down to the 'crick' and get in a little fishing."

"I thought so," she smiled at him.

Several hours later, all was done and Emily strained her eyes, peering out every window.

"Now, where in the world are they? They should be here by now," she said to herself. Everyone was waiting, enjoying the time together—everyone except Spring and Jonathon. The table was set with the birthday cake in the center and the buffet was lined with enticing dishes Emily had spent the day preparing. Suddenly, Spring came in the front door with a bang, and without looking up, headed for her room.

"Spring!" Prudence called.

She turned around and everyone noticed at once that she was crying.

"What is it, Dear?" Emily asked, rushing to her side.

"Nothing...nothing at all," she answered harshly.

"Tonight is Melony's birthday party, Spring," Heath added, confused.

She turned and left.

Emily followed her into the room that used to be

the girls' when they were small. Heath had fixed it up for Spring to use whenever she was home. Now she fell on the small bed and covered her head with the pillow, just as she used to do when she was a little girl. Emily sat beside her and stroked her back as she sobbed. Suddenly all the years seemed to vanish and Spring was a little girl again, just home from school.

It was the day that spoiled, little Wiley Mays had given his oral book report and put down American Indians so terribly. And if that wasn't enough, he'd turned to little Spring and said, "Spring Barrett could tell us all about it. She's a real Indian."

Unfortunately, that was her introduction to the truth. Both Emily and Heath had kept procrastinating and just didn't tell her that she was different. She didn't seem to remember her past, and somehow they didn't want to remind her of it. Emily felt like she was reliving this awful experience. "Don't cry, Dear...don't cry...everything will be all right...don't cry."

Spring looked up at her with swollen eyes and tear-streaked cheeks. "Why, Mother, why? What's wrong with being an Indian?"

"It's that young man, isn't it, Dear?"

"I loved him, Mother—at least I thought I loved him, until...."

"Until...?" Emily questioned tenderly.

"Mother, we were talking about marriage, but not now, never...."

"What happened, Spring?"

"Mother, did you know all about that law you spoke of the other day—that law concerning the Indian or partly Indian people in these parts?" She straightened up and spoke with a fierceness that was close to hate.

Emily shook her head.

"Well, that law, Mother, forbids the part-Indian people of these Virginia mountains to marry unless they label themselves as colored or Negro on their marriage certificates. Not only that—their death certificates state colored, and their babies are labeled as colored on their birth certificates. Can you believe this, Mother? This is Virginia law. What is wrong, Mother? I have always been proud of my home—Virginia—and all the beauty of these magnificent mountains...but Mother, how can this be the law?"

"I don't know, Dear. There are many things that are not considered justice."

Spring didn't hear her. She kept talking as if she were talking to herself. "It is not that *I* am better than or that *these* people are better than colored folk, but they *are not* colored folk. Why should they be forced to lie on their birth certificates? Why cannot they be called what they are? *To thine own self be true.* One should not lie about something so important. I would never...."

"What about him?" Emily interrupted.

Spring turned to her and shook her head. "He would...he would allow someone to label him colored and not Indian on his marriage certificate. How can I love him, Mother? Love is respect. How can I respect him if he won't stand up and fight for what is right...how can I love him?"

"But Spring, you are one hundred percent Indian. As you've said, he is only part Indian, and what was that you said about *'to thine own self be true'*? How can he know his own self like you do? Is he truly an Indian or is he a white man? What is he really?"

Spring didn't hear. She began to recite vehemently.

" *'This above all: to thine own self be true and it follows, as the night the day, thou canst not then be false to any man.'* Shakespeare's Hamlet. You remember the time I sat up practically all night reading that? I've never forgotten those words, *'to thine own self be true'*, and I will be—I *must* be," she said, not to Emily, but to herself.

"Would you like to go out and eat some birthday dinner?" Emily asked reluctantly.

Spring wiped her face with her hands and stood up, suddenly composed. "Yes, I *am* hungry and I must celebrate Melony's birthday. Of course, I must."

As they reached the door, Mary Tom burst in. "Grandma, Grandma, Jonathon is here!"

"Well, Mary Tom, you should knock before entering, you know."

"I'm sorry, Grandma, but he's got somebody with him!"

"Is that so?"

As the three of them entered the living room, all faces were on the lovely lady clinging to Jonathon's arm, and none remembered Spring's problem.

Jonathon spoke up. "This is Jessica, everyone... Jessica is my wife!" They both stood there smiling, with everyone showing shock and disbelief on their faces. Finally Heath spoke. "Well, Son, this is quite a surprise...why didn't you let us know?"

"I'm sorry if you feel like we left you out...but...well—we just decided on the spur of the moment—and just did it. Why wait?" Jonathon answered excitedly. It was apparent that he was having a hard time containing his happiness. All the while, Jessica clung to his arm and continued to smile that beautiful smile that somehow hinted at a mysterious side of this sudden event.

Spring asked, "You are Miss Smith's niece, aren't you?"

"That's right," Jessica answered, still smiling as her eyes turned to Heath, who continued to gaze at her.

Emily felt a chill run down her spine, but managed to overcome it and spoke a bit shakily, "Jonathon, Dear, you and your young wife please sit down and let us...well...let us get to know her."

All eyes were on Jessica as she made her way across the room to the couch, still clinging to Jonathon. Spring watched her also, forgetting her problems for the moment. "Somehow," she thought to herself, "I don't believe that she is *that* dependent on Jonathon—I don't think she really needs his arm for support."

Once seated, everyone waited for someone else to ask the questions that would reveal this sudden, mysterious marriage. Emily again broke the silence. "Now, where are you from, Jessica?"

"New York. I was born and raised in New York. Utica, New York."

Jonathon interrupted. "She's partly from these here mountains, though, her Mother being Miss

Smith's sister." He laughed and everyone joined him...everyone except Heath. He stared at her, and Spring studied her. Emily remained composed, and asked, "Would you care for something to drink, Jessica, and you too, Jonathon?"

"Sounds good," Jonathon answered as he got up to go to the kitchen, joining his Mother. He put his arm around her and glancing back at Jessica, said, "This is my other girl, Honey."

Jessica smiled, and Emily smoothed her apron and said, "Well, everyone, we best get this birthday party going. The food is waiting. Heath, would you please say grace, and then everyone can help themselves."

Heath's eyes caught Jessica's just before he closed them. "Lord, we thank you for this food and these, our Children. Thank you for Melony and this, her birthday. We ask that you continue to bless her for the rest of her life, as you have seen fit to do so far. Also, Lord, we ask your blessing upon Jonathon and his new...wife, Jessica. Please bless their marriage, Lord, as only you can do.... In Jesus' name, amen."

Everyone stood up and started for the food.

"I'm starving," Mary Tom exclaimed.

"You're always starving, young lady," Patrick teased.

Only Spring remained and stared at this new wife Jonathon had sprung on them. Jessica held her gaze.

"And your family, Jessica?" Spring asked coldly.

"None, except for Aunt Marianne," she answered, just as coldly.

"What happened to your parents, if you don't mind my asking?"

"They are both dead, and I was an only child. I was not so fortunate as you to have a large and happy family like this."

"You are right—I am fortunate," Spring answered.

"We are all fortunate," Ellen added as she entered the room and sat down with her plate on her lap, "fortunate to be part of this wonderful family, and we welcome you, Jessica, into the family." She smiled at Jessica warmly. Jessica suddenly felt uncomfortable.

Jonathon handed her a plate filled with meat and vegetables. "Here, my beautiful Wife, you're going to need your strength to take care of me."

"*That's* the truth," Mary Tom giggled.

By now, most everyone was seated again in the living room, balancing their plates on their laps.

"Jessica, wasn't your Mother called Betty Lou?" Spring continued. "I vaguely remember her, I think."

"Yes, my Mother's name was Betty Lou," she answered and looked at Heath.

He looked at her, full of questions, but remained silent. Emily watched.

"But I thought that Miss Smith's sister, the lady named Betty Lou, was one of the ones who was lost in the flood," Patrick spoke up innocently.

"She wasn't," Jessica smiled. "She simply used the flood as a vehicle to begin a new life. Actually, she pulled a disappearing act. Mother was quite fond of acting. In fact, she tried to make it in show business, but she just couldn't. So, she resigned herself to being a housewife, something she never enjoyed."

Emily and Heath sat very still—trying to disguise their shock.

Jonathon hugged Jessica. "I hope *you* enjoy that role."

"Was your Father from New York, Jessica?" Ellen asked. "I've always wanted to see New York."

"Actually, no, Father was from Ireland but came to New York as a young boy with his parents. However, Father died when I was only ten, and I don't have a lot of memories of him." With this, she turned again to Heath, who was listening intently.

"That explains her Irish temper," Jonathon teased.

"Irish or no Irish, all women have tempers." Clarence spoke up in jest, then looked at Prudence. "Except for my Prudence, that is."

Everyone laughed. The conversation changed from Jessica to Patrick's congregation to Melony's piano lessons to little David's teething problems and still everyone wondered about this Jessica. How would she fit into the family?

It was late before they all left. Little David was crying and sleepy as they waved to Jonathon and his new bride when they left for a short honeymoon.

The last good-byes were said and everybody went to bed. Emily wanted to talk to Heath, but decided against it. She looked at him as he sat in his favorite chair of many years. He sat very still. *No*...he kept thinking. It couldn't be. But he kept on thinking.

The next several days were unusual ones for the Barrett household. Wonderfully happy days for the honeymooners who weren't too far away, although nobody knew where. Very depressing days for Spring as she began packing again. Would she ever stop packing and unpacking, she thought to herself as she neatly folded each item and placed it in the suitcase. It was time to get on with her life.

They were puzzling days for the rest of the family as they discussed Jonathon's hasty marriage whenever they got together. Heath and Emily both went about their daily chores, but they couldn't escape that horrible thought that kept haunting them. Heath even thought about going over to Miss Smith's several times, but didn't dare. They both wanted to know the truth, but at the same time they were afraid of it. Emily was cleaning out the cupboards and thinking about Jessica when the door flew open.

"Grandma, where is Spring?" Mary Tom asked.

"She's in her room packing, Dear."

Mary Tom darted away and knocked on Spring's door. "May I come in, Aunt Spring?"

"Yes, come in, Mary Tom."

She opened the door and closed it behind her, moving toward Spring.

"Please don't go, Aunt Spring. It's so boring when you're not here. Please stay here with us."

"I'll be back, Mary Tom. You know I always come back. This is my home."

"Then why are you leaving?"

Spring looked at her and wondered how she could explain. "We can't stay at home all our lives,

Mary Tom. We have to find our own place in life and make our own homes. Would you please hand me that blouse hanging over there?"

Mary Tom sat down on the bed beside the open suitcase and looked around at all the personal things that Spring had laid out...the clothes from Virginia, the interesting clothes from South Dakota, her jewelry, especially the Indian jewelry with the many colored beads, and then her eyes caught the picture. "Oh, Aunt Spring, it's *beautiful!*"

Spring followed her eyes to the *Dogwoods*. At least, that's what she called it for now. Pride welled within her every time she looked at it, and especially when someone—even Mary Tom—praised it.

"It's the picture you did up at Lover's Leap, isn't it? You must have spent a lot of time on it, all the many times you went up there. I used to wonder how you could like doing something that caused you so much work, but now I sort of understand. I guess it's worth it."

"You're right, Mary Tom. It's worth it. I don't really enjoy the actual work of painting, but it's the end result that makes me happy, that is—if it turns out the way I want it to. You see, if I can succeed in putting down on canvas what I have up here, (she pointed to her head) then I have my enjoyment, but only then. If I cannot accomplish that, I am quite frustrated for days."

"I think I understand. Aunt Spring, why do you paint?" she asked, rather seriously.

Spring was silent for a moment.

"I think about how short life is, Mary Tom, and

all too soon it is over. I want to do something with my life that will last. I think that's why painting is so important to me. For some people—it's writing. Maybe after I'm gone, my work will live on. It will be a part of me."

"When did you first start painting?"

"Oh, I think when Father brought me my first box of crayons. I'll never forget that first box. I remember wanting to color something really special, not just an ordinary coloring book. I was never interested in them. Instead, I would create my own picture with the crayons. I think I had the same desire even then when I was so young. I wanted to do something special, not ordinary. Sometimes, it worries me though. Life is slipping by, and I still haven't done anything really special, you know, *really* special—something that no one else has done, like climbing the highest mountain or being the first woman president or just helping people in a way no one else has ever done. Oh, you probably think me strange— I think myself so sometimes."

"No, no, Aunt Spring. I want to be just like you!"

Spring smiled at her.

"I don't want to be like the other women in this family. I want to be like you. You're different. Who cares about cooking, cleaning and sewing? That's boring. Mama's boring, Aunt Ellen is boring, Grandma is boring...."

"Wait a minute, Mary Tom, that's not really fair. Everyone is different. Take your Grandma for instance. Why, she's unique in herself. She is a tower of strength...she is the knot that holds the rope together...she is the most special person in my life. Mother has given herself to others in a way that I could never do. She is totally unselfish. Her family—Father, Prudence, Patrick, Jonathon, me, you and all the rest—we're the center of her life. But she is more than just a Mother to us...she is a *friend*. She has lived an inspiring life before us as far back as I can remember. She has encouraged us to seek the deeper and more important things in life. In fact, I credit much of my own desires to her."

"Gee, Aunt Spring, I know Grandma's special, but I mean, you're different...you know...like painting, making something of your very own."

"Did you know your Grandmother writes poetry?"

"Grandma never told me that!"

"Well, you wait until one day when it's just the two of you here, and then ask her about it—she'll show you."

Mary Tom had moved over to the dresser, examining each piece of jewelry as she talked.

"Aunt Spring, what's this?" she held up a stone that had been put onto a silver chain. It was obviously a homemade necklace.

Spring reached for the necklace. "It's just a necklace, Mary Tom."

"Where did you get it?" Mary Tom's curiosity began to quicken.

"It's a gift...a gift from a friend, Mary Tom. Now, how about checking with Mother to see if we can help with lunch."

"Okay, but Aunt Spring, will you write me when

you get to South Dakota?"

"Of course, silly one, now go."

Mary Tom danced out of the room calling, "Grandma, Grandma, Aunt Spring has promised to write me when she gets to South Dakota."

Spring sat down on the bed with the stone necklace in her hand. She rubbed its rough surface and remembered him and how happy she had been when he'd given it to her. She had tried to give it back because it had been in the family for so many years, and it was a definite link to his Indian heritage. But he'd refused. Even to the end, he'd wanted her to have it. She was glad. Somehow, it was if she'd always have a little part of him with her even if she couldn't have him. She gently placed it in the suitcase.

The night before the honeymooners were due home, there was a terrible storm, and the wind whipped the trees nearly down to the ground. The rain poured in bucketfulls, and the loud thunder was earthshaking. Emily lay still in her bed, remembering another storm. She thought of Charity, and wondered if those beautiful, blue eyes could see her now. Was she looking down from heaven, maybe tucked under Jesus' arm? "I love you, Honey," she whispered into the dark that was soon lit again with brilliant lightning.

One day I'll see her again, she thought, but then another loud clap of thunder burst through her tender thoughts and brought the flood—that terrible flood—back once more. I wish Heath were here to hold me close, she thought. Suddenly another burst of thunder... and another...and another. She pulled the covers over her head. She remembered how cold and dark it was on that terrible night and how she ached. Oh, the aching...she could almost feel the rough and slimy piece of debris beneath her. It was so horrible—*so* horrible.

She sat up. I must get these thoughts out of my mind. I wish Heath was here. It was the first time in years she had gone to bed without him, but he'd gone over to the hospital to stay with his Father. It was his turn. Poor old Mr. Barrett, she thought. He was lying at the point of death. But it was not like the storm of many years ago. Heath was so good to her now and had been for so many years, but that night he wasn't there.

Betty Lou—whatever happened to Betty Lou? How many times she'd wondered that through the years, but not now. Now she knew. Had she come back to haunt her even more?

Jessica, beautiful Jessica, her new Daughter-In-Law. There was something about her—something she'd pushed way back in her mind and had been trying to keep it there, but now this storm was flinging open those doors and exposing the horrible thoughts. No—she didn't want to think about it. Why, after all these years? Why, after all these wonderful years with Heath and her family and Jonathon...*why* was this turning up now? And Jonathon—was he to be the victim? Jonathon, her baby. What was there in the Bible about that? Another ear shattering burst of thunder. She crawled back under the covers. Let me think now...the sins of the father are visited upon the children down to the third and fourth generation. She remembered reading it several times. "Oh Lord, can it be true?" she asked out loud.

Lightning lit up the room again, and she saw Jonathon's military picture on the bureau. Is it possible that she could be Heath's child? That's it. Get it out in the open. Heath's child! What a paradox! Jonathon married to his sister. No, maybe I'm going crazy, imagining all of this.

But no, there's something about her, something probably only I would see because of my love for Heath. Most likely no one else would ever see it, especially Jonathon. But what about Heath? Would *he*? She shrunk beneath the covers, the frightening thoughts crowding in upon her as the storm raged. Its power and force seemed to shake the house. She was scared and alone, but then she remembered. *"I will never leave thee nor forsake thee...."* She lay back on her pillow and smiled to herself. Silly lady, Miss Emily, why are you afraid of the storm outside or the storms within? Hasn't He been with you through all the many storms of life? Of course. She felt comforted, and for the rest of the storm, she lay still and felt that old, familiar closeness to God she'd known so often. Suddenly, she had the urge to express her feelings and rose from the bed and went into the living room. She felt safe enough to turn on the lamp as the storm was finally subsiding. She picked up Mary Tom's pen and notebook left lying on the couch, and she reached for her Bible. What did it have to say about storms? She must express her feelings...

Fear clutched at me as I lay in awe
Of Nature's twisting pain...
A sky of brilliant illuminated vastness
Sent forth its angry rain...

Suddenly heaven and earth trembled
God thundereth with His voice...
He thundereth with the voice of His excellency
A powerful and mighty force...

Hear attentively the noise of his voice
And the sound that goeth out of His mouth...
Even the storm has its source
When it rages north and south...

As the lightning lighted the world
Striking its path without regard...
I thought I heard the thunderings speak
"Be still and know that I am God."

Emily once again had found peace midst troubling waters. She took the poem, the first she'd written in years, back to her bedroom, tucked it away in her bureau drawer, and went back to bed. *Be still and know that I am God.* She repeated it over and over as she fell into a tranquil sleep. The storm subsided.

A GOOD DISTANCE away, there lay one who did not know the meaning of those words. The storm had frightened her also, and she lay wrapped in Jonathon's arms. He had not wakened during the storm. At first, she was going to wake him, but then decided against it. She wanted to be alone with her thoughts. Tomorrow was the day, she smiled to herself. Tomorrow she would see him squirm. Yes, Mother would be proud of her—hadn't she accomplished the impossible? But it wasn't so hard after all. In fact, she was really enjoying Jonathon. Could she be falling in love? Now, that wasn't in the plan. She stroked his thick, wavy hair. He is really sweet. How can I *not* care for him? Mr. Barrett...Mr. Heath Barrett. Maybe she would be making a mistake revealing herself to him too soon. Of course, she knew he was thinking the truth already—she could tell. But maybe he'd tell Jonathon and Jonathon would hate her. That was stupid. Mr. Barrett would not tell Jonathon. Of course not—he's trapped. She almost laughed out loud.

The next morning, Emily stood in her kitchen looking out on a bright and beautiful day. What is it the Bible says...joy cometh in the morning? Yes, no matter how dark the night may be, and the darkness has a way of blowing up almost out of proportion any problem, who could be unhappy looking out at the beauty God has created? The sun was shining through the trees, and the raindrops beaded on the glistening leaves. The earth had enjoyed a bath and now stood proudly displaying itself. The green leaves drew a sharp contrast with the black tree trunks and the many varieties of wild flowers as they stretched themselves and soaked up the morning sun.

"Good morning, Mother." Spring came into the kitchen.

"Spring, good morning...did the storm bother

you last night?"

"No, not really. I couldn't help but hear it, though."

"Yes, it was a terribly frightening storm. I'm surprised you're up so early. You have a long day ahead of you."

Spring hesitated before answering. "Well, I wanted to see you alone before leaving."

Emily noticed the tell-tale signs on her lovely face and wondered how much of the night she'd spent crying.

"I hate to leave you, Mother...and everyone, but I have to. I have to get away and get on with the real purpose in my life."

"I'm sorry, Dear, that things turned out the way they did, and I know you hurt deeply now—but time heals. Yes, to everything there is a season. A time to weep, and a time to laugh. You have had your share of weeping, and I feel there is up ahead for you a lot of happiness somewhere."

"I hope so, Mother. But one thing I've decided— I will never be ashamed of being Indian, and I feel there is something important I must do, and I am on the verge of it."

Emily wondered what she meant.

"I doubt it will ever happen, but just in case...just in case he ever does come by...tell him, tell him I'm with my people, serving them."

"Serving them?"

"I don't know exactly how yet. It's sort of like a gigantic puzzle lying in front of me, and it's all jumbled up, but I'm beginning to fit a few pieces together now.

You know, my people are overlooked by everyone—
the government—even themselves. It is sad to see
what has become of a once noble and proud race. If I
can, even in just a little way, restore some of that
nobility and pride—then my life will have counted for
something. I believe I'm to use the talents God has
given me...yes...God. I know something much
higher than me has given me these talents. My
painting. You know, there's such sadness and rejection in the faces of my people. I must capture this and
show it to the world—make them realize what they've
done. And not only my painting, they need someone
to speak for them...to be a voice for them, and *you*
know, Mother, better than anyone, that I'm capable of
speaking my mind. Well, I can speak the mind of my
people...." She turned and looked at her Mother.

Emily smiled at her rather sadly. "Why do I feel
like I'm losing my Daughter?"

They embraced and shared the tears.

That evening, Jonathon and Jessica arrived later
than expected, and everyone was waiting on them for
supper. Everyone except Spring, who chose to leave
early, as soon as Heath returned from the hospital.
Even with the news that old Mr. Barrett might not
make it through the week, she still left. But then,
Spring had no real love for the Barretts, and under-
standably so.

Jonathon bounced in, and the entire family could
plainly see he was still up in the clouds. Jessica was
more cool and reserved than before.

"Where's old Patrick?" Jonathon asked immediately. Though they didn't have much in common,

they were still close, the only brothers.

"He couldn't make it tonight, Jonathon," Ellen answered. "He had to call on old Mrs. Spencer, you remember her. She's very ill, and she's been asking for him."

"Yeah, I forgot about his parishioners and all that, still getting used to a Preacher Brother," Jonathon added, a bit disappointed.

Mary Tom rushed to his side. "*Now*, can you tell us where you went?"

"My, my, Little One, if I told you where, then you wouldn't have anything to think about...."

"Don't worry, Jonathon. She has lots to think about. A lot of school work," Prudence added.

"Oh, Mom..." Mary Tom complained.

"Well, Dear, we held supper for you two, so let's all get to the kitchen," Emily said with a warm smile at Jessica.

Jessica felt uncomfortable again.

The evening wore on. First supper, then talk. Jessica wondered if she would ever get the chance to be alone with Mr. Barrett. She could see that it was next to impossible to be alone with anyone in this busy household.

Finally it happened. Everyone was in the kitchen debating whether Spring would return in three months, six months, a year, or even longer. Jessica couldn't care less. In fact, she was *glad* that Spring had left. She sat on the edge of the couch and Heath was in his chair, pretending to read a magazine.

"Mr. Barrett," she spoke with confidence, "or,

could I call you 'Father' now?"

He looked up, stunned.

"Would you mind?" she persisted with a sinister smile.

"No...of course not," he answered, still not sure what she was implying.

"That's good, Father—I know Mother would be quite happy." With that she watched him squirm. He just stared at her, not knowing what to do or say. He could feel the blood rushing to his face. Just then, Jonathon walked in.

"Well, Dad, what do you think of this little prize I got?" he asked as he hugged her to him. Heath, still in shock, answered, "Fine, Son...fine."

Jessica smiled up at Jonathon with that little girl look of hers that melted his heart, and he squeezed her to him.

Old Mr. Barrett died the next day. After all the funeral proceedings, Jonathon moved into the Smith household with Jessica, temporarily. Emily and Heath moved about the house alone now. She couldn't help noticing the change in Heath lately. He seemed so preoccupied and worried these days.

One morning, she sat at the kitchen table alone and looked around her home. It was a comfort that these old walls didn't change. Everything else seemed to. Life had a way of changing, people changed, but this old cabin always stayed the same. Of course, Heath had made some good changes in it years ago, after the flood. It wasn't big enough for all of them then, and he'd added the two back rooms and did quite a bit of remodeling to make it more comfortable, but basically it was the same.

It's funny, she thought, but she had never enjoyed the new house nearly as much. Maybe it was because it sat down in the valley, all alone, without trees, hills and streams nearby. Yes, the cabin seemed a part of the mountain itself, a part of God's creation. That's why she loved it so.

While Emily sat thinking, Heath was on his way home. He had left that morning for work, but decided he couldn't go on another day carrying this burden. He must talk to Emily.

When he entered the house, Emily sensed the reason for his return. He sat down across from her. "Emily, Honey, there's something I want to talk to you about."

"Yes?"

He hesitated.

"It's about Jessica," he finally said. Emily saw the torment spreading over his face.

"She's...." Again he hesitated, groping for the right words when there weren't any.

Emily reached out and placed her hand on his. "She's yours, isn't she?"

Heath looked up, startled. "You knew?"

"Not until I met her. She has a part of you, Heath, like all your children do."

The tears began to roll down his aging face. "I'm so sorry, Honey...*so* sorry...."

"It's over now and has been for a long time," she said weakly.

"I would have told you, and maybe I should have, but after the flood, I really thought she was dead. I couldn't see where telling you could do any good, and I didn't want to hurt you, Emily. You had been hurt enough. I never cared for her, really—I want you to know that."

"I know," she said calmly.

"But what are we going to do now?" he asked. "You know, the Bible says, 'your sin is ever before you'. I've been thinking about that a lot these days. 'Whatsoever a man soweth, that shall he also reap'. How true."

"That is true, Heath, but God has forgiven you for your sin. Don't condemn yourself. The Bible also says, 'There is therefore no condemnation to them which are in Christ Jesus, who walk not after the flesh, but after thy Spirit."

"Yes, I know that, and I know He has forgiven me, that's why I have loved Him and lived for Him these many years. But still, God's laws are like the law of gravity. What goes up must come down. Whatsoever a man soweth, that shall he also reap. I sowed the wild seed, the sin, the ugliness, and now it's reaping time." He dropped his head into his hands and began to weep. "But why Jonathon? Why does *he* have to suffer?"

Emily went to him, wrapped her arms around him, and uselessly fought back her own tears.

She wiped them with her apron. "Maybe he won't. He sure doesn't seem to be suffering now. I've never seen him happier. It certainly is ironic that the two should meet and marry, but...."

"It isn't ironic, Emily. It was planned."

"What do you mean?"

"Jessica. I'm sure she's planned the whole thing to get back at me," he stood up and walked over to the window.

"Heath, why do you say such a thing?"

He turned to her. "She as much as told me so the other day."

Emily could no longer suppress her hidden fears, "What did she say?"

He told her everything.

Emily sat, quite stunned. "I find all this hard to believe, Heath. Why...how could such a beautiful, young girl want to ruin her life by marrying someone just to get back at someone else?"

"I believe her Mother fed these plans into her for many years, filled her with bitterness, and who am I to blame her—it is my fault, too."

"There is only one thing we can do, Heath."

They joined hands, went into the living room, and kneeling to the floor in front of the couch, they prayed.

Part III

Third Generation

Chapter X
Third Generation

The heavy plane lifted off the ground with its engines blasting at full speed. Spring sat tensely as its nose climbed higher and higher, forcing her head against the headrest. It pushed upward with a mighty force until it began to level somewhat.

She breathed a sigh of relief. Would she ever get used to it? How many times had she gone through the same thing? Too many times to count now. She looked out the window at the dismal skies and the gloom of Sioux Falls that lay beneath them. She was glad to be leaving.

Suddenly the plane was smothered in a grayish-green mist. She hated that feeling—cut off from the rest of the world, so helpless in this man-made invention. But then the 747 lifted above the clouds, soaring like a dove, and a glaring, bright sun lit the sky and bounced off the massive wings.

She pressed her head against the small window. A thick, puffy, glowing white carpet lay beneath them in soft folds resembling a glacier land—no—she thought, not a glacier, but cotton, like cotton candy Dad used to bring home when he'd been over to Spottswood.

Daddy—where had the time gone? Had she been so busy, so preoccupied with her own life that she had neglected him? But one *must* pursue one's own path. She still held the crumpled telegram in her hand and opening it, she read again the brief but bitter message—HURRY HOME. DAD VERY ILL! She had dropped everything and caught the first plane out of South Dakota. But was that enough? How long had it been since she'd been home? Two years? No, it would be three in May. She had meant to get home for Christmas, but that blasted banquet had popped up at the last minute. Of course, she *had* to be present. Banquets, meetings, speeches, art shows...there was always something. Her life had been so busy now for many years.

She remembered the day she'd left those Virginia mountains for good, right after Jonathan had married. Gosh, and they had just celebrated their twentieth wedding anniversary. Where had the years gone? She had left with such mixed feelings. It seemed so long ago.

She had accomplished what she'd set out to do, but was it at the sacrifice of her own life? No, she had made her choice.

All the years of loneliness, of antagonizing debates, of tangible hostility toward her, of rejection and the many times of just simply being ignored—it was all worth it now. Changes were taking place, slowly, but they *were* taking place. America was finally recognizing the oldest American of all—the Indian. He was human—he had rights—rights that had been taken away from him. America was seeing her mistake, but as nature would have it—it was too late to make it right again. He had no wide open ranges to hunt any more—there were no buffalo—he could not return to his glorious past and history. Instead, he must accept the white man's way of living—it was the only way left. But he could have pride, pride in himself, pride in his heritage.

She felt that her greatest accomplishment was that—being able to instill pride within her people—change their defeated attitudes. "Don't feel inferior to the white man—you are not. *We* are not! Did not the great White God in the sky make us all? We are equal in his sight." She had told them that over and over again wherever and whenever she spoke. She could hear herself going on and on. "Be proud of yourself—you—the first American. Our ancestors were the greatest hunters that ever lived—brave and proud men, resourceful, able to conquer the frontier and provide for their families with honor. You are their sons and daughters—you have their blood."

She could still see those hundreds of people standing that night at the Christmas banquet—standing for *her*—a standing ovation. All these people were with her now. The road wasn't as lonely as it had been those first years.

"Hello, you're Miss Spring Barrett, aren't you?" A

tall, slim girl in her twenties stood over her smiling. "I've seen your pictures in the paper, and I've always admired you so...your courage and all. Would you mind if I sat down?"

"Why no, please have a seat. And your name?"

"Jane...Jane Mayberry."

"That sounds like a good southern name," Spring kidded.

"It is, Kentucky. That's home, and that's where I'm headed now. I can hardly wait. It's been four years since I've been home."

"My, that's a long time. We're sort of in the same boat, or I might say plane. It's been a good while since I've been home, too."

"Oh, really? I thought your home *was* in South Dakota?"

"It is—but I have two homes. The other one is Virginia. In the mountains of Virginia, nestled among the tall, oak trees, is a quaint, little log cabin. That's where I'm going now."

"How romantic," the young girl said seriously.

"Are you a romantic, too?"

"I guess so. At least everyone tells me I am. I suppose it's true. I would be most unhappy if I had to live totally in reality. It can be so harsh or so dull at times. I prefer to dream, to imagine, to hope...."

"You have the right idea, Jane. Don't ever stop dreaming. If you do—life won't be worth living."

Jane stared at her with admiration. "But you're a great artist...a great leader. You have done something... something that everyone knows about. You're not a dreamer, you're a great person!"

"Oh, but I *am*, Jane. I *am* a dreamer. One must have the dream before it can ever become a reality. Ever since I was a little girl, I have dreamed that someday I would do something—something really worthwhile. I just *had* to. My life couldn't just be an ordinary life. That's why painting has always been so important to me. It allows me to dream, imagine, and hope that what I paint will live after me and speak for me."

"Oh, Miss Barrett, I love your paintings. I've seen many of them hanging in the Great American Museum in Sioux Falls. But my favorite is the one of the old, Indian man sitting on the stump by the Platt River. Such feeling is expressed in his aging face, such sadness, such emptiness."

"You *see* it! Then I have communicated. That's what's important. The old man has spoken to you from the depths of his soul. Did the stump mean anything to you?"

"Well, it seemed to be part of the old man, as if the two shared something."

Spring's black eyes sparkled.

The young girl continued, "Yes, it was if they both—the old man and the stump shared something, being cut off...both left without hope...their past wiped out...their future impossible."

"You have it, Dear." Spring was delighted. "You've grasped the meaning. So many don't. And what about the river flowing past them?"

The young girl's face dropped. "The river—it only seemed apart from them, apart from the rest of the picture somehow."

"But you're *right*. You see, the river is a sharp contrast, flowing beside the two, full of life and vigor, flowing swiftly, going somewhere, having somewhere *to* go. A symbol that life goes on—it must continue no matter what. So you see, there is hope for the old man, not for him specifically, for his life is drawing to a close and not for the tree, of course—but for their young. Many more saplings will spring up again beside the Platt River, and more sons will be born from the old man's seed. You see, they have hope yet!"

"That is what I like most about your paintings, Miss Barrett. They say something. I saw another one in a magazine a few weeks ago. A little girl with big, black eyes, and she seemed to almost be reaching out from the page. She was dressed in the usual Indian clothes, but they were tattered and not too clean, and her hair was all mussed. She was perched on a big boulder, or rock, and she was watching a large locomotive rolling down the tracks a few yards from her. I saw the contrast that time."

"Yes?" Spring interrupted with a certain amount of impatience.

"The powerful locomotive barrelling down the tracks, cutting its way across the desert with dust rolling away from its sides, making way for progress. Its cars loaded down with coal to fuel the mighty factories in the big cities...and the little girl, with fear in her eyes as she clutched the rock."

"Jane, that little girl was me."

"Really!"

"You flatter me, Jane Mayberry. I only wish everyone had your sense of perception."

"Thank you, Miss Barrett...I guess I'd better get back to my seat. It has been a real honor meeting you."

"You too, Jane. Always remember—keep on dreaming."

The young girl smiled down at her and walked away.

Spring was suddenly brought back to her reason for being there. Her Father. How ill was he? She looked at her watch and figured she should be home by evening. Her anxiety increased. She began to rub the stone that hung from her neck, then caught herself.

She lifted the necklace from her breast and smiled. Why after all these years did she still think of him, and wonder if she might see him again when she returned home? Of course, he was married most likely and probably had a house full of children. But she would always have a place for him in her heart, hidden away in a special corner. She wondered if he'd ever found out the truth. She would like to be able to tell him, but then would he really care? Probably not.

We were not of the same mind then, and most likely still aren't. But she would always be grateful for that experience because it was the beginning for her in finding herself and her purpose in life.

It was ironic, however, that he would be a descendent of her people, the Sioux. She had found out many interesting things through all her studies and research of the American Indian and his heritage—but the research that revealed that the Monacan tribes in the Virginia mountains were actually descendants of the great Sioux nation was the most rewarding. She thought of him as a brother now, no longer a lover.

Smiling to herself, she recited the words from her book: "A lover she could never see, a brother he would always be." She thought of her almost completed autobiography back in South Dakota lying in her study. But what would the last chapter hold? She was afraid to think of it.

As the large aircraft soared over the plains and headed for the Blue Ridge Mountains, Spring yearned to see her Father, but all the power of those mighty engines could not get her there in time. Death hung over the mountain cabin as a heavy mist after a summer rain.

The cabin stood out alone among the skeletons of trees climbing the mountainside. The family was gathered in the living room. They talked in whispers as Heath lay in the bedroom. The doctor was with him. All heads turned in expectation as the doctor came out, shook his head sadly and took a seat with them. He reached over and patted Emily on the hand. She responded with a weak smile and rose to go back to Heath.

She stood in the doorway and looked at that tired face, now white instead of tanned as it had always been. His eyes were closed, and he lay very still. She moved slowly toward the bed trying not to disturb him, but as soon as she sat beside him, he spoke, or rather whispered, "Emily?"

She reached out and touched him with tears in her eyes. "Yes, Dear."

"Come closer," he whispered.

She moved closer, and his right hand found hers. Then he was quiet again, falling back into a deep, tranquil sleep. She relaxed and prepared to sit there as long as he held her hand. Only when he was sound asleep again would she go out. She felt hungry, but knew she couldn't eat.

She smoothed his thin, gray hair back, remembering when it was thick and dark. He had been some charmer and some catch. How envious her friends had been when they married. And now after all these years, and yes...all those heartaches too, she was glad she'd found him. What would life have been without him? Oh, it hurt to remember those bad years, but she had a way of blocking them out and filling her thoughts with all the good times. All the love and warmth they'd shared, especially for the last many, many years. She couldn't remember how many now.

It seemed so long ago. And could she blame him totally? No. She had always felt like she was to blame also. "Whatsoever a man soweth, that shall he also reap." She'd always believed that because of her mistake—or sin—before marriage, she had suffered the heartaches.

She kept these thoughts to herself as she had always done and believed them to be the thorn that she'd had to bear. But in spite of the heartaches, life had been good to her. She had a beautiful family.

Suddenly, he squeezed her hand with what little strength he had left and looked up at her. Love flowed through those familiar eyes, the same eyes she'd looked into so many years. She fought back the tears. She must not cry. A weak smile spread over his face, and she smiled back. But then the door flew open and Jessica was standing beside them, tears flowing down her face.

"Jessica, come back!" Jonathan called from the door. His face was distraught. Emily looked at Heath, who motioned it was alright with the slight movement of his head.

"It's alright, Jonathan," Emily said, and Jonathan turned away. He was taking this awfully hard. Jessica still stood there speechless as the tears flowed. Heath let go of Emily's hand and reached for Jessica. She grabbed his hand and fell to the floor sobbing.

"It's alright, Child," he whispered and smiled at her again. "I love you."

"I love you, Father." She looked at Emily, and Emily nodded that everything was all right. Still crying, Jessica left. Emily sat back down beside him, not saying a word, but searching his eyes with love.

"Now all my Children have said good-bye except Spring. Is she here?"

"Not yet, Dear. She's on her way, though." As she spoke, she so wished Spring was here.

"If she doesn't make it, tell her I'm proud of her."

She struggled not to cry.

"I'm ready to go, Honey...and I'm looking forward to it...to see Jesus...but I don't want to leave you...." A lone tear ran down his wrinkled, pale face.

She couldn't fight them anymore, and the tears flowed as she laid her head upon his chest, and they embraced for the last time. Between sobs, she said, "But we're only parting for a little while... remember." She sat up and looked down at him, "to death do us part. But we will meet again on the other side, with Charity and Little David."

"I'll be waiting," he whispered and closed his eyes for the last time.

AS SPRING MADE her way up the mountainside in the rented Chevrolet, she wished she had her own car. Its valves didn't knock. She remembered Jonathan's eyes when she'd driven it down on her last visit. Of course, it was brand new then, and he'd fallen in love with it.

Poor baby brother Jonathan. What kind of life had he had with a crazy wife. Now, that wasn't nice. She isn't crazy, but somewhat unstable, the good doctor says. Unstable all right! Who would do the things she'd done if they were stable? She remembered the time she'd run out into the woods barefoot in the snow. It had taken more than an hour to find her, and she was almost frozen. It's a good thing she was in Virginia and not South Dakota. She would certainly have frozen there. It's different here in Virginia, and the snow is different, too.

She glanced around the countryside at the new fallen snow as it turned the mountain into a fairyland glistening white. It clung to each tiny needle on every pine tree creating a sad and forlorn look for them as they bowed their heads to the snowy carpet beneath. Every skeleton—oak, poplar, wild cherry—was now clothed in its frosty dress. Normally this scene would have brought great joy to Spring, but not today.

"Doggone it!" she exclaimed out loud, "of all the times to snow." She had been delayed in Pittsburgh due to the snow storm and had to stay over. She had tried to call, but the phones into Oak Mountain were out. "Is he okay?" she wondered. "I'll soon know." She was nearing home now, and the familiar roads brought back so many memories. Even though she'd driven these roads many times, and often in snow, she was especially cautious today. She must not get stuck. She must get home.

Her mind took over again. What if anything happened to Father? What in the world would Mama do? She couldn't imagine one without the other. It must really be something to have what they have. So many times she'd wished she could have the same thing, but it seemed she was destined to walk her earthly journey alone. Twice now love had passed her by, and wasn't it ironic that both times it was her own sense of belonging that had caused it. She was too much Indian for her first love and too much white for her second. There was still a little pain when she thought of him. She'd left him in South Dakota with his bitterness for the white man, a bitterness she couldn't live with. How could she? She'd grown up as a white person, learned how to laugh, to cry and to love, all from the white man. She would always walk that middle road, treacherously balanced between the two.

The back of the car slid a bit, and she slowed down. Even though she was quite used to driving in snow, almost constantly in South Dakota, these mountains were something else. She was almost in sight of the house now, and her anxiety quickened. One more bend. There, she could see the smoke rising from the chimney. Yes, there it was—home. It hadn't changed, the same little cabin, but...her heart stopped. Hanging beside the rough-hewn door was a wreath. *"No, no, no!"* she cried as she came to a screeching halt.

AFTER THE FUNERAL, the family hovered close to the cabin and to Emily. They would go to their respective homes for a while only to return to make sure Emily was okay or maybe just to touch base with home again. But home wasn't the same...Emily wasn't the same.

Patrick was head of the family now and took his rightful place, making most of the decisions. He was so calm and stable as he went about ministering to the rest of the family, and Ellen stood beside him adding more strength. Prudence carried her grief silently, her own faith sustaining her. She was the strength of her family. Melony had left Atlanta with her husband, Jack, and their baby daughter, as soon as she heard. Mary Tom, of course, was not there. It had been seven years now that she and her husband, Dan, had been in Africa as missionaries. David, of course, was also gone, still in Vietnam.

But there was still much activity with teenagers fleeting in and out. Ellen had given Patrick three more children, almost one every year after David. Esther was next, then Paul and then Mark. The remaining teenager belonged to Jonathan and Jessica—Heath III. My, how proud they were of him. Their first was stillborn, and then Jessica had miscarried two before Heath was finally born normal and healthy.

Everyone was concerned for the first year about whether he might have inherited some of his Mother's eccentric ways, but then they saw that this grandchild was more intelligent and gifted than all the others. His

Mother's depression and days of crying hadn't affected him either. In fact, he was so well adjusted that the other kids turned to him for leadership. Sometimes he seemed more the father to Jessica than she the mother to him. His stability was a help to her and through the years, she had begun to improve.

Oddly enough, Spring seemed to take her Father's death the hardest. In spite of the fact that she had been away from him for years, she found it difficult to accept. But, of course, he was the only real male figure in her life, and even though she chose to spend most of her life elsewhere, she always knew he was *there.*

It was almost a week now since Heath had passed away, and Emily sat by the living room window watching the snow begin to fall. How she'd always loved to watch the snow, but her heart ached today. Oh, how she missed him! Prudence and Ellen were making fudge in the kitchen, and she could smell its sweet aroma drifting toward her. Fudge was one of the few sweets that she loved, and she remembered how Heath had always kidded her by hiding it and pretending he'd eaten the last pieces.

How could she live without him? Everything was a reminder of him. Baby Emily squealed out in delight as Esther tickled her. She watched them roll and tumble on the floor. It was so sweet of Melony to name her after herself. She wondered what this little Emily's life would be like. She began to think of her own, such a full life. Would she change anything if she could? Maybe so, maybe the heartaches—but then, would she have learned all the valuable lessons if she had not experienced them? Could she have enjoyed the ecstasy of the mountains if she had not experienced the valleys?

She watched the boys, Paul, Mark and Heath, cutting up with each other just outside the window. They were really enjoying the crisp, cold air and the snow gently falling upon them. Spring and Patrick were walking out beyond the chicken house—she could barely see them. They seemed to be engaged in deep conversation. They talked a lot these days. She was happy to have her family so near, but suddenly she felt all alone.

She never dreamed she would miss him so. She remembered him lying on the bed when he had his first attack, and they knew it was only a matter of time. Paul, Mark, and Heath had gathered around his bed. She could almost hear him saying, "Boys, you see that young lady standing there?"

They had all turned and looked at her in surprise. Their youthful eyes could only see an old woman, their Grandmother, in fact. "Maybe you don't," he continued, "but *I* do. She's still the beautiful lady that I married. She hasn't changed in my eyes. You boys look for a woman like her, like your Grandmother. Don't be satisfied with less. I wasn't always the man you've known, but she stood by me even then...God only knows how. She is not only the best grandmother and mother, but she has been my best friend."

A tear dropped on the window sill as she thought of those words—some of his last. She wiped her eyes with her apron and noticed the open tablet lying on the table beside her. Somebody most likely had been reading her poem. She picked it up and remembered the day she'd written it—to give him hope, and he'd liked it, too.

In fact, he'd said it was his favorite. She read...

The Oak

Look at it standing proud and tall
Reaching for the sun
As if to say to each and all
I'm a part of this mountain

The fierce Winter winds have come
And stripped the mountain bare
Of its mystic fairyland so awesome
Now death is everywhere

But the stubborn Oak puts up a fight
And teases old man Winter so
As it clutches its leaves
and holds them tight
Determined not to let them go

Just like the Oak—my Autumn is past
My youth has vanished and gone
And winter's shadows are being cast
But life so beautiful—I will hold on!

How strongly she'd felt about those words when she'd written them. But now? Would she put up a fight like the old oak? The snow was falling thickly now with very fine flakes. She saw two figures walking up the road and smiled to herself. Though the snow prevented her from seeing their faces, she knew them by their walk. A mother knows her children. It was Jonathan and Jessica walking hand in hand. After all these years, they were still in love, even through all the despair and heartache. She remembered the night she and Heath had kneeled down on their knees in this very room and prayed for them. God had answered—in His own good time.

There for a while, their faith was tested. Jessica had definitely married Jonathon for the wrong reasons. She had wanted revenge on Heath. She wanted to hurt him and hurt him she did. Over and over, she drove cutting remarks deeper into the open wound, and gloated over them. But he always responded, "Whatsoever a man soweth, that shall he also reap."

He accepted whatever she did or said with a certain resignation that overwhelmed her, but she sought to scheme up what she could do next. Her own bitterness and hatred almost destroyed her, eating within her the way no cancer can. She sunk into deep depression and spent days on end in bed crying and refusing to get up to face the world. She would fly into screaming rages threatening to kill herself or whoever the unlucky person was with her at one of those unfortunate times.

Four times Jonathan had her hospitalized, only to have her return to the same fate again. Emily cringed at the thought of the violent scene just before her last hospitalization.

It was on a very rainy morning. Heath had already gone, and she was alone. Jessica came storming into the house and appeared in her bedroom doorway looking like a mad woman. Her eyes were wild and crazed, and her thick, dark hair was in her face. She'd stared at her, and then turned to the dresser beside her and yanked the embroidered scarf off, tumbling bottles and jars of cream and makeup everywhere. Some broke as they shattered on the hard floor.

She remembered how horrified she'd been as this wild woman came at her, no longer the beautiful daughter-in-law, but some strange and dangerous creature that lunged at her. She recalled grabbing her arms to hold her off—how strong she was! It was all she could do to keep Jessica from hurting her before Jonathan arrived. As he carried her off struggling and yelling, she could still hear those words ringing in her ears, "It's *your* fault, *all* your fault. He loved *you*, he loved you more than *me*. More than *me*, an unborn child."

And of course, she was right, but why did it hurt her so? She watched them now join in the fun with the boys throwing snow at one another. She musn't think about those times. They were gone. Jessica was different now, almost totally well, they believed. She certainly hoped and prayed so.

Little Heath had done it. She began to change when he was born. Maybe it was due some to the fact that Heath loved this little Grandson—double Grandson—so much that everyone noticed it. And why shouldn't he? Heath III was so much like him, even more so than Jonathan. Jessica had been pleased with the special attention he showed her son, and it began to soften the wound she'd carried all her life. And maybe it was because this child was so special to her—after losing three. He was hers, really hers, and she loved him dearly.

It was still hard for Emily to believe that Betty Lou

could poison her own child by feeding her such destructive advice. But then, Betty Lou was a very cold person, most likely not capable of loving even her own child as one should. Who could blame the little, raven-haired girl as she grew to center her hatred on a father she'd never known. Jessica never knew real love until she met Jonathan. Emily recalled the day she came to her with her special news. She was pregnant again—for the fourth time. How she wanted a baby! She hadn't even told Jonathan this time—afraid something might happen again.

It was the morning she'd chosen to clean out the pantry, and Jessica had sought her out. "Mother?" she'd begun.

"Yes," Emily answered, drawing the curtain aside and wondering what this could mean.

"Mother, I need to talk with you," she continued, rather emphatically.

Emily placed her apple butter jars back on the shelf and straightened up. "Come sit at the table. I'll fix us some coffee."

Jessica sat down quietly, but came to the point quickly. "Mother, do you believe the reason we have not been able to have a baby is because...because of what we are? Is God punishing me? Or is He preventing it because he knows the baby will be...well, that the baby might have something wrong with it?"

Emily had not been prepared for this. Never had Jessica confided in her or even talked about personal things. A feeling of joy swept over her as she realized that this Daughter was finally accepting her as a Mother. She thought a while before answering, wanting to be very honest with her.

"Jessica Dear, God's ways are above the ways of man. Who can know them? As to whether God is punishing you, I don't know. Have you sought His forgiveness?"

"No. In fact, I have always pushed Him from my thoughts, not wanting to believe in a God that would deprive me of my own Father."

"God doesn't control the actions of mankind, Jessica. Instead, He has given man a free will to make his own decisions. And when your Mother and Heath decided to break God's law and do as they pleased—how can you blame God?"

Jessica was very quiet.

"I guess you're right," she finally answered. "But do you believe that if we had a baby, it might not be normal?"

"I don't know, Jessica. It has happened, but then it could happen to anyone." She was thinking of her own little Charity.

Jessica suddenly began to weep. "Then it will be... it will be...I just know it...."

"What is it, Jessica?" Emily put her arm around this distant daughter for the first time.

"I'm pregnant!" she blurted out between sobs.

Suddenly Emily understood all the questions. "How far are you, Jessica?"

"Five months, I think." She continued to cry.

"Then you may carry it." She thought of the last two Jessica had miscarried before three months.

"Yes, but what's the use, when it probably won't be, won't be..." she couldn't finish.

"Jessica, do you really want this baby?" Emily asked her calmly.

Jessica looked up into her eyes and answered, "I really do."

"Then Child, I can only tell you what I would do if I were in your shoes, which I'm not."

"What?"

"If I had wronged God, I would first make it right with Him and then beg His mercy. I would call upon Him and ask Him to protect my baby and give it to me normal and healthy. I would seek His face in the morning, in the noon and in the middle of the night when I would awaken...and I would make my request known to Him. I would not cease until I held my baby in my arms...a perfect gift from God. You know, Jesus tells a parable in the Bible about a certain man knocking on his friend's door at night asking for bread. His friend will not get up and open the door and give him any bread. But the man keeps on knocking until his friend does get up and gives him some bread. Jesus says, 'Ask, and it shall be given you, seek, and ye shall find, knock, and it shall be opened unto you.' "

"How, Mother? How do I knock...how do I seek?" she asked, drying her tears.

"Do you have to get home soon?"

"No, Jonathan will not be home until later."

"Then, why don't you come and have a seat in the living room?"

Emily handed her the family Bible as she sat down on the couch. "Read God's love book to us. This is St. John. Just read it slowly and thoughtfully while you rest. I'll just sit here and catch up on my knitting."

Jessica looked at her somewhat puzzled, but began to read. She hadn't read very long before she asked, "What does this mean, Mother? In the fourteenth verse it says, 'And the Word was made flesh, and dwelt among us', and then back up in the first two verses it says, 'In the beginning was the Word, and the Word was with God, and the Word was God. The same was in the beginning with God'. Is this Jesus?"

"That's right. The Word was with God, and the Word was God."

"I never knew that," Jessica said thoughtfully.

As Emily knitted, she prayed and asked God to speak to Jessica's heart. If she made peace with God, what a blessing it would be, not only to her, but to the whole family. She couldn't blame Jessica for her bitterness and revengeful ways. She had never blamed her. She had been hurt over the reality of her birth, and her Mother had fed this hurt every day of her young life, hoping one day that Jessica would get revenge...and she had.

Her Mother had not lived to glory in it, and Jessica had found no happiness in it either. Instead, she had become more and more discontented, being so near and yet so far away from her Father. She had woven the web that ultimately caught her.

In the beginning, she had yearned to reveal her secret to the whole family, forever disgracing Heath; yet she had dared not. She was truly falling in love with Jonathan more every day, and she feared he would despise her if he found out the truth. She bore the guilt that she had not been able to give Jonathan a child. She had teased Heath so much with her threats that he began to avoid her, and this hurt her even more.

All the while that she teased and dangled him on the end of her little finger, deep down she yearned to love him and be loved by him the way he loved his other children. Oh, wretched soul that I am, she often cried aloud, what can I do? The years passed.

Emily thought as she watched Jessica read the Bible. What now?

"Mother, are you born again?" she asked.

"Yes, Jessica. A long time ago I received Jesus Christ into my life and into my heart."

"Is that what it means to be born again? It says here, 'Except a man be born again, he cannot see the kingdom of God'. I thought you had to keep the ten commandments to get to Heaven."

"No, Jessica. No one can actually keep the ten commandments. We should try, of course. God wants us to, but He knows that we are imperfect beings not capable of keeping all of them. He says in the Bible that if we break one of them, we are guilty of breaking all of them. Who hasn't broken one of them? You see, God gave us the ten commandments as a rule to go by. If He hadn't given them to us, we wouldn't know what sin is. We have to have something to go by to know when we are transgressing."

"That makes sense. I used to wonder how anyone could keep all ten of them. So the way to Heaven is not by being good, but by being born again. But I don't know if I understand all this. How can you really be born again?"

Emily smiled. "You have asked the same question that Nicodemus asked in the next verse. Please read it aloud."

Jessica read. "Nicodemus saith unto him, how can a man be born when he is old? Can he enter the second time into his Mother's womb, and be born? Jesus answered, verily, verily, I say unto thee, except a man be born of water and of the Spirit, he cannot enter into the Kingdom of God."

Jessica stopped. "I don't understand. Born of water and the spirit?"

"As you well know, what is your baby protected by right now? What surrounds him?" Emily prodded.

"Water, of course." Jessica answered thoughtfully.

"That's right," Emily continued. "Born of water is our first birth into this world—we all experience that, of course. It brings us into the family of mankind. But we are not all born of the Spirit. Only those that trust God by faith in the finished work of Jesus Christ are born of the Spirit...the Spirit of God. That brings us into the family of God."

Jessica continued reading. "That which is born of the flesh is flesh; and that which is born of the Spirit is spirit. Marvel not that I said unto thee, Ye must be born again."

"Wow!" she exclaimed. "He says we MUST be born again."

Emily was silent.

"How can you know when you've been born again?"

"Read the next verse, Jessica."

"The wind bloweth where it willeth, and thou hearest the sound of it, but canst not tell from where it cometh, and where it goeth; so is every one that is born of the Spirit."

She looked up at Emily inquiringly with those big, blue eyes of hers.

"Have you ever seen the wind, Jessica?"

"Of course not. No one has. I mean I've seen the results, but you cannot see the wind itself. Oh...I see what it means."

"That's right. You can know by your changed life. The Bible also says, 'If any man be in Christ, he is a new creature, old things are passed away, behold all things are become new'."

"Is Father born again?" she asked rather meekly.

"Yes, he is. He's been a Christian for about as many years as you are old."

"I thought so," she said, and her voice began to tremble.

Emily stood up and moved toward her. "Jessica...."

"Oh, Mother, I've been such a fool. I hate myself, and I do want to change. I want God to forgive me, but it's such a mess. How can I ever undo what's been done?"

Emily searched for the right words to say. "Jessica Dear, you can't undo what's been done. But God will forgive you and give you a new life, if you really want Him to and are willing to repent and turn to Him. Then He'll guide you in working out your problems."

"Do you really think so, Mother?"

"I know so."

EMILY RUBBED HER SHOULDER that ached with arthritis as she recalled that day many years ago.

She remembered how they had both kneeled down together on their knees and prayed. Jessica had surrendered her will and life to God at that moment, and that was the turning point for them all. God had answered her prayers and given them a healthy, normal, bouncing baby boy...Heath III.

Emily glanced out the window again and saw young Heath trudging through the snow, pulling the old, wooden sleigh behind him. He laughed that boisterous laugh of his and challenged Mark and Paul to a sleigh ride. How time flies, she thought.

She remembered how Jessica could find no peace living a lie and decided to tell Jonathan everything when Heath was just a few months old. Instead of the hurt that Jessica and Emily had expected, he took it fine and seemed to love her all the more. In fact, because of the change in Jessica, Jonathan began to open up to the things of the Lord. Shortly thereafter, he, too, walked down the church aisle and committed his life to God. As Emily still watched them standing there in the snow talking, she felt proud of them...proud of all her big family. But she wondered whether they could fill that empty spot in her life now.

The snow began to fall again, and the two came inside.

"Mother, you have a letter!" Jessica said excitedly, handing it to her dripping with snow.

"Oh, I didn't know you two went for the mail. That was nice of you. It's from Mary Tom!"

Everyone crowded around, in awe of this brave and adventurous member of the family, who had forsaken all the ordinary pleasures of life for the hardships

of a missionary. Spring picked up the discarded envelope that Emily had dropped on the table: Ghana, Africa.

The envelope kindled warm thoughts in her mind.
She understood Mary Tom to a certain degree. She was
in the same camp, where purpose in life meant more
than one's personal happiness. But Mary Tom differed
in that she was, or rather seemed to be, totally happy.
At least, her letters depicted this. Of course, she had
Dan. Maybe that was the difference. Would she ever
know?

Emily finished reading the letter out loud, which
told of the progress they were making with the native
people. There they had put down roots, making their
home in a thatched hut. The letter spoke of hardships
and trials that the rest of the family couldn't comprehend. But reaching out between the lines, the joy came
forth from the pages as a sweet fragrance blowing in the
breeze.

Prudence wiped a tear from her eye as she did
every time she read a letter from Mary Tom. "I never
thought Mary Tom the type. It's really something how
she can be so happy there. I guess she hasn't gotten our
letter yet."

Melony rocked little Emily to her as the small
child slept. "When she does, Mother, she will be so hurt
that she wasn't here."

Little did they know that far across the vast
waters, entangled in the dense jungle, Mary Tom sat
with the letter in her hand. The tropical heat enveloped
the small hut, causing it to feel like an oven. She wiped
her wet forehead with her sleeve and sighed. "I feel like

I should have been there. I feel like I should be there now to comfort them," she said quietly to Dan who was watching her tenderly.

"Mary Tom," he spoke with compassion but with a firmness typical of his missionary character, "Jesus said, 'follow me, and let the dead bury their dead'."

"I know," she answered, "and I also know that Granddad would have me here doing the will of God. You know, he was so proud of me when I told him of our plans. I remember the smile on his face. He said, 'God has been so good to me. From my seed, the chiefest of the sinners as Paul, the Almighty has chosen to bring forth a preacher and now a missionary'. He ruffled my hair the way he used to do when I was small. 'My little tom-boy', he said, 'a missionary! You'll make a good one. I always knew you'd be special, but I didn't know *how* special'."

Dan sat down across from her. "Your Granddad was a good Christian. But don't be sad, you'll meet again one day."

"I know," she smiled, and holding hands, they got up and left the hut. Dan picked up his big, black Bible, and Mary Tom smiled up at him as they went out to their people.

DAYS PASSED INTO weeks. Life went on with the family again taking up their daily tasks, but Emily found herself walking from room to room waiting any minute to hear that familiar voice. "Emily, Emily, are you there, Honey?"

Sometimes she actually imagined he was in the room, and she would turn around suddenly only to face a blank wall. She would awaken in the morning with her first thoughts to arise and fix him breakfast as she'd done for so many years, only to realize that he wasn't there for her to care for any more.

She remembered the last words she'd spoken to him..."To death do us part." Yes, it had certainly parted as a sword would a cloth, quick and final!

Spring was just around the corner, and the family was busy planting potatoes, preparing the land for expected plentiful gardens, spring cleaning and just running to and fro. Emily watched all the activity, but from a distance. Oh, they all stopped by often enough, but she found herself sort of fading away from all the things that had been so important for so long. She seemed to weaken each day and preferred to just stay at home.

One morning, she was awakened by the birds singing just outside the cabin window, and she imagined that heaven might be just like this. What was that verse in the Bible? She often had a hard time recalling these days, what was it? Birds, birds, yes...the flowers appear on the earth, the time of the singing of the birds has come...yes, it's here again. She sighed. How many springs have I seen? After getting up and going through the motions of preparing breakfast, she sat down to eat, but just couldn't. She wasn't hungry. She rubbed her aching shoulder and pushed herself away from the table.

Pulling on her sweater, she opened the front door and went outside, breathing in the fresh morning air. The dew was just vanishing beneath the warm morning sun, and the early buds of spring popping up around the porch greeted her tired eyes. She slowly moved over to the swing and sat down, pushing it back and forth gently. As always, her thoughts were drawn to Heath. She remembered the first time she had sat in this swing—just a girl on their wedding night. She could almost feel his strong arms around her, caressing her. Where had all the years gone? They had slipped away unnoticed midst the busy activities of life. She had been so busy with her family. Her family...ah, but all my babies are gone now, she thought, even my grandbabies, except for little Emily.

She smiled to herself...Little Emily. What does life hold for this little Emily? She suddenly felt an urge to climb the hill beside the cabin. Walking slowly and steadily, trying not to fall, she breathed fast and hard as she reached the top. She held onto the bench that Patrick had made and placed here some time ago. She remembered how she used to practically skip up this hill. She sat down on the bench at the foot of the grave, and leaned over to pull weeds around it.

"Till Death us do Part." The engraved words stared back at her. On his left were two small graves. Tears fell on her wrinkled cheeks, and she looked up into the cloudless sky. "Lord, it looks like I'm not much needed down here any longer. You've been so good to me. All my family's in the fold except for Spring. Don't leave her out, Lord. And if my work be finished down here, I'd just as soon be joining You...and Heath...and my babies. But Lord, not my will but thine own be done...."

The sounds of screeching tires interrupted her prayer. Someone was coming. She better get back to the house.

"BUT HOW CAN we tell her?" Spring asked with a hint of frustration in her voice.

"I don't know, but we have to. We can't keep it from her any longer!" Jonathon answered.

"Mother, Mother..." Spring called out as she entered the cabin. "Where is she?"

"Maybe she's outside—it's such a pretty day." Jonathan turned, went outside and saw her coming down the hill looking so much older.

"Mother, where have you been?" Spring demanded, coming up beside him.

"To the cemetery."

"But you could have fallen and no one would have known. Next time, please wait for one of us to go with you."

"I'm just fine. What are you two all worked up about?" She was somewhat irritated as she always was when they treated her like a child. She had been thinking about that a lot lately. Why, all those years when they were children, who took care of them? Who were the children? Why now did they think that they had to tell her what to do and what not to do? She found herself resenting it. Old age was a traitor. Instead of giving one dignity that had been earned through the years—it surprised you with this!

"Now who says we're all worked up, Mama?" Jonathan asked with a smile, knowing they couldn't hide anything from her.

"I say so," she said, catching hold of his arm and pulling herself back up on the porch.

"Mother, we have some news, and it isn't good. Why don't we go in?" Spring was trying to break it gently.

"Are the children alright?" Emily asked suddenly.

"Yes, of course."

"Why then, I think I'll just sit here on the porch awhile, and enjoy this beautiful day. You two have a seat. Look at the crocus just peeping through. It's going to be a lovely spring. I can feel it in my bones. Now what is this news that has you all worked up?"

Jonathon and Spring exchanged worried looks.

"Mother," Jonathon began rather seriously, "the highway department is, or rather has, drawn up plans to put a new road...a highway...through these mountains, over to Spottswood, and...."

"And?" Emily looked confused.

"And it's supposed to come right through this property!" Jonathon finished, glad to have it out finally.

Emily looked around quietly, first toward the mountains towering above them, and then toward the valley down below, and then at the cabin and all the familiar trees that hugged it and protected it from the north winds. She studied the uneven planks on the porch floor, and then her eyes rested on the empty rocker at the other end of the porch...Heath's rocker. At least it was considered his the last years of his life. In the early years, it was hers as she had rocked her babies to sleep.

"We've been arguing with them for the last few months, Mother," Jonathon continued, "and we've done everything we know to stop them, but, it seems they have the law on their side. Oh, they're going to pay you for it, and pay you well, but we know how much this place means to you and all...."

Another car pushed up the mountain and came quickly to a stop. Patrick and Ellen got out and approached the porch.

Spring motioned to them that the news was out. Ellen went over to Emily and put her arms around her. "I'm sorry, Mother, but we couldn't stop them. Don't you worry though, you can come and live with us. You can have David's room. He would like that."

"Jessica and I would like for you to come and stay with us, too, Mother. It would be like old times back in the valley. We've already talked about it, and Jessica is already planning on how to fix up your room."

Jonathan and Jessica had bought the land from Heath and Emily where the house had stood when the flood came. They had built a nice home in the very spot where the old house had been.

"Wait...both of you." Spring interrupted. "Maybe Mother doesn't want to live with any of us. Maybe she wants a place of her own like she's used to. With the money from the highway department, we could easily build a nice little place for her, maybe close to Jonathon and Jessica on that lot next to you."

Turning to Emily, she said, "Mother, you could have a really nice, modern house like Mrs. Baxter's, you remember."

Emily looked at Spring with a blank look on her face. Her mind had been elsewhere. "Just when is this new road supposed to come through?" she asked calmly.

"Well, they're already working down at Silas Campbell's store...maybe by the beginning of summer.

Maybe sooner, maybe later, it'd be hard to say for sure," Patrick answered worriedly.

"Well then, what's all the fuss about? I still have time to fix y'all dinner." She arose slowly and started inside. "I'm so glad y'all stopped by."

Everyone looked at each other, rather puzzled.

"Mother, you don't seem surprised," Ellen said, following her in the door.

"No, I don't guess I am. I've seen some strange lookin' fellows up here every now and then snooping around. I figured something was up."

"Of course, you don't have to decide anything soon, Mother," Ellen continued. "You take your time and make up your mind as to what you want to do, but remember Patrick, the children, and I would love to have you come and live with us."

They all had lunch together and Emily enjoyed it as always, waiting on her children and listening to their chatter. But when they finally left, she went back out to the porch swing, alone with her thoughts. Somehow she didn't feel like she would have to make that decision. She had the most peaceful feeling that when the time came, a home would be provided for her. She inhaled the fresh air and let the gentle breeze caress her. "Delight thyself in the Lord, and He shall give you the desires of thine heart...." She smiled up at the clear, blue sky, but somehow those faded and tired eyes seemed to see on beyond.

Chapter XI
The Dogwoods Are Blooming

The powerful engines started up the mountain-side, echoing through the forest and bouncing off the cliffs. The giant Caterpillar leaped forward, coughed, and proceeded to tear its way through the woods, and the mountainside shook under its dynamic force.

The usual sounds of the singing, feathered creatures were drowned by the noise of the machinery and the husky yells of the workmen. The mountain residents had scampered off as soon as the first engine had blasted forth its alien sound. Now all that was left were the trees, abundantly clothed in another year's foliage, but soon to be victims of these raging enemies. The tall, sturdy oaks that had dominated Oak Mountain for centuries were now no match for the fearless masses of steel that forged ahead, making way for progress.

"Boy, look at that bulldozer. Ain't she a beaut!" A thin, red-headed, freckle-faced youngster yelled to his friend in the next tree. The two boys clung to the trees, watching all the excitement. So great was the temptation to see these foreign machines on Oak Mountain that they had skipped school.

"Yeah, let's stay up here all day and watch," the smaller, dark-haired boy yelled back.

"My Mama will give me 'down in the country' if she catches me—but she won't catch me. What do you have in your lunch?"

Tony, the smaller boy, pulled out a crumpled, brown bag from inside his shirt. "Looks like peanut butter and jelly."

"I'll trade ya. I got baloney," the red-headed youngster proposed, aware of his influence on his young friend.

"Sho thing, Pete."

The two boys sat perched on those trees for hours, watching the earth being turned over, scooped up, tossed and trodden under. They had quit yelling back and forth because their voices were drowned by the noise. Suddenly, all was quiet. Someone yelled, "Chowtime!"

All the men crawled down from their machines and found a cool spot under the trees. The sun was directly overhead now and beating down like a summer day.

"Hey, Fred, what'd ya new, little bride fix ya for lunch t'day?" A big, burly, bald-headed man yelled over to a somewhat younger fellow with nice sandy hair.

"How about left over fried chicken, potato salad

and apple pie for dessert," the young fellow replied with a grin.

"Beats my Spam sandwiches," the big guy said with a boisterous, grinding laugh. "Maybe I need to get married again...."

"Think maybe packing your own lunch'd be cheaper, Buck," a tall, slim and wiry guy of about forty chuckled as he found a seat on the ground beside the big man.

"You're most likely right 'bout that, Elmer. I'm already paying through the nose for two," he laughed heartily.

About that time, the two boys, feeling much older than their age, sauntered up to the men.

"Well, hello young fellows, where did you two come from?" the big guy asked.

"We been watching from up there in them trees," Pete answered. "Mind if we eat with ya?"

"Sho don't. Have a seat."

The boys sat down close to the men, hoping to hear some grown-up talk. But the next few minutes were quiet as the men gulped their lunch and washed it down with coffee from large, metal thermos jugs. The slim fellow, Elmer, wiped his mouth on his sleeve and asked, "Who do ya s'pose lived here?" He pointed to a spot where someone's home obviously had stood.

"Tell me was'n old lady all by herself," the big fellow answered.

"I know who it was," Pete quickly injected, glad to have a chance to join the conversation.

"That right? Well speak up..." Elmer prodded the young fellow.

"Was old Mrs. Barrett. She died 'bout a month

ago."

"That so? Well, that was pretty good timin' if I do say so myself." The big fellow let out another one of his hearty laughs.

"Buck, I don't see where that's a bit funny a'tall," Elmer reprimanded.

"S'cuse me, brother Elmer, but you know how it is when we have to come through and somebody don't want'a move. I just thought it good timin' that she left before we got here, that's all."

Elmer shook his head at him, and the others laughed. Soon lunch was over and the men returned to their machines, bringing them to life again. They thundered forth, and the two boys scrambled back up their trees, and perched themselves comfortably to watch throughout the afternoon.

About an hour later, the boys noticed a sleek, sports car approaching with a cloud of dust behind it. It came to a stop slightly down the mountainside, and a very stylish, middle-aged lady stepped out. She was dressed in a dark gray suit with black heels, shoulder bag and ebony black hair piled on her head. She made her way up the hillside with her head held high.

"Look Pete, that lady's walking up to a graveyard. I ain't never seen no graveyard a'fore. Did you?"

"I don't think she's from these here parts," Pete yelled back. "Look at that car! Ain't that something?"

Spring approached the graves. Small clumps of dirt came rolling down the mountainside and over the cemetery, coming to rest against the engraved stones. At first, she felt anger and looked up with resentment at the workmen who hadn't even noticed her. But then she thought, "That is silly, this is progress...life goes on."

She sat down on the bench and read the familiar words on her Father's memorial: "Till Death us do Part." Then she turned and forced herself to read aloud the words engraved on her Mother's, the words she herself had ordered by her Mother's request: "But only for a Season—Together Again."

The tears began to flow down Spring's high cheek bones. "It *was* only for a season, Mama...you must have known." She began to cry harder. "I miss you, Mama...and you too, Daddy." She thought of them lying beneath the mounds of cold dirt. Oh, how she wished she could reach out and touch them again, just one more time. Suddenly she felt all alone, terribly alone. They were the closest two people on earth to her. They had reached out to her and rescued her from God knows what, and made her their own.

"Oh, Mama," she cried, putting her head into her hands. She sat there for what seemed like hours, but were only minutes, her heart breaking, being torn apart just as the earth around her was being torn apart. But then she felt a gentle breeze caress her forehead ever so lightly, almost as if it was an unseen hand, and she looked up, sensing a very real presence.

"Mama, is that you? Is it you, Daddy?" she demanded, but her voice trailed off into the forest.

"Seek and ye shall find...." What? Where did those words come from, spoken so audibly that she expected to turn around and see someone standing there, but there was no one. They had come from within, she realized, from way down within, stashed away many years ago.

"Seek and ye shall find," she repeated. "I am not alone, Mama. Someone is here with me. I don't know who yet, Mama...but I'm going to find out."

She rose from the bench, looked around, and with a smile on her face, said, "Mama, it's going to be all right...the dogwoods are blooming."

THE BEGINNING...

Carolyn Tyree Feagans grew up in Amherst County, adjacent to Lynchburg, at the foot of the Blue Ridge Mountains.
(P.O. Box 10811, Lynchburg, Virginia 24506)